THE YAHWEH GENE

N. J. SIMMONS

The Yahweh Gene
Writer/Creator: N. J. Simmons
Formal Editor: Alice Osborn
Creative Editor: Kate Damoin
Cover Design/Formatting: Damonza.com
A special "thank you" goes to the following Beta Readers:
Robert "Rob Laray" Taylor Jr. and Lataisha Shelby
Another special "thank you" goes to the following Proofreader: Gina Caldanaro

www.njtheauthor.com
njsimmonstheauthor@gmail.com

INSTAGRAM, TWITTER, SNAPCHAT:
@njtheauthor

Copyright © 2017 by NJ SIMMONS LLC

All rights reserved. This book or any portion thereof may not be reproduced or used in any manner without the express written permission of NJ SIMMONS LLC, except for the use of brief quotations in book reviews and the like.

This is a work of fiction. Any and all references to actual people, places, and things are the product of the author's imagination and are used fictitiously. Any and all resemblances or references to actual persons, living or dead, businesses, companies, events, locales, historical events, real people, real names, actual or existing characters, real places, or actual incidents is entirely coincidental.

For information regarding legal matters, please contact:

NJ SIMMONS LLC
P. O. Box 1317
Winterville, NC 28590
njsimmonsllc@gmail.com

TO YOU, THE READER.
───────────────

This story is "technically" Sci-Fi/Fiction.
What I personally like to call a
Creative Fiction, to be exact.
But it walks the fine line between
possibility and impossibility.
Imagination and reality. Natural,
and the supernatural.

~ ~ ~

This line will become more and more
blurry as you journey into the world of,
The Yahweh Gene.

~ ~ ~

Don't be alarmed when it does. This is
often how deeper truth is found.

~ ~ ~

Truth.

There's a hidden, yet obvious truth, nestled within these pages. An ultimate truth. An eternal truth. A personal truth.

~ ~ ~

A truth that you will either determine for yourself, or that will be revealed to you. Both scenarios are ultimately equivalent. No one will be able to tell you exactly what it is. Not even me.

~ ~ ~

Only you can.

You'll receive it from the Voice that echoes from both within you, and from eternity, which are essentially the same place. After you suddenly realize it, stumble upon it, or intentionally locate it, it will resonate within you:
Like a Tibetan singing bowl,
Like a Jewish shofar,
Like a church steeple bell,
Like an African drum.

Once you finish this story, I will ask you one single question regarding this "truth."

~ ~ ~

Just promise me, and yourself, something:
***That you won't stop reading
until you locate it.
Or, until it locates you.***

~ ~ ~

One of the two will certainly occur; it's simply a question of which will occur first.

~ ~ ~

*That being said,
Beyond this page,
You will find my very <u>soul</u>.*

Enjoy.

-NJ Scribe

CONTENTS

To you, the reader.................................... iii
0-0. Stories...1
1. He Is Mighty...4
2. So, This Is Life.....................................7
3. Common Good..11
4. Wormwood...20
5. He Knows Best......................................26
6. I Hear You at Night................................32
7. Just a Second......................................39
8. Deranged...40
9. Very Good..45
10. Grateful..51
11. See You on the Sabbath............................60
12. Too Soon..64
13. Talk to Me..66
14. Sabbath...71
15. Skybox..77
16. Sit Here..80
17. Jhenda..85
18. Strong Energy.....................................96
19. The Shedim.......................................100
20. Jonah Rises......................................119
21. Missed It..122
22. Trust Him Again..................................131
23. A Tiny Moment....................................135

24. I'll Hold You to It...........143
25. I'll Meet You at Eden.........155
26. Please Show Me...............159
27. Soon..........................166
28. Reality.......................170
29. Ready?........................182
30. The Cloud....................186
31. Ascended.....................190
32. The Way......................194
33. I Have to Go.................199
34. Bow..........................203
35. No Problem...................206
36. How?.........................211
37. Tomorrow.....................216
38. I NEED YOU!..................221
39. Watch Out!...................232
40. Go, Manny!...................237
41. That Spot....................245
42. Yod..........................248
43. Impossible...................257
44. Live.........................264
45. Just Believe.................269
46. Stop!........................278
47. I Can't......................282
48. It Has Begun.................291
49. Two Nights...................297
50. No Turning Back..............302
51. Command......................307
52. Watchers.....................312
53. House of Yod.................316
54. Three........................320
55. We Must......................327
56. Tonight......................329

57. No Matter What 337
58. DO YOU SEE THIS?! 342
59. Lies 346
60. Come On 351
61. Come Quickly 354
62. Write! 356
63. Sword 360
64. Do You Have It? 363
65. Come Out 365
66. Tell Me More 373
67. The Others 376
68. Blue Angels 383
0-1. More to Tell 385
Acknowledgements: 388

0-0. STORIES

A shaky voice echoes in a small space.

"THE GREATEST OF stories happen all of the time. They're all around us. Sometimes we catch them, and sometimes we don't, but this is one that I hope you catch."

A man walks into a brightly lit room, with a ceiling, walls, and a hard marble floor that are all completely white. His shoes tap on the floor and reverberate throughout the tiny area. He sits down on a wooden stool that's in the center of the room. He's anguished-looking, as if he's endured the hardest life imaginable. Perhaps this hardness has lasted much longer than a single lifetime, in fact. He has an untidy beard growing from his face in patches. His hair is wild, with gray strands here and there like small clusters of weeds in a garden. He wears an all-black suit, white shirt, black tie, and shiny black shoes. He crosses his arms and takes a deep breath.

"I won't tell you my name, or who I am just yet; that's not all that important for now. Maybe we will get to that sometime—*later*, before it's too late. What matters is the story that I must tell you. A story unlike any that you've ever heard…"

He looks down and notices that one of his shoes has a bit of ash on the toe. He stoops down to wipe it off, then sits back up and continues to speak.

"You know, a lot of people throw this word *belief* around. Belief. It's a term that you're probably familiar with to some degree. You've got three types of people in this world: those who believe, those who don't know, and those who *know*."

He smirks.

"Anything outside of that is just fantasy, right? Santa Claus. Bigfoot. Demons. Angels. *The Creator...*"

He pauses.

"You get the idea, I'm sure. Yes, *yes*. Things for children and for the ignorant; the *blind sheep* of the world, right? Humph..."

He gazes off toward one of the white walls, temporarily losing himself in thought.

"I thought so too..."

After another long pause, he refocuses and continues.

"But what is belief, exactly? You know? What is it...*really?*"

He lifts his foot onto one of the rungs of the stool, places his elbow on his knee, and props his fist under his chin in a pensive stance.

"Well, I know a story about a young man who had all of the same questions that you and I have probably had at some point or another. The *real* questions. The deep questions. The ones that people typically try to avoid."

He rubs his chin and his beard makes a scratching noise.

"It happened at the oddest of times. So much unrest, turmoil, and tension. And all of those factors brought him to the very brink of his sanity—and his *life...*"

He pauses again, this time picking at the back of his hand with his finger nail. He looks behind himself toward the back wall. His mannerisms are that of someone who is undoubtedly nervous; it's obviously difficult for him to remain still.

"I want you to pay attention to his story. Perhaps you'll question this idea of *belief* and the possibilities that may be out there; possibilities that extend far beyond our wildest dreams. Or, maybe nothing will change. I doubt it, but it's possible. You may even find *yourself* somewhere in the story…"

He curls his lips into a devious grin.

"Ultimately, I'll let you decide for yourself whether or not you *believe* what I'm about to tell you. The choice is yours, really. We always have a choice, don't we?"

He looks behind himself again as a faint yell can be heard echoing in the room.

"Yes, we always have a choice…"

He turns forward, adjusts his weight on the stool, and then smiles nervously.

"Well, let's get started…"

1. HE IS MIGHTY

THE SKY IS a dark mixture of orange and red. There are trees that have had their leaves charred away by the fires of war—only the bark remains. The smoke in the valley is thick and misty, resting just above the ground like a morning fog.

"Have you had enough, Emmanuel?!" sneers the man. He lets out a sinister laugh as he takes heavy steps toward Manny's broken and burned body.

"Emmanuel? Humph! *THE CREATOR* is with *you*?" The man kneels and lifts Manny's head from the ground. Blood trickles from Manny's nose and splashes onto the ground like red raindrops.

"*HE HAS ABANDONED YOU!* He's not here! He's left you! Your friends have left you too! It's just the two of us now..."

His voice sounds more like the low, rumbling growl of a dog than it does a human's voice.

Manny notices that the man's shadow looks totally different than his physical body. Manny can make out the outline of the man's shape and physique, but the shadow that he casts is that of a large, horned beast with broad wings.

Manny tries to speak, but coughs instead. Each breath that he takes is a laborious one. The energy blasts from the man's hands have broken about eighty percent of the bones in his body. He is bleeding internally. It won't be much longer before he dies. The pain is absolutely unbearable. He is in shock but doesn't realize it because of the damage to his skull—he has suffered a severe concussion as well.

Fog and smoke fill the entire valley. He does not recognize this man's face.

"*SPEAK!*" he yells at Manny, "speak now…or *forever* hold your peace!"

The man stands and laughs, stretching his arms toward the sky in a victorious pose.

"You'll choke on your own blood, right here in this valley… I'm going to watch you die! Look at you, all of your work for this *INVISIBLE GHOST* in the sky who doesn't care at *all* about you! *POINTLESS! A COMPLETE WASTE!* You're weak, Emmanuel… you're *weak*, and so is your *PRECIOUS CREATOR!*"

Manny manages to spit out enough blood to say something faintly. The man hears him, but can't make out his words.

"What did you say?"

Manny says it again, a little louder, but still too faint to be fully understood.

"What are you saying?! *FIND THE STRENGTH TO ADDRESS ME LIKE A MAN!*"

Manny draws upon every bit of energy and might that he has left within himself. He yells out a phrase with such clarity and authority that the man stumbles back a few steps. The words ring throughout the entire valley and echo off of its rocky walls. A small burst of light shoots from his mouth as he says it:

"IN MY WEAKNESS, HE IS MIGHTY!"

Manny looks unflinchingly into the eyes of the man as he says the words, which further infuriates him. His rage creates an orb of yellow light in the very center of his chest. He places his hands on the spot, draws the light out of himself, and holds it in his hands. He lifts it over his head and looks down at Manny's body with unfiltered hatred. His muscles bulge, and he grunts as he begins the downward motion of slamming the light-orb onto Manny's body.

His intent: **destroy Emmanuel Kohen, once and for all.**

A bright light flashes. It seems as though the heavens have taken a picture. Everything turns completely white. There is a high-pitched ringing sound.

Then, nothing else.

2. SO, THIS IS LIFE

MANNY JERKS VIOLENTLY, so violently that his head hits the wall adjacent to his bed. He thrusts and kicks, finally snapping forward and sitting up.

"Manny, it's okay, son. It's okay," a gentle voice says.

Chilly drops of sweat rest on his face as he looks into the woman's soft, warm eyes while she stands by his doorway.

He groans, places his hand onto his forehead, and hunches over.

"Did you have it again?"

"Yes, ma'am."

"The same dream?"

"It's always the same dream," he responds with his head still down.

She walks over and sits next to him on the bed.

"Manny, it's okay. It's just a dream, don't worry…"

She hands him a cup of warm tea. He takes a couple of sips and breathes deeply.

"You should get ready; the train will be coming in another forty-five minutes or so. We don't want to be late."

Martha Kohen, Manny's mother, gives off an aura of resilience and strength. She's about fifty years old. In her younger days, she was very energetic and lively, but recently, she's slowed down a bit. If kindness and compassion had a physical form, they would equate to Martha.

She's worked in the *Agri-Fields* for years now, harvesting crops on the charred land along with thousands of other *Remnants*. The constant breathing in of dust and chemicals has affected her over time; it's taken its greatest toll over the last three or four years.

She takes a breath, gathers herself, and stands up. Once she reaches the door, she grabs a hold of its handle and coughs violently.

"*Mom...*"

She raises her hand and points it toward him behind her back, anticipating the words of worry that typically flow from him whenever she has a coughing episode.

"I'm okay, son," she manages to squeeze out between coughs.

He stops his sentence.

He wishes that she didn't have to work in the Agri-Fields anymore, but they haven't had much of a choice since *Star Fall*—no one has. It's been this way for years now; for nearly as long as he can remember.

Besides, she's been harvesting for so long that she would probably be reluctant to leave even if given the opportunity. It's what she knows. It's *all* that she knows.

Manny's basically a man now, at nineteen years old, but Martha still feels a sense of obligation to him. Things haven't been easy for them, or anyone, since the devastation first happened.

He puts on his work clothes, which consists of boots and coveralls, and heads into the kitchen where his mother is now seated and sipping coffee.

"I made your favorite," Martha says.

"You always say that."

"Because it's your *favorite...*"

Beans, grits, and a cup of water. A very small portion of each. Food resources are limited, so it's rationed carefully. Because they are not in a position to eat anything else, they call what they do have their *"favorite."* It's an inside joke between the two of them.

Manny picks up a clean plate off of the counter, sits, and scrapes a little more than half of his food onto it. He slides it over in front of his mother.

"Manny, *why* do you always do that?"

"You need to eat too. So, eat up. It's your *favorite*."

She smiles and lets out a short laugh, while shaking her head and looking at him with the type of loving eyes that only mothers possess.

"Emmanuel Kohen, you are *so* stubborn," she says with a grin, "but I love you."

When they are done, they walk out of their humble and quaint apartment, down a few flights of stairs, and congregate with the others at the train post.

Men, women, young, and old are gathered there, preparing to go to their occupational destinations. Some to the Agri-Fields, like Martha. Some to the Medical Ward, to treat the millions of sick and diseased. Others, to the Reservoirs, to fight the never-ending battle of producing clean water for the entire country.

Manny, on the other hand, is on his way to *the Shield*, along with the other Remnants who are dedicated to national defense, and preventing another *Wormwood* or *Star Fall*.

The TRN-3 train approaches from the west and creeps to a stop. The Remnants pile into its doors. Manny thinks about how repetitive it all is as he watches people rush up the steps to get the best seats. Every single day is the same. No change. No variation. Every day is a mirror-image of the day before it. It's just as repetitive as his recurring nightmare. He's been having it ever since he was a child. His mother reassures him that it's just a dream, but he believes that there's much more to it. Maybe some suppressed thought, a premonition, or something else. He's never too sure about things like that.

Manny helps his mother up the steps and then to find a seat. He stands next to her, holding onto a metal arm that's attached to the train's ceiling. The TRN-3 moves down the track and Manny stares out of the window. He thinks of his dream, of his mother and her failing health, and of the repetitive nature of everything around him. It all weighs heavily on his young shoulders.

"*So, this is life,*" he whispers to himself.

~ ~ ~

His mother reaches over and grabs his hand. He looks at her. She smiles. He smiles back. It's like her eyes are saying, *"it's going to be okay, son."*

This is one of the best parts of his dull days: the fleeting moments that he gets to spend with her, the woman who gave him life, and who continues to give him life with her love and care.

Her stop is first.

The train gradually slows.

Acres and acres of dust, with patches of greenery decorating it in various places. There are canopy-covered buildings next to the patches, and a few wooden benches up front. Some of the Remnants are already in the fields working. Manny helps his mother get off of the train while others pile out of its doors and head to their work stations.

"Have a great day today, son."

"You too, mom. I love you."

"I love you *more*…"

She always responds with the same words. He believes her too.

The train doors close. She stands and waves gently as the TRN-3 crawls away. He watches her and feels himself wanting to cry. He wishes that the world was different. He wishes that she didn't have to work so hard. He sits, and continues to think as the train rumbles down the track to its next destination, *the Shield*.

3. COMMON GOOD

"THERE HE IS! Hey, Manny, look at this! I *have* to show you!"

The train has halted outside of *the Shield*, the final stop for the TRN-3 as well as other trains from the surrounding areas. An athletically built young man rushes toward him from a neighboring train at the unloading dock. There's a small gadget in his hand.

His name: Ferroq "Rock" Menden; Manny's best friend since childhood. Manny calls him "Rock" for two reasons. First, because the ending of his name phonetically sounds like the word *rock*. Second, because of his personality and physique. He's always been both very bold (even when he's wrong), and very strong—physically and in character. When they were younger, Manny and Rock would get picked on and bullied from time to time by older Remnant kids. Rock wouldn't hesitate to stand up for them both. Even though he's always been tough, he has a gentle nature and a good heart.

Since working at the Shield, Rock has taken to making things. Mostly puzzles, small figurines, and whatever else comes to his mind; he's very good with his hands; he's always been. Once, he took apart an old cell phone and made some type of electronic musical instrument that played simple songs using the phone's keypad tones as notes.

"Rock, what is it? *Please* don't tell me you've made another finger trap. My thumbs are *STILL* sore…"

Manny looks at his hand.

"Funny, but no, it's not a finger trap. Hold your hand out…"

"Let me think about it...how about, *no?*" Manny responds sarcastically.

"Just hold your hand out...come on, Manny," Rock begs.

"Rock, I swear, if this hurts..."

"Come on! Trust me! Hold it out!"

Hesitantly, Manny lifts his hand and stretches it toward Rock, who in turn looks at him with a huge smile on his face, bubbling with excitement.

Rock places the tip of a small wire that extends from the little gadget onto Manny's finger.

"Ready?"

Before Manny can take in enough air to respond, Rock squeezes the gadget.

It makes a clicking sound.

Manny feels a stinging shock course through his hand.

"OUCH! WHAT IN THE WORLD?!"

Rock laughs uncontrollably.

"WHAT WAS THAT?"

Rock is barely able to respond because of his laughter.

"It's a part of a lighter that I took apart—this little thing makes a nice little shock, doesn't it?!"

Manny laughs as he sees how hysterical Rock is.

"I'll give you a nice shock too!"

He hits him swiftly in his left arm like someone would hit their annoyingly playful sibling.

"*OUCH!* Okay!" Rock exclaims.

They laugh a little more, and then walk into the Shield.

There is a massive front gate at which they must have their faces scanned before entering. There is a row of turnstiles that will unlock once the worker's faces are recognized. People of all ages hustle through the six turnstiles like mice through the doors of a cage. There are boxes with assorted tools in them that everyone picks up once inside: a worker's kit. On a daily basis, Manny,

Rock, and the thousands of other Remnants who work at the Shield repair NRP weapons, aircraft, equipment, and vehicles. Most of these items were fully functional many years ago, but were damaged during *Star Fall*. Their work revolves around restoring these assets to an operational condition, just in case they're ever needed again. Manny and Rock are both technicians. They were trained for this since they were very young. It was necessary—*required* even.

Public education gradually stopped after Star Fall, so the Shield is all that they've known. To only be nineteen and twenty years old, respectively, Manny and Rock feel as though they've lived the lives of men who are much older. The work week is Sunday through Friday, from 6:00 a.m. until 7:00 p.m. This system has been in place for about ten years by now. It's been preached repetitively to the Remnants of *New America* that this way of living is necessary for the **"common good of the country."**

"*Fall in!*" one of the supervisors at the gate yells over the intercom.

Manny and Rock both assemble in the long line with the rest of the workers, get face-scanned, grab their kits, and head to their work station.

The work isn't difficult, but it's repetitive. Reading manuals, replacing wires, fiddling with old equipment. Typical. Boring. At least it's boring to two analytical and inquisitive young men like Manny and Rock. One of the highlights of the day is when the intercom buzzer sounds, signaling the thirty-minute lunch and leisure break. Manny and Rock usually go to the same common area that's filled with benches, reminiscent of a park or college campus.

Today, like any other day, they sit, they talk, and they eat.

"Hey, old men!"

A young woman approaches them, carrying a tray full of food. Her bright eyes shimmer at them from behind her black-framed glasses. She is dressed in customary working clothes: coveralls, boots, and a plain-colored shirt. She bounces as she walks as if tiny springs are attached to her feet. She's Rock's younger sister, Grea. Everything about her screams youth, wit, and brashness.

"Be quiet," Rock says, rolling his eyes at her.

"Umm, how about...*no*," she retorts.

She reaches into Rock's lunch tray and takes an apple.

"*Hey...*" Rock blurts out.

"*Hey* to you too!"

"So annoying," mumbles Manny.

"Hmm, 'tis true, my dear Emmanuel...*but*...you guys love me anyway!"

They chuckle.

They've been a trio since they were children. Grea, at seventeen, is younger than Manny and Rock, and she takes great pleasure in reminding them of that fact as often as she can. She works in the planning and logistics department of the Shield, which basically handles the management, transportation, and tracking of the Shield's assets and equipment. They also make sure that damaged materials and equipment found by the *Collectors* gets properly categorized and sorted. The only time that they really get to spend together is during their lunch breaks, and on Saturdays, or *"Sabbaths,"* at the International Ecclesia. The *"IE"* is a huge network of worship centers that were created after Star Fall. There is one located at the edge of their city hub, Naza.

Conversely, *"Novus Res Publica,"* or the *NRP*, was formed after Star Fall also. This unified world government was created to give a better sense of *"security"* after the United Nations, NATO, and other groups were disbanded and dissolved. It contains world leaders from all of the countries that were left after Star Fall; some of which were self-appointed, and others voted in by their comrades. The NRP initiated the building of underground bunkers, oversees the different factions of society such as the Shield, the Agri-Fields, Water Preservation, the Medical Ward, Collection, and so on, and also controls the rationing of food and resources throughout New America, and the world. The NRP and the IE are often subtly at odds with one another. There's an undercurrent of distrust, due to the way world governments functioned prior to Star Fall. Many view the NRP as *"just a new name with the same faces behind the scenes."*

There is an international military and police force that the NRP trains and controls. Those elite members of society are commonly referred to as "Nerps" for short by the Remnants. They're usually chosen at birth and are adopted into the NRP's system. The NRP attempts to have a check and balance system with the IE because it is so large, influential, and has most of the people's hearts and support. The IE is the only outlet for the Remnants. Coincidently, the Nerps have no jurisdiction in the IE, much to the disdain of the NRP. Ironically, some Nerps attend gatherings on Sabbaths at their closest IE, although most certainly don't.

The IE was formed and established by the people. The various locations have no central leader, but rather have individual city hub IE leaders, such as Jonah Price, leader of the Naza IE.

Outside of work, and the IE, there isn't much more to society. After the *"greatest tragedy in world history,"* Remnants worldwide gravitated either to some form of intense spirituality, to agnosticism, or to stark atheism. It's amazing how millions ran to an invisible *Creator* after the foundations of life as they knew it were shaken, yet others, who experienced the exact same event, ran as far away from him as they could.

Some called it a time of spiritual awakening.

It's "just life," as far as Manny is concerned. Rock too.

Grea, on the other hand, has very strong convictions about her faith, the Creator, and the afterlife. It's usually a recipe for some pretty interestingly intense discussions, like today.

~ ~ ~

Grea eats Rock's apple and reads a small pamphlet, an *Awareness Tract*, about national security. The tracts are usually arranged all around the work areas to provide "workforce awareness." Manny and Rock are disinterested. Instead, they talk about a few of the new hires.

Today's tract is a commemorative one. It's been thirteen years since *Star Fall*.

"So, then he looks at me and asks me if I can remove the connectors for him. Are you *serious?* You're a *tech!* You can take them off yourself!" Rock says in an exasperated tone.

"You should've just helped the poor kid, I used to have to take all of your connectors off for *you*, remember?!"

"Very funny. I'd like to see *you* train some of these guys. You'd understand then."

"It can't possibly be that bad…" Manny says.

Rock looks at Manny with a blank stare.

"Okay, well, it probably is…" Manny finishes.

They laugh at the statement.

Grea crunches the apple loudly and reads the tract.

"Sheesh! I hope it tastes good. Enjoy…it's on the house," mutters Rock, cynically.

"Oh, hush," Grea responds.

"Guys, serious topic. Have you ever thought about what we would do if *it* happened again? I mean, I don't even know if all of the bunkers are ready yet. I'm sure all of us up here on the surface wouldn't be able to fit down below if we needed to, *especially* if they aren't finished. Can we even trust the NRP?"

"Oh my *GOSH*…Grea, please…not today! Don't start…I'm *SO* not in the mood," Manny replies.

He snatches the Awareness Tract from her hand.

"You need to stop reading this crap anyway," he continues.

"Manny, it's the only way that we can stay abreast of what's happening in the world. Maybe you need to be *MORE* aware of what's really going on," she says.

"I said...I *don't* want to hear it," Manny says in a serious tone.

He shakes his head and places the tract back onto the table.

"It's just an honest question. Have you guys thought about it? I mean, we work for the NRP—literally the super power of the world. They control every single aspect of life as we know it, and we know *nothing* except what they tell us. Does that ever bother you? We all know about the conspiracy theories. Most people secretly believe that..."

Grea leans closer to her brother and Manny, lowers her voice to a whisper, and says, "...*the NRP was behind...*"

"*Grea, quiet!*" Rock whispers at her forcefully when he notices a group of technicians walking by just a few feet away.

She flinches a bit, looks behind her and sees them, waits for them to pass, then sits back and resumes her normal speaking voice.

"...the bottom line is...it could honestly all happen again. All it would take is for some more hackers to rise up who felt like they were doing the Creator's bidding...*oh, all-powerful and all-knowing Creator, help us bring the world to its knees again to fulfill the prophecies and please you!*"

She clasps her hands together as she says it, mimicking an exaggerated prayer with her eyes closed, head lowered, and swaying from side to side.

"We trust the NRP to protect us, but should we?" she continues.

"Grea, we *all* think about it. Every day, okay? Do you have to talk about this all of the time?" Rock says.

"Well, somebody needs to talk about it. It's a reality. This is just the world that we live in...and we can't hide from the truth..." she says to her brother.

"Nothing has happened in a long time, Grea," responds Manny.

"True, but…"

She pulls out a small black book and sits it on the table; a *Grandeurscript*. She flips to a page and runs her finger down it until she finds the words that she's looking for.

"Let's see…right here, 'this is just the start of many GREATER troubles to come,' it's right there in black and white."

"Grea, I told you—I'm *not* in the mood…"

"Well, I'm just speaking the truth," Grea says as she closes the book with a flick of her hand.

"Whose truth? *Your* truth?" Manny asks.

"*Our* truth, Manny…*ours*," Grea answers.

"Yours…like I said…" Manny responds sharply.

By this time, Rock has his head lowered, elbows on the table, and hands pressed firmly onto his forehead and eyes. He swiftly lifts his head and says, "every *DAY* with you two! Could you cut it out?! My *goodness!*"

Grea looks at him. She bites into her apple and makes a loud crunch.

"Well, *he* started it," she mumbles with a grin and her mouth full.

There's a brief, silent pause.

Rock laughs. Manny can't hold back his laugh either.

The intercom buzzer sounds again, signaling that the lunch period is over.

"Ah, perfect timing, later guys—I'm *too* thrilled to get back to work to wait any longer," Manny says.

He stands, grabs his work kit, and heads back to his work station. Grea stands as well. Rock keeps sitting there and then says, "do we *HAVE* to go back?"

"What do you think?!" responds Grea.

"After all, it's for the *common good of the country*," she says, as she snaps her legs together, clicks her heels, and thrusts her hand to her eyebrow into a salute, reminiscent of a soldier.

Rock waves his hand at her dismissively.

They reluctantly return to their work stations.

4. WORMWOOD

THE TRN-3 RUMBLES like thousands of deer racing through the woods. Manny gazes out of the window. They have another twenty minutes or so before they reach the Agri-Fields where his mother will be picked up.

He misses her.

He always worries about her during the work day, no matter how hard he tries not to. His mind wanders to her condition.

Her cough.

The aches that she rarely complains about, but that he knows she feels.

The way that her face twists whenever a sharp pain shoots through her aging spine, followed by her taking a deep breath with her eyes closed.

~ ~ ~

There's an elderly man sitting in the seat in front of Manny. The two of them face each other since this section of the train has restaurant-booth-style seating. He's seen the man fairly often, but doesn't know him; there usually isn't much talk after such a long day of work.

There's a small child, a boy, with his mother, sitting to Manny's left across the center aisle. The child is coloring in a book and periodically whispering questions to his mother while Manny attempts to not listen too closely: *"how fast is the train going, mommy?"* and *"why are your eyes green?"* to name a couple of his inquiries.

Manny continues to gaze out of the train window with his head leaning onto it. The air from his nostrils creates foggy circles with each exhale. He's exhausted.

"They used to be so green," the elderly man says, "dark green...just beautiful. Birds singing. I used to fish right over there, as a boy..."

Manny looks up at him; the man points to a rounded indention in the dusty field outside of the train window.

"What are you talking about?" Manny responds.

"Over there, the trees were once so green and lively. They were full. And there was a pond right there. My brother and I would fish there."

Loudly, and without any reservations or shyness, the young boy asks his mother, "what happened to the trees, mommy?"

Angrily, she jerks at his jacket and responds, *"shhh!* Color in your book...*quiet...*"

Manny looks at them.

The boy looks back, sheepishly, then looks down with an outpoked lip and continues to color.

"Deserts now," the man continues, "all over the country. The world. Droughts. Famines. Diseases."

"You shouldn't talk about that here, not right now," responds Manny, as he checks on the young boy again.

"London, Atlanta, New York, Tokyo, Sydney, Rome, Moscow, Cairo—*all* gone. Just our hubs. Our Shield. Our Agri-Fields. Our Reservoirs. Our bunkers. And whatever the Collectors can find..."

The man's head turns away from Manny and toward the window again as he speaks. He fixes his gaze on a handful of people who have on protective outfits with biohazard symbols and warnings on them. Their faces are covered with masks and they have large oxygen tanks mounted on their backs: *Collectors*, or as some Remnants call them, *Scavengers*. They sift through a pile of what looks to be junk on the ground a few hundred yards away.

Manny catches a glimpse of the gentleman's eyes as he seemingly stares off into space. The man's eyes are glazed over and look gray—it's like he's in a totally different world.

Manny looks at him and sternly says, *"that's enough…"*

He looks back at the boy who is coloring a little more intensely, not focusing on what he's doing, but clearly listening to the man as he speaks.

"A *war* is coming. They take our blood to test. They *know* what's coming," the man says eerily as he looks directly at Manny.

"The United Nations…NATO…*gone*. Just the NRP. *Wicked*. Darkness. It's going to come again, eventually…*Star Fall*…it's *not* over…it *always* happens again…and again…again…and again…" he mumbles.

"Sir, I said that's *enough*," Manny says a little more firmly.

"Ever since you were a child, they've trained you how to live. How to think. How to be who you are! But who are you, *really*? What's really inside of you? You *know* there's more…you *know* something is coming…you can *feel* it, can't you?"

"*ENOUGH!*" Manny yells as he slams his fist against the metal base of the window and makes a loud noise that causes a number of people to look in his direction.

The boy cries. His mother comforts him and pats his head until he calms down.

The man's gaze softens. He looks at Manny, confused, then picks up the Awareness Tract that's next to him and begins reading it as if nothing has happened.

Manny breathes heavily.

The little boy whimpers a little more.

The man continues to read the pamphlet, totally oblivious.

There's perfect quietness for a few moments.

The man looks up and notices that Manny is still looking at him. His eyes are clear now, no longer glazed-over and gray.

"Nice day," the man says with a smile as he glances out of the window briefly.

He lowers his eyes and continues to read again. Manny squints and shakes his head, not understanding the man's rant from just moments ago. Eventually, he decides to forget about the whole occurrence just as the train stops at the Agri-Fields.

Manny walks to the door and awaits his mother. When he sees her, he steps off and helps her onto the train. He walks with her to a seat; a different seat than the one he was previously sitting at.

Manny and Martha talk about their day, sharing a few laughs here and there. He tells her about Rock's little shocking-device and she finds it so amusing.

"He has *always* been such a character," she chuckles.

Eventually, she dozes off. Manny covers her with the small blanket that she usually carries with her. She's always chilly. He looks out of the window, and thinks. He thinks about the man:

> **"You know there's more. You know something is coming. You can feel it, can't you?"**

The words replay in his mind. The accuracy of them is scary.

Manny has felt uneasy and out of place most of his life, but more than ever over the past few weeks. He can't put his finger on exactly why, but it's *something*.

He picks up an Awareness Tract; they are tucked into chair pockets and scattered in seats all over the train.

On the back is a memorial page. Today is the anniversary of *Star Fall* and he didn't even realize it. He figures that's why Grea started talking about it during lunch. He suddenly feels bad about blowing up on her.

He skims through it then reads the bottom. It takes him just a few seconds to finish the paragraph:

October 27, 2047

Today, we commemorate the millions of souls that were lost at the hands of a misguided few—Wormwood. It has been thirteen years, to the day, since this terrorist group initiated their global attack: Star Fall. The innocent lives that were lost shall not have been lost in vain. We will continue to serve New America in their honor.
We will continue to work and strive for the <u>common good of the country</u>.

Someone has written on this particular tract; more than likely someone from earlier in the morning who was bored prior to reaching their work area. In the whitespace underneath the commemorative message, there is an additional paragraph. Manny keeps reading:

May they rest with perfect peace:

"Wormwood, the unrestrained star from the Great Eye, shall fall in the days of terror... soon after the earth has reached her limits, and the hearts of men have turned stony and

> *cold...the star, which gives life, shall also give death...a great death..."* ~Grandeurscript

"*Wormwood,*" he whispers as he taps the tract on his thigh.

He tosses it onto the chair across from him, checks to make sure that his mother is resting comfortably, and then leans his head onto the window.

Tears start to stream down his cheeks like tiny rivers flowing through a desert.

5. HE KNOWS BEST

"Star Fall: Religious Terrorist Group, Wormwood, Launches Global Attack"

MANNY READS THE title of the framed article above his mother's dresser. He's sitting in a chair in the corner of her room staring at it. Martha lays in her bed, propped up on her arm, her glasses lowered, and reading a small book. He enjoys being in her room. He spent a lot of time there when he was younger. He looks at her after skimming the article some more.

"Why do you keep this, mom?"

She looks over at him with those gentle eyes of hers. She closes her book and shifts her weight so that she is facing him.

"It's...just a reminder," she says while removing her glasses.

"Reminder? Why would you want to be reminded of the worst thing that's ever happened?"

She pauses, hearing the hints of resentment and sadness in his voice.

"Sometimes it takes some darkness for us to see and appreciate the light, Manny."

Manny scoffs under his breath, sits forward, places his elbows on his knees, and looks at the floor. He taps his foot nervously; he does this when he's worried, angry, or upset.

Martha rotates her legs from the foot of her bed to its side and sits up. She glances at the article, then at Manny.

"You know, those poor people—they chose that name for a reason. They thought that they were doing the will of the Creator."

"They were *insane*," Manny says sharply.

"Well, that may be true. But they weren't completely ignorant. They knew exactly what they were doing and why they were doing it. You know Manny, *wormwood* means bitterness…"

Martha scratches at her nose and looks at the article again as she pauses.

"Humph, that's exactly what they created too. Who would've thought that a group of our own citizens, and *believers* at that, were building a network right under our noses? Nobody, I mean *nobody*, saw it, or them, coming."

"And look at us now; look at the *world* now. All because of *them*," Manny interrupts with frustration in his voice.

"It's not fair," he finishes—his face stained with melancholy.

He drops his head even lower.

"They are long gone now, son. We have what we have: today, here, and now. We still have each other…and we still have the Creator…"

A pause. Manny sighs.

"Why didn't he do anything, then? If he's with us, why didn't he stop them?"

"Who, son?"

"The Creator! He's supposed to protect us, right? He was supposed to protect her!" he says with hint of aggression.

He closes his eyes. He can still see it just like it's happening right now.

~ ~ ~

He swings next to a small girl. Smiling. Laughing.

Their favorite park. The sun warms their tiny faces.

She looks exactly like him, just with longer hair.

Same nose.
Same eye color.
Same height.
Nearly identical.

The girl hops off of the swing set and runs toward Martha. She motions for Martha to bend down to her. Martha smiles and listens attentively as her little cupped hands barely cover her ear. She turns all of a sudden and darts away to an older lady sitting by a fountain who looks very much like Martha; on the contrary, Martha looks very much like her.

"Mom, we'll be right here! The pond is behind the building—she wants to show you the ducks!" Martha yells to the beautifully seasoned woman.

The woman smiles and opens her eyes wide. She gives the girl a wonderful, and exaggerated, expression of excitement, just as the girl expected. The slender, gray haired woman has such strong and defined features, just like Martha. Undoubtedly, when Martha is her age, she will look exactly the same.

The girl and the elderly woman walk behind the building.
He watches.
He continues swinging.
Minutes pass.
More minutes pass.

"Are you ready to go? We should go get them soon; they're probably still at the pond..." Martha says to him from a nearby bench.

He nods.

By now, he's on the jungle gym. He loves climbing and swinging from the bars. He drops down into the sand and walks toward Martha.

"Oh, *Manny*, your clothes are a *mess*!"
He laughs.

~ ~ ~

The skies become dark, much quicker than normal.
    A siren blares, loudly.
    People look around nervously.
    They look into the sky.
    "What is that?" A man says who is standing close to the jungle gym.
    "Come on honey, let's go," Martha says, a bit concerned.
    An explosion.
    Far away.
    More explosions.
    Closer.
    And closer.
    People are running.
    Adults and children fall to the ground in the confusion. Martha clutches Manny close to her and yells for the woman and the girl.
    The sky is red. Smoke. Fire.
    The buildings and ground shake. The glass breaks out of windows.
    Closer explosions.
    Everyone panics. A voice can be heard over a loud speaker:

> *"Find cover immediately!*
> *This is not a warning!*
> *Find cover immediately!*
> *This is not a warning!"*

Weeks pass like a swift wind.
    Martha and Manny find refuge in a school gymnasium.
    Limited food and water.
    Hundreds of people.

Search teams.

The elderly woman, and the small girl, never arrive at the gymnasium.

~ ~ ~

Manny sobs heavily. He can barely catch his breath long enough to speak.

"Why did they have to die?! Why couldn't it have been me?! It's not fair, mom! It's not fair! Where was *the Creator* then?!"

"Don't say that! You don't mean that…calm down…I know it hurts and that you're upset…"

His mother stands up and walks over to him, placing her hand on the back of his neck as she stands next to him.

"It's just not fair!"

He squeezes the words out in the midst of his uncontrollable weeping.

"I don't understand!"

"He has his reasons honey…*he* knows best," she says as she rubs his head, then pulls it closer to her waist.

Manny continues to cry bitterly. A painful cry.

Through his heaving, he manages to say, "I'm so tired of this! I'm tired…when does it stop? I don't want life to be just—*this*…"

He lifts his head and points at the window.

"Just look out there! I don't want to live like this a day longer…I just don't! There has to be more. *Something*. Anything! I mean, you're not in the best health anymore…I feel like it's up to me to make things better! *I'm tired…*"

Martha pulls his head close to her again.

"They're gone…it's just us now…I have to take care of you," he mumbles, as his voice is muffled by her shirt.

"He's taking care of us, son. Even though you may not see it right now…he is. He's there. It's going to be okay…he knows best…"

Manny knows how tenaciously faithful his mother is. He decides to not give a retort to her statement this time.

He rests his head on her waist and hugs her with all of his might instead.

6. I HEAR YOU AT NIGHT

THE ALARM CLOCK blasts like a thousand trumpets right next to Manny's head.

He sleeps with it on his pillow; he's always been a heavy sleeper.
He hits the top of it with his hand and it shuts off.
It happened again last night.
The man.
The valley.
The orb of light.

"IN MY WEAKNESS, HE IS MIGHTY!"

He grabs his head and grits his teeth like he is trying to pull the dream out of his mind.

It doesn't work.

In the kitchen, he sits at the table while his mother finishes preparing their breakfast.

"Manny, can you go to Emil's for me and get a few things before the train comes?"

"Sure. What do you need?"

"Oh, just a couple more jugs of water and some rubbing alcohol for these old joints of mine."

"Okay, I'll be right back."

"Manny...*please* be careful..."

"When am I ever not careful?" he responds.

"Your favorite will be ready by the time you get back!" she yells, as he sprints out of the door.

~ ~ ~

Two medium-sized packs of rice are wedged under his arms as he walks. It doesn't take him long to get to the bottom floor of their apartment building; he hops down periodically, skipping a few steps to save time. A few people have their doors cracked open as they prepare for work and peek out as they hear the *thud* of his boots.

Outside, the air is crisp. It's foggy. The sky is a murky gray, as usual. Off in the distance, smoke from The Reservoir's purification furnaces are pumping their fumes into the air. Manny stops to look at it for a second before continuing on. The store is only a few hundred yards away. Manny has made this trip hundreds of times over the years.

Cracked pavement.

The roads haven't been repaired since it happened. Weeds and grass once grew from the splits in the asphalt, but most of it is dead now. Brown and black debris rests in the tiny crevices beneath his feet. Most of the buildings are no longer inhabited. Rotting houses. Broken windows. Martha, Manny, and other Remnants live in a handful of the apartment buildings that are somewhat livable in their small section of Naza; there are about five or six of them in total. This is the case for pretty much all of the city hubs throughout New America, and the modern world.

He walks for about four minutes before he's at the front door of Emil's.

Before Star Fall, it was a convenience store. Now, it's used by the NRP to store supplies that will be rationed out throughout Naza.

The bell rings as Manny steps inside.

"Manny! How are you, my friend?" Denzi says excitedly.

Denzi is the store's owner and manager. Emil was his uncle.

Emil never made it to the school gymnasium either.

"Hey, Denzi, good morning. How are you?"

"Very well, Manny, very well! How is your mother?"

"She's doing pretty well."

"Good, good! Sweet lady, sweet lady! So, what can Denzi get for you today, my friend?"

"I just need rubbing alcohol and water…"

Manny drops the two portions of rice on the counter with two loud thumps.

"Ah, yes, coming right up, my friend! Come with me, it's right over here."

Denzi looks out of the front window, then closes the shades and locks the door. He then quickly walks to the back of the store ahead of Manny as Manny follows.

Trading NRP rations is illegal, but it's not heavily policed, at least not in Naza. Denzi doesn't mind taking the risk for Manny and Martha. They've always been good to him, especially during the years just after Star Fall. Martha would check on Denzi every day to make sure that he had food. She would even allow Manny to spend time with him. They would play together in the evenings, until Manny was old enough to start working at the Shield, and Denzi was old enough to take over Emil's.

Denzi fidgets through a few rows of items on a shelf in the back room, then opens a refrigerator door.

"Here it is! The freshest water the Reservoirs have to offer! You know, they work hard. Day in and day out, filtering water. Purifying it. Then they ship it by the trains to me. We get the *best* of it. Naza has the *best* and *freshest* water of *ALL* the city hubs in New America! Did you know that, my friend?"

Manny laughs.

"Denzi, you don't have to sell it to me...I've already given you the rice portions! Besides, we're miles away from another city hub...where else will I get any water?"

Denzi laughs too.

"What about the alcohol? Do you have any?" Manny asks.

"I think that I do...Scavengers brought in a large batch of items just the other day...I will check in the pile..."

"Don't call them that. They're *Collectors*..."

"Collectors, Scavengers—it's all the same!"

"Terrible, just terrible. They put their lives on the line for us. Crawling through ditches and old buildings that are probably at least a *little* bit contaminated with radiation."

"Hey, I put my life on the line too! This storage business for the Nerps can be dangerous!"

"The biggest threat you might have is a kid stealing some candy without you seeing them, Denzi..."

Denzi looks at Manny with a completely straight face, then cracks a smile.

"This...is true, my friend! This is true! They are sneaky!"

Manny chuckles again.

Eventually, Denzi finds a bottle of alcohol. He hands it to Manny, they embrace, and finally exchange their farewells.

"Thank you, Denzi...for everything..."

"No problem my friend! Be safe!"

"You too, Denzi."

They both place their hands on their chests over their hearts, saluting each other in the customary fashion.

Before long, Manny's walking back up the steps of his apartment building.

"That was fast," Martha says with a smile.

"It was, wasn't it?" he says, approaching her and holding out the bottle of alcohol for her to take.

"Thank you," she says with a mild grin.

She takes the alcohol, opens it, and massages small amounts of it onto her knees. He sits, notices that his breakfast is on the table in front of him, and scrapes half of his food onto a clean plate. He slides it to her side of the table.

She looks up and smiles.

"Don't forget, samples will be taken today…and we get more rations…"

"I remember. I wish they didn't have to do it. None of us are contaminated…"

"I know, I suppose they just want to be certain; to protect us."

The NRP administers periodic blood sampling on all Remnants. This usually happens sporadically, just to make sure that no one has been contaminated by the residual atmospheric radiation left from Star Fall. Collectors are sampled more frequently than other Remnants because of their direct contact with known ground zero areas. Small white tents are set up just inside of the gates at the Agri-Fields, the Shield, the Reservoirs, and so on. The process only takes around ten minutes. All of the blood samples are labeled, placed into silver refrigerated suitcases, and then loaded into white crates. Vehicles transport them to the NRP research facility, at some undisclosed location, for testing and safekeeping.

Martha looks down at the bend of her arm. There are scars there from where the Medics have drawn blood many times over the years—*too many*.

Manny looks at the scars, surrounded by splotches of deep purple and black. She notices, smiles, and rubs his free hand as he continues to eat.

He looks away with a light sigh. His mind suddenly fills with the sick reality that the NRP only distributes rations to those who are of working age and who are "contributing to society." Only those who are fit to work are considered eligible to receive the portions of food. Ration days and sample days coincide—if someone skips their blood sampling, they will not receive any rations.

The population of those who are homeless and starving has risen over the past few years. Manny wonders if the rations are somehow depleting, and what that could mean for the city hubs. His mother's scars and bruises are a stark reminder of their less than desirable way of living.

"I was thinking, Manny," she says with a soft voice.

"Thinking what, mom?" he says with a mouth full of food.

"Finish chewing first…"

They share a light-hearted laugh.

"I was thinking that maybe, this Sabbath…"

"Mom, come on…not this again…I should've known…" Manny says as he drops his fork into his plate with a *clank* and sits back in his chair.

"I was just wondering if you'd like to sit with me. You know? The way you used to…"

"That was a long time ago, ma…"

"I know…too long…"

"I just don't know…we will see…"

"You always say that, and when you do, it means *no*."

"No, it doesn't; it means…*we will see*…"

She breathes out of her nose and looks at him with both compassion and concern.

"Tell me why, Manny? What do you have against it? Jonah is a good man."

"I just…I just don't know if I really trust him…and I have absolutely no idea why you do…"

"He's never given any of us a reason to not trust him. What's the real reason? You can tell me, son."

"I really don't want to talk about it, mom. You're starting to sound like Grea."

She laughs.

"Oh, do I, mister? So now I'm *bothering* you? Is that it?"

She leans over the table and pinches his arm. He laughs after thinking about his statement.

"No! I'm not saying that. I just…"

"You just what?"

He fiddles with his fork on his plate and gathers his thoughts. He looks at his mother's hand as it now rests on top of his.

"I just don't know about it all. I mean, Jonah is supposed to hear from the Creator and everything, and that's fine. But how do we know that he's telling the truth? How do we know the Creator is saying anything at all? I mean, we all work throughout the week. But what about Jonah? He lives off of what we give. And then he stands up there and tells us this and that, and…and everyone just believes him! I mean, they all just take it and run with it, no questions asked…I just don't know…"

She pauses and allows the silence to soak in.

"You know, I've been praying that you would at least sit in one gathering with me, Emmanuel—the way that you used to sit with me. You used to love coming to the IE…and to be quite honest, I miss those days…more than you probably know…"

"I know, ma…I know that you pray for me too. I hear you at night; *every night*…"

She sits back in her chair and stares at him, admiring her precious son. He gazes back, then lets his eyes drop to the table as he thinks. A slow and steady stream of air exits Martha's nose as her compassion and care for him overflow. She leans back forward and rubs his hair. He smiles.

"Come…the train will be here soon…" she says.

7. JUST A SECOND

A MAN WITH very bold features and a lean physique crouches in the corner of a dimly lit room. He whispers to himself with a black book clutched firmly to his chest. His eyes are closed. Tears drip down his left cheek. He is breathing heavily.

Faintly, but intensely, he whispers:

"The time is near...when the three *fallen* will wash over this land like a putrid lake. Have I not done enough? Was there enough time? This cannot be...it SHOULD not be! He's not ready! Is he? Could he be?"

He crawls into the chair that's next to him.

"What do I do? *What do I do?!* They are coming; they're almost here! If this is what you require, I will go through it. I need your strength...I *beg* you! I beg you, *please* be with us. It's happening so quickly! Please, help us. *Please*, strengthen him..."

There's a knock at his door. It echoes throughout the room. He wipes his face and places his book, a Grandeurscript, on the desk in front of him.

"Just a second..."

He stands, walks to the door, unlocks it, and slowly turns the handle.

8. DERANGED

"FINALLY," ROCK SAYS as the buzzer sounds.

Another workday is halfway over.

Manny and Rock head to the break area. Today, Grea is already seated as they go to their normal spots; the anniversary tracts are still on the table, and of course, Grea is reading one.

Rock thumps the top of it as he sits down; she swats at his hand.

"Everyone has been buzzing about this. It's the same every year around this time," she says to Rock and Manny.

"Everyone is on high alert. Hoping that there aren't some sicko, copycat terrorists out there who want to make a name for themselves like Wormwood did," responds Manny.

"You know, I just don't get it," Rock says with annoyance in his voice.

"Get what?" asks Grea.

"I mean, there weren't any warning signs or anything? These guys were all citizens of the country; right here under our noses the whole time…"

"It makes sense, you know?" says Grea, "they were under the radar. No one suspected them. One article I read a while back said that they had *strong convictions* about the future of Old America, and the world in general. They believed that it was their *calling* to initiate what they felt was going to happen anyway—to accelerate the inevitable process. So, they started researching, studying, planning, and recruiting."

"That's true," says Manny, "there were about seven of them in all. They went to some of the top universities in Old America and studied computer science, engineering, network security, and stuff like that—real *braincases*. They formed Wormwood while they were in college and held secret meetings and Grandeurscript studies."

"*Grandeurscript* studies?" interrupts Rock.

"Yep," continues Manny, "all of them were believers. The government found a bunch of memoirs and papers from their meetings. They studied the ancient prophecies and stuff, believing that Old America was destined to fall. I don't know all of the details, but basically, they believed that it was their purpose to create that fall—they felt they were doing the Creator's *will*..."

"It's just crazy to me," says Rock.

"Very crazy," agrees Grea.

Manny continues, "after they graduated from college, they started positioning themselves to carry out their plans. They got high ranking jobs in different security industries and government positions. They got access to the defense servers and figured out all of the ins and outs. It took *years*..."

"I read about that. These guys were geniuses; *evil* geniuses. They were *so* patient. Their plan was years in the making, and I mean they planned *every single little thing,* down to the smallest detail. They knew the exact hour, minute, and second that they were going to execute *Star Fall*. They hacked into the servers, power grids, whatever else controlled the nuclear weapons and defense systems, and launched an all-out attack on Old America, Old Europe, Old Africa, part of Old Asia—the world basically. Nukes. Killed *millions* in a matter of hours..."

They all fall silent.

The only sound is Grea, lightly tapping the pamphlet on the table.

They think about where they were that day.

Manny thinks about the swing, the pond, the ducks, and the gymnasium.

He finally breaks the silence, "the ironic part for me is, you know, these guys *all* believed in the Creator. Every one of them. They made it *clear*. Faithfully studied the Grandeurscript. Totally persuaded that they were doing what the Creator wanted them to do. And then they do this *horrible* thing in *his* name, that we *all* have to suffer for, for the rest of our lives. And *then* the planet runs to *religion*? I don't get it. That's backwards! Things are so bad and broken. Nothing will ever be the same. And the world's response is to turn to this same *Creator* who neglected them, believing that he will fix everything? It's insane to me. Believers did it, and then everyone wants to become…a believer? That's stupid…"

"They were lost, Manny. They were misguided—crazy even," responds Grea without hesitation.

"You know…you're *always* so quick to defend them. I knew you would say something. You couldn't just hear it and let it go…" Manny snaps at her.

"I'm not defending them. I'd *never* defend them. They were wrong. I'm just saying that you can't blame the religions of the world for the acts of a select few. They were individuals. They made their own choices; they made their own *wrong* choices, better yet…"

"How can you not blame religion and faith, when religion and faith are what caused them to believe that their *wrong* choices… were the *right* choices?"

"That's still not a fair argument; not every believer makes the same choices they did. Again, they were individuals. No believers before them decided to hack into the defense systems and launch a nuclear attack on the world. So, you have to chalk it up to them being individuals—*deranged* individuals, who just so happened to be misguided believers…"

"Well, maybe *all* of you are misguided, *deranged* believers…" Manny concludes sharply.

"Hmm, even your *mom*, Manny? Is she a misguided, *deranged* believer too?"

She says it instinctively. She didn't even think about it, and she's not sorry for it either. She wanted him to really think about his accusations.

Manny's face glows from the blood that has rushed to his face. Grea notices, but is unflinching.

Rock becomes very uncomfortable; he is almost at the point of sweating. He didn't expect the conversation to become this heated, this intense, or to escalate so quickly. He looks at his sister who doesn't even blink. He looks at Manny, who is boiling with anger.

He looks at them both, his head turning nervously from side to side.

"Maybe we should just talk about this another time…as a matter of fact…" Rock begins to say.

Manny cuts him off as if he didn't hear a word that he said. His eyes are still fixated on Grea, and hers are still glued to him.

"So, I'm supposed to believe that some *phantom* in the sky is controlling everything? Just look around, Grea! If he was real, do you think this is his plan? This is the way he wants things to be?"

"His wisdom is *beyond* ours, Manny!"

"I don't buy it! You're living in a dream world! You need to wake up!"

"And you need to *open* up!"

"Open up? Open what up?"

"Your heart!
It's hard!
Your mind!
It's closed…"

He stares at her.

"I don't have time for this..." he says dismissively.

"You *never* do, but you will. I *know* it. I believe it..."

There's a silent pause.

Rock is still uncomfortable, but true to his character, he finds a way to lighten the mood when he feels enough quiet time has passed:

"You know, you guys should have a radio show. I bet the whole country would listen. Ooh! I know! It could be called: *GAMA in New Nazareth!* That could be the name of it! You know, they usually have some acronym as a name—it would be perfect!"

"GAMA? What does the GAMA stand for then?" Manny asks.

"Grea and Manny Arguments!"

"You are such a clown," responds Grea.

She and Manny laugh, reluctantly.

"That's one thing that we *definitely* agree on," says Manny.

He looks at her and smiles with the corner of his mouth.

She smiles back gently and taps his hand with the pamphlet.

They've been too close over the years to stay upset with each other for long. They've learned to recognize the inaudible apologies and offerings of forgiveness that can sometimes only be found in each other's eyes and body language. That's true for all three of them.

Soon, the buzzer sounds again.

9. VERY GOOD

"YOU MUST BE Jonah. Jonah Price, is that right?"

"Yes, that's correct."

"Ah, it was very, very tough to find this room. It's pretty dark in the hallways of this facility. My name is…"

"You're Damien Bell."

"Well, yes…I'm Damien! The NRP must have already contacted you…"

"They did…Novus Res Publica is very, well, *persistent and thorough*, I must say."

"That we are," Damien says with a slight smirk.

"Do you mind if my colleagues and I come in? Sit and talk for a few? Hopefully we aren't disturbing you…"

"No, it's totally fine. Come in."

"Ah, very good!"

Jonah's eyes are still faintly red from his crying out in prayer while kneeling in the corner just a few moments ago.

Three men step into the room. Jonah walks over to his desk and takes a seat. He leans back into his chair and places his hands together, pressing his two pointer fingers against his lips. He looks in the direction of the wall; it's clear that his mind is wandering. Deep thought.

"Jonah, this is Polus Hart, and this is Levi Spalding—my… *comrades*, from the NRP, you could say…"

They each lift their hands in greeting gestures as they are acknowledged.

"Nice to meet you, Polus, and Levi."

The three men walk around Jonah's office, looking at the different pictures on the walls, the small figurines, certificates, placards, and so on.

"This is a *very* nice office, Jonah," Damien says.

"Thank you. There's a lot of history in this room. I'll have to share some of it with you, one day."

Eventually they are seated. Damien sits directly in front of Jonah on the other side of his desk. Polus sits next to Damien. Levi sits off to the side of the room on a small bench.

"Well, I suppose that we should get down to it. Would you agree, Jonah?" Damien asks.

"Let's…" Jonah says with a nod.

"Well, Jonah, as you know by now I'm sure, the NRP has requested that we come here."

"I'm aware, but I'm still not fully certain *why* though—no offense."

"None taken."

Damien pauses and grins.

"To put it simply, Naza and the surrounding city hubs have become points of interest recently, from the NRP's perspective that is. Now, as far as details go pertaining to *why* exactly, I'm not for sure either…our superiors will give us more information as time progresses…however, they were adamant about us getting here as soon as we possibly could…"

"*We're just following orderssssssssssssss,*" Polus interrupts.

Polus' lisp is very pronounced. Jonah takes notice of it and looks at him for moment, but says nothing.

"Yes, we're just following orders," Damien continues with a smile.

"We are not here to step on any toes or overstep our boundaries in any way. We're simply observing, and waiting for further instructions. You're *certainly* still the leader of this ecclesia."

"*The Creator* is the leader of this ecclesia," Jonah responds.

"Why, yes. Very good! Absolutely…" Damien replies.

There is a long, uncomfortable pause. Levi coughs on the other side of the room a couple of times. Damien looks at Jonah and grins, then begins another sentence.

"Yes, very good, Jonah. Well, I suppose we should talk about how you and, *the Creator*, run the show here, shall we?"

Jonah gently releases a bit of air from his nostrils in an abbreviated laugh. He reaches into his desk, pulls out a planner, and sits it in front of him.

"There is one gathering each Sabbath, to serve the many people that live in this area: Naza, Salem, and Samaria primarily. We tend to get a few attendants from S&G from time to time also."

"Interesting names," Damien says with a raise of his eyebrows.

Jonah pauses and shifts his weight, then continues.

"I guess I should explain some of the background first. The time of *awakening* after Star Fall drew everyone back to spirituality—well, those that saw a divine hand faintly through the fogginess of tragedy, that is. A spiritual awakening. *Old America* was gone. *New America* was born. A new identity was needed. It was decided amongst the people to name the newly formed *city hubs* after ancient cities from the original holy books and Grandeurscript, whether actual or mythical; I suppose as a reminder of the truth that what once was, still is, and will always be. It took years for some of the names to stick, but eventually, they became a part of our culture…"

On the wall behind Jonah, there is a large map. He spins around toward it as he speaks.

"Salem, Samaria, Naza, and of course, S&G," Jonah explains, pointing to each of the locations on the map as he says the names.

"*Yesssssss, S&G, the Badlandssssssss,*" Polus interjects.

Jonah swiftly spins his chair back around to the three mysterious men.

"I don't call it that. I don't even like calling it S&G, honestly. But that's what the area is known as, near the Outskirts. Some of the most dangerous areas in all of New America."

"Why don't you like the name?" Levi asks curiously.

"It makes it sound as though they're all condemned. They're not all bad people, even though that's the reputation they have. Children are born there every single day. I hate that it will become embedded in their minds, more than likely, that they are lost, all because of their environment, which they have no control over— no different than the inhabitants that lived in the original two cities that its name is derived from. I suppose that I'm much like the *ancient father of faith*, constantly interceding for them…"

"There's lotsssssssss, that happensssssss there," adds Polus.

"Yes," responds Jonah, "but there are still good people there. I believe it. Some of them come here on Sabbaths, sporadically maybe, but they still come. The Creator hasn't forgotten about them, and neither will I…"

"See that!" Damien interrupts while pointing his finger at Jonah and looking at Levi and Polus, "a man of *GREAT* character! They don't make them like you anymore, Jonah! Very good! *Very* good!"

There's another brief period of silence.

"So, as you were saying. I see that the gatherings happen at noon every Sabbath, correct?"

"That's correct. There's a popular saying, *'all trains lead to Naza,'*…everyone comes here at noon, the whole world it seems. Thankfully, this old building is large enough to accommodate everyone. Many years ago, it was an athletic stadium…it obviously lost its usefulness for that particular purpose after…after it happened. Thankfully the Creator always has a way of redefining and reassigning the *purpose* of a thing…"

"Ah, I see. Now I understand why we were so easily lost while trying to find your office! So, what happens during the gatherings, exactly?"

"It's pretty straightforward. We begin promptly at noon. People of all faiths and backgrounds come here, and that's what sets the tone for the entire gathering. The communal worshipers fill the center of the stadium and the aisles. They sing and dance, and we all join in for the time of worship in whatever way the attendants personally choose. This lasts for about thirty minutes, normally. While this is going on, there is a time of personal ministry—the intercessors line the aisles praying and ministering to the people as needed. They too come from all faiths and backgrounds, and speak various languages. Sometimes, we get no further than that. But ordinarily, after the time of worship, the people give. They offer what they have…be it rations, clothing—whatever they desire to render to the Creator. Immediately after this, I stand before them and profess what the Creator has given me to say to the people."

"I see, interesting. Sounds very, *spiritual*, I suppose."

"As it should be…"

"Indeed. I do have one question, Jonah…"

"Okay, what is it?"

"Is there a plan, a contingency plan, in the case that something, well, *happens*?"

"Something like what?"

"*Star Fall*…"

Jonah pauses and taps his finger on his desk a few times.

"There's a tunnel that leads to the bunkers. We had it dug many years ago. There are openings throughout the building, and beneath each of the main sections inside the stadium. We've discussed it as a congregation a few times. Everyone is aware. Prayerfully, the bunker construction will be completed before anything happens, that is, if anything were to ever, *happen*…"

"Perfect…perfect! You've got everything under control, I see…"

"The Creator takes care of us…I'm grateful…"

Damien stands. Levi and Polus follow his lead.

"Well, Jonah, this has been a very productive and informative introduction."

Damien stretches his arm out to Jonah, who in turn leans forward over his desk and shakes his hand.

"You just tell us how we can assist you. Again, we are just here in response to the NRP's requests. We will report statuses to them weekly, and follow their pending instructions. Other than that, just let us know what we can do to make your job, *easier*…"

They walk toward the door and exit. Jonah is still seated.

"I most certainly will," Jonah whispers to himself after they leave, intentionally too late.

Down the hallway, Damien places his hands on the shoulders of Levi and Polus as they walk.

With a smile, he says, "very good…"

10. GRATEFUL

"WHEW, FINALLY A spell to rest! It's not like these blasted fields are going anywhere anytime soon! They want us to work like *dogs!*"

The woman sits down on a bench. She removes her surgical mask and a pair of very thick gloves—the type of gloves that a gardener would wear.

She is a jolly woman, with coarse gray hair that's pulled away from her face into a tight bun behind her head. She wears silver-rimmed glasses, thick coveralls, and brown boots.

Martha sits down across from her, under a tent with a white covering above them. They are surrounded by large fields of dust with spread out patches of vegetation: corn, potatoes, and beans mostly. Anything that can be grown in such harsh and limited conditions is there.

"*Old* dogs at that!" Martha replies in agreement with a snicker.

"These breaks are getting shorter and shorter. It seems like as soon as I sit down, the buzzer is screaming at us again!"

Martha pats her hand on the table and laughs.

"You are hilarious, Val!"

"It's the truth—I tell you it's the truth!"

The woman's name is Valerie, Martha's best friend over the years; they were even friends before Star Fall. That's very rare, but it makes their friendship even more special. They started their work in the Agri-Fields together purely by chance, much to their liking. She's known Manny since he was born.

"Val, how's your sister?"

"Oh, she's doing just fine, Martha. I was able to spend the last couple of weeks with her, which was good. She gets a little lonely sometimes all the way out there in Samaria, but she's doing well. I can certainly say that I've missed the IE!"

"I can understand that. I'm glad that she's doing well."

"How's my boy doing? Hopefully I can see him this Sabbath! My sister is doing much better like I said, so I plan to be home for a while."

"He's…he's doing well. He just, I don't know…he seems sad sometimes. But he's doing okay."

"Child, I understand. This world can make the best of us sad. Believe me, I know."

"I suppose you're right. I just…I just want him to be happy and really see the good in the bad."

"He will, Mar. He will. Give him time. He's a good boy."

Valerie pauses and looks off toward a tent not far from their own. A group of Agri-Field workers are gawking at a bulletin board. The heading reads:

STAR FALL: THIRTEENTH ANNIVERSARY (NEVER FORGOTTEN)

She sighs under her breath and then looks back at Martha. Martha is staring down at the bench they're sitting at, but it's clear that her thoughts are far away from the tent, and far away from the Agri-Fields too for that matter.

"Does he still have the dreams, Mar?"

Martha inhales deeply then releases the air with a *whoosh*.

"Just about every night."

Valerie nods as though she expected the response.

"I'm sure it probably gets worse around this time of year. I guess none of us have ever really gotten over it all the way…"

"I wish that we could; I wish that Manny could."

Valerie leans toward Martha swiftly, causing Martha to look her in the face.

"But that's just it, Mar! Eventually Manny will see the bigger picture of it all. How all of this, as horrible as it seems to be now, is just a little piece in a big puzzle. All of us are in that puzzle—Manny too. Wormwood, all of them. All of it means something. We just have to do the hard, hard work of figuring out what that *something* is…"

Martha smiles and looks back down toward the bench.

"He doesn't like to hear that at all. He doesn't like much talk about Star Fall, about Wormwood, the way things were before—none of it. It still bothers him, I know it. He's hurting…"

There's a brief pause.

Valerie reaches over and holds Martha's hand to comfort her. She shakes it. Martha squeezes her hand back.

"I will keep him in my prayers then—I know that you're already praying for him. Maybe mine can add a little more fuel to the fire?"

"Thank you, Val. Please do. Pray for both of us."

Martha gives Valerie a weak smile, which Valerie accepts and returns.

Martha pauses again. She rubs her own arm and inhales slowly. The wind blows bits of dust onto the bench. Martha notices. She's reminded of her reality—their reality.

"He was so young, Val. He was so young when it happened, just six years old. It's too much for any child to have to go through."

"It was too much for us old folks, so I know that it was too much for him; too much for all of them."

"I know. But it just did something different to him. It's hard to explain…"

"Well, this break isn't over yet. I'm here if you want to talk about it."

Martha offers her another sad smile.

"The explosions were so sudden. We sat in that gymnasium, completely confused and afraid for the first few hours. It was so frantic in there. No one really knew what to do. We had only heard warning sirens like that on television and in movies—those old war movies. That's exactly what it was like…"

"It was. I remember."

Valerie lets out a low moan and closes her eyes, remembering that day and her own pain, along with Martha. Martha places her hand on her head. She sees the whole tragic movie again in her mind.

~ ~ ~

"Where's Granny? Where's sisser?" Manny's small voice demands, "what's happening, mommy? I don't like fire. I'm scared mommy. Where's Granny and sisser?"

"Just calm down honey, okay?"

He tugs her arm with tears streaming down his face while she yells at the policeman.

"Sir! Excuse me! I need you to listen to me! They are still out there! My mother and my daughter! My mother looks very much like me. My daughter is about his height, and…"

"Ma'am! There's nothing that I can do right now! We are trying our best; please go inside the gymnasium, ma'am. We have everyone that we can out looking for missing people, but you *have* to step inside, ma'am…*please*…"

Martha bursts into tears and picks Manny up. He curls up into a ball on her shoulder. Afraid. Confused. He's one of hundreds of children feeling the exact same emotions.

Martha dashes into the building.

Not a single person inside is sanitary. People are covered in blood and ash. The smell is repulsive, nearly unbearable. The scents of smoke, urine, feces, and vomit waft through the air. Clothes are torn. Faces are distraught. It's frenzied. People are stumbling over one another. Children stand outside the doorway, crying and screaming, alone and disoriented.

After a few hours, the volunteers and medical personnel are able to create a faint sense of safety and solace. There are many who are still asking where loved ones are. They are asking what happened. There are about five televisions on the walls of the gymnasium that policemen have brought in so that everyone can stay up-to-date with the latest developments.

No solid answers, just frightening phrases being used repeatedly over the television speakers:

"Global attack."
"Unprecedented."
"Act of terrorism."
"The *worst* event in world history."

The President gives some speeches. The United Nations is going to meet that evening, and so is NATO. Prayer vigils are being held around the world: Africa, Asia, Europe, Australia, everywhere. Everyone is affected.

~ ~ ~

"Sir, I haven't been able to locate my mother yet. Have there been any others brought in?"

"No, ma'am, not lately. There's a list being kept at the front desk down that hallway; maybe there's something there?"

"Come on Manny…"

They walk down the hallway. He's tired and hungry. He's sleepy.

"Is sisser okay? And Granny? Is sisser up there, mommy?"

"They're going to be okay sweetie. Let's go and check the list to see if they've come to join us yet. Okay? Sound good?" she says with a trembling voice and forced smile, while choking back her tears.

Their names aren't listed.

They never joined them.

Never.

~ ~ ~

Martha has mentally returned there and can't seem to find her way back. She recalls the conversation that she and Manny had just a few nights after that moment. It still brings a heavy sadness to her heart.

~ ~ ~

"What? What do you mean? They *have* to come be with us, mommy!" Manny says with tears rolling down his tiny, plump cheeks.

"They *have* to come, mommy!"

He runs toward the large doors.

She chases him. It's evening. It's raining.

"Where are they, mommy? *Sisser! Granny! Sisser! Granny!*" he yells into the moist night air.

He calls for them while sprinting to nowhere.

She chases him through the rain, crying.

There are people standing at the door and watching them.

She stops and drops to her knees, overwhelmed with grief. He hears her whimpers intensify. Unaware of how to respond, he stops running. He turns and walks to her, looking into her eyes, which are the same distance from the ground as his own now.

"They are with the Creator now, Manny…"

Her cry overtakes her. Her head drops.

She lifts it again.

"He wanted them to be with *him*…they are with *him* now, honey…"

The words shake Manny in a way that a child should never be shaken.

His eyes widen and dart back and forth as his brain attempts to process his mother's piercing words. Unaware of what to do, he tilts his head back and yells at the top of his lungs into the blanketing sky:

"I *HATE* HIM, MOMMY—I HATE HIM SO MUCH!" "*THE CREATOR ISN'T REAL!*"

The words strike her heart like a bolt of lightning.

~ ~ ~

Valerie touches her hand, noticing that Martha is in a distant place. Her touch is a rope that lassos Martha and pulls her back to this world. Martha smiles out of courtesy and a sense of obligation.

"We sat in that gymnasium for weeks, Val. The pain I saw in his eyes—I couldn't bear it. He was so hurt and angry. *So* confused. He couldn't understand how this could happen. He loved them so much…"

Valerie says nothing. She just nods her head.

They fall silent again, another one of the many times that silence has spoken volumes in their conversation today. Martha forces herself to perk up.

"Ah! I'm not going to fall into this trap again. Every anniversary we all do this! We start moping and reminiscing and re-living it. *Not* today..."

The words are like hands that forcefully choke her cry to death just moments before it overpowers her.

"You're right, Mar...you're so right! No use in going back to the past. We've *got* to keep moving forward!"

"We do! We do! In fact, do you remember the *good* old days... not the bad ones, but the *good* ones?"

Valerie hears the words and journeys to another world. A happier world.

"Yes! Before *all* of this. I'm convinced that we didn't know how good we had it!"

"You're right! That's usually how it goes, doesn't it? We don't appreciate what we have until we lose it..."

"You've got that right!"

"We had cars, not these trains. And television! Oh, how I miss my *television*!"

"Me too! Can't forget grocery stores!"

"Oh! I would spend *hours* in the grocery store, picking out everything I needed to cook that evening. And of course, a few things that I *didn't* need."

Valerie pats the table with her palm and releases a hearty laugh at the statement.

"Ah! I miss it so much!"

"So do I. Shopping centers, malls, restaurants—even schools. I would take Manny every morning and kiss him on his cheek just to watch him wipe it off as he walked into the building."

"Yes, my little Eric would do the exact same thing..."

Valerie falls silent before she completes the phrase and stares off as if she's suddenly become lost. She slowly lowers her head. Martha reaches over and grabs her hand, offering the same consoling gesture that Valerie extended to her just moments ago.

"He's in a better place, Val…"

"I know, Martha."

As she says it, she looks around at their surroundings.

"At least we have the IE—it gives us all hope. Even those who don't fully believe, or just don't believe at all," Martha says.

"Yes, I agree. Jonah is such an awesome leader. I'm so grateful for him."

"So am I. I just hope that Manny can see it eventually."

"He will, Martha, he will."

"Thanks, Val. You know, he used to *love* the gatherings when he was really young, ironically…"

"Did he now?"

"Yes, absolutely. I remember it. I think it's the size of the IE that bothers him. The IE is so large; it seems to just swallow you up when you walk in. And the people—*so* many people…I think he feels lost in there…out of place…"

The buzzer sounds.

"Well, you know what that means," Martha says sorrowfully.

"Yes, I do…*mush on, mush on!*"

Martha laughs loudly.

"Val, you are a riot! I'm *so* grateful for you…"

"And I'm grateful for you, sweetie!"

Valerie places her hand on Martha's shoulder.

They exchange smiles once more, then walk back to the fields.

11. SEE YOU ON THE SABBATH

"I DON'T UNDERSTAND why it's such a big deal to go. Manny is probably right," Rock grumbles to Grea.

The work day is over. Manny is still inside the gate putting his tools way and cleaning up his work area.

Grea and Rock await their train. Rock stands with his shoulder propped against a metal support connected to the train platform. Grea is sitting on the edge of an elevated sidewalk area.

"Rock, Rock, Rock...*you* know just as well as I do how important it is. It's all we have..."

"I hear what you're saying. But I mean, let's be honest. What difference has it really made so far? You know? What difference have you seen? Things are the same way they've been since we were kids."

Grea looks off into the field beyond the Shield and lets out a laugh of unbelief as she shakes her head. She's quieter than she normally is—a little *too* quiet.

"What is it?" Rock finally says.

She rubs her eyebrow, then looks over at her brother.

"You just don't get it. Or maybe you do, and you just like to pretend that you don't..."

"Get what?"

"That we're not in this alone. That nothing is coincidence; not even Star Fall..."

~ ~ ~

"What if it is, Grea? How would you handle it?"

It's Manny. He joins them at the train stop without either of them noticing.

She pauses again. She draws something on the ground with a small stick. After a few seconds, she looks up at Manny and says, "and what if it isn't? How would *you* handle it?"

Manny smiles, unable to deny that her response was quite witty.

He lets out a short breath and looks down in thought, but says nothing. He stoops, picks up a handful of pebbles, and begins tossing them into the dusty field in front of them. Rock joins him.

"I look at it like this," Rock says, "if the *Creator* is real, he will honor the fact that we at least come, right? I mean, that has to at least count for *something*."

"Good point, Rock, *good* point," Manny agrees as he glances in Grea's direction.

"It *would* be a good point, *if* it were true," Grea responds sarcastically.

They laugh.

"That's like coming here to the Shield, day in and day out, but not working. Never touching a single piece of equipment or weapon—just sitting in the break area all day long. Eventually, someone is going to complain and it would start a whole list of issues."

Rock tosses a small pebble at her but she dodges it.

"You know it's true. And not just that, but ultimately, you'd be hurting the people who may eventually need the equipment. That's how I look at it. Who am I hurting if I don't interact and get involved with what the Creator is doing? Even if it seems like he's been really quiet and motionless for a while..."

Manny tosses a pebble at her too. She laughs.

"You get a kick out of this don't you, Grea?" Manny says.

"Of *course*, she does," Rock adds.

"I'm just stating facts, old men. You should be ashamed of yourselves! Sitting up in the skybox every Sabbath, doing *who knows* what…"

"Hey, we have a good time. And like I said before; at *least* we're there," Rock says, mockingly.

"You should really hear Jonah out. He's awesome," responds Grea, as one of Manny's pebbles hits a metal sign and makes a *clank*.

"*Sheesh*, you sound like my mom," Manny interrupts.

Grea completely ignores him and continues.

"He's got a good heart. Super humble, friendly, and approachable. But beyond that, I know that the Creator speaks through him. He's personally told me things that only the Creator could possibly have known about me; things that I haven't told *anyone*. He's spiritual, very spiritual. It's pretty intimidating, but not in a weird way. Just in a way that makes me respect him. Is that why you avoid him, Manny? You sense it too, huh?"

Manny stares at her. The truth in her statement pierces him. He tries to pretend that he's unaffected.

"I don't avoid him. I just, don't really have much to say to him I guess…"

"You *totally* avoid him, but *anyway*. He's like a symbol of hope. I know that we're not supposed to put our trust in others… only in the Creator…but Jonah *really is* chosen. It's obvious that the Creator uses him."

The train approaches and slows to a stop in front of them with a grinding, metallic sound.

"I *don't* avoid him," Manny says as they separate.

Manny's train is to their left, Grea and Rock's train, to their right.

"*You do!*" Grea yells out with her finger in the air, "see you on the Sabbath!" she continues, just as she boards the train, still wagging her finger.

Rock pushes her inside the train door gently. Her hand emerges, pushing him back in his chest. He looks over at Manny and tosses both hands up as if to say, *"what am I going to do with her?"*

Rock climbs onto the train and the doors close.

Manny laughs to himself and shakes his head. The Shield's front platform is empty now. The sun will be setting in a few hours. Manny still has one of the pebbles in his hand. He stares at it and eventually tosses it back into the pile that it came from.

"Are you coming, son? It's time to go. Getting late," the conductor says to him.

He's an elderly, peaceful-looking man. He waves his hand, motioning for Manny to get on.

"See you on the Sabbath," Manny says to himself in a delayed response as he finally boards.

12. TOO SOON

"HOW WILL WE know who he is?" Levi asks his comrades.

The train has booth-style seats, similar to a restaurant. All of the trains do. They are very modern on the inside, but dusty and corroded on the outside. The TRN-13 is heading to Eastern Naza. Inside, Levi sits directly across from Damien and Polus.

"We won't. We just have to trust that Master will reveal him to us," Damien responds.

Levi nods and glances toward the window. He is the newest to this union.

"You *sssssstill* have much to learn about the *Ssssssssssshedim*," adds Polus.

"He will…in due time," Damien says.

The train rumbles forward. It's beginning to get darker outside. Levi watches the clouds as they zoom through the sky. Clearly, he's still thinking.

"What happens after we figure out who he is? What do we do then?" Levi asks timidly.

Damien clears his throat. He picks up a glass that is in front of them on a small table and examines it. Levi looks at him with a puzzled glare. Damien places the glass back onto the table, then reaches into his breast pocket and pulls out an ancient-looking flask. It's made of mostly metal, but has wooden areas that are covered with carvings and engravings that look to be in an archaic language. There are skulls, bones, cryptic symbols, and other shapes on it.

Levi tries his best to not stare at it.

Damien pours some of its contents into the glass—it smells putrid. A bubbly, thick, burgundy liquid. Damien picks up the glass and drinks; his eyes glow a bright and deep yellowish color for just a few seconds as the drink apparently satisfies him. He closes his eyes, tilts his head back, and sighs with gratification.

"Point him out to me if you locate him. That's all. I will take care of it from there…" Damien finally responds.

Levi nods, and looks back out of the window toward the clouds.

Damien hands the flask to Polus, who pours some of the liquid into a glass as well and drinks it. It affects him the same way. He holds it out to offer some of it to Levi. Damien lifts his hand and stops Polus.

"It's too soon…" Damien warns as he takes the flask from Polus and places it back inside of his breast pocket.

"The Sabbath is coming. We may be able to find him during the gathering at the IE. Another day or so. When we go, we must blend in. Just be watchful…"

13. TALK TO ME

THE TRN-3 ROLLS toward Naza. They've made their stop at the Agri-Fields. Martha is sleeping in an uncomfortable position next to Manny. He stares out of the window, as he often does—thinking. He looks over and notices his mother's position and gently pulls her closer to him so that she can rest on his shoulder. After they arrive at their apartment building, he helps her off of the train, up the stairs, and into the living room to her favorite chair.

"*Take a seat, young lady...*" he whispers softly.

She's still drowsy.

He kneels in front of her, removes her work boots, and replaces them with her comfortable slippers. They are all black and look much like karate shoes, which he often jokes about. He stands up after he's done putting them on and does a traditional martial arts bow with his fist pressed against his palm.

She chuckles.

"You're so silly..." she says.

She taps his leg with the back of her hand as he walks past her.

They both look forward to evenings when they can sit and talk after work for a little while before bed.

In the kitchen, he starts making some warm tea for her on the stove.

Martha has dozed off again.

While the tea is being prepared, Manny is in his room putting away his clothes as thoughts float around in his mind. He reflects on the day. He thinks of his friends. He contemplates the upcoming Sabbath. But mostly, he thinks about his conversation with Grea.

Eventually, the teapot whistles.

Martha hears it and awakes as Manny comes back into the kitchen. He pours two cups and returns to the living room. He places one of the cups in front of his mother and says, "here you are, sensei…"

"Oh, *hush*! Leave my shoes alone!"

They laugh together.

Manny sits down on the couch across the room from Martha. He hangs one leg over the chair's arm, places his tea cup on the table, and lies back with his forearm over his face.

"Tired?" Martha asks.

"I am. Long day," he replies.

"Don't I know it…" she says.

They sit quietly for a few moments.

Martha leans forward and turns on an old radio that is on her table.

Static.

"You know that nothing's going to play, right?"

"I know, I just like this old radio. It helps me to remember…"

She sips her tea.

"This is good."

She takes another sip.

"Manny, I nearly forgot to tell you, Valerie asked about you today."

"Oh, did she? Tell her that I said hello when you see her tomorrow."

"I sure will."

"How's she doing?"

"Oh, you know, she's *Valerie*…"

Manny giggles.

"Yes, she is."

"She's doing pretty well. *Still* a comedian. I'm glad that she still has her sense of humor…after her sister's little, *episode*…"

"That's really good. I'm glad too."

"We talked about the Sabbath for a little while, and the way things used to be…"

Manny falls silent. The pressure in the room changes.

"I told her how you feel about it…"

Another long pause.

"Why do you always do that, ma?"

"Do what?"

"You bring up the IE, and Jonah, and all of this stuff. I don't want to hear about that all the time. I hear *enough* about it from Grea…"

She waits. She drinks more of her tea. She looks at her son with loving and understanding eyes.

"Manny…"

"Yes, ma…" he sighs.

"When you were born, I remember being so overjoyed. Val fell in love with you. She was so happy for me—for us. You had me wrapped around your little finger from day one. You still do…"

Manny moves his arm momentarily and looks over at her. He smiles. He puts it back over his face.

"Manny, talk to me…"

"I *am* talking to you."

"I mean, *really* talk to me, Manny. What is it? Something troubles you and has troubled you since…since it happened. The dreams…well, nightmares, I guess. The anger that you don't talk about. The discomfort and frustration when anyone brings up the IE, or Jonah, or *the Creator*…"

"Can we not talk about this tonight, mom? Please?"

She pauses again.

"Okay. I won't press it. But could you at least do an old woman one little favor?"

"And what exactly might that be?"

"Come help me get up; it's time for me to go to bed. The Agri-Fields will be waiting for me tomorrow."

He sits up and picks up his cup of tea. He puts his pointer finger in it to make sure it's not too hot, then drinks it all, quickly, with three large gulps.

"Goodness…I don't know how you do that…I have to sip mine," Martha says.

"Takes years of practice, sensei…"

She waves her hand at him in a quick dismissive motion and giggles.

He picks up her tea cup as well.

"Be right back. Then we'll get you to bed."

He takes the cups into the kitchen and washes them quickly. He blows out the living room and kitchen lamps, but leaves the hallway lamp lit.

He goes back into the living room, helps Martha up, and slowly walks her down the hallway.

Just before she enters her room, she stops and turns to him. She places both of her hands on his shoulders.

"Will you at least think about it? For me?"

"Think about what?"

"Sitting with me, this Sabbath. You know, the way we used to when you were young…"

He breathes out of his nose and looks her in the eyes. He cannot deny that he loves this woman with his whole heart.

"I'm not asking for a definite yes. Just an, *I'll think about it, because you're the best mother in the world*, that's all," she says meekly before he can offer his response.

Manny smiles.

"I'll think about it, because you're the *best* mother in the world," he answers.

She grins, lets out a faint squeal of happiness, and quickly claps her hands a couple of times.

"Thank you! Have a good night honey, okay?"

Manny giggles at her reaction.

"Goodnight ma, I love you."

She touches his nose with her pointer finger and says, "I love you more…"

14. SABBATH

MARTHA ALWAYS WAKES up early on Sabbaths. She has no other choice except to rise early during the week for work, but she is usually up even earlier on the days like today.

Her routine is always the same. She goes into the kitchen and makes breakfast, knowing that Manny will be up soon. When she's done cooking, she places it neatly onto the kitchen table and covers it with a paper towel or napkin. Then, she goes back into her room and pulls out a very old and dilapidated Grandeurscript that she's had for years now. She reads for a while, and then she kneels beside her bed and whispers prayers that eventually become loud enough for Manny to hear.

Manny gets up not long after her. The combination of being able to hear her talking to the Creator, and the smell of "his favorite" coming from the kitchen, are enough to pull him out of his sleep.

He didn't have his dream last night. It was a good night's sleep.

"Morning," he says as he passes her room and walks to the kitchen.

She's sitting on her bed, closing up her Grandeurscript.

"Good morning sweetie."

It's not long before they are downstairs waiting for the train.

Everyone is outside, just like it's a work day, except, the people are happier. The atmosphere is very different. There's a lot more conversation. A lot more peace. Everyone is upbeat. Everyone except Manny.

Martha places her hand on his shoulder and rubs it gently.

She doesn't say much, but she knows what he's feeling and thinking.

He feels no different than he does any other day.

She wishes that Sabbaths gave him the same peace, joy, and hope as they do everyone else.

He touches her hand, looks at her, and gives her half of a smile.

The train approaches and they board it.

~ ~ ~

The ride is about twenty minutes.

The IE is located at the edge of Naza, which makes it easily accessible for not only the Naza Remnants, but also Remnants from the surrounding city hubs.

For the last five minutes of the ride, the train climbs a very steep hill, *Sinai*: the place where, *"the Creator speaks to his people."*

Children on the train rush to the windows. It never fails. It's an experience that they all look forward to.

All of the trains merge at Sinai. To the left and right, all of the other trains can be seen making the very same climb. The children point and wave in excitement. Once upon a time, Manny did the same thing. Even now, he smiles when it happens.

One of the children hops onto Manny's lap out of pure excitement and places his finger on the window. Manny jumps from being startled, and then laughs.

"Micha!" a woman screeches from behind Manny's head.

The child's mother rushes to him and picks him up.

"I'm so sorry, he's just..." she says.

"It's okay, ma'am..." Manny says reassuringly.

"Micha, tell him you're sorry..."

"I sowwie!" the little boy says with a huge smile on his face, and then runs down the aisle toward another group of children in the back of the train.

Manny smiles again. The woman chases after him.

Manny looks out of the window once more.

"All trains lead to Naza," he whispers to himself. His mother is in the seat in front of him, still giggling about the little boy who just jumped into his lap.

Finally, the trains reach the top of Sinai and the IE can be seen.

It's not rundown and falling apart like many of the other buildings in Naza. The community came together to repair and renovate it after Star Fall. Everyone values it and wants it to be taken care of properly. There is a level area at the very top of Sinai which resembles a volcano with its opening filled in and flattened out. This is where the IE sits, dead center of a few rows of trees and bushes; some of the only trees and bushes that still grow in Naza.

It's absolutely stunning, considering the state of the rest of the world.

Everyone exits the trains. They laugh, hug, talk, and cry; everything that you could expect from a group of people who have only a few precious things left in life to hold on to. Manny helps his mother off of the train; they stand on the platform.

"Mar!"

Valerie approaches from behind them.

"I was looking for you!" Valerie says.

"Val, hey sweetheart!"

They hug each other like reunited sisters.

"Manny, I know you're not going to just stand there! Come here! Give Auntie Val a hug! I haven't seen you in weeks!"

Manny smiles and obeys.

"How's your sister doing, Miss Val?"

"Oh, she's doing good—*really* good."

"I'm glad to hear that."

"So am I, Manny! So am I! It's good to see that you're doing well too...Mar and I were just talking about you the other day at work..."

"Oh, you *were?*"

Manny looks at his mother. She looks back and makes a feigned expression of innocence.

"Umhm. Nothing bad. You know that I have to check on you from time to time...that's all. Well, we'd better get inside and grab seats, I don't want to have to sit too far back! Come on! I've been missing this place!"

As they are walking inside the lobby, Manny sees Grea and Rock walking into a different set of entrance doors.

"I'll be right back," Manny says hastily while in the process of darting off toward the doors.

"Manny, where are you..." Martha blurts out.

Before she can finish the sentence, he's surfing through the crowd to get to his friends.

"Rock, hold on!"

Rock turns his head, recognizing Manny's voice, and tries to find his face in the crowd. Finally, he sees him.

"Manny!"

"Hey, Manny!"

"Grea! How long have you guys been here?"

"Not long, we're just now getting off of the train," Rock answers.

"Mom and miss Val are over here," Manny says, pointing to where he just came from.

"Okay, we're coming," Grea says.

In a few moments, they're all standing together in the lobby. People are still pouring in. They all talk with each other for a while and then move farther inside. Even though they've all been in this building countless times, it always has a sense of newness for each of them. It's unexplainable.

The Naza IE is gigantic. It captivates and impresses with little effort. Professional sports teams once played in the stadium during the Old America era, so it's extremely spacious. There's decorative artistry on every wall that's been collected and salvaged: paintings, pottery, sculptures, and carvings. The building swallows everyone who enters. The atmosphere is a cross between a very prestigious museum, a movie theatre, and a governmental facility. All of the aisles lead directly to a large platform which is the main stage. Behind the stage, there are numerous large screens. The stadium has coliseum-style seating that stretches up many feet above the floor.

All of the seats are different colors with small numbers on the backs of them.

There are men, women, and children of all ages, who are wearing matching shirts, lining the rows and greeting people as they enter.

High above the floor are a few rows of balcony seats that look exactly the same as the floor seats, except they tower over the entire arena. There are concrete steps that lead to them. Above the balcony are the *skyboxes*. They look like white, cube-shaped, bird houses fixated high in the air. Those who are uninterested in the gatherings, and in *the Creator* for that matter, typically go to the skyboxes. That's usually where Manny and Rock can be found, along with other occasional believers, non-believers, those with nagging spiritual questions, and those who once had questions, but have grown tired of them and quieted them altogether.

They reach the stairwell that leads up to the skyboxes. Rock doesn't hesitate sprinting up them. Manny stalls. Martha stalls too. It's a moment that only the two of them notice. Grea and Valerie continue walking to their seats close to the front.

Manny thinks about his mother's words just days prior:

"Will you at least think about it? For me?"

She waits. He smiles at her and reluctantly shakes his head. She smiles back, and nods gently. She lifts her hand to her mouth, kisses her fingertips, then gently blows on them in his direction.

He touches his chest above his heart, then turns and disappears in the stairwell.

15. SKYBOX

THIN LAYERS OF cigarette smoke hover like tiny stratus clouds just below the ceiling. Mostly men are here, but there are a handful of women also. You feel like you're walking into a nightclub, or a bar, and someone is about to ask, *"so what are you having, the usual?"*

There's a tile floor with a black and white checkerboard pattern, similar to one that you'd see at a barbershop. Tables are sporadically arranged throughout the room. All of the skyboxes are similarly organized. This one is Manny's favorite. It's positioned directly in front of the center of the main floor. The window that is facing the main floor is dirty, but still clear enough to see through fairly well.

Card games, board games, profanity-decorated conversations, and middle-aged men taking naps—commonalities in this, "sinner's paradise."

Manny is mostly comfortable here, but not completely. He figures that he'd be even *less* comfortable sitting with his mother down below on the main floor, so this is the better of the two options. Rock enjoys the card games; poker to be exact. It makes him feel like an adult, *officially*.

"A lounge for the lost and indifferent."

Manny has heard that phrase on a few occasions. It doesn't really bother him.

One of the regular attendees wrote it down on a sheet of notebook paper and taped it onto the wall, many years ago. It's still there.

"Five-card-draw, or straight?" a pudgy, balding man says to Rock as he and Manny walk into the room.

A cigar hangs from the man's lips as he shuffles a deck of cards.

He is looking at Rock with squinted eyes, studying his potential opponent.

"What's the difference?" Rock asks him with his head to the side and eyebrows lowered.

"Heck, your guess is as good as mine…I just like the way it sounds…"

They nod at each other and say, *"straight,"* simultaneously.

Manny sits at a table near them and watches the cards fly back and forth. Neither Rock or the man appear to be fully sure of what they're doing.

A younger woman sits across the room drinking something from a plastic cup. Her hair is messy, her pants and shirt are both dirty, and her skin is noticeably soiled. Manny assumes that she could be a *Collector*.

Collectors are typically filthy in comparison to other Remnants; the nature of their work makes it so. It's no different than Agri-Field workers having a cough, Medics having dry hands from constantly wearing latex gloves, Preservers having shiny skin from water filtration fumes, and Shield workers having oil-stained hands and fingernails from the greasy electrical equipment that they repair—nearly everyone shows some physical sign of their occupation.

Manny looks at his hands briefly as he thinks about it.

The woman gazes at the wall behind Manny, saying nothing, and sipping from her cup periodically. She's like a zombie.

A couple of small children play with marbles in the hallway.

A light hangs just above the card table, flickering.

Three or four gentlemen at a table behind Manny have an animated discussion about whether Medics, Collectors, or Preservers have better jobs.

Manny takes it all in. He always does.

The gathering will be starting soon, he can see the countdown through the cloudy glass. It appears to go so slowly. Manny remembers when he would sit on the main floor and listen attentively, but that was years ago. Jonah would speak for what felt like just a few minutes. Manny loved it. He never wanted to leave gatherings when they were over. They seem to last much longer now, and he can't wait to leave. He's not even sure of what happens in there these days—whether it's exactly the same, or if it's changed at all.

Grea, Miss Valerie, and his mother always say how *amazing* it was. They always get something precious from it: a catch phrase, a quote, a thought. Something. He's just happy that neither of them really pushes him to come inside, even though he knows they each desperately want him to.

A soft but strong voice breaks the solitude of his thoughts.

"Hey...can you *stop?*"

Manny looks in the direction that the voice came from.

It's her. The young woman in the corner. She's looking directly at him; no longer gazing off in the distance in a trance. Her eyes are piercing. It's eerie.

Before, she seemed to be lost, like she was under the influence of some type of medication. Now, she is completely aware and conscious.

She says it again, looking Manny straight in the eyes.

"Yes. You. *Can you stop?*"

16. SIT HERE

> *"A man came as a witness long ago, during a critical time...he was a witness of a great light that has shined into the darkness of humanity since the beginning...he came so that others could eventually see that light, and believe. He himself wasn't the fullness of the light, but he was the foreshadowing of it...he came to show its possibilities, and draw others to it..."* ~Grandeurscript

LEVI, DAMIEN, AND Polus stand in a side hallway just beyond the main floor. Levi is scratching himself uncontrollably. Polus is noticeably uncomfortable and adjusts his shirt collar; he's scratching as well, but not as much as Levi.

"I don't know if I can *take* this," Levi says.

"Just relax, take deep breaths. Don't focus on the itching," Damien responds.

"It feels like my *skin* is *crawling*! Why?"

"*It'sssss* because so many of them are gathered together," Polus responds.

"*He'ssss here...*"

Polus spews the words as he looks up toward the stadium's ceiling through the cracked door that they're standing behind.

"I hope this is over soon," Levi says as he jerks at his blazer and rolls his head around in his best effort to find some relief.

"Just relax," says Damien.

"Be watchful…*the Witness* is probably out there somewhere…"

Levi and Polus both nod in agreement.

They open the cracked door and enter into the main floor area. There is a long aisle that encircles the main stage. The lights are dim. They walk around the aisle as there are hundreds of people seated in the stands as far back as they can see. Most of them have their hands lifted in the air. Many are crying out phrases and words in various languages:

> *"Glory to the Creator!"*
> *"Allah Hu Akbar!"*
> *"Deus Est!"*
> *"Aleluya!"*

People of all languages—of all ethnicities and nationalities are lifting their voices and praising the same Creator, in their own, personal way.

The trio navigates through the aisle, maneuvering past individuals who are either praying, singing, crying, kneeling, or completely lying down prostrate on the floor and mumbling words. The sound is enchanting.

There are men, women, and children decorating the aisles and waving colorful banners in the air. Although the auditorium is dimly lit, it's still bright enough to faintly make out people's faces. There are about eight men and women arranged around the main platform who are playing various instruments: horns, flutes, and large drums that must be played with open palms. There is somewhat of a mist beginning to form in the room. It is hard to tell whether or not the mist is naturally occurring, or *supernatural*. The room is not hot, so it's probably not likely being produced from heat or humidity; the often-shifting atmospheric patterns in the land are not to blame this time.

Large numbers appear on the screens above, starting at one minute. They go backward, second by second. When it's down to fifteen seconds, Damien stops walking and points at three open seats off to the side of the platform.

"Sit here," he says to his comrades as he scans the auditorium.

"We have the best vantage point of everyone here from this spot. We can see what Jonah sees…"

As they take their seats, the numbers count down even further.

5…

4…

Levi fiercely scratches at his neck again. Damien looks at him. He stops.

3…

The room falls dead silent. Everyone who was up in the aisles or performing their own personal form of worship finds their way to their seat.

2…

The music stops.

1...

The lights in the auditorium dim even more, and spotlights point to center stage.

No one makes a sound.

Perfect silence.

Muffled footsteps.

Mechanical noises.

An opening appears at center stage and a compartment elevates from it. The door of the compartment opens, and out walks Jonah. He doesn't believe in glorying in one's self or worldly pleasures. His clothes are tattered, as they normally are, but they still fit him fashionably because of his physique.

His jeans have small tears and dark spots on them. He has on a dark green military-like shirt, and a tactical jacket with lots of pockets all over it. His black shoes are laced all the way up and fit perfectly under the cuffs of his jeans. Jonah walks forward to the microphone stand that's at the front edge of the platform. When he reaches it, he says a single statement with the type of refined clarity that only he can muster:

"Our Creator is *great*..."

The room erupts with applause, cheers, screams, and praises. The noise can probably be heard for miles. With a bright smile that seems to add additional lighting to the room, Jonah lifts his hands to quiet the crowd and signals for them to be seated.

"Well, he really *must* be great, based on that response!"

The crowd laughs, and so does Jonah.

"Whelp," he says with a clap of his hands, "let's get started. The Creator has really laid a *lot* of things on my heart to share with..."

He pauses as he looks over to his right and sees Damien, Levi, and Polus seated there. They look completely out of place. They stare back at him. Damien smiles back slyly and nods gently. Jonah takes in a small breath and then turns his head back to the crowd. His eyes scan all around him as he looks at the hundreds, maybe thousands of people.

He continues, "…with you today, so I suppose we should begin. Let's take a look at the Grandeurscript…"

17. JHENDA

"Excuse me?" Manny asks the woman with the Styrofoam cup.

"I said, *can you stop?*" she responds matter-of-factly.

"Stop what?"

"Stop picking your lip; it's annoying. Actually, it's kind of disgusting…"

Manny looks at his hand as he pulls it away from his face.

He picks at his bottom lip when he's nervous or in deep thought.

"Well, sorry that it bothered you so much…"

"It's okay. Thanks for stopping," she says with a wink.

She smirks and then taps her pointer finger on her cup.

"What's your name?" she asks.

"Emmanuel. Or, just Manny. Manny Kohen. What's yours?"

"Jhenda."

"Nice to meet you, Jhenda. Nice name," Manny says.

"Thanks, Emmanuel, *Manny Kohen…*"

"Do you have a last name?" Manny asks.

She takes another sip from her cup without breaking eye contact with him.

"Why does that matter?"

"I…uhh…I guess it doesn't, I just figured that…"

"I'm kidding…it's Boyd," she says in the middle of his stuttering.

"Oh, okay…Jhenda Boyd…got it," Manny says, relieved.

Manny moves his chair closer to her. As he does, he looks over his shoulder and sees that Rock is totally preoccupied with his card game; he doesn't even notice Manny moving.

Jhenda sits her cup down next to her.

"So how come I haven't seen you up here before?" Manny asks.

"I don't always come. And when I do, I usually don't sit in *this* skybox. This one's the busiest, I think. I usually go to one of the ones on the corners…"

She points to the side of the room in the direction of the corner most skybox.

"Oh, I see. Why's that?"

"Less people. Less noise," she says blandly.

"Makes sense…"

Manny looks at her pants. They're torn in many places; one of her pockets is almost ripped completely off. She notices him looking at her pants and looks down at them along with him.

"Yes, I'm a *Scavenger*…"

"What?" Manny says, a bit caught off guard.

"You were about to ask, right?"

"I'm sorry. I didn't mean to…"

"It's okay. Really. Don't apologize. We're like unicorns—people don't expect to see us without our gear on."

She smiles. As she does, Manny feels a little less embarrassed about his staring.

"What's it like?"

"What, being a Scavenger?"

"Yes. Well, no, a *Collector*…"

"Scavenger is fine…"

"You guys are okay with that name?"

"It's not offensive, I mean, we do sort of *scavenge*, right? Besides, everyone has a moniker: Scavengers, Greasers, Harvesters, Preservers, Needlers, and the list goes on. The world will always have a name for you; the important thing is deciding what you will answer to…"

"Humph," Manny says with a look of mild surprise and a grin.

She changes positions and leans in a little closer to him.

"You want to know what it's like, huh?"

"I…I suppose?" he stutters.

"Just imagine waking up every morning before the sun is even out…"

She pauses and gazes at him. She doesn't blink.

"…climbing out of your warm bed and dropping your feet into boots that are as cold as concrete in the winter…"

She continues. Her face is completely emotionless.

"Imagine not even showering until the week is over, because you know that it's pointless. Then, putting on a twenty-pound hazmat suit and walking out of your door, knowing that you won't be back until it's dark again; that's *if* you make it back. Climbing hills covered in sewage and bacteria for hours and hours: either in the hot sun, or snow, or a downpour of rain. The weather is fickle, and you're constantly exposed to it. Rummaging through lakes filled with red, radioactive water, while inside your suit you're covered in sweat…and tears sometimes. Imagine dragging old rusted car parts, wood, batteries, scraps—pretty much anything that you can find that may be somewhat useful, for *miles*, to the nearest collection bin. Always having to ride the *Scavenger Train* everywhere you go, separate from everyone else because of your odor, and because of how everybody thinks of you. Imagine children staring at you. Pointing. Being afraid of you when your suit is on…*and* when it's off…"

Manny is silent.

"So, *basically*, it's not so bad!" she says loudly all of a sudden.

As she does, she slaps the top of Manny's thigh with her hand. He flinches and jerks his leg away from her in response. She laughs to herself.

"You make it sound so—*appealing*," Manny replies, sarcastically.

She picks up her cup with a smile and nod, then sips. Manny looks at the cup.

"What is that stuff anyway?"

"Oh, this?" she says as she looks inside of it and swirls the liquid around.

"It's homemade—for my stomach. I think I inhaled some chemicals a while back. I was young. My stomach gets really upset sometimes, but this helps."

"Oh, okay," he says.

She drinks a little more, then places the cup down next to her again. She lifts her arms into the air and stretches, then rubs her belly with a long exhale.

"What about you, Manny?" she asks as she looks over at him.

"What about me?"

"What's it like being a *Greaser*? Working at the Shield? That is where you work, right?"

"How'd you know?"

She points at his hands. Manny curls his fingertips toward his face and takes a look; there's grease under his fingernails.

"Oh..."

"Told you. We *all* have a name..." she responds with a smile.

"Well, it's not so bad. Rock and I both work there..."

He points at Rock. He and the other gentleman are still playing cards and being excitedly loud.

"We fix stuff all day, basically. Making sure the Nerps have what they need. Weapons. Aircraft. Equipment. Vehicles. A lot of it probably comes from you guys: metals, parts, engines, batteries. We use what we can and store what we can't. Not as exciting as being a Scavenger, I guess..."

"I guess not. But probably safer," Jhenda says with a weak smile.

"I guess so," Manny replies.

Jhenda picks up her cup, finishes her drink, then stands. She tosses the cup into a recycling can next to her, then yawns and turns toward the large window behind them that faces the main floor. Jonah is pacing back and forth across the stage. His arms and hands move swiftly; he's very animated when he speaks. Jhenda places her finger on the glass.

"His job is better than both of ours though, I have to say."

"You think so?"

"I *know* so. What's better than giving the Remnants of an entire region a reason to keep living? A reason to keep waking up in the morning?"

"Hmm," Manny says.

"I mean, he's introducing people to the Creator. Reminding us all that we're not down here lost and alone. Afraid maybe, but not lost, and not alone…"

Manny breathes out of his nose forcefully. Not exactly a scoff, but close to it.

Jhenda looks at him.

"What is it?"

"I just…don't know," Manny says, almost sadly.

"You don't know what?"

Manny points up to the ceiling and looks up at it simultaneously.

"I don't know about, *him*. I don't even know for sure if he's real, sometimes, honestly. I don't know…"

"Really? Humph. *That's* surprising…"

"Surprising? How come?"

"I don't know. You just, seem like someone who would believe…"

"I used to. A long time ago."

"What changed?"

"*Everything* changed…"

There's a brief moment of silence. Manny rubs his hand on his knee cap.

"What about you. Do you believe?" Manny asks.

"Oh, absolutely. I'm certain that he's real…"

She points up to the same spot in the ceiling that Manny did.

"How do you know?" he asks.

"I mean, it's clear. How else did all of this happen? The planet, the universe, all of it. It didn't just pop up, and if it did, something had to cause the *pop*, right?"

Manny grins and looks toward the floor.

"I guess…maybe…"

"Who knows. I just think there's someone, something, *somewhere* out there," Jhenda continues.

Manny scratches his cheek.

"I'm not sure about that, Jhenda. It sounds nice. I'd like to believe it, honestly. But I don't know. If there was really an all-knowing and all-loving Creator out there somewhere, it seems like he, she, or it would be a little more involved with us, the creations, if it cared about us the way people say…"

She looks at the floor and thinks.

"I understand that. I'm no expert, but maybe there are just reasons and truths that we don't understand completely. I can remember times that I've done things, and in retrospect, thinking back, I don't know *why* I did them. I say to myself, *what in the world was I thinking?* You know? But I did it, can't deny it. If I can't figure me out all of the time, then I'm *sure* that I can't figure the Creator out all of the time either."

Manny continues to look down, but nods, unable to not at least acknowledge that what she just said makes sense.

"Manny…"

He looks up at her. Her eyes pierce him. The moment stands out to him in an unusual way. She opens her mouth to speak and it's as if everything else falls dead silent around him:

"It's possible for someone to be real...to exist somewhere, and for us to just not know them, yet. In your case, it's possible to have just lost touch with them or to have forgotten about them after pushing them away. Time and distance can have that effect on any relationship..."

Manny stares at her with his mouth slightly open. She grins. She looks away and scratches the back of her neck. Eventually, she looks back at him in a confused yet amused way, because of his gawking. His eyes haven't left her, and he hasn't blinked once, in at least ten seconds. He's still processing.

"What are you staring at?" she says, slightly laughing.

The words still resonate deep inside of Manny. He mentally grounds himself and then shakes his head.

"Nothing. Sounds like you should be sitting inside with Jonah and the rest of them instead of up here in the skybox with us."

"Oh no, no, no. I don't belong in there."

"Huh? Why not?"

"I don't really belong anywhere…"

"Everyone belongs somewhere, right?" Manny responds.

"Maybe…" Jhenda says.

They look out of the glass and see everyone beginning to leave. When the stadium starts rumbling, they know that the gathering is over.

The large monitors say:

"Go with the Creator, and he'll go with you."

"If only he really would," Jhenda says as she looks at it.

"What do you mean?"

"If only the Creator really would go with people like me. I think Jonah should correct it to say *some of you*, or maybe even *most of you*. I think that would be more accurate."

Manny says nothing. A part of him burns deep inside, badly wanting to say, *"he'll go with you too, Jhenda…he already does…"*

He has no idea why, but he feels an extreme urge, an undeniable yearning to say it. The words ring inside of his heart and head. It's not even that he necessarily believes it's fully true, but it's more about the fact that he hates when people feel hopeless. He's felt hopeless. He feels hopeless. He knows how lonely it can be; how scary it can be.

He dismisses the thought and chuckles.

"What is it now?" she asks as a result of his laughter.

"It's just funny. You apparently believe in the Creator, but it's like you distance yourself from him."

"Well, not really. Do I think there's something out there? Definitely. But I guess I just don't think he wants anything to do with me. And that's okay."

"How do you know that? Why wouldn't he want anything to do with you?"

"Well, because I usually don't want anything to do with me—it's simple really."

The sentence punches Manny in the chest.

Jhenda approaches him and pats his shoulder with a grin.

"Come on, let's go, *Emmanuel*…everyone's leaving…"

She turns and heads toward the skybox exit, leaving Manny standing there bewildered and intrigued.

Rock has just finished his card game and is standing up from the table. He looks over at Manny who isn't standing too far away from him. He notices the exchange between he and Jhenda, cocks his head to the side, and drops his eyebrows in a puzzled expression.

"Who's she?" Rock asks while walking up alongside Manny, and at the same time pointing at Jhenda as she walks away.

Manny looks at him with a roll of his eyes.

"Long story…"

Manny, Jhenda, and Rock walk downstairs and find Miss Valerie, Martha, and Grea. Manny introduces Jhenda to everyone and they all greet her warmly.

The hallways, aisles, and front lobby are crowded. There's always a traffic jam of people as they exit the IE on Sabbaths due to one of the customs: Jonah loves to go to the exit immediately after gatherings and personally greet as many people as he can. He's there today, shaking hands, smiling, and speaking to everyone that he can get close to.

Everyone loves it, except Manny of course. He does his best to avoid Jonah as he exits. He tries to see exactly where he is so that he can walk out of a different door. Sometimes it works. Today it doesn't. As the group departs, Jonah is standing right there awaiting them. He hugs Miss Valerie, Martha, Grea, and Jhenda, then gives Rock a hearty handshake.

Manny reluctantly approaches the door.

"Manny!" Jonah greets him enthusiastically as he grabs Manny's drooping shoulders with a wide grin on his face.

"How are you? It's always so good to see you!" Jonah exclaims.

"Hi, Jonah. I'm okay, I guess…"

"You guess?"

"I'm…I'm doing well, Jonah…how are you?"

"Well, I'm doing well, Emmanuel."

Jonah makes brief eye contact with a few people who are exiting and waving at him. He waves back with a smile.

"The work is never done, but I love it. I'm grateful for the call," he says while still looking at the smiling faces of people as they walk out.

"Aren't you grateful for it, Manny?"

"Grateful for what?" Manny asks.

"The call..." Jonah says as he locks eyes with Manny again, unflinchingly.

"The call?" Manny asks with a squint.

Manny's eyebrows are lowered as he contemplates what Jonah could be talking about. Jonah does this often. He'll say some cryptic phrase—something that makes Manny think that Jonah's mind is either too advanced for him to comprehend, or that he's spent too much time in closed rooms filled with the smoke of scented incense, and it's affected his brain.

He smiles at Manny and simply says, "hmm...it's *so* good to see you, Manny..."

He looks back and sees the group waiting for Manny.

"Well, go on. They're waiting for you. They need you more than you know. And take good care of your mother, Manny. I will see you next week."

"O...okay, Jonah..." Manny mumbles.

Manny walks away, looking back momentarily at Jonah. He's speaking to another family by now. Jonah stoops down and rubs the head of a young boy. Manny remembers being that little boy years ago, but things have certainly changed. When Manny reaches the others, they all begin walking toward the trains. Miss Valerie, Grea, and Martha are ahead of Manny, Rock and Jhenda.

"What was that about?" Jhenda asks Manny while they walk.

"What was what about?"

"That little chat you just had with Jonah. It was pretty awkward looking..."

"It wasn't awkward."

"It was, but, okay..."

"Manny's *always* awkward," Rock interrupts.

"Whatever, Rock..."

"Hey, it's true!"

Jhenda smiles and lowers her head to better watch her step.

Every Sabbath, after everyone leaves the IE, crowds of people go to an area called *Eden*—a large gardened area not far from the IE. In fact, it's just a few miles east of it. There are merchants there who barter for food, lots of benches, a walking trail, and even a few buildings which survived Star Fall and are still mostly intact.

Eden is equally as beautiful as the area around the IE and the IE itself. Ironically, just beyond the cliff of Sinai lies a section of the Outskirts. It's astonishing that sometimes in life, the most wonderful and attractive things can be in such close proximity to what's perceived to be vile and despicable.

"Jhenda, why don't you join us in Eden today?" Manny's mother suggests.

"Thanks, but…umm…no thanks, ma'am…"

"Why not?" Grea asks hastily and unashamedly.

The group looks at her, silently rebuking her for being so straight-forward.

"What?" she whispers as she looks back at them.

"Well, it's just not where I need to be. I'm an S&G—how many of *us* do you see in Eden on the regular?"

Everyone is silent. They look back and forth at each other.

"Exactly," she continues.

"Thank you so much for the invite though. You're all really nice people. Nice meeting you Manny, and everyone. I'm sure I'll see you all again…"

No one protests. They respect her decision.

She walks away. The rest of them head to Eden.

18. STRONG ENERGY

BEFORE LONG, MANNY and the others are stepping off of the train and into Eden. There's a large garden directly in front of them with a paved walkway going directly down its middle and in a number of directions within it.

"It's like another world," a teenaged girl says as she stands on the platform.

The group moves toward the benches located just a few yards away from them.

"Val and I are going to look at what the merchants have today. We'll be back," Martha says to the group.

Manny looks at his mother out of the corner of his eye.

"Oh, relax. I won't trade for anything; I have nothing to trade," she says with a grin.

Within moments, they've vanished into the crowd.

"Well, who was she?" Rock says as he sits on top of one of the benches.

"Who? Jhenda? She's a Scavenger—I mean Collector—well, *Scavenger*, that comes to the IE from time to time, I guess? First time meeting her, so I don't know much. Did you know that they're okay with being called *Scavengers?* Oh, and did you know that they call us Greasers? *Greasers!* Can you believe it?"

"She seemed, I don't know, *strange*, but not so strange at the same time," Grea interjects.

"What? What does that even mean?" responds Manny.

"She's just *different*, I guess. But not in a bad way. It's like she knows a lot. Perceptive. Aware."

"I got that too, like she's reading your mind, but not letting you know," adds Rock.

"Exactly!" exclaims Grea.

"She seems decent though," says Manny.

They sit and talk for a few moments. Grea talks about the gathering and what Jonah taught. Manny and Rock halfway listen, but not really.

"Sure, that's *nice*, Grea," Rock says over the last few words she muttered.

"So rude…" Grea says as she slaps her palm on the table and jerks her head toward him.

He sticks his tongue out at her.

They sit quietly for a few moments, which can only go on for so long with Rock around.

"I'm bored," Rock blurts out.

"Me too," replies Manny, "let's walk around. We still have about an hour before it's time to go anyway."

They get up and begin walking toward a large group of tents where the merchants usually are. There's still a crowd of people all around them, but they maneuver their way through. They walk past a wooden structure with a decorative presentation of beautiful flowers surrounded by colorful stones arranged on top of it. Manny picks up three of the stones and juggles them as they walk.

"I never could quite get the hang of that," Rock says as he watches.

He turns around and grabs three stones of his own.

"Always a competition. Such *boys*…" Grea says with a giggle.

Rock drops one of his stones, and then the others.

"Aw, poor thing! Keep at it, you'll get it one day!" Manny says while laughing.

Rock gently tosses one of his stones at Manny in retaliation, but he dodges it. This causes him to laugh even harder. He spins in a circle while juggling to highlight his mastery of the talent.

"Show off..." Rock says.

While Manny isn't paying attention, he bumps into someone. The stones drop to the ground with three light taps. Manny stumbles and nearly falls himself.

"Excusssssssse you..." a mysterious and creepy voice hisses.

It's Polus. Levi and Damien are walking alongside him.

Manny pauses and says, "I'm so sorry, sir, I didn't mean to..."

"It's quite okay, don't mind it," Damien interrupts with a smile. As he does, he stoops down and picks up the stones.

"You're pretty good at juggling, I see," Damien says, holding out the stones for Manny to take.

Manny cups his hands and places them underneath Damien's just in time to catch the stones as he drops them.

They look into each other's eyes. Everything around them fades into silence as they focus; peering into and studying each other's very souls. Neither of them even so much as blinks or breathes during the silent exchange.

"Thank you," Manny finally mumbles.

"Ah, no problem! Very good..."

There's another quick moment of irregular staring.

Damien sticks his hand out to Manny for a shake.

"I'm Damien, by the way. What's your name?"

Manny gathers the rocks into his left hand to free his right then shakes Damien's.

"I'm...Emmanuel..."

"Hmm, *Emmanuel*? That's an interesting name...you probably hear that a lot, I'm sure."

"I suppose," Manny says with uncertainty.

"Hmm, very good. Well, we'd better be getting along. Nice meeting you, *Emmanuel*..."

"Thanks…same," Manny says.

The three men continue on their way. Manny, Grea, and Rock continue on also.

"Awkwaaaaard," Grea says jokingly, after a few moments.

"Very," Manny replies, glancing back at the three men.

~ ~ ~

Just across the field, Levi looks at Damien. He seems to be thinking.

"What is it, Damien?"

"I believe that was him…" Damien says softly, looking straight ahead.

Polus stops abruptly.

"Him? That boy? The *Witnesssssssss?!*"

Polus turns and points in Manny, Grea, and Rock's direction.

"Quiet! And don't point! Keep walking…" Damien demands.

They continue on.

"He had a very strong energy, I could sense it. There will be another full moon soon. We will ask Helel to confirm it then, but I'm almost positive that it was him…"

"Damien! Are you sure? How do you know?"

"I'd know my own…" Damien yells as he turns swiftly and grabs Polus' collar.

He pauses and gathers himself. He looks at his hand clutching Polus' shirt, then releases it, brushes at it, and adjusts it as if it were an accident. Levi and Polus wait for him to finish his statement.

"…it's him. Trust me. We need to summon Master—*soon.*"

19. THE SHEDIM

THE SUN SETS. Valerie and Martha have returned to the group. As is the custom, everyone leaves Eden at dusk. Sabbaths are the only days that they all get a chance to ride the train together—Manny at least appreciates that much about Sabbaths. On the ride back, everyone falls asleep except for Manny and Grea, who happen to be sitting next to each other.

Manny looks out of the window at the sky. Twinkling little stars are peeking through the burgundy and gray blanket above them.

"Pretty, isn't it?" Grea says.

Still peering into the heavens, Manny responds.

"Yeah, really pretty."

Rock is snoring. They both notice him at the same time. Manny chuckles. Grea shakes her head with a smile.

"You know, Manny...I understand..." she says, as her laughter subsides.

"What do you understand?" he says as he turns his head to her.

"I understand how you feel sometimes, well, *most* of the time. I even think that I know why you feel it..."

"What do you mean?"

"The doubt. In *here*."

Grea points to the side of her head at her temple. She glances back out of the window and into the sky.

"It doesn't make sense to me either all of the time."

Manny is silent, but listens carefully.

"You know, when our mom passed, I hated the Creator. I think I hated the idea of a Creator more than anything."

Manny nods. He thinks of the gymnasium. His grandmother. His sister.

"I didn't know why the Creator would take her from us, or any of those who were taken away. That's exactly what happened; they were *taken* from us. And how can a loving Creator allow that? It didn't make sense. It still doesn't make sense. But for some reason, I can't shake this feeling of deep…powerful…*love* that comes from somewhere out there, you know? I mean, it just grips me from time to time. Like he's real, and he cares, and that there's a reason for it all…"

Manny keeps listening. He looks at her facial expressions while she talks. Her honesty and transparency move him.

She extends her hand, and touches his chest with her pointer finger.

"In here. That's the only place that matters when it comes to believing for me. I can feel it in here, even when it doesn't make sense up here…"

She touches her temple again as she finishes the sentence and sighs deeply.

"But I don't know. I guess it will make sense one day, right? I mean, this is all temporary. All of it. This whole life as we know it. We'll find out the *ultimate* truth eventually. If there is one, that is. I think there is. And I think it's him…"

She tilts her head toward the window and the sky for a few seconds, then back to Manny. They exchange a silent smile. Slowly, Grea's smile transitions into a straight face.

"I miss her, Manny. I miss her *so* much…"

Tears form in Grea's eyes. Manny puts his hand on her shoulder. She falls over into his side and he puts his arm around her. She cries. Manny cries too, quietly. He briefly glances at Rock as he sleeps. Manny knows that he hasn't gotten over the loss that he and Grea have both suffered either, although it's been many years.

People never bring up Rock's mother to him. He never speaks of her. Grea only mentions her occasionally, and even when she does, it's never in any great detail.

Their mother was injured very badly during Star Fall and never fully recovered. A few years after, she passed away. Rock and Grea bounced from home to home with friends and relatives for a short time, and even temporarily lived with Manny and Martha. As they got older, they began to take care of themselves.

Eventually she's asleep. Manny is still wide awake. He looks at the sky as the stars sparkle like specks of glitter on black construction paper.

"Are you real?" he whispers.

A part of him expects a reply.

A part of him doesn't.

No reply comes.

~ ~ ~

Soon, they reach their stops.

Val reaches home first.

"I am tired!" she whispers enthusiastically. Martha briefly wakes and giggles at her friend's quiet exuberance. Almost everyone on the train is sleeping so whispers are most appropriate.

"Bye, Val, I'll see you in the morning," Martha says to her.

"All right then. Bye, everybody!" Valerie says quietly.

She gets off and disappears into her apartment building.

Grea and Rock are next. Grea wakes and buries her head into Manny's side in a playful way. He laughs. She hugs him and whispers, *"thank you…"*

He smiles back.

Rock wakes, says nothing, gives Manny a heart-salute with his eyes closed, and staggers off of the train as Manny chuckles at him.

Rock and Grea disappear into their building as well.

Manny gets up and goes to sit next to his mother. She lays her head on his shoulder while hugging his arm. When they reach home, he holds her hand as they exit the train. Once they get upstairs, he guides her to her room, takes her shoes off while she sits on her bed, and places her covers on top of her after she tilts over onto her pillow.

"Goodnight mom. I love you."

"I love you more."

"I know you do."

He kisses her forehead, turns off her light, and goes into his room.

Manny lies flat on his back for about an hour.

Thinking.

Thinking some more.

Remembering.

Eventually, he's asleep too.

~ ~ ~

The next morning isn't much different than every morning. Neither is the one after it, or any of the days for the remainder of the week. Nothing changes significantly until the following Friday.

~ ~ ~

While sitting at breakfast, Martha says, "samples and rations today; I know that you don't like it, but it's time again…"

"Uggghhh…" Manny grunts.

Envisioning the endless lines of Remnants, rude Needlers, and the rows of white tents, Manny eats his breakfast a little more slowly today. Eventually, he and Martha are downstairs and the TRN-3 is approaching. He holds her hand while she maneuvers her way up the steps, then she stops to look at him. She can see the apathy on his face. His head is dropped down toward the concrete, frozen in time. He doesn't notice that Martha is staring at him. Side by side but worlds apart.

After a gentle touch on his cheek from her warm hand, he finally looks up at her and she whispers, *"it won't be so bad..."*

He smiles and places his forehead on her shoulder.

Admittedly, riding the train is probably one of Manny's favorite things to do. It gives him time to clear his head for a while; to not be bogged down with thoughts or tasks. He can sit, ride, and gaze out of the window. He can allow his mind to freely wander through the far reaches of his own imagination, and he always takes full advantage of it.

At the Agri-Fields, his mother gets up, and he follows her to help her down the steps as he normally does. As she reaches the bottom of the platform, she turns and waits, knowing what will come next.

"I love you," Manny says.

She grins and giggles like a schoolgirl and lifts one leg in the air, jokingly. He chuckles at her antics.

"I love you more!" she says.

He waves as the train doors close. She waves back, holding her small white bag at the bend of her elbow. He sits back in his seat and resumes his journey into his deepest thoughts, and the peace of his own wonder.

After his train stops at the Shield, Manny lets out a deep sigh as he sees the white tents. Long lines of men and women with tattered clothing, soiled hands, and smudged faces decorate each tent's entrance.

"Okay, here we go," Manny mumbles as he steps down the TRN-3's steps.

Once inside one of the tents, the actual process never takes too long, but it still isn't something that he looks forward to. He's never really cared much for needles, or the *Needlers* for that matter. They're probably his least favorite of the Remnants. He thinks they're rude: not all of them, but certainly most. More importantly, the whole sampling process is a harsh reminder of the worst time in his life—in everyone's life. Manny stands in line and starts to remember.

~ ~ ~

"Mommy, I don't wanna!"

Martha stands in a long line of people inside the gymnasium. Manny is in her arms squirming.

"I don't *wanna!*"

"Emmanuel, calm…*DOWN*…okay?!"

It's been about two weeks since the blasts. A handful of doctors, nurses, and emergency medical technicians have managed to gather some supplies: syringes, a few medicines, antibiotics, and first aid kits. There are tables set up inside the gym and people are being given flu shots, antibiotics, and other much needed treatments; small children are the top priority.

"Ma'am, is this your son? My what a handsome little fellow!" the young nurse speaks to Martha as she makes her way to the front of the line.

She has beautifully tanned skin, jet black hair, and the whitest teeth imaginable. She can't be much older than a college student would be.

"Yes, he's mine," Martha says, trying to muster up a bit of joy in her voice to drown out her sadness and worry.

"Well, what's your name cutie pie?"

Manny looks at her for a moment, frowns, then tosses himself onto Martha's shoulder and whimpers.

"Calm *downnnn* honey…I'm so sorry, his name is Emmanuel…"

"That's such a nice name."

After some wrestling, Martha is able to get Manny into the chair and roll his shirt sleeve up. The woman thumps a needle with clear liquid inside. She rubs his arm with a cotton ball soaked in rubbing alcohol.

"It's cold…mommy! It stings!"

"I know honey, I know. It will be okay! This will keep you from getting sick, that's all…"

The nurse tosses the cotton ball into the trash can and turns back to Manny with a smile.

"Okay, sweetie, here we go," the beautiful young nurse says.

Moments before the needle punctures young Emmanuel's soft and youthful skin, setting off a chain reaction of disdain for all things related to needles, doctors, and the like, Martha looks into his eyes and says, *"it won't be so bad…"*

~ ~ ~

"Last name, sir?" a middle-aged yet very fit woman says with a stern face.

She's one of the NRP Medics; a *Needler*. Manny snaps out of his daydream; the voice startles him.

"Kohen," Manny replies.

She points to a table labeled: "H—K". Her whole demeanor is that of a dictator, or a stern school teacher. Manny scoffs lightly, to which she responds with a raise of her eyebrows and a jerk at the elbow of her rigid, outstretched arm, accentuating the fact that she's telling him where to go. She looks over at the table with the sign.

"It's right there…"

Manny shakes his head at her, then walks toward the table.

The stations are set up just beyond the entrance, categorized alphabetically by last name. An older woman sits behind the "H—K" table with a huge smile on her face, and a much warmer presence than the Needler that he just spoke to.

"Sit right here, sir," she says, seemingly showing Manny as many of her teeth as she can.

He smiles back slightly.

"Do you have a preference?"

"Excuse me?"

"Your arm, sir. Do you prefer one arm over the other?"

"Oh, my right arm is fine…"

She rolls his sleeve up, rubs the area with rubbing alcohol, and prepares her needle.

Manny closes his eyes.

He trembles slightly, and the woman takes notice.

"It won't be that bad," she says with another warm smile.

Once done, Manny stands and pulls his sleeve back down. The bulge of the bandage is visible.

"Leave it on for maybe an hour or so," she says to Manny when she notices him looking at it.

"Yes, ma'am. Thank you."

"Oh, dear, so polite! You must've been raised by a *good* woman!" she says as she hands him a small, red, rectangular card.

"A nice Needler for once…" he thinks to himself.

He takes the card, smiles, and walks to the back of the tent.

Here, there are tables with various food items and large brown bags. There is a sign above the tables:

RATIONS

These tables are categorized by last name as well. Manny presents the red card that he received from the Medic to the gentleman at the table; proof that he gave blood today. The man inspects it, and then nods.

Manny picks up one of the brown bags and stuffs food into it: rice, grits, beans, bread, water, a few fruits, a few vegetables, and a small portion of meat.

Manny picks up two of the meat portions, which are processed somehow and packaged tightly in plastic.

The man slams his hand on one of the packets.

"*One!*" he says with his pointer finger in the air, giving Manny a visual aid to accompany his strong instruction.

"Okay, okay! *Sheesh*," Manny responds.

Manny walks away from the area rubbing his arm and lugging the brown sack over his shoulder.

"Aw, poor baby," Rock says as he walks up next to Manny, "does it hurt, sweetheart?"

Rock touches the bulging area on Manny's arm.

"Cut it out!" Manny says, jerking away from him.

Rock laughs.

"I *hate* these things," Manny says as he looks at his arm.

"Me too, but hey, I'd want to know if I was contaminated, so we've got to do what we've got to do. I mean, look at this place—it's probably *crawling* with radiation."

Rock picks up a piece of rusty scrap metal and tosses it aside as he says it.

"And if age has anything to do with the likelihood of being at risk for contamination—you two should *DEFINITELY* be grateful that we get sampled often!"

It's Grea. She makes the statement as she walks between them and strikes both of their arms with her palms. Not hard enough to hurt them too badly, but just hard enough for them to react.

They both say, *"OUCH!"* simultaneously.

"Oops, *sorry*…old men!"

The remainder of the day goes by fairly normally. Work. Lunch. Conversation.

The only thing that's out of the ordinary is the fact that Manny has felt uneasy all day. He's not certain why, but things just feel a bit different. He determines that he must be negatively reacting to the blood sample taken earlier in the day.

While waiting for the trains that evening, Manny, Rock, and Grea talk as they usually do.

"What is it, Manny? You've been more quiet than normal today. Has the shot bothered you that much? Are you getting sick or something?" Grea asks.

"I don't know, I was wondering the same thing. I just feel weird, that's all. I'm not exactly sure why. It's probably just the shot, like you said. I'm all right though, honestly."

"Are you sure you're okay?" Rock responds, sounding worried.

"I'll be fine…"

He moves his bandage aside and looks at his arm. He sees that it's healed, so he tosses the bandage into a metal can beside the gate.

"IE tomorrow. This week has gone by so fast," Grea says.

"It has. I wonder if Jhenda will be there. What do you think, Manny?" continues Rock.

"Not sure. She said she doesn't always come. She may be there though, hopefully…"

Manny's train arrives first today.

"Feel better, Manny," says Grea as he steps on.

"Thanks, Grea. See you guys in the morning…and I *do* mean you *guys*," Manny says, staring deviously at Grea with a smirk.

Rock laughs.

Grea tries to hit him with a rock, but the door closes. The rock makes a *tink* on the glass window. Manny looks out of it at her, pointing and laughing.

~ ~ ~

The work day draws to a close at the Agri-Fields as well. The white tents are being taken down. Valerie and Martha are sitting on a bench waiting for their trains to arrive.

"It was so good to see Manny and the kids last weekend, Mar. *So* good to be home at the IE again. I'm really looking forward to tomorrow," Valerie says, looking out across the field at the sun setting.

"I knew that you'd miss it!" Martha responds.

"Oh, I certainly did!"

They sit on their favorite bench. Martha has her leg propped up on the seat portion. She massages her calf. The air is crisp. The sky is quickly darkening. Valerie scratches her shoulder and looks around. She sees only a few people, aside from themselves, who are left inside the gate.

"You feel that, Mar?"

"Feel what?"

"I don't know, the air just feels different this evening, I'm not really sure why…"

"It's a little windy and cool, I guess."

"Hmm, yes, maybe that's it…"

Off in the distance just over the horizon, Valerie can see a large white circle beginning to climb higher into the sky.

"Well look at that. You know, I'm sure the moon is always just as big, bright, and beautiful, but I'm just now really noticing it."

Valerie points directly in front of her toward it, in order to get Martha to turn and look. Martha adjusts the way that she's sitting, looks over her shoulder, and sees it.

"Wow, it's pretty. And *enormous*."

"Sure is. It's really standing out tonight."

They take a few seconds to admire it. Eventually they hear a sharp, metallic screeching sound in the background that breaks them out of their trance.

"Well, there's my ride, Mar! I'll see you in the morning!"

"Okay Val…I'll see you tomorrow…goodnight!"

"Goodnight!"

Valerie walks away.

Martha sits and gazes at the moon a bit longer.

She thinks of Manny.

She remembers life before Star Fall.

She prays for a few moments.

She thinks of Manny again.

Her train comes.

She leaves.

~ ~ ~

A few miles away in a hidden and secluded area, Damien, Polus, and Levi are together in a small building with only a few rooms in it. There's a five-pointed star drawn on the floor with yellow chalk. Other symbols are drawn sporadically around and inside of it. A large circle has been drawn around the star and is touching all five of its points. A black candle sits in its very center. Levi notices the full moon as he stands against the wall and looks out of the window into the night sky. Polus is carving a small opening in the ceiling with a long metal object while standing in a chair. Damien begins to walk around the room, lighting various black candles arranged in different places.

"Hurry, Polus," Damien says calmly but firmly as he lights another candle.

The tiny flames flicker; the three men's shadows dance on the walls to the silent rhythm of candlelight.

"The Shedim…it's time that we teach you more, Levi…" Damien says.

Levi turns from the window and looks at him.

"*Shedim* is one of the many names that was given to us, but it is one that we embrace. Often misunderstood, but still revered, and *feared*," Damien continues.

"We were *Watchers*. Protectors. Messengers to all of creation. We have been here since the beginning, just not always in this form. We weren't always bound to living in these physical bodies. We were betrayed by the one who created us…"

"Who betrayed us?" Levi asks.

"Hisssssssssss name is *YAHWEH*," Polus interrupts.

Damien looks at Polus and nods in agreement. He speaks again as he turns back toward Levi:

"Yes, the Creator, *Yahweh*. That's one of his names. He has many. He betrayed us, long ago, believing that we betrayed him first."

"I don't follow," Levi responds.

"You've forgotten, that's all. It will still take a few days for your memories to come back to you. That always happens with a new *conjuring*…"

"Conjuring?"

"Yes. Since we fell, we've been forced to dwell on this planet. Being that we aren't bound by physical bodies, we are able to possess and control the weaker and lower creations…and in special cases, we inhabit those who call us to them willingly, or *conjure* us…"

Damien stops and looks at his arms, then mid-section, then legs and feet.

"This is nothing more than a shell…with limitations…but because of our, abilities, we can exceed those limitations…once we *ascend*," Damien says.

"This all sounds and feels so familiar…" Levi says, rubbing his forehead.

"Indeed. It will come back to you. You recently possessed the body that you're in now, through a *conjuring* ceremony. We had to rush to do it, in order to accomplish our mission here in Naza. When we take possession of one of them, our memories are lost for a period of time. After a while, they will come back to you. Little by little."

"I see. So, what's our mission?"

"*Helel Ben Shahar*, our leader, our *true* master, has sent us here in order to find and destroy the *Witness*, Yahweh's chosen one. All we know is that he will arise from the IE here in Naza. He is the only real threat to Helel in these last days. He could cause serious troubles if we do not stop him first—the sooner we find him, the better. He hasn't *ascended* yet. He hasn't realized his abilities…his powers…his *true* self. He's still lost, insecure, afraid, and weak. In fact, he's turned from Yahweh; he hates him, deep down inside—anger, unforgiveness, doubt, and bitterness eat away at his soul. If we can find him soon and take care of him while he's powerless, our mission will be simple. If not, it will be much more difficult; he's chosen by Yahweh and will be given great wisdom, strength, and authority, just like us…"

"You said that this…*Witness*…is chosen? Chosen for what?"

"Chosen to keep the world free from Helel's reign. Helel is the true ruler of this world. All that is here rightfully belongs to him. This is why we were cast out long ago. Helel rebelled against Yahweh. He realized that he was just as great as Yahweh…in fact, *greater*…but Yahweh is very selfish and jealous. He forced him out of his presence, and we chose to follow Helel; therefore, we were *all* forced to leave the Kingdom, and became the *fallen* Watchers.

Yahweh wants this world and these people for himself. Although he is the Creator, he made us *all* creators, much like himself. He hates us because we awoke to the truth of who we are!"

Damien grunts and pauses for a moment, noticeably upset. A low and quiet growl rumbles in his belly for a few seconds. His eyes glow yellow, faintly.

Once he regains his composure, he continues:

"He's chosen the Witness to be his hand in the earth. Helel has chosen us to be his hands in the earth as well. Helel is the greatest among us Shedim..."

Polus climbs down from the chair. The hole that he has carved allows the moonlight to shine into the dark room onto the floor. The circle of light is about the size of a quarter, and is about five inches away from the candle in the center of the five-pointed star. Damien looks at the moon's light on the floor. He points to it. Levi looks on as he does.

"We've been called not only the Shedim, but *demons*. Originally, the word was *daemons*, or *day moons*; moons of the day. The world has misunderstood us, just as Yahweh has misunderstood us. They embrace the sun. We embrace the moon and its contrasting, but equivalent power. One governs the day, and the other governs the night. Life is full of dualities. Light and dark, yin and yang, plus and minus, and many more examples. Secrets, ancient wisdom, and the deepest mysteries are usually hidden in plain sight, only being revealed those who can see beyond the obvious."

Damien takes a step closer to Levi.

"We are the true lights of this world—the children and followers of Helel. You'll remember it all soon, don't worry..."

Levi listens closely. The words resonate. Such a familiarity.

The quarter-sized circle of moonlight has moved closer to the black candle; it's within a couple of inches now.

"Come, it's time. Kneel here. Remember everything that you will see tonight and do exactly what Polus and I do," Damien says to Levi.

They each kneel down at points on the pentagram. Damien and Polus begin chanting in low voices at the level of a whisper, *"Helel Ben Shahar..."*

Levi chants with them. Polus stands up and walks to a table in the corner. He reaches inside of a large clay jar that's on the table and pulls out a small, black snake. From the snake's squirming, Levi can tell that it's alive. He walks to the center of the star and pulls the sharp metal object that he used to carve the hole into the ceiling from his pocket. Without flinching, he punctures a hole in the snake's side. Levi cringes a little as he watches out of the corner of his eye. Damien is still chanting. Polus holds the snake over the candle, squeezes it, and allows its blood to drip down into the star's center. He walks back over to the clay jar, places the snake's corpse inside, licks the blood from his hands, and then kneels back into his position and continues chanting.

Levi is extremely uncomfortable, although he feels that he shouldn't be.

Their chanting grows louder.

Levi opens his eyes and looks back and forth at Damien and Polus. They have become very intense, squeezing their eyes tightly shut and saying the words louder with each iteration.

Levi looks at the spot of moonlight as it crawls closer to the candle.

When it meets the center of the star and touches the candle, the thin line of smoke rising from the candle's flame expands with a quick burst of energy like a firecracker has exploded.

It startles Levi and he jerks back away from it. The small burst transforms into a tiny cloud of yellow smoke that rises just above their heads. The smoke expands and illuminates from its center.

When Levi first hears the voice, it feels as though it is coming from within him and all around him at the same time.

"MY CHILDREN…"

Deep.
Low.
Spookily.

Levi feels a heavy, dark, spiritual presence in the room. It covers him like an invisible blanket. He immediately closes his eyes and is afraid to open them again.

"Master, Helel…"

Levi can tell that it's Damien's voice which responds.

"Master, we must confirm who the *Witness* is. We know the time of his ascension must be near. I believe that we have encountered him on the Sabbath, here in Naza…his name was…"

"Emmanuel…yes…" Helel interrupts.

"Yes, Master…Emmanuel," Damien finishes.

Levi can barely gather his thoughts. Everything inside of him wants to get up and run out of the door.

"Emmanuel is the Witness. He is the one upon whom the hand of Yahweh lies…"

"I could feel it, Master. I could feel that it was him, I just wanted to be certain…"

"YOU MUST HURRY!"

The voice of Helel suddenly booms inside the room, and inside Levi's chest. He's completely petrified as he listens.

"We can't afford for him to ascend. You *MUST* stop him. Do *not* fail me…"

"Yes, Master…yes…" Damien replies, crouching in timidity and slight fear.

"Be mindful of the *seer* named Jonah as well. I have given you the power that you need. And as for *HIM*…"

As the word, *HIM,* is spoken by Helel, Levi feels a frigid coldness come all over his body; he knows that Helel is addressing him.

"ASCEND HIM…"

"We will, Master," responds Damien.

The presence in the room lifts. The yellow glow that Levi could see so strongly beyond his closed eyelids fades. The smoke clears as the light of the moon passes beyond the candle.

The three men sit in silence for a few moments.

Damien looks over at Levi.

"We must move quickly."

Nothing else is said for the remainder of the night.

~ ~ ~

Miles away, Manny wakes up with a jolt. He's been dreaming more intensely tonight than at any time in the past that he can remember.

He stands up from his bed and rubs his head. His heart is racing. His shirt is soaking with sweat. He removes it and tosses it into the corner of his room.

As he turns, he sees his mother standing at his door. He sighs.

"How long have you been there, mom?"

"About ten minutes. Are you okay?"

"I'm fine."

She walks into the room and sits on his bed. She rubs his back.

"They're just dreams."

"I know. Sometimes, I just wish I didn't have them anymore…"

"I know you do."

He scratches his chin and looks at the clock on his dresser.

"Gosh, there's no point in going back to sleep now…" he says.

"You're right," Martha says with an exhale.

"We may as well start getting ready. It's nearly time to go to the IE. I'll start breakfast."

She stands and walks to his door. She stops.

"Oh, by the way," she says as she turns back to him.

"I'm making your favorite…"

He smiles at her, drops his head again, and closes his eyes as she walks down the hallway toward the kitchen.

A few moments later, as he prepares to get up and start getting dressed, he looks out of his window.

The moon is full and bright in the sky.

"Wow," he says in admiration.

~ ~ ~

At the very same moment, Jonah too awakes with a jerk and sits beside his bed.

His eyes are filled with tears.

He kneels and fervently prays:

"Emmanuel. *Please* draw and teach him. Prepare him. *Please*. Protect him…"

20. JONAH RISES

It's 11:50 a.m.

Manny and Rock are in the skybox. Rock sits at a card table and Manny is close by, looking out of the large glass window from side to side.

"Do you see her?" Rock asks him as he shuffles a deck of cards.

"No. She must not have come today."

He sits down next to Rock and watches him as he deals the cards across the table. Manny's mind roams. He thinks about his dream and how intense it was the night before. Rock notices.

"Manny…"

Manny doesn't hear him. He just stares off in the distance.

"Manny?"

Still no response.

"Manny!"

"I hear you," he finally responds with a jolt.

"What's your deal? Are you okay?"

"I'm fine. Just thinking…"

"Thinking about what?"

"Just, these dreams…"

"Oh. You had it again last night or something?"

"I did. I barely slept…"

"You know, you're the only person I know that's consistently had the same dream since he was a kid. I remember when you first told me and Grea about it. Some guy standing over you and hitting you with a big ball of light or something, right?"

"Yeah, something like that…"

"That's pretty weird. Ever thought about talking to Jonah about it?" Rock asks.

"What! Talking to…no…*no* way…"

"Why not? He may know what it means or something. I mean, isn't the guy talking about the Creator in the dream? Jonah talks about the Creator all the time. He may have…"

"Rock. *No…*"

"Sheesh, okay, I was just saying…"

"You're always just saying…"

Manny stands up and approaches the door.

"Your panties are all in a bunch today…" Rock says, flicking the cards a little more aggressively now.

"Whatever…I'm going to the bathroom," Manny says with a dismissive wave of his hand.

"Fine…" Rock says, returning the hand gesture.

Manny walks out of the skybox and the door closes behind him. He walks along the balcony railing just beyond the skybox's entrance and hesitates. The people are still praying, singing, crying, and murmuring. He looks down at them for just a few seconds and thinks, *"what's the point?"*

The restroom is just around the corner. He walks in and stands at the sink, staring into the mirror. He studies his own face. A few blemishes. He looks older than he actually is. He could pass for twenty-five or so, easily.

He thinks of Grea and her constant picking.

"Old man, huh…" he whispers to himself as he pokes his chin out, turns his head from side to side, and studies his face a bit more.

The water from the sink is cold. It runs over his hands like water over rocks at the top of a waterfall. His eyes are closed—the cool liquid hits his face like a wave crashing onto the sand at the beach. He turns the faucet off, wipes off with a towel, and then heads for the door.

While walking out of the restroom, he thinks about his mother. He knows that she is somewhere down below with Miss Valerie and Grea. He walks past the same balcony, but stops at it this time. With his arms draped over the railing, he scans the crowd, looking for his mother. He tries to remember exactly what she wore. The stadium settles. Manny's eyes are drawn away from the crowd and to the stage. It's been a *very* long time since he's watched Jonah elevate from the center of it. It used to excite him. He feels a bit of faint anticipation attempting to rise in his heart, but tries to ignore it.

The aisles clear.
The voices in the building weaken to whispers.
The lights dim to a faint glow.
Complete silence.

Jonah rises.

21. MISSED IT

THE AUDITORIUM IS perfectly quiet, except for the mechanical noise of Jonah's elevator. The door opens and he steps out. The slow taps of his steps echo throughout the large space.

Tap.

Tap.

Tap.

The microphone whistles gently as he adjusts it.

"Well! Hi, everyone! I wasn't expecting to see all of you today…"

The room bursts with laughter from all sides. Even Manny cracks a smile at Jonah's charisma and sarcasm from the balcony, still with his arms draped over the rail. He's not looking for Miss Valerie, Grea, and his mother anymore.

"But no, seriously. I'm always amazed at you all. With all that you do throughout the week, you find the time to come and gather here. It's amazing. *You're* amazing, and I'm humbled that each of you desires to come here, together. You each have hearts of pure gold. Give yourselves a hand, seriously; please, you deserve it…"

Everyone applauds and cheers. It lasts for about twenty seconds.

"Sheesh, so full of pride you all are!" Jonah says.

Again, laughter fills the room.

"Relax, relax! I'm just…*serious*!"

More laughter.

"Okay, I'm kidding, I'm kidding. But you all truly are amazing. Thank you, thank you, and *thank* you…"

Jonah walks back and forth across this platform every week, drawing everyone's attention and piercing them with every word that comes out of his mouth. Today will be no different. He's truly gifted as a speaker and a teacher. If there is such a thing as a "calling" to do something in life, he is certainly called to speak, teach, and lead.

Manny watches and listens, something that he hasn't done in years.

"You know, guys, I have to share this story with you if you'll allow me. Just last week, I had the pleasure of sitting with an elderly woman who stuck around for a while after our gathering. She's a beautiful soul; such a youthful and bright smile. She actually may be in here, so I hope she doesn't mind me sharing our conversation. It actually leads me into the two main topics that I want to address today. The first is this…"

He stops his movement and looks directly at the crowd from center stage:

"Is this so-called *Creator* even real?"

Manny shifts his weight from one foot to the other. He wasn't expecting Jonah to be so blunt. Jonah continues:

"I mean, really. We've all thought it, right? We've all wondered it, even if we haven't said it out loud…"

Jonah points up to the ceiling.

"Is there really some all-knowing, all-seeing, all-powerful being up there that is involved in every little thing that we do? Is he watching our every move? Are there really angels, or some form of higher intelligence, all around us, keeping a record of our good and bad decisions? When we die, do we really stand before the Creator in judgment?"

Jonah steps backward—a single, long, and slow step.

"Or, is it a myth?"

Total silence.

"That's what this beautiful elderly lady and I spoke about. We'll call her *Rosa*. That was my great-grandmother's name. I love that name. Rosa looked at me with those soft eyes, that perfect smile, and said to me, 'Jonah, son, I've lived *many* years. I remember the way things used to be. I remember Star Fall and all of those people who died. I remember what it felt like to lose those who were closest to me. I even remember how we all came together and started to rebuild this world. I saw how many of us got filled up with faith and started to come here, and go to the other IEs all over New America—this broken, but beautiful country of ours. In my life before all of this, I was a scientist. I was in laboratories all of the time, doing experiments, doing research, you name it. From the time I was young, I've always struggled between faith and science. Jonah, son, sometimes I wonder…is the Creator *really* real, and if he is, how do we know?'"

He walks back to the podium, masterfully building suspense as he speaks.

"I thought about her question, long and hard. When I thought that I had a decent enough answer, I simply told her, 'that's a tough question, and to be honest, we won't know until we transition to the next phase, whatever that may be, I suppose. I can say this much though, I remember being in science class and learning about the theories of creation, the *Big Bang*, and so on. We learned that everything that exists can be put into four basic categories: time, energy, space, and matter. All four of those things shot into existence in a single moment, and they've been expanding ever since—that's basically the way science puts it, if I remember correctly. You probably know much more about it than I do, I'm sure. It's like a big balloon that's been having air blown into it since the beginning of time…'"

He pauses.

"She looked at me and smiled, then said, *go on, son*. So, I went on, 'if all that exists exploded into existence all of a sudden, then that can only mean one thing; someone, or something, not limited by the boundaries of time, energy, space, and matter had to initiate the *bang*...someone had to start *blowing into the balloon*...'"

A few sighs of understanding can be heard throughout the crowd. Even Manny tilts his head to the side, twists his mouth, and nods in semi-acknowledgement of the logic.

"She looked at me and said, *'well, Jonah, that makes sense, I have to admit.'*

We talked a little more and then eventually she left. Even though she was gone, her question stayed with me all night long—actually, all *week* long. It reminded me of all the times that I've personally doubted the existence and involvement of the Creator. That may sound like a shocker, but I have. I do. I've wondered if it's all inside my head. I usually try to come back to the conclusion that he must be real. That leads me to my next and final point..."

He scratches his chin and scans the room.

"If the Creator is real, then why?"

He pauses and allows the question to sink into their minds, then continues:

"Why did things happen the way that they did? Why did he allow Star Fall? Why are there Remnants in the Outskirts, and amongst our city hubs, who are starving and homeless, when everything that we do is supposed to be for the **common good of the country**? Why would a *good* and *merciful* Creator allow that? What does it all mean?"

Jonah walks back to the front of the platform, closer to the people. He doesn't speak again until he is all the way there. He sits down on the edge of the stage and allows his feet to dangle.

"We're just having a conversation today; a heart-to-heart…is that okay?"

Many in the crowd nod, and respond with sounds of affirmation and agreement.

"*This* book…"

He holds up his Grandeurscript.

"How do I know that it's real?"

He looks at the book.

"How do we know mistakes weren't made during the great merging? How do I know it's not a compilation of mythological and allegorical stories that have been collected over the centuries? How do I know that it hasn't been used to control us? There are *proven* instances of belief systems, and of the original holy books that our coveted Grandeurscript was derived from, being used as a means of psychological control over groups of people throughout history. I won't get into all of it today, but some of it, I question myself…"

He pauses. He lowers the Grandeurscript into his lap and looks at it. The words grab Manny like one million hands. He's saying much of what Manny has thought about for quite a while now.

"I think we've missed it. We've all missed it in the past. I will say that I have probably made the biggest mistakes of all concerning the Creator, or at least the concept of the Creator. Can I be honest with you all? Right here and right now? The truth is, *I don't know.* I don't know how any of this works with complete certainty. I don't have all of the answers. I don't know if our faith and beliefs have been tainted over time or not…"

Jonah breaks and chuckles to himself; he's entertained by and shocked at his own transparency.

"But I completely and wholeheartedly believe that there is someone or something out there that's beyond us. I do know that love is the most powerful force I've ever experienced. I do believe that there is a force of love out there that we understand as the

Creator, which responds to us and that is within us all—every one of us…"

At that moment, Jonah glances up and looks directly into Manny's eyes. Manny had no idea that he could even see him up in the rafters, high above the crowd and the stage. For about five seconds, they stare at each other; neither of them blinks. As uncomfortable as Manny is, he cannot take his eyes away. Something about the moment pierces him. Jonah's words, his presence, the atmosphere in the building, his stare; they all captivate him in a way that he's never felt. *Ever.*

Jonah stands from his seated position on the edge of the stage. He turns and looks at Damien, who is sitting to his right, with Polus and Levi. Damien stares back at him; unflinchingly.

For just a second, Damien looks up at Manny as well, then he turns his eyes back to Jonah. Jonah begins speaking again:

"I know that many of you are of different backgrounds. Some of you couldn't care less about some invisible being in the sky who controls the universe, *supposedly*. Heck, some of you might believe that there are *orange penguins* out there somewhere that sustain existence…"

A few in the crowd chuckle.

"I have the exact same questions that you do the majority of the time. I can honestly say that. Thankfully, since the great merging, we are peaceable and accepting of one another, for the most part. We understand that everyone is an individual and has a personal way of relating to the Creator, according to the way that he has designed us individually. Although, most of us still hold true to our former religious systems, or the religious systems of our direct lineage. That's understandable; I have no problem with that. But I stand before you and ask you a question. One simple question…"

He stands, walks back to his podium, and flips through a small notebook. The room is dead silent. Manny is locked in place—frozen. It's like time has stopped in its tracks. Everyone is hanging on to Jonah's every word, *especially* Manny.

"If there really is a Creator, and he has all knowledge, all power, is everywhere at the same time, and can do any and everything…"

He pauses again. Everyone is on edge.

"…then which of the old religions would he be faithful to if he lived among us?"

The room is completely still.
Everyone ponders.
A deep quiet.

"That question came to me not long after Star Fall. I lost faith. I couldn't understand any of it anymore—I had no desire to either. But eventually, I realized that if the Creator is real, then he *has* to be so much bigger than my mind is able to comprehend. To create billions of galaxies, most of which we more than likely have no idea about. To make the world as complex as he did. To make us as diverse as we are…then there *has* to be more to him than we can *totally* understand…"

He scans the room.

"If I can fully comprehend him, and if there is no more to him than that which I can fit into this human-sized brain, then is he *really* eternal?"

Jonah stops, allowing there to be another moment of awkward silence, on purpose.

"We will never completely figure the Creator out. But we can be confident that he has figured us out; that he's figured *you* out. Every single, solitary one of you. And me. He knows exactly how to reach you, at the right time, right where you are. He can reach you. He *will* reach you. If this great and all-powerful Creator is real, then he's more than capable of proving himself, I'm sure. He doesn't need me to do it for him…"

Jonah glances at Manny once more, then completes his statement:

"…and, He will."

The words shoot through Manny like lightning.

"I used to be judgmental. Closed-minded. Self-righteous. Not anymore. I realized that a lot of times, my uninformed actions actually pushed people away instead of drawing them. The Creator is so much bigger than we realize—than I once realized, and still realize. That's true, even if he only remains a concept to many of us. Who knows, maybe in his infinite wisdom, he chooses to only reveal himself as a simple concept to those of us whom he specifically designed to be conceptual thinkers…"

He pauses, staring into the crowd and saying nothing. He places the book back onto the podium then looks down at it and scratches his head for a few seconds.

"The Creator is not limited to my thoughts. He's not limited to my human efforts to prove his existence. It's best that I step aside and let him prove himself. In other words, if he truly is *the Creator*, I should, we all should, let him be just that. He is more than capable of doing so…"

Manny is pierced by the statement. He zones out, not really hearing much more of what Jonah says. In fact, Jonah only speaks for maybe another forty-five seconds before his soliloquy is over.

~ ~ ~

"What are you doing here?" says a voice from behind Manny.

Manny doesn't hear it.

He stares at the screen above the platform, his arms still draped over the balcony railing.

"*Manny?*"

No response.

A hand grabs his shoulder and pulls him from behind.

22. TRUST HIM AGAIN

"Manny, what are you *doing*?"

It's Rock.

"Nothing...I just...I just went to the bathroom, and then I stopped here..."

"You've been gone for a long time. I thought something happened to you."

"No, I'm fine."

"You look sick. Are you *sure* you're okay?"

"I'm okay."

"Okay, well, it's almost time to go. I've got to go back to the skybox to grab my jacket."

"I'll walk with you," Manny says as he glances down at Jonah one last time before walking away.

It's not long before they're on their way into the crowd of individuals leaving the IE. Jonah is waiting again. This time, he's not greeting many people. It's like he's looking for someone; distracted, peering over the tops of people's heads as they exit. He's shaking hands without looking effectually into people's eyes as he normally does; it's *very* unlike him. Grea, Miss Valerie, Martha, and Rock are each recipients of one of his half-hearted farewells also.

Jonah stops Manny and gives him a firm handshake.

"Manny, *there* you are..." says Jonah.

"Hey...hey, Jonah," Manny responds, a bit suspiciously.

"I saw you today, up on the balcony," Jonah says, peering into Manny's eyes.

"Oh...yes. Right, I was..."

Before Manny can finish the thought, Jonah cuts him off.

"What did you hear?" Jonah asks, still piercing him with his eyes.

Manny is caught off guard.

"Well, I...uhh...I heard pieces of what you were saying. I went to the restroom and stopped there for a little while...why?"

"Manny. I have something to ask you."

"Okay. What is it?"

"Do you sleep well at night?"

"What kind of question is that?" Manny responds semi-defensively, again caught off guard.

"I'm sorry, that's quite rude of me I suppose. I apologize. But I just sense that lots of things are happening with you, and have been for quite a while. Dreams. Deep thoughts. Unusual feelings. Things like that, maybe?"

"Well, I mean..."

Before he can respond, Jonah interrupts him again.

"You're very introspective, Manny. You're a young man of many thoughts, and emotions, and deep wonder. Have you ever wondered why? And your dreams...I know that you have them..."

Manny is speechless. He has no idea how to respond.

"Manny. It's time. I can't explain it all to you now, but it will all become clearer every day from this point forward. Okay? Trust him again, Manny. Trust him...as best as you possibly can..."

Manny stares at him blankly.

"Go on...go on with the others...I will talk to you soon..." Jonah says.

Manny begins to walk away from Jonah completely confused and with his mouth open.

Seconds later, he feels Jonah's hand grab him by the arm.

"Manny?"

He turns and looks at Jonah. Jonah motions with his head toward Martha, Rock, Valerie, and Grea.

"Take good care of them, they need you more than you know, *especially* your mother…"

Still unsure of what to say, Manny walks away and joins the others.

~ ~ ~

Manny is quiet for the majority of the evening after they arrive at Eden—thinking.

Thinking about the night before and the intensity of his dream.

Thinking about the things that Jonah said during his time of teaching.

Thinking about how Jonah behaved after the gathering.

He barely pays attention as Grea and Rock talk at the table. Martha and Valerie are away again, walking through the merchant tents.

"What's your deal?" Grea finally says, noticing Manny's obvious distance.

"Huh? Oh…nothing. Just, nothing. I'm thinking, that's all…" Manny replies.

"Well, *obviously*…but about what?" Rock says.

"A lot…" Manny responds dryly.

Silence.

"Well, don't tell it all at one time; I can hardly keep up," Grea remarks.

Manny smiles.

"Nothing, it's okay. Really…"

~ ~ ~

Across the field, Damien, Polus, and Levi are seated.

"That was him, up on the balcony during the gathering. *Emmanuel*. Jonah looked right at him."

Damien says the words with satisfaction, gazing off in the distance, rubbing his fingers together.

"What do we do now, Damien?" Levi asks.

"We wait. We wait for the perfect opportunity to clip his wings before he can ever take flight…"

Levi pauses and looks at the ground for a moment.

Finally, he asks, "what does *that* mean?"

"*That meansssss, we mussssssssst kill him…*"

Polus says it with a straight face, then nothing else is said between the three men.

~ ~ ~

As the evening comes, the people at Eden disperse.

Manny and the others are back on the train headed to their modest homes.

The sunlight fades behind large gray clouds on the back row of the sky.

23. A TINY MOMENT

Although they are but tiny things, *moments* are still extremely powerful. There are some that happen far too fast for us to process at the time of their occurrence. In other words; they're a blur. We don't realize the true depth of their significance until we look back and think about how they set off a chain of events—a ripple effect that altered the courses of our destinies. Or perhaps, those moments don't change anything at all. Maybe their sole purpose is to highlight a predestined path that was set for us long before our birth.

~~~

Maybe our lives were already plotted and pre-determined, and *moments* simply help us to see the map more clearly and accurately.

Everything seems normal today; nothing is out of the ordinary at first glance.

Manny eats his "favorite."

He talks to Martha.

They wait outside for the train.

Manny helps Martha on.

He stares out of the window and thinks.

Usual.

"Do you think that you could run to Emil's for me this afternoon, Manny?" Martha asks softly.

"Sure, I can go as soon as we get back."

"Okay, that will be good. We need some more water. I want you to get some vinegar too, if you can find any."

He looks at her and twists his face.

"Vinegar?"

"Umhm…"

"I'll try…"

She giggles at his response.

The two of them get quiet again. She usually tries to not say too much to him in the mornings; she knows that he's in his head and doesn't want to disturb his thoughts.

After a few moments, Martha looks down the aisle at an elderly woman. There's a large blanket under the woman's arm. Manny notices her too. The woman looks up and smiles at them.

Martha sees a picture of herself in an instant; herself in the years to come. Clearly the woman is exhausted already and the day has not even begun. Manny looks at Martha, then immediately looks away. He's bothered—thinking about her toiling in those dusty fields for hours upon hours.

Her knees.

Her cough.

The Agri-Fields approach quickly through the windows. Martha stares at the canopy-decorated field in a trance-like state.

"Mom," Manny says.

She continues to stare. Thoughts zip through her mind like a fleet of Grand Prix race cars. She's not as focused today.

Something about seeing the elderly woman, an older version of herself, has completely smothered her conscience.

She wonders about her and Manny's future, not for the first time, but in a new and more profound way. Manny wonders what she might be thinking about, but chooses to not ask.

"Mom…" he says again.

She sits there, motionless. The train slows to a stop. Many of the Agri-Field workers are already beginning to stand and approach the doors. Manny touches Martha's shoulder.

"Mom?"

"Yes…yes honey?"

"Are you okay?"

"Oh, I'm fine. Just letting my mind wander for a bit…"

"We're here," Manny whispers to her.

"Well, yes…yes we are, aren't we?"

She stands, grabs her blanket, folds it, and tucks it under her arm. She looks at the elderly woman again as she passes by, who has fallen into a light sleep. For some reason, she feels compelled to touch her shoulder. She does so. Gently, so as not to wake her.

"I'll see you this evening, mom. I love you."

"I love you more…"

She steps down to the platform beneath her.

~ ~ ~

It's like clip from a movie that has been manipulated with high-end technology and software. It happens in real-time, slow-motion, and in fast-forward, simultaneously, in Manny's mind.

Maybe Martha's mind is still wandering?

Maybe the image of the woman is still superimposed over her cognizance?

She misses a step.

She lands—*hard*—onto the concrete with a thud. Her blanket unfolds and lands next to her.

She only hears murmurs and a few short yelps and gasps.

Her hands, shoulder, hip, leg, and foot all begin to hurt immediately.

Sharp, stinging pains.

Manny stands there, gawking at her, completely uncertain of what to do and speechless.

She grimaces. The pains are deep. Her knee is bloody. So are her hands. Pieces of loose gravel are lodged in her skin.

"I'm okay...I'm okay," she says, reflexively.

Manny is still frozen.

She struggles to stand up as a handful of people attempt to help her.

Manny's mind comes back to the real world in that instant. He pushes a few of the people aside. He's frantic. He quickly stoops down and begins lifting her up.

"Ouch! I'm fine, Manny...o*uch!* Really...I am..."

She can barely stand—her leg. It hurts so much that she can't hide it in her expressions, as badly as she would like to. People stare at her, and at Manny. She looks deeply into Manny's eyes.

"I'm okay, really. I will be fine..."

"No! Mom, you *can't* go to the Agri-Fields today..."

"What? What do you mean? I *have* to, Manny..."

"*NO!* You can't. We have to get you back home. I will tell the conductor that..."

"Manny, No…"

She strains to lift her arm and places her hand on his cheek.

"I have to go. I *have* to. I don't have a choice…"

"But…"

"No *buts*. I will get through the day, and tonight we can tend to everything else. Now go. You have to get to the Shield. *Go*. I mean it, Emmanuel…"

The crowd of people at the train's door disperses. Manny still stands there, looking into his mother's eyes. She motions for him to get back onto the train.

"Go on now…I'm okay…I'll see you this evening," she says, just before biting her lip to offset the aching.

He backs up the steps while holding onto the rail.

The doors close.

The train pulls away.

He watches his mother limp toward the tents, still clearly in pain. For another few moments, he continues standing at the door. A voice rings out over the train's intercom system:

"Be seated, *please*, sir…"

He sits. His mouth hasn't closed yet. Fear. Anger. Frustration. They all course through his veins like immunity shot vaccinations. The train rumbles along, leaving his mother farther and farther behind. He can't think clearly. He impulsively decides that at the very next stop, he's going to get off the train, no matter where he is, and walk away. Away from it all. Away from everything. Not to any particular place. Just *away*. Wherever *away* is.

He's done.

Helplessness and hopelessness both consume him like twin raging fires.

The single person that means the world to him, he can't protect.

Dying is a better option than living at this point.

He's thought about it before, but not as intimately or desirously as he is right now.

He wishes it. *Longs* for it.

Death.

Death would be easier. It's probably peaceful.

He figures that he's already died twice before, inside.

Once during Star Fall.

And again, just moments ago.

The third time should be a charm.

~ ~ ~

Thoughts flood his mind to the point of psychologically drowning him.

He visualizes his mother's face, in pain as she lies on the ground.

A tear dribbles onto his cheek.

He thinks of *the Creator*. He thinks of how he wanted to give him a chance, but it seems that he can't even protect him and his mother. He can't even free them from the lives that they are forced to live. He can't even save the world from the state that it's in, yet he's supposed to be the world's savior?

Another tear.

Death.

His only option.

The next stop.

He's made up his mind.

There's a storm raging inside of him and nobody notices, though there are people all around him. Oblivious, clueless, and unaware people; locked into their own worries, concerns, and cares.

Manny is invisible to them.

~ ~ ~

He visualizes it.
    He'll get off of the train.
    The very next stop.
    He'll walk.
    And, he'll die.
    Somehow.
    Quickly.
    Painlessly.
    Radiation?
    Does radiation poisoning hurt?
    Or maybe he'll do it himself.
    Train tracks?
    A leap from an abandoned building?
    Remnants have done it before.
    He's seen it in the Awareness Tracts from time to time.
    Suicide prevention.
    Medic counselors.
    He's heard the rumors and stories.
    Maybe the Outskirts?
    By the hands of a Wayward?
    Perhaps the stories are true.
    He doesn't care anymore.
    It makes him no difference how.
    As long as the time is: soon.
    Today.
    Now.
    He's weary.
    He's had enough.

~ ~ ~

Then, he sees it; at his absolute lowest point, ever. And when he does, everything changes for him, and for everyone else in the world, forever; from that **moment** forward.

A tiny **moment…**
…that contained eternity.

24. I'LL HOLD YOU TO IT

"...ACKNOWLEDGE THE CREATOR, AND YOUR PATH WILL UNFOLD."

THE SENTENCE IS incomplete, but the few words that are left dive into his pupils. The color of the text is fading, but the impression it leaves is stronger and bolder than Manny could have prepared himself for.

He's never noticed it; this tattered, rusty, and worn billboard. A large portion of the sign's wording is torn off—completely missing. Only the last part of phrase is still readable. As much as he's ridden the train, and as many times as he's passed this very section of Naza while gazing out of the window, he's never seen it before.

It had to have always been there, but today it strikes him like a thousand sledge hammers. An eerie calmness comes over him that he can't shake. He's heard or seen these words in the past it seems, but can't remember where.

As the train passes, Manny's eyes stay glued to it. He turns his head as it zips past the window, then he stares at the back of it. It's supported by rusty metal and rotting wood. He keeps watching until it becomes a small brown speck.

Eventually, it's completely out of sight.

"ACKNOWLEDGE THE CREATOR, AND YOUR PATH WILL UNFOLD..."

He replays it in his mind, over and over.
His heart is calm now; strangely calm.
He no longer sees the fallen image of his mother.
He won't get off at the next stop.
He won't die; not today.

~ ~ ~

The majority of the day is a haze to him after he reaches the Shield. He pulls tools from his kit, unscrews panels, fidgets with equipment, and pulls at wires, but his mind is still on the train—the moment when he saw the billboard.

At lunch, he reaches the bench first. As soon as the bell is done ringing, he sits.

He pulls a piece of paper out of his pocket; the back of some torn out page from an electrical manual. He digs into his other pocket and retrieves an oil pen. He writes with his attention fully concentrated on what he's doing.

Just then, Rock and Grea approach.

"Beat us here I see, *old man*," Grea says.

"I haven't seen you all day, you must've been in one of the side shops," Rock interjects.

No response. Only intense writing.

"Hello? Earth to Manny? Manny, do you copy?" Grea continues as she waves her hand in front of his face.

He never lifts it, he just writes more intensely.

Grea and Rock look at each other and shrug at the same time. In a synchronized motion, they both tilt their heads to the side and attempt to read what he's writing. He has drawn a large rectangle in the shape of the billboard.

Inside of it, he's written in bold, capitalized letters:

"ACKNOWLEDGE THE CREATOR, AND YOUR PATH WILL UNFOLD."

"The heck is this?" Rock says as Manny turns the paper toward them so that they can read it clearly.

"Where is this from? *Tell me...*" Manny says.

He sounds exasperated and desperate. Grea squints and moves her head closer to the paper. She looks at Rock with a very confused expression on her face. She looks at Manny with the same expression.

She looks back at the paper, then picks it up.

"*No* way," she says in disbelief.

"What?" Manny says.

"No *freaking* way..."

"What, Grea? Tell me? Do you know what it is?"

"Do you realize what that is, Manny?"

"No! That's why I'm asking you! I've seen it somewhere before, but I can't remember where. What is it?"

"Manny, this is from the Grandeurscript...why are *you* writing it?"

"Well, I saw it today, on a billboard. Right after mom fell..."

"Wait, what? Miss Martha? Is she okay?"

"Yes, I mean, no. Well, she'll be okay, I hope...I'm not sure. She fell down the steps off of the train today..."

"Oh my *goodness!* Manny..." Grea says, placing her hand on her chest and widening her eyes.

"I won't know anything for sure until tonight. I was going to take her back home, but she insisted on going to the Agri-Fields anyway. But this...I saw this on a sign right after that, and I haven't been able to stop thinking about it. What does it mean?"

"Well, I tell you what, both of you have lost me; this is too much," Rock says as he sits down on the bench and drops his forehead into his hands, completely overwhelmed.

Grea pulls her Grandeurscript from her bag and turns to the passage.

"It's right here…"

She reads it aloud:

"…YOUR HUMAN KNOWLEDGE WILL ONLY TAKE YOU SO FAR; ACKNOWLEDGE THE CREATOR, AND YOUR PATH WILL UNFOLD…"

Manny looks at it. Grea and Rock study his face. After a few moments of silence, he finally says something:

"I used to read this when I was really young. *All* of the time. I remember it. Of all days, why did I see it today? I've never even seen that billboard before. Not once. The train passes by that same area every single day, and I've never noticed it."

"Seriously?" Rock asks.

"Yes, seriously."

Manny has a blank look on his face. Neither of them is sure what to say next.

Luckily, the buzzer sounds not many minutes after, relieving the awkwardness.

"I'll see you guys later…" Manny says as he rises from the table, still consumed with thoughts.

"Guy and girl…that is…" Grea says as he walks away, almost hoping that he'll turn and smile, or say something witty in return.

He doesn't.

He simply returns to his work station.

He thinks.

His mother.

The billboard.

Grea and Rock don't see him for the rest of the day.

He stays to himself.

Manny's train is the last to come. When it does, he leaves the gate, and hastily boards, hoping to not bump into anyone that he knows.

During the ride home, he looks out of the window the entire time, mentally replaying the scene from earlier, repeatedly. He remembers where the billboard was. Inside his pocket, he still has the scrap piece of paper that he scribbled the cryptic message on. He pulls it out and studies it:

ACKNOWLEDGE THE CREATOR, AND YOUR PATH WILL UNFOLD...

The cleared-out section of land that the sign was located in is quickly approaching. It's getting dark now, but there is still enough sunlight to make out a large billboard.

"It should be right around this curve," he says to himself.

He cups his hands around the sides of his eyes and presses his face against the window as close as possible to maximize his vision.

The train rolls out of the curve.

Nothing.

Manny stands. His mouth opens wide. He walks down the aisle sideways, agitatedly looking out of the window. The hair on his arms and neck stand at attention. People stare at him. Most everyone else is exhausted from the day and half asleep; Manny is a rude disturbance. He moves all the way to the back of the train, looking out of the window searching for the billboard. He accidently bumps into a man who has his leg extended into the walkway.

"Hey, watch it..." the man reprimands.

Manny doesn't respond. His eyes are fixated on the spot that he passed earlier—the spot that he is *certain* that he saw the sign.

Still, nothing. It's not there.

Confusion grips him suddenly and firmly.

"What? Where is it? It was right there!"

His face begins to sweat.

He stands at the back of the train and tries to process how a huge billboard could vanish into thin air in just a matter of hours. Did the Scavengers take it down? Did a sand storm pass through and destroy it? Nothing makes sense. There isn't any evidence that it had been there at all. Not even holes in the ground that would have supported its legs.

"How?"

Before he knows it, the train is slowing to a stop.

The Agri-Fields.

His mother.

He comes to himself and rushes toward the door, remembering his mother's fall earlier that day. People are already crowding on.

He doesn't see her. Finally, after just about everyone is on, he looks onto the platform and sees two figures; one leans on the other.

"Miss Val?"

"Manny, hey there, sweetheart…"

Her face is dropped low. He's never seen the bubbly and energetic woman so solemn. Martha leans onto Valerie's side with her arm around her shoulder. She's clearly still in pain.

She limps toward the train's door. Manny dives under her other arm and helps her up each step. She twists her face. Pain.

About two full minutes pass. They've gotten her to a seat. Valerie says nothing. She looks at Martha, rubs her arm, hugs Manny, then exits the train.

Manny sits next to his mother, the doors close, and the train scuttles away.

Her head is low, along with her eyes. Manny looks at her arms and legs. Bruises everywhere. Her skin is now a collage of purples, reds, burgundies, and blacks. He doesn't say anything. He doesn't want to upset or disturb her. She falls asleep.

At home, he helps her off of the train, up the steps of their building, and into their door. It takes her about two hours to shower. He sits in his room the entire time, fighting back tears.

When she's done, he helps her into her bed. The only words that they exchange the entire evening are:

"*I love you…*"

"*I love you more…*"

In his room, all night long, he stares at the sheet of paper.

ACKNOWLEDGE THE CREATOR, AND YOUR PATH WILL UNFOLD.

After a few hours, he falls asleep.

~ ~ ~

The next morning, there's no smell of *"his favorite"* coming from the kitchen. He wakes and goes to his mother's room. She's still asleep; much later than she normally would be. He doesn't disturb her.

He cooks, he leaves her a plate of food, and he leaves to catch the train.

On the way to the Shield, he waits for the moment that he will pass by the place that he saw the billboard. He wonders if he somehow just missed it the evening before.

Maybe it was darker than he realized.

Maybe he overlooked it.

The train finally reaches the plot of land just beyond the Agri-Fields after what seems like hours.

Still nothing. It's gone. Utterly gone.

There's no sign of a billboard EVER being in that spot.

"Am I going crazy? I can't be—I *KNOW* that I saw it there..." he says softly to himself.

~ ~ ~

For the next few days, Martha's condition doesn't get much better. She stays at home and sleeps. Manny makes sure that she has whatever she needs from Emil's, and he does all of the cooking. He rubs ointments and creams on her arms and legs to treat the cuts and bruises every evening.

"Thank you, sweetie," is her response each time.

He smiles sympathetically and nods whenever she says it.

Every day, without fail, Manny looks out of the window of the train on his way to the Shield only to see that the billboard is still nowhere in sight—and apparently never was. Confusion is an understatement. How does a billboard just disappear into thin air? Better yet, how did he see a billboard that was possibly never there?

At lunch, he writes the mantra on sheet after sheet of scratch paper and daydreams. In the meantime, Rock and Grea talk about a handful of Nerps that they saw moving lots of boxes out of the Shield earlier that morning.

"It was so weird. I can't remember ever seeing them here during daytime hours. I assumed that they always came either late in the evenings, or super earlier before we get here," Grea says as she cracks her knuckles.

"I know what you mean. I don't remember ever seeing them either. It looks like they were moving some of our finished parts, maybe radios and night vision goggles and stuff. I saw a few crates of ammo too," Rock says.

"I hear that they distribute it throughout all of New America, at what's left of the bases. I've also heard that lots of it goes straight to the bunkers...but I don't know..." Grea continues.

"Me neither," Rock responds as he turns to look at Manny, who is writing feverishly.

"Seriously? Still?" Rock says.

"Don't start," Manny quickly and sharply responds without even so much as looking up.

"You're still writing this stuff? Maybe you just didn't see anything, you know? Maybe you just had one of those weird moments, like when an old memory comes to mind, and you imagine that you're seeing it right then…"

"Maybe he's right," Grea adds.

"I mean, it was a pretty traumatic day already with your mom falling and all. It could've just been in your head…"

"I know what I saw! It was there! It was right there out of the window, I *know* it was! I'm not going crazy! I know that I saw it!"

"*Sheeeeeshh!* Okay, okay! Relax! You saw it—*maniac!*"

Rock lifts his hands and leans backward as he says it.

Grea laughs.

"It was there…" Manny mutters while lowering his head to write again.

"I don't know, Manny, maybe it's something you could talk to Jonah about, you know?" Grea says.

"What? No! *ABSOLUTELY* not…" Manny sharply replies.

"Why not? I mean, it's from the Grandeurscript, and maybe it's something he's experienced before…the whole, *seeing things that aren't really there?*"

"Quiet. And no, I'm *not* talking to Jonah about *anything…*"

"All right, suit yourself…"

"Well, it's time to get back to work you two—I'm going to beat the buzzer. I've still got some wiring to repair, and I don't plan on working too hard for the rest of the day."

Rock stands and stretches.

"You *never* work too hard," Grea responds.

Rock sticks his tongue out and thumps a small metal washer at her. She blocks it with her arm, picks it up from the table, tosses it back at him, then stands and proceeds to her work station also.

"Okay…I'll see you guys later on then," Manny says while still seated at the table.

Manny stares toward the front gate.

"*Jonah? Psshh. They're crazy,*" he says to himself.

"Or maybe *I'm* crazy…"

~ ~ ~

When he arrives at home that evening, Martha is in the kitchen, attempting to cook and clean. Manny pauses at the door and looks at her. She sees him.

"Oh, hey there! You snuck up on the old lady…"

She coughs painfully.

Manny drops his bag, walks over to the sink, and picks up a towel. He hands it to her, and she finishes her cough with it pressed to her mouth.

"I can do that. You should sit down and rest, ma…"

"Oh, such a *worrier*…"

She sits in one of the kitchen chairs closest to the sink. She coughs more. She rests her head on her hand. Manny starts washing the dishes.

"So how was work today?"

"It was just work," he answers, blandly.

"Oh, don't I know it…"

As Manny cleans the dishes, Martha notices a piece of paper poking out of his back pocket. She gently pulls it out without him noticing.

"What's this?"

"What's what?" he asks without turning.

"This…"

He turns and sees what she's holding.

"Oh, that. Remember, what I was telling you about the billboard?"

"Ohhh, right, right. Yes, I remember…that's certainly something…"

She looks at the paper, then looks up at Manny.

"So, are you going to talk to him?"

"Talk to who?"

"To Jonah…"

"Gosh, you sound like Grea…"

She laughs.

"Well, I suppose she's very intelligent in that case."

"She sure *thinks* so…"

They both laugh. Manny stops washing dishes and sits at the table across from Martha.

"I just don't know. Even if I did want to talk to him, I wouldn't know how to explain it, you know?"

"Hmm, I see."

She thinks.

"I think I know how," Martha says.

"How?"

"Just explain it…" she responds as she smiles and gently rubs his hand.

She has the uncanny ability of creating comfort when he's most uneasy.

"I only understand the basics of the passage, and I've told you as much as I can about it. Sometimes, the road ahead isn't clear. In fact, oftentimes that's the case. But it's those times that really prove to us that we've been guided all along. That's when we have to quiet ourselves, and everything around us, and find our answers deep inside—find the Creator deep inside. That's when the path unfolds right before our eyes, and we'll realize that we've been on track the whole time, even when we felt most lost. Much easier said than done, of course. But if we acknowledge that there's truth out there, then somehow, some way, that truth will draw us. The divine will take over when our humanity reaches its limit…"

Silence.

"Wow. You're so wise. If you're not careful, I may just start believing again…"

She laughs and coughs.

"That's what I'm hoping, honey…"

She finishes her cough, then takes a moment to look into his eyes. Love and compassion rise up in her like a tiny swelling ocean inside of her heart. She refocuses and pulls her mind back into the conversation.

"Now, why you saw it on a billboard, that doesn't exist—*that's* where Jonah comes in. You've got me stumped there."

"I'm stumped too," he says with a lighthearted laugh.

She touches his hand gently again.

"Just think about it."

He inhales and his nostrils flare.

"I'll think about it…" he says with an exhale.

"Promise?" she asks.

A pause.

"Promise…" Manny says.

She squeezes his hand with hers and smiles.

"Okay. I'll hold you to it…"

25. I'LL MEET YOU AT EDEN

"YOU'LL HAVE A perfect opportunity today. You *know* that he's going to stop you and talk to you—he always does," Rock says, scratching his chin, and looking at Manny from the corner of his eye.

"I don't know, Rock…"

"What is there to not know? Just *tell* him…"

"Tell him what? *Everything?* I can't. I won't have time. All of those people. No, I just can't."

"Well, you *have* to do something. You've been bugged about it all week long. You have to say something. Maybe, I don't know—maybe just tell him that you'd like to talk to him some time later, even if it's not right then."

Manny lets out a long, slow sigh.

Rock isn't playing cards in the skybox today. He and Manny sit off to the side.

Today feels strange with Martha not being down in the crowd somewhere. Her fall has really taken its toll; she never misses attending the IE on Sabbaths. She's still too weak and in too much pain to do much more than sit at home, cook a little, clean a little, and sleep. She's mentioned the NRP and the ration laws a couple of times, but Manny usually cuts her off with, *"we're okay. I'm able to work. We're fine. Just rest…"*

Grea and Rock constantly ask Manny about her and offer to help if either of them need anything. Having them there makes it much easier for Manny to deal with. He knows that he can depend on them; he's always been able to.

~ ~ ~

"I agree, it just makes sense to at least try to talk to Jonah about it; I certainly would if I were you. I'd at least ask him if he had any ideas or knew of an explanation. Billboards with Grandeurscript passages don't just pop up, and then disappear..."

It's Jhenda. She's in the skybox again today and Manny is thankful for two reasons: he wanted to see her again, and it also affords him another opportunity to tell someone what happened. She has fresh set of ears and an unbiased perception.

"I don't know, maybe you are crazy," was her first response.

Then, it was, *"maybe they're right...maybe it was just inside your head."*

Manny's response remains the same: "I know what I saw; it was there."

They talk about the possibilities in greater detail for the next few moments. Chemicals in the air and food supplies, water pollution, fatigue, stress, a hallucination, UFOs. Any possible reason behind Manny's experience is entertained, no matter how seemingly absurd or farfetched.

"Well, it certainly wasn't us," Jhenda says, "no Scavengers were even assigned to the edges of the Agri-Fields that day. There's nothing there, firstly, and secondly, what are we going to do with a *billboard*?"

Manny's head is lowered and both of his hands are on the top of it.

"I'm not going crazy..."

"Well, hold on a second, let's not jump to any conclusions..." Jhenda says jokingly as she touches his shoulder.

The three of them snicker.

Once the gathering is over, they wait for Grea in the stairwell. She eventually appears in the crowd. Everyone is together again, except for Valerie and Martha. Valerie decided to stay at Manny's apartment with Martha again for the day, which puts Manny's mind somewhat at ease.

The four friends approach the exit.

"*Dun-dun-dunnn,* moment of truth," Rock says dramatically as if introducing a climactic movie scene.

"Shut up," Manny shoots back.

When Manny reaches Jonah, they peer at each other. Jonah looks intense just as he did during their last awkward encounter.

"How are you, Manny?" he says, sincerely.

"I'm—I'm okay, Jonah."

Jonah moves his head from side to side and studies Manny's face.

"Are you sure? You look troubled, is everything okay?"

Within milliseconds, Manny considers pouring out the contents of his heart and mind to Jonah. He envisions the entire scene:

"I'm not okay, Jonah. I keep having these weird dreams that I don't understand. My mother fell and got hurt pretty badly, and I'm worried about her. I saw this billboard with a Grandeurscript passage that I used to read when I was a kid, then it vanished, and I'm afraid, Jonah—I'm afraid because life doesn't make any sense. I don't know what to do! I want to believe in the Creator, but I don't know how to. It's hard for me to believe in what I can't see, feel, and know for certain. I'm confused. I'm frustrated about the way things are. There

has to be more, Jonah. There has to be more to life than this! I'm tired...I'm so tired."

"Manny! Are you okay?"

It's the third-time that Jonah has called him; this time with his hands on both of Manny's shoulders, shaking him. Manny has been daydreaming for a few seconds now and didn't notice; Jonah's shaking snaps him out of it.

"*Yes, I'm fine!*" he spurts.

"It's like you were in a trance. Are you sure that there isn't something you'd like to tell me, Manny?"

"Uhh...I'm sure...thanks...thanks Jonah..."

Manny hurriedly frees himself from Jonah's grip and swiftly walks away.

When he's taken about seven short, quick strides, he stops in his tracks. He just can't just let himself leave, still carrying this great burden. In a split-second, he musters up the courage to turn around and ask Jonah to talk.

At the moment he turns, he sees Jonah facing him. Before Manny can say a single word, Jonah speaks calmly but firmly to him:

"*Manny, we can talk about the Grandeurscript passage this afternoon; I'll meet you at Eden...*"

With that, Jonah turns away from Manny and continues greeting people like he didn't say anything at all. Manny is frozen in place. He's so shocked that he wonders if it really happened, or if he imagined it altogether.

Manny watches Jonah for a few seconds, greeting his congregants, smiling enthusiastically, and talking jovially.

Manny immediately turns back around and darts to the exit.

26. PLEASE SHOW ME

MANNY SITS ON the train having no idea what to expect at Eden.

He's already let Grea, Jhenda, and Rock know what Jonah said to him earlier. They're just as surprised and curious as he is. Jhenda has actually joined them this time, partially out of pure intrigue. It's her first time in Eden. Her face is plastered to the window of the train, much like the children.

"I can't *believe* it, it's so amazing," she remarks at least four or five times.

After they reach Eden, Rock and Grea decide to head off at the merchant's tents. Manny paces back and forth beside one of the benches. Jhenda stands near him, still in awe of the splendor of Eden.

"S&G looks *nothing* like this. This place is so…beautiful…"

"Yea…" Manny says weakly.

"So many people. I guess I'm used to it being crowded, just not this clean and organized."

"Umhm…" he responds, half-way paying attention.

Jhenda looks at Manny. He's still pacing.

"You should just try to relax."

"It's kind of hard to do that," Manny murmurs.

"I can imagine. But hey, what's the worst that could happen—him confirming what we all believe anyway?"

"What's that?" he says as he stops and looks at her.

"Well, that you're *crazy*…"

Manny grins, looks away, and resumes pacing.

"Good, at least you're still able to smile…"

At that moment, Jhenda looks up and sees a train stopping about two-hundred yards away from them. She taps Manny's shoulder and points at it. As she does, Jonah steps out of its door.

"Well, here he is," Jhenda says.

Manny looks at her and lets out a slow stream of air from his nostrils.

"Just, tell him, okay? You don't want to hold anything back when the moment to let it all out finally comes…"

She pauses.

"This is one of your moments. Get the answers you've been waiting for; the answers that you *need*…"

Manny nods.

"I'll see you later," Jhenda says as she touches Manny's shoulder just before turning and leaving to give them privacy.

As she walks away, Jonah waves at Manny. Manny waves back. Jonah points at the benches just behind Manny as he walks toward him. Manny turns around and sits. Jonah sits next to him with a long sigh.

"*Finally*, a second to relax. I've been on my feet all day," Jonah says.

He leans backward, arches his back, and stretches.

"So, Manny, how are you? Goodness! It still blows my mind how quickly all of you have grown up. I remember when you were just a boy. I was a young man myself then, not much older than you are now. What are you, eighteen?"

"I'm nineteen now, since a few weeks ago."

"Gosh! See what I mean? Time flies…"

Jonah reaches into a bag that he's brought with him and pulls out a few books while he speaks. He places them in front of him on the top of the bench then looks into Manny's eyes.

"So, how are you? How are you *really*, Manny?"

"Well…I'm okay…I suppose?"

"Be honest with me, Manny. Let it all out, like Jhenda told you…"

"How do you…how did—how do you know?" Manny says as he drops his eyebrows in bewilderment.

"Well, certain things come to me, you could say. We'll get into that too, eventually. But let's hear what's been on your mind and troubling you first. Oh, and how's your mother? Is she recovering well?"

A multitude of questions suddenly arise in Manny's mind. How does he know about Martha being hurt when he's never shared it with him? Did Miss Valerie tell him? Well, she couldn't have, she's been staying with Martha at home every Sabbath. Maybe Jhenda? Unlikely, they never talk for more than a few seconds after gatherings. How could he possibly know?

Manny quiets his questions momentarily and responds.

"Well, she's not doing too well, but I'm hoping that she'll be okay."

"Right. She's a little older now, so it will take a little longer for her to heal, but she'll pull through. Try to not worry about her. Now, tell me about what you saw that day on the train…" Jonah says, clasping his hands as if he's a therapist.

"I…wait, how do you know that I saw something?"

"Manny, it's okay. Tell me…"

Jonah looks down and starts to flip through the pages of one of the books he's brought. There are three of them. One is a tattered and worn Grandeurscript. The other two are notebooks. Manny glances at them and can see that each page is completely full of words and symbols, even beyond the margins. The handwriting is messy, so he can't clearly make out what any of it says.

Jonah looks up and catches Manny looking at the pages.

"Manny, what did you see—the day that your mother fell?"

"Right. Right. I was on the train, heading to the Shield. I was really fed up, and mad, and frustrated. She had just fallen, and, things just didn't make sense to me anymore. Things haven't made sense to me for a while now actually, to tell the truth..."

"What things?"

"Just, *things*, you know?"

"Be open, Manny. Let it out—that's the only way. Cups that are full already can't be filled anymore without being emptied first. Say it. You were angry with the Creator, right? That's if there even is a *Creator*. But how could there be, with us having to live the way that we do? How could he love us, yet allow something like Star Fall to happen? How could he just sit back and allow *millions* to die, right?"

Manny peers at Jonah, speechless.

"Am I right, Manny?"

"Yes. That's how I felt, well, how I feel..."

"Okay, and then what happened?"

"I saw a billboard."

"Go on."

"And it had this on it."

Manny reaches into his pocket and pulls out a crumpled piece of paper:

ACKNOWLEDGE THE CREATOR, AND YOUR PATH WILL UNFOLD.

Jonah studies it, then smiles and places it back on the bench top.

"Umhm...I see...and then?"

"Well, that's it, I guess. I saw it and felt like the weight of the world lifted off of my shoulders. It was kind of weird. I haven't been able to stop thinking about those words ever since. I used to read it all the time when I was really young. As a matter of fact, my grandmother was the one who…"

Manny stops speaking all of a sudden and his eyes drop. Jonah stares at him.

"I understand," Jonah says.

Manny picks up the paper and examines it. He flicks at its edges with his fingertip.

"You haven't dreamt since you saw it either, have you?" Jonah asks.

Manny is done being shocked that Jonah seems to know so much about him without the information ever being told to him, at least not by anyone that he's aware of.

"No, no I haven't actually…now that I think about it," Manny says, tilting his head to the side in thought and recollection.

"I thought so. Well, here's the thing Manny. I can't tell you everything just yet, but very soon, you're going to discover a lot more than you probably ever expected. The time is very close—the time that I've waited for, well, that we've all waited for, for a very, *very* long while."

"What time? What do you mean Jonah?"

Jonah grins and nods. He opens another one of the notebooks and flips through its pages in search of something. Jonah speaks as he looks:

"Ever since I was a child, I've been really *in tune,* if you will. I've always had this feeling that there was more out there—more to life than what we see day to day, probably much like you…"

Manny nods but his face remains blank as he listens carefully.

"When I was really young, I had a lot of experiences that I considered to be *supernatural,* I suppose. Nothing that was too outrageous necessarily, but things that I just knew couldn't have been mere coincidences. I attributed those things to a higher power—the Creator. That was the only explanation that made any sense. I took it as a calling to share this "spiritual intuitiveness" and "metaphysical sensitivity" with the world, which I did. I studied everything; every belief system that you can think of. *Everything*. In fact, it was the perfect time to do so. The years before Star Fall were divided. Everyone sort of did what seemed right or best to them: religiously, socially, and morally. Everyone followed their own path for the most part. There was no consensus at all. This gave me a sense of freedom and liberation, but at the same time left me extremely frustrated..."

"Frustrated? Why frustrated," Manny asks.

"Well...I could do what I wanted and believe what I chose, but there was no standard; no *single* path. I figured that everyone couldn't be perfectly correct about their ideas, right? But everyone couldn't be wrong either, could they? What if *everyone* was wrong?" Jonah suggests, then pauses.

Manny scratches his neck and stares down at the table in thought; Jonah continues:

"I wanted to be sure. I wasn't satisfied with being really sharp and wise, but still incorrect in my perceptions of spirituality, of life, of existence...of the universe. I wanted answers. I wanted to know the truth. I wanted to know the *way*..."

Manny doesn't blink. His heart, mind, and soul are drawn in and he's completely focused on Jonah's words.

"Even while leading others, a very small group at the time; I would secretly question if *any* of it was real, or if what I perceived as the Creator was all in my head. Year after year, I was in turmoil inside, and no one knew. I didn't feel that I was getting any answers until..."

Jonah hesitates and seems to drift away.

"What happened?" Manny asks anxiously.

"*Every* single night, I started to have a dream. The exact same dream. It started then, and has persisted on a regular basis ever since..."

Manny's heart rate picks up.

"What happens in the dream?" Manny asks nervously.

Jonah looks into Manny's eyes like a child would look into their parent's eyes after accidentally breaking their favorite vase. He turns the notebook around so that Manny can read it:

October 15, 2034

"This was just a few days before Star Fall, right, Jonah?"

"Yes, keep reading…" Jonah says as Manny's eyes refocus on the notes:

I don't understand. For the past three nights, I've had this same dream every time I close my eyes. I don't know what it means? I'm running, somewhere in a valley. I'm trying to get somewhere. The sky is red, and it's foggy—it looks like a war scene. I run, as hard as I can. After I get over a tall hill, I see two men. One is on the ground, bloody, beaten, and bruised. The other stands over him, and he's yelling something. I can't make out what he's saying. I'm running toward them, I think that I'm trying to save the one who is on the ground. Then, a voice booms:

"IN MY WEAKNESS, HE IS MIGHTY!"

…the whole valley rumbles and shakes. Rocks and debris fall from the valley walls. The man who is standing becomes furious. He creates a large yellow light that comes out of his body. He holds this light above his head and throws it down onto the man on the ground. Then everything turns white. I don't know what this means. Who are the two men? Please show me…

27. SOON

MANNY STANDS UP in shock. He looks at Jonah like he's seen a ghost. Not knowing what else to do, he starts to walk away.

"Manny, Manny…wait…" Jonah pleads.

Manny stops but does not turn around. He's breathing heavily.

"Manny, please sit…"

He turns and goes back to the bench without making eye contact with Jonah.

"Jonah, how can this be? I've had this *exact* same dream since I was a child…"

After a few moments of quiet, Jonah speaks again.

"A few days later, Star Fall happened. I assumed that the dream was a symbolic warning; a premonition of some sort. As time went on, I became increasingly influential as a speaker amongst Remnants. More and more Remnants came as the city hubs were formed, and we eventually moved to the stadium once the IE was officially established. Your mother began to regularly attend not long after it was first formed. You were very young, but I remember you. As soon as I saw you one day in a gathering, I knew that you would grow to be the young man that I saw, well, that I see, in my dream. I began to write everything down; I knew that it would be important for me to record it all…"

Jonah flips a few pages forward, then turns the notebook back to Manny:

October 3, 2047

"This was a little over a month ago," Manny says, then he reads:

Tonight, I woke up from the dream again, only after the bright flash and everything turning white, something happened that's never happened in the dream before. I saw a cloud-covered sky. I felt like I was flying through them. Then, I stopped in midair, and written on the clouds, in what looked like black smoke, I saw the words...

"ACKNOWLEDGE THE CREATOR, AND YOUR PATH WILL UNFOLD."

...while I read the words on the cloud, a soft voice said, 'THIS IS NOTHING MORE THAN A SIGN, OF WHAT IS TO COME,' ...that's when I woke up...

~ ~ ~

Manny is silent again. Jonah clears his throat.

"How can this be, Jonah? I don't understand. You wrote these things down long before the events actually happened. How could you have possibly known?"

"I don't fully understand it either, Manny, but it's happening. My notebooks contain much of what I've been able to pick up over the years. I've written most of everything down ever since Star Fall, like I've told you. Sometimes I have dreams. Sometimes it's an out-of-the-blue thought. Sometimes it's something that just stands out to me in an unusual way. Regardless of what it may be, I write it down, believing that it's the Creator's way of speaking to me."

Manny stares at the books.

"A few weeks ago, three men from the NRP came to join our IE. They are not good men; that's all that I can say for now. There's something happening in the world, Manny, something big, and *you* play a *huge* part in it, whatever it is. I don't know exactly how, or why, but I do know that you play a critical role in what's to come. It's not time just yet, but I will give you these notebooks when the time comes. And that time is very, *very* close."

Manny drops his head.

Disbelief, overstimulation, fear—he feels all of them.

Jonah points back at one of his notebooks.

"The billboard was never there Manny…it was a vision. You saw into the spirit-world, and your mind created something physical to try to compensate. Different cultures throughout history have called it many things: the *third eye* opening, an awakening, a revelation, tapping into higher consciousness, and so on…"

Manny rubs his head.

"So, what happens now?" Manny asks.

Jonah smiles.

"That's entirely up to *him*," Jonah responds as he points to the sky.

"Over the next few days, everything will become clearer. I'm sure of it. We will be in touch…"

Jonah collects his books and stands.

"Wait, wait…so that's it?"

"Were you expecting more?"

"Well, yes…yes, I was…"

"Manny, you already have the answers…in here," he places his finger on Manny's chest, "and, in here," he finishes as he touches Manny's forehead in the area directly between both of his eyebrows, but slightly higher.

"Just keep your ears, your heart, your mind, and your eyes open. You saw the billboard and that was just the beginning.

You're already on your journey; you're on your path. We all are. We have *always* been…"

Jonah has shaken Manny's hand, walked away, and is boarding the train again within minutes. Manny watches him leave, and thinks.

"So…how'd it go?" a soft voice says.

Grea has sat down next to him without him realizing it; he has been sitting alone and lost in thought for just about three minutes prior to her arriving.

"Well, I know a little more and a little less at the same time."

"Figures…" she says, popping her knuckles and lightly laughing to herself.

Manny looks at her hands and twists his face.

"That doesn't hurt?" he asks with his eyes squinted.

"No. Feels good actually," she responds, as she pops another knuckle after thrusting her hands toward his face.

"How could he just leave without telling me *everything*?" he asks her as he scratches at his ear.

Another voice rings out from behind him.

"Did you at least ask what you needed to ask, and say what you needed to say?"

It's Jhenda. She and Rock approach and take seats.

"I did, I think? Most of it, I suppose…"

"Well, then, it was worth it, right?" Grea asks.

He doesn't reply.

"So, what now?" Rock asks.

"I'm not really sure, but I think that I…*we*…will find out, soon enough…"

28. REALITY

AT HOME THAT evening, Manny sits and talks to his mother for hours at the kitchen table. She wants to know every detail about all that she's been missing. He tells her about the conversation he had with Jonah at Eden, he even tells her about how he watched the gathering from the balcony at the IE weeks ago, which he hadn't mentioned to her before.

"You watched the whole gathering?" she asks.

"Pretty much…"

"My goodness, Manny."

She touches her cheek and curls her lips into a smile.

"That makes me so, so very happy. It's been such a long time since you've done anything like that; listened to a message, I mean."

"It has, I suppose…"

She rubs his hand. He looks at her bowl of homemade soup—chopped vegetables, boiled water, and a bit of salt from Denzi.

"You should finish…"

She coughs, painfully.

"I'll try."

Before long, she starts to nod. Manny watches her head drop and then dart back up toward the ceiling a few times as she fights to keep her eyes open.

"Come on little lady…it's time for bed."

She lets out a long sigh and gestures in agreement.

He tucks her in affectionately and kisses her forehead. As he walks out of her bedroom door, he looks at the top of her dresser and pauses. Her old tattered Grandeurscript sits there like a statue. He takes another step but hesitates again. He looks back to see her with her eyes seemingly closed. He grabs the Grandeurscript and hurriedly walks out of the door like a child stealing a piece of gum from a convenience store. She sees him through her squinted eyes and smiles again, too pleased to be able to hide it.

~ ~ ~

When Manny goes into his room, tosses the small book onto his bed, and changes his clothes, periodically looking over at it. For a few moments, he leans his elbow on his dresser and stares at the Grandeurscript, trying to remember if it's the same one that his mother would carry when he was a child. It was actually given to her by his grandmother. He's pretty sure that it is.

Finally, he sits down on his bed and takes it in his hands.

He flips it open and starts to explore the worn-out pages. Hours roll by effortlessly. It's been so long since he's read this book. Different passages stand out to him and put him in the same state of mind that he was in when he first read them.

Suddenly, he's an innocent child again—an innocent child full of belief, faith, and optimism. He grins every so often, remembering how he felt years ago as he would sit up at night with his grandmother while she would read the very same tattered book to him like a compilation of bedtime stories. No passage, however, stands out as vividly as the one that has been resurrected in his mind over the past few days; the earliest one that his grandmother taught him:

ACKNOWLEDGE THE CREATOR, AND YOUR PATH WILL UNFOLD...

He thumbs back to it intermittently, each time reading it like it's the first time he's ever laid eyes on it.

He remembers the billboard.

He remembers Jonah's notes.

He eventually finds himself asleep, yet still aware.

He dreams.

He sees the valley again, but it's different tonight. He feels more *in control* inside of the dream. He knows what's going to happen. He looks around the valley, trying to see details that he normally would miss.

The dark figure approaches.

Manny strains to move his body. Nothing. He tries to stand up, but can't. He struggles to see the man's face, but he's still unable to make out enough of his features to identify him.

"The Creator has ABANDONED YOU! He is not here, Emmanuel!"

Manny feels fear, resentment, anger, and doubt course through him. He notices the man's shadow. He knows that he's not just a man, but something more.

"*SPEAK!*"

The pace of his heart accelerates.

"You're *weak*, Emmanuel...you're *weak!*"

He closes his eyes, anticipating the words that are soon to come—the whole scene is like a damaged record that has repeated for thirteen years.

"*FIND THE STRENGTH TO ADDRESS ME LIKE A MAN!*"

Maybe it's pride. Maybe it's courage. Maybe it's faith.

The words swell like an ocean inside of Manny. He feels energy from within him and all around him collect inside of his belly. He feels like he could just burst into an explosion and light up this entire valley.

In a sense, he does, but the explosion comes out in the form of a phrase:

"IN MY WEAKNESS, HE IS MIGHTY!"

He hears the echo bounce off of the walls of the valley and sees the man stumble backward. Manny can feel heat and energy emanating from the man's body—pure hatred. The yellow glow forms faintly in all of the man's limbs and then flows toward the center of his chest, becoming more and more intense as it does. In a single motion, the man draws the energy out of himself and lifts it high into the air.

Fear shoots through Manny again.

The yellow ball of light hurts Manny's eyes as he braces himself for impact.

~ ~ ~

Just as the destructive energy is about to crush Manny's frail body, at the point that he would normally wake up, he feels himself moving at a speed faster than he's ever traveled.

His eyes are closed.

When he opens them, he's traveling through what looks like a tunnel in space decorated with stars all around it.

His body stops abruptly. He's hovering over his city hub, Naza.

He sees a multitude of people, including his loved ones: Jhenda, Grea, Rock, Martha, and Miss Valerie. He even sees Jonah and the IE off in the distance. He sees the Shield, the Agri-Fields—pretty much everything that he knows, all in one panoramic scene.

He hears a whistling sound just above him.

When he looks up, many metal with trails of smoke behind them are plummeting toward Naza.

"What?" he says to himself in confusion.

"Bombs? Missiles?"

He flies up a little higher toward them. He tries to stop one of them but it passes right through his body; he's like an intangible ghost. He tries to stop another one by flying next to it and catching it, hopefully to redirect it. His arms pass right through it.

He flies down to the ground and tries to warn them all—he screams:

"RUN, EVERYONE! RUN! GET AWAY! LOOK!"

He points up toward the deadly armaments falling from the heavens. The people just smile and talk to each other without a care in the world. They can't hear him at all. He attempts to grab Rock as he fusses with Grea about something. His hands pass through him too. He tries to pull his mother's arm as her and Valerie sit at a bench and talk about planting gardens. His hand grabs onto nothing as it closes.

He panics.

Within seconds, the bombs hit their mark.

Fire. Screams. Smoke. Explosions.

None of them survive.

~ ~ ~

Manny is back in the tunnel now.

He's crying, painfully.

Everyone he knows and loves have just been killed right before his eyes.

He weeps bitterly.

He's distraught.

A few more seconds pass and then his body abruptly stops again.

~ ~ ~

A familiar scene.

He floats in midair toward a swing set. He sees a small boy, next to a small girl. Both of their faces shining as they yell with joy.

"*No,*" he says to himself.

"*No, no…*"

They look exactly alike—twins.

The girl hops off of her swing and runs toward a woman; Martha.

Younger, healthier, and happier perhaps, but it's undoubtedly Martha.

The girl runs to an older lady now.

He feels an overwhelming sense of love for them, coupled with an inescapable feeling of powerlessness to protect them.

They disappear behind a building. Manny weeps again as he hears the whistling in the air.

The sky darkens.

The sirens blare.

Fire. Screams. Smoke. Explosions.

He's afraid to look up again.
So, he doesn't.

~ ~ ~

He's in the tunnel again, too exhausted to cry anymore.
He's still.
Solemn.
Silent.
Thinking about all that he just saw—apparently, his future, and then his past.
He doesn't want to accept either, but believes that he doesn't have a choice.
When he stops for a third time, he is overlooking the entire world. He can make out the massive continents of the earth based on their shapes. He can see the bright and beautiful oceans, the plush green land, and the thick, fluffy clouds.
He realizes that this must be the way the earth once looked in the past. The oceans are no longer blue and the land is no longer green—not since Star Fall.
Closer views of the various places around the world flash before him.
People are happy, full of joy, smiling, and excited.
All over the world, there is harmony, not perfection, but harmony.
Manny watches children at play, adults driving automobiles, and families enjoying sunny days. He sees elderly people in parks playing chess, teenagers with backpacks and skateboards at shop-

ping centers, parents picking their children up from school, men working in factories, highways lined with cars; all over the world.

Then, the whistling again.

He closes his eyes just as the sounds of bombs bursting fill his ears and the scents of fire, smoke, chemicals, and gunpowder fill his nostrils.

When he opens his eyes again, he sees the world that he now knows, with a thick gray fog surrounding the planet, flame-charred land that is brown and mostly void of vegetation, and rust-colored oceans that closely resemble the dreary earth that they surround.

~ ~ ~

In an instant, he's gliding through the streets of Naza, swooping past his own apartment building.

Rusted fire hydrants and street lights that are no longer functional line both sides of the streets. He sees two motley women in an alley to his right as he passes by. They are both sickly thin, with gray and black streaks in their hair, along with mud and bits of paper and ash. They crowd around a brown metallic barrel with burning newspapers inside of it. They rub their hands together for a few seconds, then place them palm down just over the fire—close enough to burn them if they leave them there for too long.

They peer at Manny with sad eyes.

The embers continue to float into the air.

~ ~ ~

Now he's zipping through the air like someone pressed time's fast-forward button.

He slows down, on another street where the buildings have chipped blue paint.

"*Salem,*" he says to himself.

It's been years since he's been here, but he recognizes the blue buildings, which are only located in Salem.

He floats to a nearby a window.

A man and woman are inside having one of those arguments that doesn't seem to be any less of an argument even though neither party is yelling.

"It's not going to make a difference, I'm telling you," the man says.

"What do you mean? Why wouldn't it?" the woman responds.

"Because it *WON'T*, Gloria. It just won't. There's nothing that I can do…"

"Ray—she's my *sister*, Ray," the lady says with a trembling voice and moist eyes.

The man lowers his head.

"Gloria, we can't. We just can't. The NRP only distributes rations based on the number of Remnants within a household who are contributors—those who can work. You're no longer able to, and we have two young boys. Your sister can't work either. We…"

The man looks at the woman with tears in his eyes.

"I love her too, Gloria, but we just *can't*…"

The woman loses all control and falls into the man's arms, crying as hard as a woman can cry.

Manny is unable to hold back his emotions.

~ ~ ~

Again, he soars through time and space.

Abruptly, he stops, high in the air.

He moves toward the ground, closer and closer, slowly.

He wipes tears from his face with his shirt as he drifts downward, his body horizontal and perfectly parallel to the land beneath him. Eventually, he's close enough to make out what looks like a large pile of clothes in a ditch.

"*S&G?*" he says to himself in his mind.

The closer he gets, the more certain he is that he's in *the Badlands.*

The dusty fields and their deep blood red clay make it clear.

A long line of bulldozers, driven by Nerps in protective gear, push large piles of clothing into a gaping ditch, one by one. The wind is blowing sand, so it's difficult to see anything clearly. Manny covers the top of his eyes with his hand to keep the dust out. Bulldozer after bulldozer pushes more and more clothing into the ditch and it's filling quickly.

Manny descends, closer and closer.

"What is this?" Manny asks himself as he sees a small wooden sign that says: **Burial Grounds**, with an arrow pointing to where the bulldozers are going. Manny's eyes open wide and his heart races.

He can see that these are not just clothes, but people, limp and lifeless, being pushed into the ditch like rag dolls. Maybe they were exposed to radiation?

Perhaps they died of malnutrition, as many do, due to the lack of support from the NRP to feed those who are unable to contribute to New America through work—*Waywards,* as they are so dismissively called, as opposed to *Remnants.*

He smells the penetrating stench of death and decay in the air.

He can hear the buzzing of flies.

Corpses. Thousands of them, piled upon one another like human rubble.

He cries again, deeply and sorrowfully.

Pain, despair, famine, disease, war, homelessness, and destruction. It's his world.

He zooms through the sky once more, and then through the tunnel. He feels warmth all around him. He can faintly see a bright light drawing closer from behind his eyelids. When he opens them, he is rushing toward what has to be the sun, or some other star.

He can't stop.

~ ~ ~

He presses his arms downward onto his bed so hard that he pushes himself up into a plank position.

Deep breaths.

Covered in sweat.

When he realizes that he's in his room, he eases himself down and turns to a seated position on the side of his bed. His head hurts. The Grandeurscript has fallen onto the floor; he picks it up. When he does, he hears his mother coughing in the next room. It's getting worse; harder and raspier, lately. Sometimes there's blood.

His heartbeat picks up again, pounding in his chest like a bass drum in a cave.

The dream is his reality.

The fear.

The hopelessness.

The inability to protect those closest to him.

His constant, pressing, and weighty reality.

A reality that he can't seem to escape, even when he's asleep.

~ ~ ~

The billboard flashes before his eyes in another vision. A relapse:

ACKNOWLEDGE THE CREATOR, AND YOUR PATH WILL UNFOLD.

He can't control it anymore. A lump forms in his throat. Emotion bursts out of him like lava from the mouth of a volcano. He quickly drops to his knees and buries his head in his pillow to keep his weeping as quiet as possible. He sobs while pressing his face harder into it. His chest expands and deflates like bagpipes.

"*Why?*"

The only word that he can manage to squeeze out between his sobs.

29. READY?

AFTER ABOUT TWO minutes of trying to calm himself, he is able to speak again. He whispers with intensity as he lifts his head from the pillow but keeps his eyes closed. Drops of moisture shoot from his mouth with each agonizingly forceful, yet quiet word.

"I don't know how *any* of this works! I have *no* idea! I'm trying to not hate you…I'm trying to believe that you hear me! I don't even know what to say; I don't even know if you're *REAL*…"

He cries a bit more with his head buried again.

"I'm tired! I'm so tired of this! I don't know what these dreams mean…I don't know *why* things are the way they are! And mom…mom's *dying*…"

Raw emotion continues to burst from him. Mucus and tears saturate his pillowcase. Every bit of faith, hope, belief, and strength that he hasn't yet thrown away, or had stolen from him, is poured into this moment.

"If you're real, and if you can hear me, then why won't you *HELP* me? Please! Please, *help me*…"

Just as the wave of sentiment comes over him again, he manages to mutter out:

"I SURRENDER!"

Manny's cry comes from deep within him. His entire body shakes. Thirteen years of pain, disappointment, loss, anger, and frustration are being discharged in a single instant.

~ ~ ~

In the midst of one of the most transparent moments of his life, something happens inside of him. He can't explain it, but the sudden calm that he felt on the train the same day that he saw the billboard comes again; and this time it's far more pronounced.

He stops crying abruptly.

He feels like he could stand up and just float away.

Booming from deep inside, he hears a *Voice*:

"EMMANUEL…"

He moves backward from the bed.

He's not sure if it happened in real time, or if he simply imagined it. It's strong enough to be an audible voice, yet internal enough to be a deep thought. Maybe it's just in his head? He's quickly losing his grip on what's real and what isn't.

It's late at night. He hasn't had much sleep. He could be imagining things.

"Mom?" he says with a slight excited fear as he turns toward his door.

He leaps up and walks swiftly to Martha's room to see if she has called him. She's sleeping peacefully—a rare occurrence for many days now.

He walks back into his room and sits down on the bed.

Again, *"EMMANUEL…"*

Stronger this time, and with more volume. More intensity. Manny quickly stands up and looks around his room, expecting to see someone there. He feels like the sound is being projected into his mind with a transmitting device of some sort. He panics. He's never experienced anything like this. There aren't many people that address him by his full name: only people that have just met him, his friends on occasion—usually jokingly, and his mother, when she's serious, or angry. He's confused and worried. Maybe he really is losing his mind? Maybe Grea was right.

Once more, *"EMMANUEL..."*

Even stronger this time. Undeniable. Clear.

This *Voice* originates from within the intangible parts of him, but radiates outward, ferociously. He imagines that his mother can probably hear it and may awaken from her sleep. It overshadows all of his other thoughts, feelings, and even his panic attack from just moments before. It shoots through him like cool water. If there's a specific physical location that's reserved for a soul, this is where it echoes. Penetratingly. Not soft or hard. Not high or low-pitched. An internal sound that he's never heard. A distinct vibration, commanding his attention.

The sound rumbles from somewhere inside of him.

His head?

His heart, perhaps?

He's unsure.

He doesn't know what else to do, except answer.

"Who—who are you?" he says nervously as he sits down on his bed again.

The deep impression, *the Voice,* responds from inside of and all around him at the same time:

"YOU KNOW..."

Manny blinks quickly. It's hard from him to process the fact that he just received a response from within himself.

"*...Creator?*" Manny whispers with a fine mixture of certainty and doubt.

Manny waits. Seconds pass that feel more like hours. His chest and stomach begin to quake uncontrollably, and then the internal sound is released again:

"I AM…"

The voice resonates from the hollows of his chest.

At the very same time, tangible warmth envelopes him. The heat is immediately followed by a soothing coolness. The two sensations take turns being the strongest, creating a rhythm.

He closes his eyes in an inexplicable sense of satisfaction.

He giggles to himself, unable to conceal his pleasure and the joy that he feels.

He begins to cry again, overcome with emotion. He feels like he's just reunited with a parent that had abandoned him. Or better yet, that he had abandoned.

His gleeful weeping is stamped out by:

"*Are you ready?*"

He wipes his face with his shirt, still on a high from the past few minutes.

"Ready for…*what?*"

30. THE CLOUD

SMALL SPECKS OF light fill his vision. Very faint at first, and then brighter by the second, like a tiny galaxy is forming right in front of his eyes.

Brighter.

Brighter.

Eventually, the light completely covers him. He can feel the heat of it. Then a jolt. He's rushing somewhere—up.

Higher.

Faster than he's ever moved.

His body is weightless.

No gravity.

He's floating.

He opens and closes his eyes repeatedly, but all he can see is the brightness of the white light surrounding him. He swings his arms attempting to grab on to something, but there's nothing there. He panics. The lack of control over his body overstimulates him. The white light turns blue now, and he speeds up. Much faster.

~ ~ ~

Manny feels himself separating; literally being torn apart, but not in a painful way.

He can't speak. He tries to produce sound, but nothing comes out.

Eventually, he relaxes in the moment, realizing that his fighting is doing him absolutely no good. He gradually becomes aware of what's going on around him. The light dims. After a few blinks, he opens his eyes and realizes that he's still inside his room.

The feeling of separation continues until his consciousness separates from his body—a translucent version of himself now stands beside his bed. Oddly enough, he doesn't panic; it feels natural. He looks around his room, feeling as light as a feather. There's no doubt in his mind that he could take flight right now if he wanted.

It feels much like a lucid dream, but he's completely aware that this is a very *real* experience.

He looks over at his dresser. As he walks toward it, he notices that his feet do not make any noise on the floor beneath him. He doesn't feel the soles of his feet making contact with the floor at all in fact; there's no sensation whatsoever. He looks at the clock on top of the dresser.

It's 3:00 a.m. on the dot.

He reaches out to touch it and his hand passes right through both the clock and the dresser. He pulls his hand back, looks at it, and can see the shadowy image of the clock through it. He turns back toward his bed. He looks at himself still sitting there; not completely him, but his shell. As he draws closer, he reaches out to touch his own face. His eyes are glazed over—he's utterly still. As he expects, his hand passes through.

Then, the Voice, again:

"THE WAY..."

Deeply and powerfully.

A soft wind blows all around him. He can't feel it, but he knows that his physical body can—he watches his shirt flap gently. A tunnel appears just above him as he looks up to the ceiling, identical to the one that he saw in his dream.

He rises toward it. Slowly at first, and then in the twinkling of an eye, he moves at what has to be the speed of light, or close to it.

He's zips up the center.

Faster.

Faster, until there is no sound.

He's moving so quickly that he feels perfectly still.

He bursts through a collection of clouds, which are joined together to create a single, gigantic cloud. All of his momentum stops; he's staring at the sky while his body is levitating parallel to it.

He's never seen it so blue and beautiful.

The sun shines brightly in the center of it.

It's magnificent.

Music. Voices. Laughter. Conversations.

It sounds like the inside of a busy train station with lots of people conversing, but he can't see where all of the voices are coming from. Nothing but the clear sky. They must be behind him; underneath him. His body rotates away from the sun and toward the cloud that he just blasted through.

Something else is carrying him. He's not turning on his own. An invisible force cradles him. He can feel it all over him; all around him.

Finally, he sees them.

~ ~ ~

He can't recall a time that he's ever seen this many people in one place at one time.

Some sit in chairs. Others stand and speak candidly. Millions of different scenes layered on top of one another; separate but connected. Every ethnicity, culture, complexion, age, shape, and size of the world, all right there on top of the cloud. Elderly men and women, young boys and girls, and everything in between. Some are dressed in modern clothing. Some are wearing ancient traditional garb from long passed civilizations that Manny has never seen. Their clamor is loud. Walking, talking, singing, running, playing, and dancing.

Within seconds, it all stops. Every face present looks up toward Manny in a synchronized fashion as he floats in the air above them.

Not a single sound.

Not a single word.

He can feel the uneasiness creep up his spine like a large, hairy-legged spider.

His eyes lock with a short balding man who is wearing a colorful blue and white robe. There are worn out sandals on his feet. He has a graying beard. His skin is wrinkled and tanned, but there is a youthful glow in his eyes. He smiles at Manny and nods gently. Everyone and everything around the man blurs and he becomes all that Manny can see.

With lightspeed, Manny's body takes off toward him.

Bracing himself for the collision, Manny closes his eyes.

31. ASCENDED

THE THREE MEN walk swiftly through a secluded section of the Outskirts. They cross a dusty field that's lit by another full moon.

"It's too late," Damien says as he leads the group. His tone is urgent.

"How? How is it too late?" Levi asks.

Damien stops swiftly and darts his head around to look into Levi's eyes. He releases a low-pitched rumble from his belly—a demonic snarl. His eyes glow yellow for just a brief moment, then he yells:

"Because he's already ascended! That's why!"

He catches himself and lowers his tone. He looks up at the brightness of the moon and says:

"I felt it. Just a moment ago. He's joined with him..."

He turns and they continue walking.

"Damien, what *sssssshall* we do now?" Polus asks.

"We have to ascend Levi tonight. We can't wait any longer; it's time. The Witness will become more powerful as time passes and as he is trained and instructed."

For the next couple of minutes, the men don't speak. They charge across the field as quickly as they can; for brief intervals, they jog. Damien is the most rushed as they search for an unknown destination; he trots feverishly and produces a clanking noise that comes from the breast pocket of his coat.

Most of the land has lots of debris and litter—this is clearly an area that the Scavengers have not ventured into often, if at all.

There are many hills, patches of brown grass, and weeds that decorate the terrain.

The three men reach a clearing that is out in the open and mostly flat. Damien stops. He raises his hand motioning for Levi and Polus to stop too. They become still and everything becomes quiet, except for the distant howl of a few wolves many miles away. For a brief moment Damien gazes up at the moon again; its light blazes back down onto him relentlessly. He closes his eyes and inhales slowly, then releases the air in the exact same fashion.

"This will do…" he says.

Damien reaches into his pocket and pulls out the same antiquated metal flask from weeks ago. He opens it, takes a sip, tilts his head back, and spews the liquid into the air creating a red, misty cloud. The scent of the fluid is unbearable. Levi covers his nose to block its stench.

"What is that?" Levi says just before coughing twice, then sneezing once.

Damien places the flask on the ground next to him and then stands and stretches his arms high and wide into the air.

He looks at the moon again.

He looks at Levi.

He looks at Polus.

Polus nods in return.

Without hesitation, Damien and Polus lunge toward Levi and tackle him to the ground. He attempts to push them away, but they both have far more strength than him; superhuman strength. His efforts are pointless.

"Hey! Hey! What—what are you doing?! Let me *GO!*" Levi yells.

Damien lets out a sinister laugh while on top of Levi.

"You don't get it, do you! Stop *STRUGGLING!*" Damien yells.

Damien stands up once Polus has positioned himself on top of Levi with Levi pinned down on his back. Polus is holding both of Levi's wrists and uses his shins to hold down his legs.

"You don't understand how *NECESSARY* this is! You don't know what's ahead! But soon…very soon you will! *This*…"

Damien picks the flask up and points it toward Levi.

"*This*, is necessary…"

He stoops down beside Levi.

"Let…let *go* of me! *GET OFF!*"

"*STOP* it, Levi! Stop it now! You *must*! He's getting stronger—but so shall we!"

Without warning, Damien thrusts the opening of the flask into Levi's mouth. A gurgling sound can be heard from probably close to a mile away in this deserted land. Burns appear on Levi's face as the majority of the acidic liquid spills onto his cheeks and chin as he moves his head back and forth—choking on the concoction. He coughs, but Damien continues to pour. As he does, Damien also whispers some type of spell into Levi's ear. It's a foreign and forgotten language; perhaps one that has never been spoken amongst mankind on this planet.

Smoke rises from Levi's face like that from a candle as the acid burns become deeper. His screams are painfully loud, but then they become something else. He starts snarling like a wild animal. The pitch of his yell changes to one that an unnatural creature would make—a growl, or a roar of some sort. His body bulges, and his eyes turn bright yellow, much like Damien's do at times. Damien finishes the final words of the hex, then stops pouring and stands up.

"Yes, yes, that's it; it's *happening*," Damien says as he watches Levi transform.

He must have poured gallons from this flask, which couldn't possibly hold more than a pint. It's enchanted in some way. At the very same moment, Levi thrusts Polus into the air off of his body with a surge of new, untapped strength. Polus lands on his feet about fifteen yards away with reflexes that are inhuman, then walks up next to Damien.

Levi's growl becomes so loud and strong that can be heard all the way in Naza. Off in the distance, lamp lights and candle lights appear in apartment building windows as the inhabitants hear the beastly noise.

The yellow glow in Levi's eyes becomes too bright for Damien and Polus to look directly at. Damien turns his head and notices Levi's shadow. Although Levi is still in the form and shape of a man, his shadow resembles that of a dragon. The silhouette of a large, winged creature, with a long jaw and fangs for teeth can be seen on the ground. Bursts of flames and smoke pour from its nose and mouth. It has talons on the bottoms of its robust legs, and a tail that extends at least ten yards.

Levi stands and says, *"what has happened to me?"* with a deep, distorted voice.

He stretches his arms and looks at his own shadow.

The beastly silhouette stretches its wings—they span many yards beyond the reach of his arms. Damien looks at him with a sly smirk on his face.

"You've *ascended…*"

32. THE WAY

MANNY'S EYES ARE closed. The stench of animals is all around him. The wind blows gently, mingled with particles of sand that strike his face. It's hot—he can feel the heat of the sun as it warms his skin under at least three layers of clothing. He places his hands in front of him and feels the strong back of a very large horse as he sits atop of it. He hears the footsteps of men and the hooves of other horses walking alongside him. They speak in a language that he's never spoken or heard, but oddly enough, he understands every word of it. He opens his eyes, blinks a few times to allow them to adjust to the sunlight, then looks at his hands—hands that he's never seen before. He feels older. His movements feel slower than he's accustomed to. He looks to his right and sees his reflection on the shield of one of the men who is walking next to his horse. He gasps.

The man from the Cloud.

"What is this?" he says in this unknown language.

It's Aramaic. He knows the language, but why? *How?*

One of the men turns to him and says, "what is what, sir?"

"Oh, nothing," Manny says dismissively.

He looks around at the scenery of this unfamiliar place. The landscape is beautiful. Afar off, there are women in a field harvesting grains. They are unusually dressed. Manny looks at his own clothing: a large robe, a few layers of thinner robes, and other garments underneath. One of his garments has four long fringes hanging out at its four corners.

The group keeps traveling down the road as Manny sorts through what's going on.

"Where am I?" he thinks to himself.

There are many looped ropes hanging on the sides of the horses that he and some of the other men ride on—Manny takes notice of them. Others carry ropes in their hands. He hears a few of them speaking in the Aramaic tongue:

"I'm *sure* they are there, in the next city. We will find them," one says.

"You're right. We've gotten word of those who follow this, *feigned messiah*. We will put an end to this foolishness, once and for all. Shall we not?" another says.

The man looks up at Manny. Manny looks back at him with a blank gaze.

"Shall we not?" the man says again, looking directly at Manny.

"We shall," Manny finally says. It comes out as if it's out of his control.

His soul is trapped inside the body of another man—apparently, the same man that he just saw in the clouds and crashed into.

~ ~ ~

Not more than a few seconds later, the temperature suddenly drops, the sky darkens rapidly, and all of the horses become startled all of a sudden.

"Whoa, boy! Whoa, whoa!" the men say to the horses.

With a loud crash, the sky splits open and an unfathomably bright light shines on the men. It happens too fast for any of them to brace themselves. Manny falls from the horse and onto the ground. He blinks rapidly.

Nothing.

He's completely blind. He panics. He can hear the horses fleeing. He can hear the men all around him crying out in shock and surprise. Then, everything falls dead silent.

A voice booms from the sky:

"WHY ARE YOU FIGHTING AGAINST ME?"

Manny instinctively knows that the voice is speaking to him. It's the same voice that he heard come from within himself while in his bedroom; he undoubtedly recognizes it.

"Is it you, Creator?" Manny says nervously, shielding his face.

The Voice responds:

"Yes, I AM…"

Manny blinks fiercely, trying to see. He weeps.

The men around him exclaim, "do you hear that? It is the Creator!"

The Voice in the sky booms again:

"Go to the city that you were headed to, and then I will tell you what to do…"

Clouds quickly rush in and cover up the light, then silence falls over the land.

The men, completely startled and not knowing what else to do, rush to Manny's side and help him up. At the moment they touch him, Manny is back in the tunnel. He realizes that whenever he's inside of it, it allows him to travel through space, time, and different dimensions.

"The Way," a voice whispers, as he zips through it unfathomably quickly.

He stops. He's inside of a house now, one that he can't see, but he can sense. He's still blind. Manny places his hand on his eyes and feels a thick, crusty substance covering them. It feels raw to the touch, but it isn't painful. He senses that he's waiting for someone. There are a few people around him, eating and talking. He's sitting in a room close to them, but separate from them.

He hears footsteps approaching the door of the hut, then there's a hard knock.

The door rumbles open.

~ ~ ~

"Hello, dear friend."

Manny lunges forward when he hears the voice.

"I am looking for…"

"I'm right here!" Manny exclaims, cutting the man off.

"Ah, there you are…"

The man approaches him while the rest of the household falls quiet.

"Brother, the Creator has sent me to you so that you can receive your sight and be filled with his spirit…"

The man lifts his hands carefully and places them on Manny's eyes.

There is a loud crackling noise.

Thick, scaly sheets of dead skin fall from Manny's face.

Manny blinks furiously.

Once his eyes adjust to the light in the room, he looks into the man's bright, smiling face and says, "I can…*I can see!*"

The room cheers in excitement. Manny weeps again.

A sinking feeling comes over him; the feeling of falling backwards.

Everything around him quickly becomes dark.

He's traveling through the Way again.

He feels new.

He feels like his eyes truly have been *opened* to things that he didn't know existed.

With an abrupt ceasing of motion, he's hovering inside of his room again, this time with his back toward the floor and his face toward the ceiling. His body tilts forward until he is in a vertical position. A gravity-like force, unseen but powerful, draws him back to his body.

He attempts to fight against it. He doesn't want to go back. The freedom that he feels being outside of his physical body is far too liberating—he wants to stay in this state forever. The more he thinks about how free he is, and the more he attempts to pull back from re-entering the hollow shell of himself, the stronger the force is that pulls him back into it.

His soul leaps back into his body with a jolt.

His heart is beating faster than it ever has.

He places his hand on his chest over his heart to feel its pounding.

He looks at his clock: 3:00 a.m.

Before he has a chance to take his eyes away, it blinks 3:01.

33. I HAVE TO GO

THE ALARM BLARES in his ear. He can barely move his arm to turn it off. His entire body is sore. It takes all of his energy just to squirm across the bed and reach it.

He rubs his hair. Every one of his muscles feels overworked. He sits, and remembers the night before. The horse, the light, the blindness—*the Way*. He drops his face into his hands and takes a couple of deep breaths, trying to reconcile whether it was a dream, or if it all actually happened.

It happened. He's sure.

After crawling out of bed, he walks down the hall and looks into his mother's room. She's still fast asleep, so he decides to make breakfast himself; he's been doing this a lot lately. He'll leave her a plate too; she won't get up until sometime after he's already gone.

His train ride is a quiet one. Today is gloomy—typical. He looks for the billboard again, just out of habit. Still nothing.

At the Shield, the white tents decorate the entrance again. People enter and exit them like ants, with the latter group holding their arms.

"*Gosh*, not today," he grumbles.

After his sample is done, he walks to his work area biting his bottom lip to offset some of the pain running up and down his arm. As much as the shots have hurt in the past, today, it's twenty times worse. He can barely take it. That coupled with all that's happening in his mind is a recipe for deep and solemn introspection. All day long, Manny seems very distant. Rock is the first to notice.

"Are you okay? You look sick?" Rock asks him.

"What? I'm perfectly fine."

"You don't look it. You haven't shaved or anything. Seriously, are you *really* okay?"

"I'm okay, Rock. Thank you…"

They don't speak much during their shift, which is unusual. On a normal day, they'd laugh and entertain the wildest of ideas while working. Not today. Manny is in a daze—in a faraway world with no intentions of returning. He can't get last night off of his mind, or the past few weeks for that matter.

"Hey, old men!"

Grea approaches the lunch table while Rock and Manny sit in silence.

"Hey, sis," Rock replies with a hint of sadness in his voice.

Manny's head is lowered. Grea ducks down to try and make eye contact.

"What's wrong with him?" she says to Rock, "he looks like a serial killer—I've never seen his beard before."

Rock shrugs and shakes his head in response.

"How many times do I have to tell you guys, I'm *FINE!*"

Grea puts her hands up with her palms facing Manny.

"Sheesh, okay! But you look like a wild man. You don't look fine at all…"

Manny scoffs. Grea relaxes her demeanor and exhales.

"You know that you can always talk to us, right Manny? We've been here your *whole* life. You don't have to guard yourself from us the way you do the rest of the world. We're not going to judge you. We may joke a lot, but we love you, Manny…"

Manny looks up at her, blinks, and then looks down at the table again. He sighs.

As the air leaves his lungs, his defensive wall leaves with it. He rubs his forearm and glances at Rock, who is nodding his head in silent agreement with Grea.

"Guys, something happened," he finally says.

It's like a pressure valve is released in that moment. His whole body loosens up.

"What happened? Did you see something else on the train?" Rock asks.

"No, last night. Something happened. I doubt that you'd even believe me if I told you…"

"What happened Manny? Tell us," Grea urges.

"I don't know how exactly to put it, but I…"

He looks at them both and shifts his weight in his seat.

"You what?!" Rock says impatiently.

"I talked to the Creator. Well, the Creator talked to me. I think? We talked to each other…"

Rock and Grea's mouths both drop open. They look at each other at the same time, then refocus on Manny in a harmonized manner.

"I'm sorry…*what?*" Rock says.

"There's no easy way to say it, so I'll just say it. I basically left my body. I mean, I was literally looking at myself—my spirit, or soul, or *something*. And then, I flew into this tunnel and ended up in the sky somewhere…maybe heaven? And there was this huge cloud with millions of people. I went into one of them and it was a man from the Grandeurscript. I think I remember the stories about him. It was real, guys. I know it sounds crazy, but it was real. I was there. I could feel everything he felt and see everything he saw. I was connected to him. Then, I came back into my body, and basically no time had passed. Then I spent the next, I don't know, it must've been hours, just talking to the Creator…*all* night long, until I eventually fell asleep. His voice is deep down inside of me. I have no idea how, or why, but it is. I know it sounds crazy, but it's the truth…"

Manny catches his breath.

Neither Rock nor Grea say a word.

Grea taps her finger on the table.

Rock stares at him blankly.

"Okay, Manny, seriously, I'm worried about you. I know that you've been stressed, your mom is sick…maybe you should see a Medic," Rock finally blurts out.

Grea looks totally puzzled and only makes a few "uhh" and "umm" sounds of bewilderment.

"No, that's not it, something is *happening* to me, or *has* happened to me. I don't know, but I've got to talk to Jonah again. I've *got* to. He'll know what to do…"

Manny sits and soaks in his own frustration.

Not having the answers that he wants, coupled with Rock and Grea not understanding or believing him, tip him past his boiling point.

He slams his hand on the table, hard.

"I HAVE TO GO!"

Rock flinches. Grea jerks back a few inches.

Manny quickly stands up and walks toward the front gate—they've never seen him this bothered before about anything.

"Manny, where are you going?! The trains won't be here for hours!" Grea pleads.

"I don't know…I've just…I've got to *go!*" he yells back without turning around.

They watch him as he pauses just before the gate, looking from side to side. There's not a single yellow and black Nerp uniform anywhere to be seen. He hastens to the turnstile and maneuvers his way through it, quickly and carefully.

Before long, he disappears from their sight.

"Should we go after him?" Rock says.

"No, he needs time," Grea responds, "let's just give him time…"

34. BOW

HIS PACE IS hurried. He's angry, tired, sore, and afraid. The tiny tornado of fear and confusion swirls around inside of him and he can't slow it down. He heads toward the central part of Naza, not sure of where else to go. He's miles away, but he figures that he should cross a train stop at some point.

The air is crisp. It's fall again. The farther he walks, the more he realizes that his impulsive departure from the Shield may not have been the wisest decision.

"What was I thinking?"

He folds his arms and his teeth chatter. He continues to walk.

"Grea and Rock probably *really* think I'm crazy now," he mumbles to himself.

"They just don't get it…I mean, how could they?"

A few more steps.

"Jonah. I've got to talk to Jonah…"

With his head down, he thinks, and thinks. He studies the hard dirt and broken pavement beneath his feet. He listens to his boots as they clunk on the ground, one step after the other.

"Look up…"

It rings inside of him like a gong. *The Voice.*

When he lifts his eyes, an old deteriorating building is about one-hundred yards away. He's seen it before from the train—an old decrepit department store. What was once a parking lot is now chipped and cracked pavement with sand lodged in all of its gaps. He stops.

His eyes lock onto a rusty light pole. The lantern at the top of it is broken. Only a few jagged edges of glass are still attached to the metal branch that protrudes from its highest point.

"Bow..."

The sound comes from within him again. Without even meaning to, Manny repeats the word out of his own mouth, robotically.

"Bow..."

His eyes are fixated on the light pole. He feels a surge of blood and a burst of adrenaline throughout his body; a cool, rushing, windy sensation. Time slows down and nothing is in his view except the light pole; nothing else exists to him. He's sensitive to everything around him.

Everything in the universe feels like it begins and ends at the core of him.

He's connected to it all, but completely unfocused on any of it. The energy of the word forms in the intangible parts of him, exits his mouth and pores, and then expands all around him. He's never felt such power.

~ ~ ~

He hears the sound of metal bending, quietly at first, and then with more force. It's a sharp, penetrating sound. He watches as the pole leans toward him. Gradually at first, then faster, until its metallic arm is touching the ground. The metal rings like a bell on impact. He snaps out of his trance and steps backward, his jaw loosely hanging open.

"What? How...how in the *world*?"

He continues stepping backwards until he bumps into something solid.

"Manny! Watch out, what is *wrong* with you?!"

He turns around swiftly, breathing heavily.

35. NO PROBLEM

"JHENDA? WHAT ARE...WHERE'D you...where'd you come from?" Manny says.

He looks behind her and sees a group of Scavengers on the far end of the parking lot. He didn't notice them before; he had been walking with his head down the whole time.

"What the heck are you doing all the way out here?" she asks.

"Jhenda, did you *see* that?" he says, ignoring her question.

"See what?"

"That light pole just..."

He points to it. It's still leaning toward him on the ground.

"That pole just..."

Jhenda looks at him with her eyebrows pulled down as low as they can be and waits for him to finish his statement.

"It what, Manny?"

Hesitation. He figures that he doesn't want to risk another one of his friends assuming that he's losing his mind, *especially* if he actually is.

"Uhh, never...never mind..."

"Are you sure?"

He looks back at the pole. He turns back toward Jhenda.

"Yeah, I'm sure..."

They both start walking in the same direction that Manny was headed originally.

"So, what are you doing out here?" he asks her.

"We were collecting some metal from this parking lot, but we're done for the day. I was headed to the train stop that's not far from here, then I looked up and I saw you of all people. So, the better question is, what are *YOU* doing out here? Shouldn't you be at the Shield?"

She tucks her protective mask under her arm.

"Well, I was, but it's a long story…" Manny says, dropping his eyes.

"Oh, I'm *sure* it is."

As they walk, Jhenda's suit makes rubbing noises every time she moves. Manny looks at it and chuckles.

"Isn't that thing uncomfortable?"

"Very. It's not bad when it gets cold out though—keeps us warm. But in the hot seasons, *sheesh*!"

"What's it made out of?"

She stops, looks down at her pants, and lifts her legs one at a time.

"You know, I'm not even really sure. It protects against radioactive materials though. As long as it keeps doing that, I really don't care *what* it's made out of."

They laugh.

They walk on, silently for a while. Eventually, Jhenda looks up at Manny's face. She can tell there's so much on his mind.

"I wonder what's going on in that head of yours," she says.

He smiles at her.

"So do I…"

"Well, you shouldn't keep it all in, not all the time anyway," she suggests.

"Sometimes I think that maybe I should."

"Humph, I know what you mean."

They become quiet again for a bit. The only sound is the thudding of their boots, and Jhenda's suit.

"I still can't believe you left the Shield. I'm surprised the Nerps didn't stop you," Jhenda says, looking at the ground.

"Well, no one was on post when I left—probably at lunch or something," Manny replies, looking at the side of her face.

"I suppose," she mumbles.

With the events of the past few weeks constantly beckoning his attention and thoughts, Manny has been on edge. But today, during this walk with Jhenda, he's calm for a change. It's nice. He enjoys the ease of the moment.

After more silence, Manny finally starts opening up.

"Weird stuff has been happening Jhenda, stuff that I can't really explain..." he says with his face dropped to the ground again.

She doesn't immediately respond. She thinks about his words. She gives him time to breathe and release. She can sense that listening is far more important than giving advice, her thoughts, her suggestions, or her opinion right now.

"I don't really know. I can't be going crazy. I really need to speak to Jonah."

He scratches at his neck, then looks at her. She looks back with a slight grin and nod, letting him know that she heard him. He realizes what she's doing. He appreciates it. He smiles and nods back.

"I don't know what to do; I've been seeing weird things, feeling weird things, and hearing even *weirder* things..."

He looks at her again to see if she'll react. She just continues to walk and nod.

"I've got to talk to him again—Jonah."

They don't speak much more for the rest of their walk. They finally make it all the way to a train stop that was a few miles away from the abandoned department store and the light pole. There are about four trains docked at the station.

"Either of these heading to S&G?" Jhenda asks one of the conductors, who is standing on the platform smoking a cigarette.

"Yep, Jim is."

The man points to another man who is on the other side of the tracks. He waves at them when he hears his name.

"I'm going to Naza," the first man says as he releases a puff of smoke from his mouth.

"Good," Jhenda responds.

"We've still got about ten minutes before we pull out, but you're free to load up when you're ready," the husky gentleman says just before taking another pull of his cigarette.

"Okay, thanks sir," Jhenda responds.

Jhenda and Manny sit down on a bench that's against one of the walls. She bends down, adjusts her boot, and lets out a moan of relief.

"Are those uncomfortable? They look uncomfortable..." Manny asks.

She makes a face at him, being that the statement is clearly axiomatic. He laughs.

She sits back and takes a deep breath. They both rest their eyes on the landscape. The conductors finish their cigarettes and thump them into large metal bins that are on the platform. There are small whirlwinds of dust swirling out in the field beyond the platform. The sky is gray, as usual. Ever since the atmosphere was damaged by the nukes, and the majority of the oceans were polluted, it's very rare that a clear blue sky can be seen—if ever.

"Manny, before you go, are you okay? Honestly?"

Manny moves his head and breathes out of his nose lightly, as if he expected the question.

"Yeah. Yeah, I'm fine."

"Manny..."

She presses her knuckles against his thigh. He looks into her eyes. Her face is covered with both gentleness and firmness.

"Are...you...okay?"

He pauses and looks down. After a couple of seconds, he just looks at her without giving a response. She moves her hand and looks beyond the trains toward the miniature dust tornadoes.

"Okay. I understand. Just know that I'm here…and I'm positive that Rock and Grea are too…and of course your mom…"

She touches his shoulder.

"You're not by yourself Manny…and it's going to be okay…"

He nods with his face pointed back toward the ground.

They both stand and walk to their respective trains. Manny's is closer, so he climbs the steps first. Jhenda maneuvers around it, and walks toward hers. Manny stops halfway up, like he's forgotten something. He hops back down. Jhenda is now about halfway to the other train.

"Hey, Jhenda!"

She turns around, swiftly, and a little alarmed; her suit makes a squeaky noise in the process.

"Yeah! Yeah?"

"Thanks. Thanks for everything, okay?" he says with a grin.

She smiles and puts her hand on her chest just over her heart; a salutation that many Remnants give as a symbol of love, acknowledgment, and respect.

"No problem, Manny. No problem…"

They climb onto their trains. Soon, they are gone, in opposite directions—but still, the same direction, in a way.

36. HOW?

MARTHA IS ASLEEP when Manny arrives. It's earlier than normal, and he doesn't want to alarm her unnecessarily; he tries to stay quiet as he walks to his room.

He steps on a soft spot in the wooden floor. It creaks. He hesitates. She moves a bit, but rolls over and falls back asleep. He keeps walking, more carefully now, and enters his room.

He closes his door and takes his time removing his work clothes, still quietly and carefully. He puts them all away neatly, and then looks around his room with his hands on his hips.

"I need to clean up in here..." he thinks.

He looks around some more.

"Maybe tomorrow..."

He lies down on his back with his face to the ceiling.

"The Shield. I can't believe I really just walked out of, *the Shield.*"

He laughs to himself about how outlandish the thought really is. He's never done that before. He's thought about it often, but he's never done it.

"Rock will *NEVER* let me hear the end of it," he says with a chuckle.

Normally, none of the Shield's supervisors or work leaders come to his area. He, Rock, and those in their group have worked there for so long that it's not as strenuously observed as some of the newer groups. They're pretty much autonomous. Nerps are stationed at the gate sporadically, but quite often they're easily distracted and wander off someplace.

He thinks of his walk to the train stop with Jhenda.

He thinks of the light pole.

"Weird. So weird. How in the world did I do that? I did do that, right? I mean, it did happen, didn't it?"

He's certain of it.

While contemplating the day, his eyes catch his mother's Grandeurscript. It's atop the dresser with one of its corners hanging off of the edge. He stares at it for a few moments and then looks back toward the ceiling.

"On the Sabbath, I'm going to talk to Jonah," he thinks.

"I mean, I'll just approach him and say, *hey, Jonah, I need to talk to you again.*"

He plans it in his head. He closes his eyes and pictures the IE. He envisions himself walking into the lobby and seeing Jonah.

"I have to talk to him…"

In the very center of his thoughts, the Voice speaks his name from inside of him:

"MANNY…"

Automatically, his eyes are drawn to the Grandeurscript on the dresser—it's like it's calling him. He stares at it again for a few seconds. Finally, he swings his legs around into a seated position on the side of the bed with his elbows resting on his thighs. He sits there, tapping his fist inside of his palm. He stands and retrieves the book, then sits back on the bed.

He holds it in his hands; the imitation leather is cold to the touch. He looks around his room, still afraid from the last time that he was in here alone. The intense experience of leaving his body and traveling through different dimensions, was just as frightening and uncomfortable as it was exhilarating.

His eyes lock back onto the book. He flips it open to the introductory page:

THE GRANDEURSCRIPT

Herein lie stories and wisdom which have existed since the beginning of time. They have been compiled, translated, and presented here for the edification of all who may read. Man, woman, and child, from generation to generation, from culture to culture, and from civilization to civilization, may now have their eyes opened to the truths of the universe, as expressed by the Creator, to and through all creation.

Manny thinks about the words for a second. He's read this a few times in the past, but it seems to strike him differently now. He continues flipping through the Grandeurscript, feeling each of the delicate pages with the tips of his pointer, middle, and ring fingers. He stops at a page that stands out to him. The heading at the top reads: **Departure.**

He grins a little.

"I remember this story...let's see, where is that part at?"

He runs his finger up and down the surface of the thin sheet.

"There it is..."

He begins to read in the middle of the page:

"You brought us all the way out here to die, didn't you? You should have left us in the land of the golden kings if you wanted us dead!"

> "...but the man told the people, **listen! Don't lose heart! Keep yourselves calm and don't move...**"

As Manny reads, he begins to smell the faint scent of salty sea water in his room.

> "...the Creator is on our side and
> will fight for us, you'll see..."
> "...tell all of the people to get ready to go!"
> "...when the time is right, lift up your rod
> and hold it just over the water..."

Manny starts hearing the yells of a mass of people all around him. He drops the book onto his lap and darts his head back and forth in the dimly lit room.

There's no one there. Just him.

He picks the Grandeurscript up again and continues reading:

> "...then, the night came, and the puffy cloud
> turned into a raging fire of light..."

Now, the strong aroma of smoke and fire fills Manny's nostrils. He drops the book again and covers his face with his arm. He coughs heavily, but there is no smoke in sight. His eyes leak. He wipes them with his hand. He stands. He opens his door expecting to see flames.

Nothing.

He feels his heart leaping inside of his chest. After a few moments of perplexity, he walks back over to his bed. He rubs his forehead. The odor of smoke is gone now. He sits down, picks up the Grandeurscript, and looks for the page that he was on. Once he finds his place, he keeps reading:

> *"...the man lifted his hand and rod over the water...and a roaring wind came..."*
>
> *"...at the very same time, the prince stepped into the waters...head-deep..."*
>
> *"...the wet ground became bone-dry all of a sudden..."*
>
> *"...the water miraculously stood up on both sides like two towering walls!"*

The book flies out of Manny's hand and hits the wall. He falls over onto his side, landing on the other end of the bed, then rolls onto the floor. Paper, clothes, pillows, and all types of items are being thrust about Manny's room. A powerful gust of wind is blowing—out of nowhere.

"WHAT IS GOING ON?!" he yells.

He holds his hands up, shielding his face from the things that are flying at him from his dresser. His alarm clock falls to the floor. His dresser is tilting over and nearly falls on him; he catches the front of it with his foot before it does.

"STOP!" he screams as loudly as he can.

The wind recedes until his room is calm again. He sits there, panting. His face is covered with sweat. He looks at the Grandeurscript yet again. He closes it swiftly, then tosses it across the room as if touching it will burn his hands.

"How?!"

It's the only word that he can manage to get out of his mouth.

37. TOMORROW

FOR THE NEXT few days, Manny experiences much of the same. He and his mother's Grandeurscript are inseparable, but he only reads it privately, for obvious reasons. Each time he does, he tangibly experiences whatever is happening in the stories firsthand. He can hear, smell, feel, taste, and even see the events that he reads about. Clairvoyance, clairsentience, and clairaudience, all combined. The words burst to life through all of his senses.

Martha notices the change in him, but she hasn't experienced any of his *adventures* first hand. He's careful to be alone whenever he takes his journeys into the pages of this obscure book. He's learned more in a week's time than he has in all of the prior years of his life. It draws him like a spiritual magnet, each single day.

There's an open field behind his apartment building. He would often go there when he was younger and play; it's been a very long time since he's frequented the area until recently. He spends just about every evening after work there now, much to the surprise of Martha.

"Manny, are you okay?"

"Yep, I'm good mom!"

"Are you sure? You'd tell me if you weren't, wouldn't you?"

He smiles at her sneakily.

"Of *course*, I would!"

He kisses her forehead gently and then he's out of the door before she can say anything else. He bounces down the steps and around the dusty concrete walkway that surrounds his building.

There's no one else outside. He wonders where the words in these pages will take him today. He keeps the Grandeurscript inside of a black backpack that's constantly strapped onto him like a turtle's shell.

"Well, I guess this is what I've prayed for. He's yours now, clearly," Martha prays softly as she stands in the kitchen, looking out of the window at him as he charges to the field.

"I guess I'll have to find another Grandeurscript," she says with a slight chuckle as he disappears from sight.

Raging wars and battles, tumultuous storms on the sea, fire falling from the sky; they all occur as Manny sits on a large stone, day after day, in the secluded field. The stone that he sits on is now charred with visible ash; possibly the same ash that was said to have consumed a well-known ancient city. A puddle of water has formed a few feet away too; perhaps the very same waters that were said to have swallowed the whole world long ago. The more that he reads, the more he's drawn in. He spends hours at a time there, daily, without a break. There is a huge burden in his heart to share all of this with Jonah the very next opportunity that he gets.

"*Sabbath…this Sabbath,*" he says to himself as he concludes his reading one evening.

~ ~ ~

Grea and Rock notice the change in Manny too. He does his best to conceal everything that's been happening until he gets the opportunity to speak to Jonah. There has to be an explanation for these supernatural occurrences. He doesn't want to alarm his friends any more than he already has. He knows that they already worry about him, but it's hard to hide what he's feeling.

At the Shield, lunch has come quickly today, as it usually does on Fridays.

Grea is already seated at their bench by the time Manny and Rock approach. She's eating a slice of packaged and processed meat.

"Hey, isn't that mine? I thought I left it at home?" Rock says.

She wipes her mouth and lifts her head. Both of her jaws are full. Bits of food fall out of her mouth as she attempts to respond.

"So, *sue* me," she says in a muffled voice just before taking another bite.

Rock squints at her and then pokes his finger through the meat, making a huge hole in it as she holds it.

"Hey, cut it out!" she yells at him.

Manny and Rock laugh and sit down across from her. She continues eating.

"Eww, you're disgusting! I can't believe you're still eating that...I stuck my finger in it and all..."

"No, *you're* disgusting. *I'm* just hungry!" she snarls back.

She darts her eyes over at Manny.

"So, how's it going today, old man?"

He lifts his eyes, looks at her, tilts his head to the side, and shrugs his shoulders.

"Not too bad. What about you?"

She puts the meat down and finishes swallowing.

"It's been okay. Some Nerps came to pick up a big shipment of equipment today. A bunch of crates full of, well, I'm not sure what they were full of honestly. That kept me pretty busy."

"I understand," Manny responds.

Rock butts in.

"I forgot to ask earlier Manny, how's mom doing?"

Manny hesitates for just a moment before answering.

"Not good and not bad either. She sleeps a lot. I was able to get a few meds from Denzi the other day. That helped a little, I guess."

Rock nods with a hint of concern on his face.

"Well Manny, let us know if either of you need anything or if there's anything we can do," Grea says with a serious tone.

"Thanks, Grea…I will…"

They sit and banter about nothing for a little while. Grea's hair. If the Nerps ever wash their uniforms. The time that they put rocks on the train track when they were children and were afraid that they'd derail it. Manny eventually breaks the flow of the discussion:

"I'm going to talk to him again, tomorrow. Right after the gathering…"

"Who? Jonah? Really? What about this time?" Rock asks him with surprise in his voice.

"Well, just…stuff. You know?"

"No, not really. You don't tell us anything anymore. You just act weird all of the time. You're not so bad today, but most days, you're *weird*…"

"*Very* weird," Grea agrees.

Manny laughs.

"Glad to know that you think so highly of me!" Manny exclaims.

He claps his hands together a few times as a sarcastic sign of appreciation.

"No, but really, I know that I've seemed a little off lately. I'm sorry for that. There are just things, interesting things happening, that—I don't know, that I wasn't expecting. Things that I can't explain…"

"Well, are you going to tell us about it, Manny? We're your friends," Grea says.

"I will. I will, after I figure it out a little more. As soon as I get a chance to talk to Jonah. Ever since I walked out of the Shield that day…"

"I *STILL* can't believe you did that. I'm shocked that the Nerps didn't stop you," Rock interjects.

"Me too. Funny thing is that I ran into Jhenda the same day, not long after that."

"Seriously? Where was she?" Grea asks.

"Well, she was out in the field with some other Scavengers. They had just finished for the day. I saw her right after I…"

He stops abruptly and suddenly appears to be very uncomfortable.

"After you *what*?" Rock asks.

"Right after I…after I passed by this old abandoned parking lot…"

Grea makes a face at him.

"Sure," she says with a squint.

Manny makes a quick dismissive gesture, then continues speaking.

"The point is, I'm going to talk to Jonah one last time. There are some specific things that I want to ask him, and then I'll give you guys all the details. Okay?"

"I suppose that we'll allow it," Rock replies.

Manny and Rock both look at Grea. She's picked the meat up and is eating again.

She notices them staring at her.

"What? That's fine, do what you want…" she says with a full mouth.

They laugh at her. She laughs too.

Manny looks at Rock when the laughter settles; he solemnly peers back at his best friend since childhood.

"Tomorrow," Rock says.

"Tomorrow," Manny responds.

The buzzer sounds.

38. I NEED YOU!

THE SABBATH HAS arrived.

Manny wakes up with a jump—the knocking on the front door surprises him.

"It must be Miss Val..." he thinks while rubbing his eyes.

He swings his body around in order to get out of his bed. He lowers his head, rubs his face with his hands, takes a few deep breaths, then finally gets up as a second round of knocks ring through the humble apartment.

"Jonah," he says to himself when he realizes that it's the Sabbath.

"Today..."

After he trots down the hallway and opens the front door, Valerie is standing there with the biggest grin he's ever seen. Her plump cheeks shine from the creams and oils that she uses to moisturize her skin. She's around his mother's age, but her skin is healthily tanned and youthfully beautiful.

"Manny!" she says as she grabs him tightly with both arms and hugs him affectionately.

"How are you my boy?"

With a laugh he responds, "good morning Miss Val...I'm doing okay today..."

He welcomes her in and she sits at the kitchen table. As she does, she coughs forcefully a few times, much like his mother.

Manny pours a glass of water and places it on the table in front of her.

"Oh, oh thank you. Those dusty fields have gotten to us old birds over the years," she mutters just before taking a few large gulps.

"Would you like anything to eat?" he asks.

"Oh, no, no…I'm stuffed! I had two bowls of grits before I left home! You can save your rations, but thank you just the same! How's Mar doing?"

"She's…not too bad…"

"Hmm, okay. She must still be sleeping. I should keep my big mouth shut!"

Manny laughs again.

He steps into his room to get prepared to catch the train to the IE. When he passes by his mother's room, he sees that she's still asleep. Once he returns to the kitchen, he sees that Valerie is tidying the kitchen.

"Miss Val, you don't have to do that…" he says with a hint of sadness.

"Oh, *hush*! I was cleaning this place when you were still a *child*! I don't mind helping out. It's okay! *Really*!"

He humbly nods his head, realizing that the help is beneficial.

"Thank you, Miss Val," he says.

He walks toward the door then turns to Valerie as she washes a pot in the sink.

"Take care of her for me, will you?"

"I sure will! Don't you worry about a thing, sweetie! Now, you get on to the IE…tell us about it when you get back, okay?"

"I will," he says.

Manny turns and closes the door.

~ ~ ~

He's nervous during the entire train ride. He thinks about all of the events that have happened over the past few weeks: the light pole, his times of reading his mother's Grandeurscript; it all just seems like so much.

Will Jonah think he's crazy too?

"Probably," he says to himself with a shake of his head and light snicker.

The trains have climbed Sinai, and people stir across the IE's grounds like a swarm of gnats, as can be expected. It's winter now. Ever since Star Fall, summer can turn to winter, and vice versa, within a matter of weeks; it's presumed that the radiation polluting the atmosphere has made it so. It's very unpredictable.

Manny maneuvers through the crowd. All of the Remnants look much like a school of fish attempting to swim through a narrow creek.

By chance, his eyes catch Grea and Rock.

"You're out of your little mind!" Grea says to Rock as she throws her hands into the air.

"What? How does that not make sense to you? You're cuckoo, that's the problem…" Rock shoots back.

Manny approaches.

"What are you two arguing about now?" Manny asks as he grabs both of Rock's arms aggressively, startling him.

"Whoa! Manny?!" Rock yelps.

"Ha! That's exactly what you get!" Grea says, reveling in the fact that Manny scared her brother.

"He's an imbecile," she continues, pointing at Rock, "but he doesn't realize it, unfortunately…"

Rock shakes his head and looks over at Manny.

"I'm trying to explain to her that if I were to save up enough rations, I could probably bribe one of the train conductors into letting me borrow one of the trains! I've always wanted to take one of them down Sinai with the brakes off. I bet it's so fun! Hey, he may even let me keep a train overnight if I throw in some meat portions…you think!?"

Manny pauses and looks at Rock with a face of confusion and bewilderment.

"See, I told you," Grea says as she lifts one of her hands toward Rock with the other on her hip.

"*Imbecile!*" Grea and Manny say in chorus as they turn to enter the building.

The trio laughs about the exchange when immediately they hear a fourth voice behind them:

"Hey! Wait up!"

They turn and see Jhenda bouncing toward them.

"Jhenda!" Grea exclaims first as she reaches out and embraces her. Manny and Rock greet her too, and then they continue into the IE.

"We were hoping we'd see you," Manny says with a grin.

"Really? Why?" she asks, matter-of-factly.

"I mean, we just…were, I suppose?" Manny stutteringly responds.

Rock and Grea both snicker.

"Well, here I am," she says as she pushes Manny's shoulder and grins widely.

The four companions talk amongst themselves in the midst of the surrounding multitude. When they reach the stairwell, Grea hesitates. She looks toward the main floor, and then back at her brother and friends.

"What is it?" Rock asks.

"Well, it just feels weird, you know?"

"What feels weird?" Jhenda asks.

"I mean, I'm so used to Miss Val and Miss Martha always being here. It feels sort of funny sitting down below, *alone…*"

"Oh, well, you're always welcome to come up to the skybox with us," Manny suggests.

"It's pretty cozy up there, actually," Jhenda adds.

Grea pulls her jacket sleeves over her hands and cracks a few of her knuckles, contemplating her decision.

Rock has already started walking up the steps.

"Well, are you coming or what? I've got some card games to win. Us heathens don't bite—not *all* the time anyway!"

His words and subsequent laugh echo in the stairwell.

Grea lets out a loud sigh of disdain and rolls her eyes at her brother's remark.

Manny and Jhenda laugh.

"Come on, girlie, you'll like it," Jhenda says, placing a hand on Grea's back.

And with that, the group marches up the steps. They can see their warm breath mixing with the cold air as they huff and puff on their way up. Rock cups his hands and blows into them; so does Manny.

~ ~ ~

Grea has only been in the skybox once before, and it was so long ago that she barely remembers it. They were all still very small children. The IE had just been completed and everyone in Naza was there taking a tour of the new facility, led by a very young Jonah.

She only remembers climbing up onto the counter right beside the large window and tapping on the glass. She was enthralled by the view, peering down at the main floor and all of the lights in the aisles. Without her even noticing, Jonah had stealthily grabbed the back of her shirt, just to prevent her from wandering down to a section of the glass that was open. He continued speaking, explaining how the gatherings would run, but motioned with his head so that Martha would notice in a subtle, clandestine fashion.

"*Grea!*" Martha exclaimed as she grabbed her under both armpits and pulled her away.

Jonah looked at her and laughed as she was hoisted onto Martha's shoulder. His smile was bright and captivating, and has remained unchanged over the years. This is her earliest memory of him, and is the image that is burned into her conscience concerning his character—one of wisdom, leadership, and genuine care for others.

~ ~ ~

Her second visit isn't nearly as impressive. Her arms are crossed tightly and pulled in snuggly to her chest. Her face is a bit twisted. She lifts one hand and places her fingers under her nose—the smell is rancid as far as she is concerned.

"Ugh! It's so *disgusting* up here! Why is it so dirty?"

"It sure beats the Outskirts! You'll get used to it," Jhenda says while she laughs.

~ ~ ~

In a cold and dark back hallway, three men stand and wait. Levi's clothes no longer fit. His arms and legs are bulging; his shirt and pants are now skin tight. Every time he exhales, there is a light snarl. His eyes are bloodshot as he looks out to the main floor area.

"Today?" Levi says.

His voice, now more of a growl than an actual voice, is quite intimidating. He stands about six feet and eleven inches tall, as opposed to the five-foot, seven-inch frame that he possessed before his *ascension*. He looks back at Damien who is standing behind him and next to Polus.

Damien simply nods at him in response.

"*Yesssss,*" Polus agrees.

"I wish that I had ascended much sooner—we would have been able to stop the *Witness* many moons ago!"

Rage rises up in Levi's heart like an overflowing river, suddenly and bountifully. He strikes the cement wall next to him with his palm, breaking away chips of the hard surface; they crumble and fall onto the floor. A hole is left in the shape of his abnormally large hand. Damien steps toward him quickly and pats his upper back, as if patting a pet beast.

"Calm," he whispers softly.

Levi whimpers like a canine, letting out a low-pitched squeal. His heavy breathing drops back down to a low and airy grumble.

"In due time, brother. We will deal with the seer first, as Helel has suggested. And then we will focus our attention on the Witness."

"Sssssshould we go inssssside? It sssssshall sssstart sssssoon," Polus says.

"No. No, not today," Damien answers.

Suddenly, the mechanical metal sound can be heard over his voice. The crowd cheers as Jonah's elevator rises from the floor. He steps out with his hands raised, and then he claps them together a few times, greeting his congregation.

For a brief moment, Jonah pauses. He glances over in the direction of the three men behind the curtain. Damien takes in a breath and moves his head, so as to not be seen. Jonah drops his hands, still looking toward the curtain. He's considering something; expecting something. Then, he turns to the crowd.

"Come. Let's go," Damien says. The men hurriedly walk out of an exit at the end of the hallway.

~ ~ ~

Grea sits, with her arms still folded, trying to make herself as tiny as possible, hoping that a bug or rodent won't leap onto her. Her eyes are locked on her brother. He shuffles cards, laughs, and speaks loudly. Jhenda is stooped next to her. Manny sits on her other side. Grea's expression is one of total disgust as she watches Rock's demeanor and antics.

"Look at him, I bet he's like this all the time up here, isn't he?"

"*All* the time," Manny laughs.

"I never learned how to play," Jhenda says.

"Me neither. I'm sure it's not hard though, I just never took the time to really *play* it. But, I get the concept. It's just card counting, basically…I'm sure that I could be really good if I wanted to be…" Manny responds.

Grea and Jhenda both look at him with unconvinced expressions, then they turn to each other and laugh simultaneously.

"I'm serious," Manny says with a grin.

They sit and talk for quite a while. About rations. About the Shield. About when the term *Scavenger* was first used. Manny becomes distracted and Grea notices.

"What is it?" she asks him.

"Nothing."

"You're still going to talk to him, right?"

"I have to…"

The few moments prior were a nice time of relief from his thoughts, but that time of ease has passed. He considers what he needs to say, how he needs to say it, whether or not Jonah will believe him, and of course, if he's really going crazy.

"*Ahhhhh!*" Jhenda yells as she jerks her leg forward while still stooped.

"What?!" Grea says, thinking that she must've been bitten by some pest.

"Pins and needles!" Jhenda says loudly.

"What? What are you talking about?" Grea responds frantically.

Jhenda jumps up and wobbles around in a circle.

Manny laughs.

"Her leg must've fallen asleep."

"Oh, gosh! She scared the heck out of me!" Grea says, placing her hand on her chest.

"My legs are getting tired too. Do you think the gathering is close to being over? Must be by now, right?" Manny says.

Grea and Manny stand up. Just behind them is the glass window; Grea takes a look out of it.

"You're right. Can't believe I actually spent the whole time up here instead of down there," Grea says.

As she talks, there's a young boy, no more than about twelve years old, walking down the aisle as people cheer and clap. Jonah sits on the edge of the stage, beckoning for the boy to come closer.

"This is *amazing*, you all! This is what it's all about! Right *here*!" Jonah says excitedly into the microphone.

The entire stadium is ecstatic. There are hundreds of people all around the boy, cheering, and clapping; people from different backgrounds, who speak various languages, and who have their own avenues of spiritual expression.

The boy takes a few more steps, looks around, stops, then covers his face with his hands. Tears burst from his eyes like pressurized water from fire hydrants that have had their caps broken off. Women, men, and other children cry along with him; others shout praises and prayers. It's extremely intense and emotional; there's a tangible sensation of joy and compassion in the air.

Manny, Grea, and Jhenda watch the entire scene from above. Even they are captivated by the moment. Manny thinks to himself about how admirable it is for such a young child, who probably has just as many unanswered questions as he does, to be bold enough to step out from the crowd and express that he wants more; more of whatever the Creator has to offer.

The boy finally reaches the stage.

Jonah embraces him.

The room falls silent.

"We're going to pray with, with...what's your name, young sir?"

Jonah bends his head down so that the boy can whisper into his ear.

"...with *Jeremiah*!"

The room erupts again.

Since the glass window is open, everyone in the skybox can hear. Without even realizing it, they have stopped their card games and side conversations, almost in an act of unintentional, yet inherent reverence. Jonah speaks again after he motions with his hands for the assembly to quiet down.

"Jeremiah, do you mind if I pray with you?"

The boy shakes his head, then bows it as he holds Jonah's hands.

"Creator, we thank you today, for Jeremiah. We thank you that no matter who we are, no matter how old or young, and no matter where we come from, we can always come to you. We're so glad that we don't have to use fancy words, and that we don't have to know everything, or anything at all about you, but we can just say with a sincere heart, that we want to know you, be close to you, and be with you. That's Jeremiah's prayer today. He wants more of you..."

As Jonah speaks, he notices that Jeremiah's body is beginning to tremble. He opens his eyes, but continues his prayer.

"He offers his very life to you today, Creator. Instruct him, lead him, and guide him. Remind him that he has already been accepted as your

> *own because he comes from you. Teach him who you are, by teaching him who he is..."*

Jeremiah's body shakes more fiercely until it's noticed by the first few rows of people who are just behind him. They've opened their eyes to watch him too.

Without warning, Jeremiah blurts out something in the middle of the prayer. He's close enough to Jonah's microphone for the entire building to hear it:

"CREATOR, I *NEED* YOU!"

With that, his body falls limp onto the floor. Grea is crying profusely now. So is Jhenda. A few others in the skybox have stood up to watch too, with tears streaming down their faces.

Manny, however, can't believe his eyes.

His face is completely flushed.

39. WATCH OUT!

AT THE MOMENT that Jeremiah falls to the floor, a large, hideous, dark entity flies through one of the walls in a ghost-like fashion toward the stage.

Trails of black and gray smolder follow it as it swoops through the crowd, snarling and breathing puffs of smoke, ash, and flame from its snout. It appears to be easily ten feet tall. It's wearing a long black cloak which fades into a smoky translucent substance as it flies. Manny can't mutter a word at first; fear and terror grip his heart as he watches on helplessly.

The entity lands and towers over the body of Jeremiah. No one sees it apparently, except for Manny—not even Jonah.

"He's okay, he's okay! Just give him some space…he's fine…" Jonah says nervously as a few people rush toward Jeremiah to help.

Those who stood up slowly return to their seats, comforted by Jonah's reassurance. Jonah continues to pray, fervently, after looking around the room.

He feels that something is off; something is wrong and he knows it, but he doesn't want to alarm the crowd.

"I need you all to pray…pray with me, for Jeremiah…" he says to the crowd.

People all around the room lift their voices at the same time: shouts, cries, and prayers in various languages all waft through air. Jonah cannot see what Manny sees, but he can feel a dark presence all around Jeremiah as he lies on the floor, his body twitching every few seconds.

The entity stands, snarling, growling, and roaring over the boy. Its talons are as long as an eagle's. Its face is dark and twisted. Its eyes are blood red. Long yellow fangs hang from its mouth. There's a bone-like structure protruding from its forehead, and it has a snout much like that of a pig. It wears chains—black and silver chains around its neck, and they hang down to its upper abdomen.

Manny panics, and yells:

"HEY, WATCH OUT!"

Grea jumps.

"What is your *problem?!*" she whispers at him vehemently.

Some of the people on the main floor look up toward the skybox momentarily before turning back to Jonah and Jeremiah. A few in the skybox chuckle lightly and whisper from behind him.

"Kid's crazy," one man says.

Rock has now come to stand at Manny's side. Not sure of what to say or do, he just stands there, studying Manny's demeanor; his face is flushed and he's quivering.

The beast looks back at Manny, its entire body rising and falling with each laborious breath. Manny is in shock, and gets more and more flushed by the second. He's sweating and feels feverish. Everyone sitting on the main floor is still praying. Jonah continues to analyze Jeremiah and prays too.

The large creature, still staring at Manny, laughs with a heavy, bellowing voice. It lets out a roar, then turns back to Jeremiah and lifts its colossal hand into the air. Manny can see that it intends to strike Jeremiah with its talons, which look like the teeth of a bulldozer's shoveling blade. Manny can no longer stand still.

Without hesitation, he runs out of the room, much to the surprise of those with him in the skybox. Grea, Rock, and Jhenda have no idea what to do except run after him and scream his name repeatedly.

"*Manny! MANNY!*"

He ignores them and yells down at the crowd from the upper deck, flailing his arms in the air.

"*HEY!*"

Nearly everyone below turns and looks up at him; even Jonah notices the commotion that Manny's causing. Manny runs around a path that encircles the top level of the arena between a metal rail and another row of stadium seats.

He runs as fast as he can, still yelling:

"*HEY! HEY!*"

His friends are in hot pursuit. He goes for about fifty yards and stops at an angle that allows him to be best seen by everyone in the stadium.

"WATCH OUT!"

He yells it with every fiber of his being. The entity stops again and looks up at him, this time infuriated. Manny is still the only one who sees him.

The beast grunts and shoots a puff of fire from its snout. Then, it leans back and lets out the most intimidating sound that Manny has ever heard—clearly not a noise that a human being, or anything of this world for that matter, could ever produce. Large leathery wings sprout out from the beast's back and it takes flight directly toward Manny.

Manny steps back. Jhenda, Grea, and Rock stand a few feet away from him, reluctant to get too close, afraid that he could possibly lash out at them. The beast flies at Manny with great speed. Manny falls backward to the ground, covers his face with both hands, and closes his eyes, certain that this creature intends to kill him.

"*STOP! NO! NO! NO!*" he screams.

When the beast is close to the railing, still in mid-flight, there is a bright flash of light, and a crashing sound.

Metal.

Ripping.

Tearing.

Groans of agony and terror.

He hears rumbling and tussling around him, and then stillness.

Quietness in the entire stadium.

Only the sound of Grea, crying.

"Manny, what is *wrong* with you?" she sobs.

He drops his arms from his face, opens his eyes, and sees Grea sniffling.

He sees Rock and Jhenda, both startled and a bit fearful.

He peeks down through the bars of the upper deck railing and sees the entire room looking up at him.

He sees the boy, Jeremiah, standing there next to Jonah, and *smiling*.

Their eyes lock.

Manny sees peacefulness in Jeremiah's face—a glow.

Finally, Manny glances at Jonah, who looks both nervous and exceptionally pleased, oddly.

~ ~ ~

Warmth hits Manny's face as he remains on the cold concrete floor of the upper deck, outside of the skybox. He sees a bright glimmer on his right side. He turns his head in that direction and observes the most beautiful being that he's ever laid eyes on.

~ ~ ~

Tall, strong, and adorned with the purest, whitest, and most brilliant metallic armor conceivable. It's decorated with ropes and cords of silver and gold. The being appears to be faceless, simply because the light that's emitting from it is nearly blinding.

Manny covers his eyes.

The light settles, gradually becoming less intense.

He's able to see the being more clearly.

This creature, which has a set of slowly-flapping white and golden wings of its own, stands boldly and regally with one foot on top of the crumpled body of the creature that was on the verge of attacking Jeremiah, and ultimately Manny.

It's dead.

There is a wound in its back that must have come from the bulky sword that the divine being is holding. A viscous green substance pours from the creature's body, mouth, and snout, onto the floor. There are stains of the same substance on the shiny being's sword too.

The glowing presence looks at Manny and smiles.

Seconds later, a poof of blue smoke engulfs both creatures, and they vanish.

40. GO, MANNY!

MANNY JUMPS UP and runs as quickly as he can into the restroom. He lowers as much of his upper body as possible into the sink and flushes his head with cold water, as if doing so will rinse away everything that he just saw.

He feels sick; physically sick. Rock has quietly creeped in behind him and stands by the door, watching with his mouth wide open, clueless about what he should say. Grea and Jhenda stand by the door outside. Everyone in the congregation is murmuring. There is a constant hum coursing through the whole building:

> **"Who *was* that?"**
> **"Did you hear that guy up there?"**
> **"What *happened*?"**
> **"What's going on?"**

The ripples of unrest throughout the IE intensify.

Jeremiah is standing up now, smiling nonchalantly at Jonah; a few seconds later, he turns away and goes to his seat. Jonah looks at the boy walk away with his eyebrows dropped lower than normal—contemplating. He's acutely aware of what may have just happened. He's seen spiritual deliverances and cleansings before, but not quite like this. The whispers grow louder as everyone looks toward the balcony of the upper deck, trying to figure out who was yelling and why. Jonah, being a "master" of mastering moments, turns and steps up to center stage.

"Everyone, everyone! Listen, we've experienced a great thing today! This young man has come to a place of relating to the Creator, in his own way; that's something to certainly be celebrated!"

A few in the crowd clap their hands, then more, and more.

"Oh, come on, we can do better than that!"

Applause and cheers erupt around the building.

"I think that we've certainly accomplished what needed to be accomplished for today, so it's a perfect time to depart, and to reflect. Spend time with your loved ones, your friends, and your families. Let's prepare for the week ahead, and be ready for next Sabbath. Go with the Creator, and he'll go with you..."

With that, Jonah starts to maneuver his way through the aisles, attempting to get to the entrance as quickly as he can.

~ ~ ~

"I'm *fine*," Manny says when he catches a glimpse of Rock in the mirror.

"Manny, you're not *fine*! What happened back there, I mean you were..."

"*I said I'm fine!*" Manny blurts out as he scoops another handful of cold water onto his head, staring into the mirror at his bloodshot eyes. He looks over at Rock, who is still patiently standing by the door. Manny lowers his head.

"I'm sorry...I'm sorry. I don't know. I don't know what just happened. I can't explain it, okay? Something is...*happening*. Something *has* happened..."

He looks back into the mirror, "*...to me.*"

"Well, what do we need to do?! We're your *friends*, Manny! We're your friends..." Rock replies affectionately and emphatically.

"Nothing! *Okay?!* You can't do *anything!* I need to talk to Jonah..."

Manny turns swiftly, darts right past Rock, and exits the door.

He passes Grea and Jhenda with haste. They can barely get out the initial sounds necessary to formulate their questions and concerns. Manny leans over the balcony rail and looks at the dispersing crowd. He focuses, trying to catch sight of Jonah somewhere. Anywhere.

His friends stand behind him and watch him as he searches the crowd in a panic. Without warning, he takes off for the stairs.

"Manny!" Grea yelps.

He pays her no attention and continues on his mission to find the only person in the world that he feels can give him any guidance right now. They chase after him. As soon as they reach the lobby, Jonah is positioned off in the distance, looking from side to side just as frantically as Manny is. Jonah sees Manny first and rushes toward him, yelling his name over the murmur and chatter of the crowd.

"Manny! Manny! Over here!"

When Manny turns, he's shocked a bit and his face shows it. Grea, Rock, and Jhenda make their way down the stairwell just in time to see the whole exchange.

"Manny, Manny, do you have a moment? Can we talk?"

"Yes. Yes. Please..."

"Good, follow me. Excuse me, everyone!"

They speed away to Jonah's office. The three friends gawk at each other as the two men disappear in the commotion of the hundreds of people in the lobby. After a few moments of quiet between them, Rock looks at Jhenda and his sister and says, "well, that went *extremely* well, wouldn't you say?"

"Rock, *quiet*..." Grea says.

~ ~ ~

"Sit. Sit. We haven't much time..."

Manny looks around the office like a toddler in a toy museum. He's never been in this section of the IE. He notices all of the plaques and picture frames, the hundreds of books, the nice wooden desk, and the scent of incense lingering in the air. Jonah points at the chair that is directly in front of his desk. Manny sits, still gazing all around him and taking in as much as possible.

"You saw them? You actually saw them?" Jonah asks, as he goes behind his desk and picks up a small wooden box with a curved engraving on its top.

"How'd you..." Manny begins to say, but stops himself, remembering that Jonah tends to know what he seemingly shouldn't, and couldn't for that matter.

"Yes, when the boy went to you...I saw...well, I don't know *what* I saw..."

Jonah places the box on the table in front of Manny, and Manny studies the engraved symbol. He's never seen it before, but for some reason, there's a certain familiarity that he senses; it's as if deep down inside he knows what it is, or once knew and has just forgotten.

Jonah starts to grab books and papers from his bookshelves. He flips through the pages as he picks them up one by one and either says, "no, no, no," or, "yes, this one," as he works his way around the room.

He places the ones selected onto the desk in front of Manny along with the box.

"Manny, you're seeing into the unseen world. The spiritual world. It's just as real as this natural world...more real, actually..."

As he talks, he continues to scramble around his office, grabbing papers, books, and different items. It's like he is preparing for something. He starts stuffing many of the things he's collecting into a large black safe that's sitting in the corner of the room.

"The spiritual world?" Manny asks.

"Yes. The world of hidden, invisible forces that act upon this natural realm of existence at *all* times. The world that most, if not *all* religions and belief systems have tried to connect with, comprehend, and explain throughout history. It's not a new phenomenon. Faith, belief, and so on have been around since the first humans walked this earth. From the very beginning, we've been trying to reconnect with the Creator. Reconnect with the source. Or, maybe the Creator has been trying to reconnect with us..."

He stares at Manny.

"Everything is connected, Manny. You, me, the planet, the universe, the spiritual world. *Everything.* You are connected to everything, through your soul. Your life-force. Your energy. You're already eternal. *YAHWEH* is eternal."

He looks into Manny's eyes, studies him, and then picks up the items that he just placed on his desk. He gives Manny the small wooden box, a handful of notebooks, and some sheets of loose paper that he's stuffed into a binder.

"Open it," Jonah says as he places his finger on the small box with the engraving.

Slowly, Manny opens the box. There is a folded and crumpled sheet of paper inside. He picks it up. Underneath it, there's a small key with the same curved symbol from the box's lid engraved onto it. He picks the key up and rotates it around between his fingers. When he unfolds the paper, he realizes that it's a map.

"You must go here," Jonah says, tapping his finger on a circled area, "use the key and make sure you're not followed; you can NOT be seen..."

Jonah turns away and grabs more things, then packs them tightly into the safe.

"Wait, what do you mean? Where does this lead to? And what's this key for?"

Jonah keeps working, ignoring Manny's questions.

"I've only seen unconscious glimpses of the world that you see while in a conscious state Manny. That's mind-blowing. I've waited for this day for so long. We all have. You'll understand more, once you get there…"

"Get where?"

"Just follow the map…"

Jonah stops and turns to Manny.

"Have you heard him yet? Have you heard his voice?"

Manny makes a nervously shy expression.

"I…I think so. I mean, well, yes. Yes, I have…"

"What about *the Cloud*? Have you been there already?"

"All right, Jonah. Stop. How do you know all of this? How do you know?! This was the whole reason that I wanted to come to you today, to tell you about all of these things. But you know already? *How?!*"

"We don't have enough time. Take this key, Manny. Take it, and follow the directions on the map…"

Jonah walks slowly over to Manny. He places his hands on Manny's shoulders and slows his speech, ensuring that Manny hears every word. He stares into his eyes with every bit of seriousness and sincerity that he can.

"Helel and his Shedim have been after you since you were born, Manny... ...but so has the Kingdom...so has the *King*..."

Manny's heart rate slows down. The words dig into him.

Jonah moves his hands to Manny's face as he stares into his eyes and continues to talk. He holds him as a father would hold his son while explaining an important life lesson, cupping his cheeks and chin with both palms.

"They all know how critical you are. You're needed. Don't forget that truth. No matter what lies ahead. You've been chosen.

And you've been given everything that you need to accomplish the tasks that are in front of you. It's already inside of you, because *he* is now inside of you. Don't faint, no matter what happens from this point forward. I believe in you, we all do, but you have to believe in you too…"

Manny is silent. Jonah's hands still cup his face. They stare unflinchingly into each other's eyes. Jonah doesn't look away until he's certain that his words have completely set in like concrete in Manny's soul, then he lets him go.

"Manny, it's *imperative* that you go to this location, and don't waste any time," Jonah says.

He resumes amassing materials and shoving them into the safe.

"Jonah…who is *Helel?* And what are…"

Jonah doesn't even look in Manny's direction.

"The map, this key, and these few papers and books, Manny. They contain the answers that you're looking for; at least, the *beginning* of the answers that you're looking for…"

When the safe is full, Jonah lowers it into a compartment that's been cut into the floor.

"It will all make sense…just go to that spot…"

At the very moment that Jonah closes the door to the floor compartment and pulls a rug over the top of it, his body shoots up like an arrow.

"*Oh, no…*"

His eyes dart around the room quickly, and then he focuses them on the door.

"*They're here…*"

Manny is even further confused at this point.

"Manny, you have to trust me…quickly, get up! Get up!"

Manny jumps from his chair as Jonah hastens over toward him. Manny stuffs the items into his bag, then Jonah pulls him to the back of the room. He moves a fairly large statue of an angel aside, revealing another small door that's attached to the floor.

"You have to go through here, Manny. Crawl all the way through until you reach the end of the tunnel. This is an unfinished portion of the bunkers. Go, Manny…and do *not* come back here, no matter what you see, hear, or what may happen. You must *promise* me…you're *too* important…"

"But Jonah…"

"PROMISE ME!"

Manny has never heard Jonah yell before. He's never seen him like this. Such fierceness and seriousness. He's always an extremely mellow and kind-hearted person, like a lamb.

Today, he is a lion.

"I promise," Manny mutters softly.

"Now, GO!"

Footsteps approach from the hallway. It sounds like an army marching.

"Go, Manny…go!" Jonah whispers forcefully.

Manny crawls through the trap door, and Jonah places the statue back on top of it.

Manny peeks through a crack in the floor.

At the moment he does, Jonah's door bursts open.

41. THAT SPOT

"*GRAB HIM!*" DAMIEN screams as he rushes into the room.

Levi, Polus, and about six Nerps flood in right behind him. Four of the Nerps tackle Jonah to the floor. He doesn't fight them.

Damien kneels down beside Jonah with a sinister smirk on his face.

"Very good, very good!" he chuckles, "I'm so sorry, Jonah," he continues as he rubs him on the head.

"You're hereby under arrest, for treason against Novus Res Publica. I hate to do this, but you know how these things go…I'm just following orders…"

"To *HELL* with you, Damien!" Jonah grunts while a Nerp's knee is buried into his upper back.

Damien laughs.

"Very good!"

He looks up at one of the soldiers and motions his hand toward the door.

"Take him…"

They pick him up and march out of the door. Polus and Levi follow, leaving Damien in the office alone.

Manny sits in the dark hole. He keeps peeking through the cracks in the floor, trying to not breathe too heavily. He can't believe what he's just seen.

Where are they taking him?
What did he do?
Why is all of this happening?

All questions that circle in his mind.

Just as Damien turns to leave the room, he hesitates. He leisurely turns around and looks back at the statue in the corner.

He takes a few steps toward it. Manny holds his breath, terrified.

Damien stands just over the area that Manny is just beneath.

Silent.

Not moving.

Not breathing.

Damien places his finger on his chin and peers at the statue. He reaches out with both hands and adjusts it, like someone with a compulsive disorder would adjust a slightly crooked picture.

"Very good," he says with a devilish smile.

He walks out of the door.

Manny hits his head a few times with his palm and blows air from between his teeth. For a second, he imagines that this is what losing one's mind feels like. He feels fear and uncertainty grip him again.

He fights his nearly overwhelming emotions off and gathers himself.

He looks around inside the dark tunnel. It's cold and damp. There is a putrid slush under him as he squats down in this trench. There are three separate directions that he can go. He notices that one pathway has a faint light that the others do not, so he crawls in that direction. The splashing and crunching of the icy sludge is much like a rank iced coffee; similar in color, but with an unbearable scent.

"These pipes must funnel the IE's septic network," he thinks.

He crawls through the maze of metal pipes for what feels like hours. Periodically, he panics and cries along the journey, but something in him pushes him to continue. It's so dark. Gradually, the faint light at what must be an exit becomes brighter. He picks up his pace and crawls like a mad man with all of the strength and energy he has.

He finally reaches an opening and stops for a second to close his eyes and catch his breath. His hands and legs are numb from the cold. A round metal door is just above his head that's connected to a wheel that must be unscrewed to open it. He does so, and pops the top open with a slap of his open hand. He climbs out with a few grunts, then stands on the icy ground. His clothes are covered with a dark oily substance. He strips away his top layers, drops them back into the tunnel, closes the tunnel's lid, wipes his face and eyes, then lets out a long, slow sigh of relief.

He thinks of Jonah's words to him:

"It will all make sense…just go to that spot…"

42. YOD

"I CAN'T BELIEVE this. I can't believe that I'm even out here. Where am I going? What was I *thinking*?!"

He's walked for miles.

"Jonah's crazy. No, I'm the crazy one for listening to him and going through with this. What if there isn't anything out here?"

Periodically he looks at the paper in his hand, with its faded arrows and lines, and the faded circle that was probably once a bright red, but is now more of a weak pink. He stops and turns to look behind. The IE and Eden both look like a tiny scene in a snow globe. His feet are throbbing inside of his boots. He hears the crunch of the ice capped sandy surface of the ground and patches of nearly frozen grass beneath him. The wind blows bits of cool, icy debris into his face. His clothes are still damp. Stains from the gunk from the tunnel are still on him. He folds his hands into his oversized sweater and trudges along. His book bag dangles from his back like a leaf from a tree branch.

After another mile or two, in between struggling to follow his makeshift map and straining to see through the mild winter windstorm, a wave of emotions comes crashing down on him. He's in the middle of nowhere, going somewhere that he's never been, and wouldn't know how to get there even if his map was perfectly written. The wind picks up all of a sudden and blows large chunks of snow into Manny's face, making it difficult to see even two feet in front of him. His eyes close and panic rushes into his heart. His eyes fill with tears immediately, and he cries a cry so deep that his chest trembles. He covers his nose and mouth with his sleeve to try and muffle it to no avail. Finally, he succumbs and drops to his knees, sobbing.

~ ~ ~

He's exhausted. So much has happened to him over the past few months. Far *too* much in his opinion. Everything that was once secure has changed. Everything that he thought he once knew, he no longer knows. He imagines himself dying in this frozen desert, maybe even in this very spot. The world is crumbling all around him, and everything inside of him is crumbling along with it.

Then, like a shockwave, *the Voice* booms inside of him in that instant:

"STAND..."

An immediate and familiar calmness fills him up from the inside and his tears stop.

He lifts himself to his feet.

The wind slows to a dead and eerie peacefulness.

~ ~ ~

There's a wooden building directly in front of him.

He looks from side to side, as if trying to catch a glimpse of someone who dropped it there, then hid themselves away. He hadn't seen this structure at all, until now.

"What is this? Where did this come from?" he says to himself.

As he approaches, he notices a blue squiggly symbol faintly painted on the door; the same symbol that is etched on the key that Jonah gave him. He pulls the key from his bag, holds it up to the door, and compares the two markings.

The same.

Cautiously, he slides the key into the door, turns it, and hears a loud click. The door creaks open and he watchfully steps inside. The wind blows ice inside, so Manny quickly closes the door. There's just enough light coming through the small window on the back side of the cabin to see large objects, like a table, and some chairs. He blows into his hands and rubs them together to warm them while looking around, timidly. A beaded chain hangs from the ceiling.

He pulls it.

Click.

Nothing.

He feels his way around the room and stumbles across an old vintage oil lamp. Luckily, there's a book of matches right next to it. He strikes one and lights the lamp. He walks around the room and looks at the numerous bookshelves that line the walls. There's a large table in the corner with stacks of paper and notebooks on it. He also notices a small cot in one of the corners, with a pillow and a thick black blanket on top.

"*Does Jonah live here?*" he asks himself with a heart full of curiosity.

The plethora of books, notebooks, papers, diagrams, posters, and so on, easily number in the hundreds—possibly thousands. Most of it is handwritten with pens and markers. There is a group of notebooks on the table, all bound together with a thin rope. They each have a different title scribbled on their covers. He remembers that Jonah gave him a handful of notebooks that look much like these, so he pulls them from his bag. He starts to read through the titles:

"The Messengers and Watchers"

"Things to Come"
"Star Fall"
"NRP Handbook"
"IE Origins"

As he browses through them, he selects one entitled, **"The Shedim."**

He flips it open and peruses. There are images and descriptions throughout the book.

~ ~ ~

"The Hebrew term for demon is Shedim..."

"The Watchers (angels) who fell became the Shedim (demons)...the one-third which followed Helel Ben Shahar (many names)..."

~ ~ ~

He continues to read and finds a hierarchy with the names of the chief Shedim listed, along with their subordinates, based on different cultures, traditions, and belief systems.

~ ~ ~

"The war has never been a natural one...the true battle happens in the unseen world...powers and energies that cannot be comprehended by the naked eye and closed mind...natural things only experience the effects of spiritual things..."
"Demons, Jinn, Shedim...they are all the same... simply different names within different cultures..."

> "They emulate the Watchers who remain with the Creator...but revere Helel as their true master...they follow the same order that they did before they fell..."

~ ~ ~

Manny stops for a second and looks around the room.

"*This is crazy. I've never known about any of this,*" he thinks.

As he continues flipping through the pages, he reaches a section that has sketches of different dark forces that have been active in the earth for ages. The drawings have a great amount of detail and look very realistic.

"Jonah is a *really* good sketch artist," Manny murmurs to himself.

He sees creatures that look reptilian like large snakes or lizards.

Some look like beautiful, enticing women.

Some of them are bound to the seas.

Some are drawn flying in the air.

Some are as small as insects.

Others, as large as buildings.

There's a beautiful woman who has the heading *"Vulithina"* above her head.

There are even two which are twins, a male and a female. Underneath them the caption reads, *"Dar'Nicibus and Si'linibus."*

One page depicts a dark, horned, winged entity, with chains hanging from its body. Manny drops the book onto the floor and steps backward away from it.

"What?! It *can't* be..."

He takes a second to settle himself, and then picks the book up again. He turns back to the page and studies the creature.

"That's it. *That's* what I saw earlier today..."

~ ~ ~

"...*Ra'zazel*..."

~ ~ ~

Manny closes the notebook and places it back onto the table with the rest. On the wall, there are diagrams drawn on large posters and held into place with nails and tacks. Manny reads them like some archaeologist deciphering hieroglyphs.

One looks like a diagram that would be found in a science book. It has equations written next to it. Directly underneath it is the same squiggly symbol from the door and the key. There's another sketch. It has two long and winding bars on both sides and smaller bars connecting them going down the middle, like a twisted ladder. It looks vaguely familiar, but Manny doesn't know much about it; it's been years since he's had the privilege of studying something as *frivolous* in his world as science. There are words written beside it; a short sentence:

THE YAHWEH GENE:

"No one can connect with the source, the Creator, or themselves, without faith, love, and truth...higher consciousness requires transcendence of self, of hate, of envy, of fear, and of doubt...faith is necessary... the seed of supernatural consciousness resides in the core of the mind..."

In large bold letters above it are the words:

"ASCEND"

Beneath it is the curved symbol again. Next to it is another word:

"...Yod..."

Manny says it aloud.

"Yod?"

In small print beside it, he reads:

"Yahweh...one of the many names of the Creator... YOD is the first letter of this name in the Hebrew language...I AM...find self in the source..."

He pulls out the key and looks at it again.

"So that's what it means..."

He continues to look at the diagrams. One depiction shows a burst of flames coming from a person's hands. Another shows a group of people flying over a large body of water. One in particular takes his breath away.

In it, there is a cartoonish scene of a man standing in a valley holding a ball of light above his head. Another man lies on the ground just in front of him. An eerie reminder of his recurring dream.

"Strange," he whispers.

In another drawing, there is a long cylindrical tube. It is decorated with lots of pencil-drawn stars and leads to a group of clouds.

Positioned on the clouds are small circles of different shades; they must represent people.

"The Way" and *"The Cloud,"* are written above the sketch.

Manny grabs a few of the sheets of paper from the desk and the handful of flashcards that are next to them. He sits on the cot in the corner and studies them.

Some of the papers have Grandeurscript passages written on them. He unzips his bag, pulls out his mother's Grandeurscript, and starts to cross reference them:

**"Right after these terrible and difficult times...
...The sun will fade out, and the moon itself will be covered by darkness...
...the past shall be erased and the earth will be polluted...
...the skies will remain gray and sadness will live in the land...
...the very stars will plummet from the heavens above, and the celestial powers will quake, leaving the planet devastated, permanently..."**

"Star Fall?" he whispers, and then continues to read.

"The seer came up and voiced himself to the Creator...*if you are truly the Creator, then show us...prove that you're with us...answer me, I beg you, and prove to these people who you are and who I am*...at that very moment, fire fell from above and burned up everything in its path..."

Manny immediately smells something burning in the room, but there's no fire in sight.

"Not again…" he says after pausing, but continues.

> "There's a huge difference between the tough times that we experience now, and the good things to come. The world is excited! Can you feel it? We're in a holding pattern; the whole universe is! The Creator rules over all, and the anxiety builds every single second concerning what's to come. Creation is in its third trimester. We're all pregnant with purpose, and the gestation period is almost over! The universe itself is pregnant with a coming glory! It's not just about the external things though, it's really about the things that are inside of every one of us. The essence of the Creator is within every single one of his creations…within us all…within *you*…"

He puts the Grandeurscript back into his bag, places the bag next to him, and starts meditating on the words.

Then, it happens again.

43. IMPOSSIBLE

HE FEELS THE separation begin. Everything slows down completely. Soon, he's looking into his own eyes as he sits on the cot. Sure enough, when he looks up, he sees the star-encrusted tunnel above his head. He's not as nervous as he was the first time; he even leaps to assist the pull when it begins to draw him in like reverse gravity.

When he reaches the Cloud, he sees the millions of faces again. He hovers above them for a bit. A group of children look up at him, all wearing pure white robes. They wave at him with smiles and laughs.

Manny's eyes catch a fairly young man with a short scruffy beard. His physique is like that of marathon runner: lean, youthful, and sturdy. The young man nods and turns his body completely toward Manny as he quickly flies toward him.

They collide, producing a burst of light.

~ ~ ~

Manny shields his eyes from the sunlight like someone who has just arisen from a deep slumber. He blinks a few times until his sight adjusts. He smells the salty scent of the sea. The air is warm, but not humid. Rays of sunlight kiss his skin like millions of butterflies landing on him simultaneously.

He's in a crowd and there's a lot of murmuring and whispering.

"Hey, sit down!" someone yells in a dialect and language that Manny's both unfamiliar and acquainted with.

He somehow senses that the voice was directed at him. He turns. A man is seated on the ground with other men nearby. The man's hands are out to his sides in an impatient expression as he stares into Manny's eyes. Manny's assumption was correct; the man is talking to him.

"Sorry—*sorry*," Manny responds, in the same ancient language.

Manny plops down on the grass at the edge of a circle of men. A few yards away from them are groups of women and children. Manny notices them because one of the men yells to the group, "is my wife there? Ah, I see her! I *love* you, my love!"

Someone next to Manny says to an elderly man, "he's the *messiah*, I tell you! I hear that he raised a young girl from the dead… the daughter of one of the men from the synagogue!"

A younger man interrupts, "don't be a fool! No, he's not! What proof do you have? What proof does ANYONE have?"

Another young man approaches from behind them and sits next to the first two.

He says, "oh, dear brother, it is a wonder that we come from the same womb! He is *indeed* the messiah! You'll see! Just listen to his words…"

At that moment, Manny notices their eyes move toward the front of the large crowd. The voices around him become quieter. The whispers and conversations recede.

Manny turns his head and sees a man, no more than in his late twenties or early thirties, approaching a hill. He walks by the people, touching their outstretched hands as he passes. His smile is brilliant and liberating. There's something captivating about him; his presence alone attracts the crowd.

Some start to cheer:

"Teacher!"

"Master!"
"Rabbi!"
"Our King!"

Eventually, the entire mass is clapping, waving their hands, whistling, and yelling praises. Once he reaches the top of the hill, the man lifts his hands to quiet them.

They obey his silent command.

He begins to speak, and all eyes are locked on him. His words are stirring and enchanting; Manny gravitates to his energy and feels like he's about to explode inside. He can tell that everyone present feels the exact same way. It's much like when Jonah speaks at the IE, only amplified—infinitely.

The man walks through the midst of the people now. He continues teaching and speaking as he does. He makes eye contact with everyone that he can as he navigates around the seated assembly.

He's walks in Manny's direction.

Now, he's standing directly in front of Manny, but is looking away.

He stops speaking.

He turns to Manny.

He stoops down until he and Manny are eye level.

They stare into each other's eyes, face to face.

He speaks:

"I've not come to destroy any of the old ways or teachings. I've come to continue the works that were begun by the Creator. I can speak to you completely honestly and transparently; all that exists, and even the universe itself, will not lose a bit of its essence before every word of old, which has been decreed

by the Creator into eternity, is fulfilled...I AM that fulfillment...and so are you..."

He addresses the crowd, but he never takes his eyes off of Manny. Any other time, Manny would be uncomfortable, but instead, he's extremely calm. Everyone in the crowd turns and looks at them. The man reaches his hand out for Manny to take it.

He does.

Before he can blink he is back in the Way.

But not for long.

~ ~ ~

The stars slow down and his speed decreases. He is now with a small group, crowded around the same captivating man from the hill by the sea. The men around Manny speak to their leader as he tilts his head down and leans against a wall with his hand on his chin. One man speaks up louder than the others. He's brawny and firm, yet gentle in the eyes; he reminds Manny very much of Rock.

"That Shedim, it was too strong for us..."

The others join in.

"Yes, Master. Yes, it was too strong!"

"You have not trained us for that type of battle!"

"What went wrong?"

"What shall we do now?"

The stronger of the men speaks up again. The others quiet down to hear his words to their master, "why couldn't *we* destroy it?"

The man lifts his eyes and addresses the entire group, but looks directly at Manny:

> *"Simple...you didn't have the faith. If you have even one drop of faith, you can do things that you've never imagined. Believing is the key. Believing when you have little to no evidence naturally. Believing when it's easier to doubt. You can shake the foundations of the planet if you believe...the entire universe will bend to your will...you can move the unmovable...and do the unthinkable..."*

With a flash of light that starts from the man's eye, Manny zips away into eternity once more.

~ ~ ~

Manny's soul materializes in the small cabin out in the middle of nowhere. His consciousness rushes back into his body. He pants like a wildly exhausted winter hound that has just run miles across cold mountainous terrain.

There's a loud hum in the room. His bookbag, which is partially leaning on his thigh, gets increasingly warm. He looks down at it. In seconds, it gets so hot that he's certain that it must be on fire. Quickly, he tosses it onto the floor. Light gray smoke pours through its open spaces and mesh skin.

The hum stops.

The smoke stops.

Reluctantly, he opens the bag.

To his surprise, his mother's Grandeurscript is now coated in pure gold. It's much heavier now. Its pages are no longer worn. The ink is fresh. The same curved "Yod" emblem is etched into its cover.

Just like the door.

Just like the key.

"This is insane..." Manny whispers.

It's too much for Manny to take in at once.

He handles the transformed book in his hands in total awe.

For the next few moments, he lies back and thinks.

Reality hits him like a tidal wave after a few more minutes of contemplation and analysis of the golden Grandeurscript. While he lies on his back on the small cot with his eyes closed and the heavy golden Grandeurscript on his chest, he thinks of his friends.

He thinks of his mother.

"Oh no! I've been here for *HOURS...*"

He hurriedly puts all of the things back where they belong, stuffs the Grandeurscript back into his bag, tosses all of the notebooks back onto the table, and blows the old lamp's flame until it disappears.

He locks the door behind him, and takes off for Naza.

[Miles away, at Eden]

Grea, Rock, and Jhenda walk toward the train deck, away from the benches and merchant tents.

"Let's just go to Miss Martha's before it gets too late. The last train is about to leave it looks like. We can just wait for the knuckle-head there. He'll *have* to come home eventually," Grea urges.

Jhenda stops in her tracks.

"Wait, I don't know if his mother...you know? I don't know if it would be okay if..." Jhenda stutters.

"Don't worry, you're like family now," Rock reassures her.

"Family?" The word is foreign to Jhenda. Ever since the blasts, she's been a nomadic recluse.

"Well, yeah...Miss Martha thinks the world of you already," Grea adds.

"Well, how do you know that?" Jhenda asks.

"She said so, the day that she first met you. When we were leaving, she said, *'that was a sweet young lady. I certainly hope to see more of her. Make sure you all make her feel welcome. She's going to be like one of mine too, eventually, I'm sure…anyone that Manny takes to usually ends up being like one of mine'*…"

Jhenda looks astonished.

"She…she *really* said that?"

"See! It's just like I said. You're like *family*!" Rock finishes.

They board the train and head for Martha's place.

44. LIVE

HE JOGS A bit, then walks a bit. He does this for miles. No trains run this late, so he has to get home by foot. It's close to nine o'clock at night and he's still at least ten miles away from Naza.

"Gosh, it's going to take *hours*. I know they're worried about me…"

The air is even more cool and crisp than it was when he first left the IE hours before. It's dark, but everything around him has a bluish glow; the brightness of the moonlight peaks through the scattered gray clouds. It seems close enough for him to touch. The stars twinkle all around it like glitter on a black canvas. He passes by a large tree that has lost all of its leaves long ago. The branches are brittle and cracked. It looks like it was once sturdy and full of lush vegetation, perhaps before Star Fall; certainly not tonight.

"It's freezing…"

He says the words through chattering teeth as he looks at the tree, still thinking about how quickly the temperature has dropped since he left the IE.

Without warning and with no apparent lapse of time between when the words exit his mouth and when he sees it; the tree, from the ground up, ices completely over.

Manny stops and his mouth drops open. He listens to the cold crackle of the ice forming over the tree's bark; a very thick and defined layer.

He cautiously walks over to it in complete amazement.

He touches it.

Solid.

Cold.

Another thought comes into his mind out of nowhere; an inspired thought. Unsure of why he thinks it, he feels the insatiable urge to just say it out loud anyway.

He takes a couple of steps back and says:

"Live…"

Immediately, the ice breaks away in large sheets and the bark becomes lively and colorful. The branches thicken and small buds shoot from its skin. Leaves pop out and create a rustling sound in the cool night air.

Manny falls down to the ground and looks at it in bafflement.

Large, ripe apples form and droop from the branches of this newly re-born tree, which now looks completely out of place compared to its surroundings. Manny stands up and plucks one of the apples. He looks at it. He squeezes it and feels its plumpness. He bites into it with a loud, juicy crunch.

"This tastes—*WOW!*"

He's never had an apple this delicious; those that the NRP provides aren't nearly this good. He wipes the juice from his mouth and laughs heartily.

"I cannot believe this!" Manny exclaims.

As soon as he says it, the apple rots in his hand.

The tree returns to its withered and dry state.

The leaves fall and disintegrate on the ground.

Manny is shocked, again.

~ ~ ~

Whatever it is that's happened to him is more real than he imagined. Jonah must've had an idea about this all along; he must've been preparing for it for quite some time. Maybe that's why he's been hiding away out in the Outskirts, taking notes, studying, writing, and researching. Maybe he knew all along.

Manny paces, and scratches his head. He looks at the tree again.

"*Live!*"

The tree immediately returns to its state of bearing the most beautiful and delicious apples imaginable.

He laughs.

He looks down at the ground.

"Water..."

The icy ground beneath him melts. It pools into a small pocket that the earth has formed and becomes clear; it's like it has purified itself. Manny stoops down, removes his glove, and scoops some of it into his hand. He sniffs it. He tastes it. Far better than what the Preservers provide from the Reservoirs; nearly perfect, if perfection can even be attained.

Manny stands up with another laugh, blown away by these newfound *abilities*.

And then, tears. Lots of them. He cries, not out of sadness, but amazement.

Thoughts and feelings of unworthiness and gratefulness overwhelm him.

"...you can shake the foundations of the planet if you believe...the entire universe

will bend to your will...you can move the unmovable...and do the unthinkable..."

He whispers it to himself with a grin, remembering his conversation with the man from his spirit-lapse. No matter what happens from this point forward, he knows that nothing will ever be the same after tonight.

Just as he starts to approach the tree to take another apple, it dawns on him:

"I've got to get home! Mom is going to KILL me..."

He turns back toward Naza and resumes his rush home. At the same moment that the thought of getting home as quickly as he can hits his mind, a gust of wind blasts into his back and lifts him off of the ground. He's taken by surprise. He looks behind him and sees nothing. Again, he thinks about his need to quickly get home. Another gust—longer and more pronounced this time. He looks down as his feet dangle in the air just above the earth. This time, when the wind stops, he tumbles to the ground and does a forward roll.

"This is absolutely CRAZY!"

He stands. He focuses his mind and closes his eyes. When he does, a strong wind comes again from behind him and he rises into the air, riding on top of it. He grins and yells at the top of his lungs. It doesn't take long for him to master maneuvering his body through the air like he's been doing it his entire life; it feels uncannily natural.

He leans forward and soars through the sky like an eagle. Still yelling with utter joy, he climbs higher and higher, almost to cloud level. He does a few dips, dives, barrel rolls, and loops.

After he's high enough, he looks down at the entire city hub of Naza. He stops and hovers; the wind sustains him in his position as he controls it with his thoughts. He peers down, squinting, studying the planet from miles above, looking for something specific.

His eyes catch a small cluster of buildings.

"There it is…"

He locates his section of Naza, and without hesitation, he jets toward it, poking holes in the bluish-gray clouds that hang in the crispy night firmament.

45. JUST BELIEVE

HE LANDS IN the area just behind his apartment building, the same place that he goes to study at evening—a hard landing; his thighs and feet sting.

"I've got to work on that..." Manny says with a chuckle.

He scurries around the building and up the steps, breathing heavily. It's nearly pitch-black outside. Grea, Jhenda, and Rock are all sprawled around his living room. Grea wakes up first; she hears keys jingling as Manny struggles to get them into the key hole.

"Manny? Is that you?" Grea whispers as the door creaks open. She begins to stand and squints in the darkness to try to make out the silhouette entering the apartment.

"What are you all *doing* here?" Manny exclaims as he lights a large candle, unsure of what else to say; he's a bit startled and wasn't expecting them to be there.

"Wait, whoa, whoa, *WHOA*...what are we *doing* here? Where have you *BEEN* is the question!" Grea says somewhat loudly.

"Shhhhh! *Goodness!* Keep your *voice* down!"

Rock rolls over on the floor.

"Ughhhh, is that Manny?" he says, still half asleep.

"YES! It's *RUDE* Emmanuel Kohen! *What are we doing here? I can't believe you just said that...*" Grea grumbles as she folds her arms tightly across her chest.

Now Jhenda pops up from the couch.

"Are you okay? Where've you been?" Jhenda says.

"It's…it's sort of a long story…"

"Well, *clearly*! We have all night," Rock responds.

By now, Martha is making her way out of her bedroom and into the hallway. When she gets into the living room, the lights are still dim so she can't see well. Her limp has gotten worse—she's in much more pain now than she was a few days ago.

"What's going *on* out here?" she asks while looking at Grea who's the closest to her.

Grea points at Manny. Martha's eyes slowly drift toward him as he stands by the door.

"Manny! Oh my *goodness*…are you okay? What *happened*?"

She makes her way to him as quickly as she's able and grabs a hold of him. She squeezes him with the little strength that she can muster; he wraps his right arm around her in reassurance.

"I'm okay, relax. I'm okay! It's a long, long story…"

"Well, tell us what's going ON Manny! We were worried sick…"

"It's okay, mom. I promise."

"Manny, they told me about what happened at the IE earlier. I just…I'm worried about you? What *really* happened?" Martha asks in a voice sprinkled with concern and fear.

Manny releases his mother and motions for her to sit down. They all take seats around the room and stare at Manny. He rubs his neck while looking at each of them, then begins to speak:

"Well, it started at the IE. I saw, well…"

He pauses and looks at each of their faces again. They stare back blankly, waiting for him to continue.

"There's no easy way to say it, so I'll just say it. I saw a Shedim and a Watcher. That's why I lost it a little…I had never seen either before…"

Silence.

"Wait, a *what*, and a *what?*" Rock responds.

"A *Shedim* and a…well, a demon and an angel, basically…"

Another pause.

"Okay, he's *sick*, guys. Seriously. Rock, you were right. What do we do now?" Jhenda says, looking at both Rock and Grea.

"I'm not sick, I'm being serious! I saw them, and the angel killed the demon. And so, I went to Jonah afterwards, and he gave me a key, and a map, and he had a bunch of notebooks and papers...and..."

They all stare at him with puzzlement stitched onto their faces.

"...and I got into this underground trap door, which led to a tunnel in a part of the bunkers, and then those guys from the NRP busted in, and they took Jonah..."

Grea puts her hands on her face. In her mind, she's watching her best friend completely lose his sanity. Manny tends to ramble when he gets excited, so they let him finish before they interject or ask any more questions.

"...and so, I went to this place, outside of the city, and it had all of these books, posters, and Jonah's research, and I had another out of body experience, and now I have these abilities. I left to come back here, and brought this apple tree to life, and then I flew home..."

No one says a word for at least ten seconds. They all stare at Manny, partially waiting to see if he is going to burst out laughing and tell them that he's joking.

He doesn't.

"I know it sounds crazy. I wouldn't believe it either, but... it's true..."

"Wow," Rock finally says, "I didn't know it had gotten *this* bad," he finishes.

"I'm telling the truth! Okay, I'll just show you..."

Manny looks around the room, searching for something. He spots a candle in the corner that isn't lit.

"*On,*" he says confidently.

When the word leaves his mouth, the candle bursts with flame and brightens the entire room far beyond the brightness that a candle should be able to create. The light is blinding. Everyone covers their eyes and turns their heads away.

"*Off,*" he says.

The fire fizzles out within a few seconds.

"*What the heck?!* How did you do that?" Jhenda says as she opens her eyes and lowers her hands.

"How *DID* you do that?" Grea adds.

"That's not all…"

Manny stands up quickly. Rock's mouth is wide open, still in shock over the candle. Manny walks to the center of the room and stops.

"You know, over the past few weeks, I've done a lot of reading from your Grandeurscript, ma…"

Martha nods her head reflexively, looking just as confused as Rock.

"I've remembered a lot of the things that I used to think about, and ask about, and pray about when I was a lot younger… the things that I got away from as I got older, and more bitter, I suppose…"

He scratches his head and looks down, a bit embarrassed.

"But it's been good. It really has, lately. Better. I remember a lot of it. I remember all of the things that I used to know so well. It's all been coming back to me. Like, when the believers were in that room. Waiting, unsure of what would happen next, feeling abandoned probably. Feeling lost and confused. Possibly doubting. But then there was a wind…"

A tear forms in Martha's eye as she listens to her son. She couldn't be any prouder than she is right now. There's even a gleeful smile on Grea's face. She's speechless. Rock isn't totally sure what's going on, but he's never seen this side of Manny before. There's something powerful about him. His confidence.

His demeanor. He feels like he's looking at a man that's standing eight feet tall. Jhenda feels what Rock feels. She gets a glimpse of Manny's authority and leadership. She admires it, and there is nothing that she wouldn't do to support and back him in whatever decision he chooses to make, trusting that leading isn't just something he does, but it's a part of who he is, when he's absolutely sure of something.

Manny lifts both of his hands above his head.

He closes his eyes.

He takes in a deep breath.

"LET US FEEL YOUR WIND…"

A faint noise can be heard off in the distance. It sounds like it's miles away, but is approaching them like a runaway train that's lost its emergency breaks. It rapidly increases in pitch and volume. Everyone looks around, attempting to determine what it is and where precisely it's coming from.

There are three candles sitting on a table just in front of Manny. They flicker on all of a sudden. The noise keeps growing; it sounds like a tornado by now. In the next few moments, a very strong gust of wind blows into the room, swiftly and powerfully. A blue mist circles through the entire apartment and around Manny. It enters and exits his body repeatedly. His head is tilted back and his arms are still raised in the air as it happens.

The wind blows Rock backward in his chair. Martha is blown backward in hers as well, almost to the point of it tipping over. Jhenda is blown off of the couch and is pinned to the floor. Grea is stuck between the couch's arm and the deep corner between it and the cushion. They all scream, but the wind is too strong and loud for anyone's voice to be heard.

For a short while, they can do nothing accept acquiesce to the wind's will.

Manny lowers his hands, and the wind subsides.

When everything calms, Rock, of course, is the first to say something:

"WHOA! WHOA! WHAT IN THE WORLD WAS THAT?!" he exclaims.

They adjust their clothes and pick things up from the floor.

Rock jumps up and bear hugs Manny. Manny laughs.

"How is this even *REAL?*"

"It's the Creator. *HE* is real. He's so much bigger than we've ever dreamed or imagined. I don't know why me, but he's proven himself to me. He wants to use me…to use…*us*…for something…"

Grea, Jhenda, Rock, and Manny continue to pick up things around the room and place them back where they belong. Martha helps for a while too, until she gets very tired. She lets out a long sigh as she sits down and rubs her leg through her gown; only Manny notices her. Sadness and pity come over him. Then something dawns on him. He makes the face of a young man who has just had the brightest idea of his life.

He walks over to her as she sits in the chair that's next to the kitchen table. He kneels next to her and holds her hand with a smile. She smiles back and rubs his head then allows her caress to fall to his cheek.

"Look at you…" she whispers, proudly.

"How is it?" he says, touching her knee.

"Well, I manage," she responds as her expression changes.

She rubs the damaged leg once more.

"Let me see it," he requests, unflinchingly.

"Oh, no, no. It's fine. Really…"

He looks at her with as serious of a face as she's ever seen him give her.

"Let me see it, ma…just trust me…"

"Manny, don't. Don't…" she says when she realizes that he's not letting it go.

"Just trust me…okay?" he urges her.

There's such a peace and joy in his eyes that she can't say no again.

The others have finished straightening up the room; it's quaint and cozy again. They all enter the kitchen to see what Manny and Martha are talking about. They can sense that the moment is a serious one, so they remain quiet.

Martha complies with her son's request and carefully lifts her garment, just enough for her bruised leg to be exposed. It's a variety of colors: reds, purples, blacks, and blues; they all decorate her once beautifully tanned skin. She still has a few scars on her hands as well, but the leg wounds are most noticeable.

Rock and Grea casually look away, not wanting to make Martha any more uncomfortable or embarrassed than she already probably is. Jhenda doesn't. She stares as Manny prepares to do whatever it is that he has in his mind. Martha notices Jhenda's face. She's sorrowful. She can feel Jhenda's pity for her. When Jhenda looks up and they make eye contact, Martha does her best to reassure her with a smile.

"Okay. Are you ready?"

"Yes, Manny."

"Mom…"

"Yes…"

She looks into his eyes and sees a freedom that she hasn't seen since he was a little boy asking her every question that popped into his young mind, before the blasts.

"Just believe…" Manny whispers.

He smiles at her as she feels warmth surround her. At the very same time, Manny reaches his hand out and touches the center of the bruised area on her leg. The warmth intensifies, so much so that the room glows with a pulsing light. Grea, Jhenda, and Rock are startled all over again. They back away from Manny and Martha. The event lasts for just ten seconds or so, and then the room returns to normal.

They can't believe their eyes.

"*Miss Martha?!*" Grea exclaims as she raises both of her hands to her mouth.

Martha stands up and wraps her arms around herself with her eyes closed. She opens them and grins until her once wrinkled cheeks poke out like two tiny red balloons.

"Oh, my *goodness*! She looks twenty years younger," Jhenda says in astonishment.

Had they not witnessed it themselves, none of them would have believed it. Just moments ago, her entire frame was crumpled over. She limped when she walked. Her skin was tough and showed only faint signs of a once thriving beauty, which was quickly fading away into the recesses of time. Her hair resembled grayish cobwebs entangled in the dull branches of an oak tree.

Now, her cheeks are rosy, her eyes are bright and clear, and her hair is a thick, vibrant red. Her skin looks like high quality fabric, tightly wrapped around the curvy contour of an African drum.

Martha stands before them, completely transformed.

"Well, Jhenda, I have to say, I *feel* twenty years younger too!"

She lifts her dress and spins in a circle on one foot. The group laughs with shock and wonder in their voices. She immediately turns to her beloved son.

"Oh, *Manny*..."

She places her hands on his cheeks and smiles with tears in her eyes.

"I knew that he was real. But *this*...this is..."

She looks down at herself. She feels like she can leap, and run, and dance, the way that she did as a young woman.

"How did you...how did I..."

Manny shakes his head and places his finger on her lips.

"Just, *believe...*"

The group stays up all night, into the wee hours of the morning, talking, laughing, and admiring Martha's revitalization. They spend a brief time praying together too.

Even Rock leads one of the small prayers of thanks to the Creator. They realize that it will be time for work in just a few hours. They decide to all catch the TRN-3 instead of Rock and Grea attempting to get back home first. Jhenda decides to catch it with them too; she can catch up with the other Collectors at one of the stops on the way to the Shield.

The day has certainly been less than ordinary.

But none of them expect what's to come in just a few more hours.

46. STOP!

THEY WALK DOWN the steps and speak to each other cheerfully.

Jhenda can't take her eyes off of Martha.

"I just can't believe it. I mean, I saw it...but *how*? How is it possible?" she says.

Manny laughs with a glimmer in his eye.

"You know, I actually don't know for sure, but..." Manny says as he points up to the sky without finishing his sentence.

Jhenda looks up too.

"This is just insane! Like, you have super powers basically!" Rock says.

"Well, I wouldn't say all of that..."

Their eyes catch the TRN-3 as it approaches like a gigantic metal worm.

"Train's almost here," Grea says amongst all of the other voices in the crowd just in front of Manny and Martha's building.

People migrate toward the train doors as it slows to a stop. Manny and the others are near the back of the crowd, still chatting. About a minute passes and they start to hear noise coming from the front of the crowd, close to the train. People are knocking on the train's door and yelling:

"Hey, open up!"
"What's going on?!"
"Open the door, conductor!"
"We're going to be late!"
"What's your problem?!"

The rest of the crowd looks toward the commotion. The train is still sitting perfectly still and the doors haven't opened yet, which is unusual. No one wants to be behind schedule and then have to deal with any repercussions from the supervisors or Nerps; they don't want their rations to be jeopardized.

More knocking. More yelling.

"I wonder what's going on?" Rock says.

"I'm not sure," Jhenda replies.

Martha moves her head from side to side trying to see.

Manny's face turns a little pale.

Grea notices.

"Hey, are you okay?" she asks, "you look sick all of a sudden..."

"*Oh no...*" Manny mutters with his eyes still locked on the doors of the train.

No sooner than he says the words, the train doors are ripped open and Nerps rush out of it like fire ants from a disturbed dirt mound. They begin grabbing anyone close to them and tossing them to the ground. They have short yellow and black batons which match their uniforms. The batons produce a surge of powerful electric current. Whenever one is used on a Remnant, they become petrified and as stiff as wood. After shocking someone, the Nerps look at a display screen that's attached to their uniforms on the inside of their forearms.

"*It's not him!*" some of them say.

"*Check this one! This may be him! Quickly!*"

Manny grabs a hold of his mother, Grea, and Jhenda. Rock is standing in front of the group and spreads his arms out to shield them.

"What in the world is going on?!" Rock exclaims.

"What's happening, guys? What is this?" Jhenda says loudly.

The crowd disperses. Everyone runs. One of the Nerps notices and sends commands over a radio that's embedded into his suit. They are equipped with state-of-the-art technology. All of the Nerps hold their batons in the air and strike them against each other. As they do, an electric force field forms and encircles the crowd.

A handful of people are already too close to the force field by the time it fully forms and can't stop running in time. As soon as they encounter the circular fence of controlled lightning, the energy knocks them to the ground—unconscious.

"What do we do?" Martha says while crying.

Jhenda and Grea are both huddled together with her, holding each other and weeping. Rock still stands before them.

Manny breathes heavily; sweat pouring from his face.

~ ~ ~

In the very next moment, Manny is standing in front of Rock. None of them remember him moving, but things were happening so fast, that it's hard to recollect the details.

They do however remember what they heard:

"STOP!"

About twenty people who are directly in front of him fall to the ground. The force field that the Nerps had created disintegrates. The entire crowd freezes, Nerps included. There is total calm, and all eyes are on Manny. No one is sure how he produced such a strong and intense sound from human lungs and vocal cords. They aren't even sure if he produced it; it's like the word came from the sky and landed on all of them. No one moves an inch.

"You're looking for me. Leave these people alone..." Manny says authoritatively.

Manny walks toward the Nerps. After snapping out of his bewilderment, Rock grabs Manny's arm.

"No! No, Manny, you can't go with them—I won't let you!"

Manny looks back at Rock.

"It's okay…it's okay. Watch out for them…"

He points at Jhenda, Grea, and Martha.

"I have to go…"

Rock looks at them, then looks back into Manny's eyes; he sees certainty and conviction like never before. He finally nods and says, "okay…okay, I will…"

Manny turns back to the Nerps who have now split into two lines, both leading to the door of the train on both sides. Manny walks past them cautiously. Once he reaches the steps, he looks back one final time. Everyone in the crowd is still motionless and staring. Not a sound is made, except for the sobs of Grea, Jhenda, and especially Martha.

He catches Martha's eyes.

He smiles at her weakly, then turns, and steps onto the train.

After all of the Nerps are inside, the doors close, and the TRN-3 coasts away.

47. I CAN'T

THE TRAIN STOPS after a long ride.

Manny's been blindfolded nearly the entire time. He could've freed himself, but chose not to; he wants to see where this goes. The Nerps march him down a path with a hard surface. They walk into a building with hollow corridors that produce a distinct echo. They take an elevator up a few floors. He listens to the breathing of the Nerps and tries to count how many there are—at least twelve. They walk him into a room, seat him, and snatch his blindfold off. He looks around and notices a surgical table, a desk, and a stool in front of him; he's in some sort of medical facility.

"Stay put," one of the Nerps says.

They exit the room.

Manny sits there at ease. Understanding his abilities now, he's not worried. Although, he is very curious about where exactly he is and why he was brought here. He ponders it, but can't come to any solid reasons or conclusions.

Three Nerps walk back into the room. They grab him by his arms and legs. Again, he doesn't fight them. A woman in a long white lab coat walks in with a needle. She sticks him in the arm and withdraws a blood sample, then they all exit.

Manny sits up and looks at his arm.

"Heal," he whispers.

The small hole closes and the bit of blood evaporates.

He grins.

He waits for at least thirty minutes. The room is cold. The walls and ceiling are white. He's never liked being in medical facilities, or anything that resembles one; and he certainly doesn't like needles. He thinks of the gymnasium for a second.

Footsteps tap in the hallway. A handful of Nerps enter the room, along with six other people dressed in long white lab coats. A dark-skinned man stands in the center of them. He is bald with a salt and pepper goatee, and glasses that make him look very sophisticated. His smile causes Manny to want to smile back at him—he has a friendly and inviting presence.

"Hello, Emmanuel! I'm Doctor Ahmad. I'm sure you're wondering why we've brought you in. I hope that it wasn't *too* abrasive or alarming."

He has the thickest accent that Manny's ever heard.

The doctor approaches Manny and stretches out his hand; Manny shakes it firmly.

"Hello, Doctor."

"Nice to meet you finally, *Emmanuel*. That's a good, sturdy name. I like it! Mind if I have a seat?"

Dr. Ahmad points at the stool in front of Manny.

"Not at all...go ahead..."

He sits, rubs his thighs, and smiles at Manny again.

"I guess I'll get right to it."

He looks down at a clipboard that's in his hand and adjusts his glasses.

"As you know, we take regular blood samples from all Remnants, to make sure that no one has been exposed to radiation or any other fallout from Star Fall. Those samples are analyzed, the data is recorded, and we track them to ensure that significant changes do not occur over time. Big changes are red flags, and could mean that someone is either contaminated, or at risk of being contaminated. We want to protect all of the Remnants, so it's just a precaution. Does that make sense, Emmanuel?"

Manny stares at him while he processes the doctor's words.

"Yes, doctor."

Dr. Ahmad continues.

"Okay, good. Good! Well, we've noticed some...*interesting* things in your past few samples, to say the least..."

Manny shifts his weight in his seat.

"Interesting? Interesting how? Have I been contaminated?"

"No, no, relax. Your samples aren't showing any signs of major health risks, but, well, it's difficult to explain..."

"Is something wrong? Please tell me if there's something wrong with me..."

Manny feels panic beginning to overcome his heart. His abilities have become a distant thought now.

"Emmanuel, relax! You're perfectly healthy. We've just seen something that we can't fully grasp just yet..."

"I don't understand."

"Neither do we, but I'll do my best to explain...ladies and gentlemen, could you give us a moment, please?" Dr. Ahmad says as he turns to the others in the room.

The Nerps, physicians, and nurses quietly leave. The final one, a petite nurse with the most beautiful and vibrant gray hair Manny's ever seen, closes the door behind her.

"To properly explain, I have to give you a quick crash course in genetics—my life's work."

"I'm listening..." Manny says curiously.

"Good. Trust me, I will make this as quick and simple as possible. I'm pretty good at that. I have a five-year-old daughter who *constantly* asks what I do at work every day..."

Manny grins and nods.

"Okay, so here we go..."

Dr. Ahmad slides in his chair closer to Manny.

"As human beings, all of our body parts, bones, skin, hair, and so on—are made up of cells. They are the smallest structural and functional units of our bodies. I mean, the things are *teeny tiny.*"

Dr. Ahmad squints and pinches his fingers together as he says the words, causing Manny to grin again.

"Each cell has *liquid stuff* called *cytoplasm,* a nucleus, and is surrounded by a cell membrane. They make up everything about us. Now, inside of the nucleus, you have what's called a chromosome. You've probably heard that term before."

"Yes, I think that I have."

"Good! Good! Chromosomes are basically little pieces of genetic thread made of acids and protein. You've got X and Y chromosomes. They determine whether someone is male or female; XX for female, and XY for male."

He pauses and looks into Manny's eyes, attempting to discern whether or not he understands. He appears to, so Dr. Ahmad continues.

"Now, the chromosomes carry our genetic information; our genetic code. It's like the recipe for a person. *Human ingredients,* in a sense; the things that determine eye color, hair color, and everything else about us."

"I understand," Manny says.

"Wonderful! Okay, so chromosomes are made from something called *Deoxyribonucleic Acid,* better known as DNA."

"Oh, okay, yes. I've heard that term too."

"I figured that you probably have. Same thing; it's just our *human recipe* basically. I won't bore you with any more of the monotonous details, but let's just suffice it to say that DNA is made up of a bunch of segments called genes. Genes are the building blocks of us all. That's it in a nutshell; now, you're a geneticist!"

Manny peers at Dr. Ahmad blankly.

"Have you found something wrong with my DNA—with my genes?"

Dr. Ahmad pauses. There's a brief silence.

"You're not easily distracted are you, Emmanuel?"

Manny gives him a half grin. It's about as much as he can muster to conceal his worry and concern.

"I'm getting to that. So, we understand chromosomes, DNA, and genes now; a little better anyway, right?"

"Right…"

"Well, the Naza Medics noticed a few things that they can't explain from your past few samples. They sent me the results a couple of weeks ago. I'm from New Ethiopia, and I'm considered the top geneticist in the world today. I've been doing some research and tests, and I've never seen anything like it. That's why I flew in from overseas; that's why I'm here in New America. I wanted to meet you in person and share these things with you."

Manny nods, finally understanding why Dr. Ahmad has such a heavy accent.

"What's wrong with me?"

Dr. Ahmad looks at him with sympathy.

"Manny, there is a specific gene encoded in our DNA that has been a mystery to the science world for a very long time. There are a lot of speculations, theories, and inconclusive studies about it, but to be blunt, we don't fully know what it does or how it functions. What we've seen over years and years of tests and observations is that we see more of this particular gene in people who believe in a higher power…people who believe in some form of the Creator…and less of the gene in people who do not. Again, that's inconclusive. We were instructed to observe it more after Star Fall, at the request of the NRP…"

Dr. Ahmad looks away.

"What are you saying, Doctor?"

"Emmanuel, from the time that you were a child up until about two or three weeks ago, your records have shown that you had a very low count of this, *mystery gene*."

Dr. Ahmad rolls his chair over to the wall, pulls down a white screen, and turns on a projector. He pulls some clear, laminated sheets from his clipboard and places them on the projector, showing colorful images with years above each picture.

"These images are your blood samples, with the gene that we've discussed colored in blue. I will scroll through them year by year…"

Manny looks at the images as Dr. Ahmad scrolls and sees small splotches of blue here and there over the years of his life, starting with age eight.

"Now, here are your samples over the past few weeks…"

When Dr. Ahmad shows Manny his sample from two weeks ago; nearly the entire image is covered in blue. He takes in a deep breath, remembering that it was around that time when he experienced his first *spirit-lapse*.

"Your body started to randomly produce large amounts of the gene, very rapidly. Although it's extremely unusual, it wouldn't be a cause for any type of alarm. What *is* alarming however is that not long after that, it looks as though the genes have, well… mutated…"

"*Mutated?*"

"Yes. Your body has apparently begun to produce proteins and genes that we've never seen before in the history of genetics. We have no idea how it's even happening, but there are clearly brand-new genes in your system that were never there before, or anywhere else in the world for that matter…*ever*…"

Dr. Ahmad pulls up three images side by side showing blue, red, and purple colors.

"These images are your samples from two weeks ago, one week ago, and this morning. Your original genes, shown in blue again, have begun to merge with these other brand-new mystery genes, shown in red, and are forming a *completely new* gene, shown in bright purple…"

Manny stares at the charts with his mouth dropped open.

"To put it simply, your body is producing lots of the original mystery gene, plus a brand-new mystery gene, and the two are fusing together to create a *third* mystery gene..."

Manny is dead silent. His mind is racing.

"You haven't shown any health issues; no problems whatsoever. You don't show any physical changes. Nothing. It makes no sense. We've never seen *anything* quite like this before. As I said before, we are already uncertain about exactly what the original gene does, aside from the spiritual and religious theories that have been proposed in the past. But I have to admit, we are *totally* clueless about what happens when these genes spontaneously couple with new genes that we didn't even know existed."

When Manny glances at the chart again, it clicks. One of the images looks exactly like the sketch that he saw at Jonah's hideout just the night before. He can't take his eyes off of it.

"THE YAHWEH GENE..."

Manny says it to himself, just loud enough for Dr. Ahmad to hear faintly, but not loud enough to understand what was said. He does however hear him say the word *"gene,"* and something before it.

"I'm sorry, Emmanuel? What was that?"

"Nothing, nothing, Doctor Ahmad..." he responds nervously.

Dr. Ahmad notices that Manny is very antsy all of a sudden, and then Manny's face goes completely blank; he looks like he's completely lost touch with reality.

"Emmanuel?"

No response.

"Emmanuel!"

Nothing.

Manny's consciousness is being sucked into a vacuum.

He hears the Voice echoing all around him:

"YOU MUST GO...YOU MUST GO...YOU MUST GO"

Finally, he snaps out of it as Dr. Ahmad calls him once more: *"EMMANUEL!"*

"Yes! Sorry. Umm, I have to go. May I go now?"

Dr. Ahmad is the one who appears nervous now.

"Well, Emmanuel, I'm sorry...but I *can't* let you go..."

"What do you mean you *can't*? You can't let me go? I need to...I need to get to the Shield. I'm late."

"Oh, don't worry. I'm sure that your absence will be excused today."

"Then, I need to get home..."

Dr. Ahmad makes his way toward the door. He cracks it open and motions with his hand. The Nerps and those in lab coats pour back into the room.

"I'm afraid that it's a bit more, *complicated*, than that. We... we actually, have orders from the NRP to...well...keep you here for just a *little* longer..."

As he talks, the people who just came into the room move in front of the door to block it. Some stand at Manny's sides, at a safe distance. Manny looks at one of the Nerps—he is firmly clutching his baton.

Manny drops his head and thinks. He wonders if he should use his powers. Maybe blast them with a strong gust of wind and knock them unconscious? Perhaps just crumble the entire building? He feels himself getting both angry and nervous; a dangerous combination, especially for someone with his unique skills.

Just then, Manny hears a high-pitched tone in his ears.

Time slows to almost a complete standstill.

Then, the separation.

Manny's consciousness steps out of his body as it has the few times in his recent past; he's gotten a bit more comfortable with it now. As he scans the room, everyone looks like statues. Their movements are so slight and delayed that it takes them several seconds to complete the simplest task, such as a blink, or an inhale.

Manny watches in amusement for a just a little while, then he searches for his entrance into the Way.

There, he sees it, to his right against the wall.

He gets a running start and dives in.

48. IT HAS BEGUN

MILLIONS OF FACES peer up at him from this beautiful cloud that he's come to enjoy.

He feels free here.

A man is standing afar off, waving his arms frantically in the air. He has a long beard and wears a knitted brown cloak. There's a youthful hope in his eyes. Manny's body is drawn in by an unseen force toward him. Just before they collide, the man smiles at him and nods as if to say, *"yes, me…you've found me."*

Manny accelerates.

A bright flash.

Quiet.

~ ~ ~

Manny's eyes open and he's at a gate just outside of an ancient city, waving his arms just as the man had done on the Cloud only moments before.

It's dark.

Two figures are approaching in white raiment.

When they are close enough, Manny feels the weight of their presence; a power that he's never sensed. It's as if there's a pressurized force field all around them; like the force of gravity increases as they get closer. This force pulls Manny down into a bow before them.

"I beg you, come and stay at my house tonight...*both* of you," Manny pleads.

"No thank you. We'd like to stay in the town square instead."

"Sirs, I *beg* you, *come* and stay with me..." Manny pleads.

The two beings look at each other. One of them nods at the other, then they both nod at Manny. The three turn and walk into the city.

~ ~ ~

Time lapses.

Now, they are sitting around a table, inside of a quaint home, speaking in a jolly fashion, and eating delicious food.

Then they hear footsteps outside; *many* of them.

It sounds as though an army is approaching. Manny stands up and looks out of the window; he sees hundreds of men, young and old.

They surround the house, yelling at the inhabitants:

> *"Where are they?!"*
> *"Where are those two men?"*
> *"Bring them! Give them to us!"*

Manny steps outside and holds his hands out, attempting to calm the rambunctious mob.

"Brothers, no, no! I cannot do that! Please, do not act this way! Leave these men alone!"

"Move aside! They belong to us!" the crowd continues.

Manny hears his door open, and then a strong hand pulls him from behind. He leaves his feet momentarily.

He's back inside the house and the door has closed. One of the men stands between him and the door. The other stands next to him. The two men glare at each other once more and nod, just as they did at the gate of the city.

All of a sudden, their faces begin to shine like diamonds and light up the entire room. The one near the door bursts into light beneath his garments. Manny covers his eyes. The man turns toward the door and lifts his hands as the yells and jeers continue to pour in from outside.

A loud hum, then brief quietness.

Manny runs to the window and looks out again:

"What has happened to us?!"
"I AM BLIND!"
"Help us! We cannot see!"
"What type of witchcraft is this?"

The men and boys are groping around, trying to find the door to the house. They have no vision whatsoever.

Manny is sucked back into the Way in an instant.

~ ~ ~

He comes through the wall of the medical facility and sees Dr. Ahmad still moving his lips. He sees himself on the table sitting patiently, surrounded by Nerps, doctors, and nurses. He steps back into his body.

~ ~ ~

"We're sorry, Manny," Dr. Ahmad continues.

"But we must…"

Without a word more, Manny jumps up from the table. Everyone backs away from him. His entire body gradually starts to shine as bright as the sun with a loud humming noise and everyone in the room covers their faces.

Manny lifts his hands.

They scream.

Blindness.

All of them.

They hold out their hands to feel their way around. Terror and shock are in their voices. Manny quickly maneuvers through them and heads for the door. Dr. Ahmad has fallen to the ground and is crawling, trying to find his glasses in a panic. As Manny passes him, he touches his head. Immediately, Dr. Ahmad's sight is restored. He looks at Manny. Manny smiles back. Everyone else is still blind and bewildered.

"I'm sorry, Doctor, but I've got to go..." Manny says as Dr. Ahmad peers at him, still crouched on the floor with his jaw dropped, and nodding his head quickly and nervously in agreement.

"You should go too. Go back to your home and to your family," Manny says.

And with that, he exits the room.

Dr. Ahmad hurriedly picks up his glasses, puts them on, stands, then looks around at all of the others blindly feeling around and shrieking in a confused horror.

He gathers his clipboard and runs out of the room.

~ ~ ~

As time passes, another thirty minutes or so, they all regain their sight. They ask each other what happened. No one is sure. The door swings open forcefully. The entire room jumps to attention with their heads lifted high and their eyes straight forward. Footsteps click across the room.

"Where...is...he?"

The voice is Damien's.

Levi and Polus have entered with him, but both stand off to the side.

"He...he got away, sir," one of the Nerps responds. He has many more badges on his uniform than the others. Damien lets out a slow breath.

"And the Doctor?"

"He's gone too...sir..."

Damien closes his eyes, lowers his head, and rubs his forehead like he's just developed a spontaneous migraine. Moments later, in a fit of rage, he makes a tight fist and begins panting heavily. He lets out a fierce, primal yell, turns, and lunges toward the row of Nerps standing just behind him.

His fist pierces the closest Nerp to him; a fairly young and athletically built man. Blood squirts from his chest. Levi and Polus back up; so does everyone else in the room. The Nerp's hands drop to his sides and he falls limp, seeing Damien's glowing yellow eyes as a final sight.

Damien's hand slides out of the Nerp's chest as the body falls to the floor. Damien kneels beside the corpse and studies it for a few seconds. He reaches into his breast pocket and removes his flask. Without flinching, he gathers some of the deceased Nerp's blood into the flask, and then returns it to his pocket.

He stops, and looks around the room. No one dares to make eye contact with him.

He holds his arm out.

"Your coat," he says, with his hand pointed toward one of the female nurses to his side. The woman nervously removes her lab coat and hands it to Damien as his fingers flick, motioning for her to hurry.

He takes the piece of clothing and wipes the blood from his hand and arm. He continues looking at the Nerp sprawled on the floor, then nonchalantly tosses the bloodied garment onto his lifeless corpse.

"Find him…" Damien says with a low voice.

No one moves.

"NOW!" he yells.

Everyone runs from the room except Levi and Polus. Damien stands with splotches of blood still left on his hand.

He notices it, then sucks some of it from his fingertips.

"It has begun," Damien says.

49. TWO NIGHTS

ABOUT TWO WEEKS have passed.
No one has seen or heard from Manny.
Not even Martha.
There's been an endless search for him; an officially documented manhunt orchestrated by the NRP in all regions and city hubs of New America. The number of Nerps stationed at each of the worksites has been increased, primarily at the Shield. The unrest and tension lingering in the air feels strangely like the days just after Star Fall; it's all too familiar.

Manny's friends have been in dismay; they're broken-hearted about his absence and uncertain of his safety. Martha has taken it harder than any of them. Even though years of youth and health have been returned to her, she'd give it all back in exchange for him in a second.

They spend their evenings at Martha's apartment now—Grea, Rock, and Jhenda. Staying with her has been their attempt to console her ever since Manny was taken. In the process, they have brought a faint sense of solace to each other. They've pretty much moved in, and Martha welcomes them with open arms; it keeps her mind occupied. When all of them are together, it's a little easier to get through the increasingly difficult days.

~ ~ ~

It's afternoon. Martha is sitting with Valerie at lunch and can't seem to stop crying.

"I just don't know what to do, Val. They *took* him. Right in front of me—they took him. I don't know *where* he is..."

"You've *got* to pull yourself together! Come here," Valerie responds as she leans over and wraps her arms around Martha like a mother bear protecting her cub.

"Now listen to me, Manny is strong, and he's smart. He's going to be okay. Don't worry yourself..." Valerie says.

~ ~ ~

A few miles away, Grea paces around the lunch table at the Shield. Rock stands with his foot resting on the seat and his hand on his chin.

"This is crazy! We have to find him, Rock. We have to!"

"I know, but how? I mean, where do we even start?"

"I don't know," Grea says.

She's exasperated. She looks up at her brother.

"I don't know...but we've got to do something..."

~ ~ ~

Many more miles away, close to the city hub of Samaria, a group of Collectors dig through ditches retrieving rusty containers of gasoline at an abandoned gas station. Jhenda is with them. She's preoccupied with Manny's well-being too, like her newest friends—her newest family.

"Hey..." a man says, but Jhenda doesn't hear him.

"Hey, Jhenda!" he says again, louder this time.

She looks up.

"Here!" he says as he hands her two very large containers to place into their transport vehicle.

She takes them, drags them across the sand, and sits them onto a pallet that will be hoisted into their truck. She leans on the side of the lift and looks off into the far distance where she can see a small cluster of buildings. It's Naza.

"Gosh, Manny…where are you…"

~ ~ ~

In that instant, they all hear it as clearly as if it came from right beside them, or from behind them:

"I'm okay, you all…I'm okay…"

It's Manny's voice; inexplicably and distinctly, Manny's voice.

~ ~ ~

Jhenda looks around frantically; she even stoops down and looks under the truck that she's standing next to.

"Manny?!" she screeches.

~ ~ ~

Grea and Rock stop talking and their eyes widen. Grea stops pacing and Rock pops up to attention. He looks at Grea.

"Did you hear that?" Rock says, confused.

"It's Manny? But…where is he?" Grea responds, equally bewildered.

~ ~ ~

Martha jumps so unexpectedly that Valerie lets out a light squeal and snatches her arms away.

"Manny? Manny?!" Martha says desperately.

"What's wrong?" Valerie asks.

"Manny! It's Manny! I just heard him!"

Valerie scrunches her face up and cocks her head to the side as she looks at Martha.

~ ~ ~

Each of them hear him, much in the same way that Manny hears the Voice, from a place deep inside:

"Hey, you all. I know that this is all VERY weird, but I'm okay. And yes, it's really me. I can't explain everything right now, but soon I will..."

~ ~ ~

Rock looks at Grea and says, "gosh, he sounds like Jonah now. That's *totally* something that he would say. How is this happening?"

"Quiet! Just listen!" Grea blurts back at him.

~ ~ ~

Martha cries even harder, with her quivering hands to her mouth.

"Girlie, what is wrong?" Valerie says with lots of concern.

"*Shhhhhhh...*" Martha says, stretching her hand out toward Valerie to quiet her.

~ ~ ~

Jhenda is stooped low to the ground like a trained soldier listening to the ambient noise around them for reconnaissance purposes. She closes her eyes to better focus on his voice and take in every word.

~ ~ ~

"I will meet with you all at mom's, two nights from now. And please, please...don't worry about me. I'm safe. I will see you soon..."

~ ~ ~

With that, they continue their day with a little bit more peace, and a *lot* more confusion than they had before.

50. NO TURNING BACK

THE NEXT COUPLE of days speed by. They all anticipate seeing Manny again as he promised—none of them doubt that he will keep his word. It would literally have to take the earth completely falling apart to prevent him from coming. The only scary thing is, the world falling apart isn't too farfetched; it's already happened once before.

"*How was it today?*"

This is usually the first question asked by one of them every single afternoon.

Between the random interrogations, being constantly monitored at work and on the trains, and even a handful of Nerps being stationed outside of their building, none of them feel completely safe or at ease. Manny's a wanted man, literally. They don't know about what happened at the NRP medical facility at all; all they remember is seeing his eyes peering back at them from the train weeks ago, surrounded by Nerps.

As much as they've talked about it over the past couple of evenings, they still can't come to any solid conclusions aside from, as Rock has said, "something has happened to him…something *big*…"

That evening: they sit, and they wait.

It's nighttime, and Manny is soaring high above in the air. He slows down as he approaches the center of Naza and spots his building. He can clearly see the yellow and black uniforms of Nerps stationed outside of it; their batons sparkling in the moonlight.

He hovers for a moment and watches them, then drifts to the back of the building and lands as softly as he can, so as not to be heard. He walks to the side of the building and sees a Nerp pacing back and forth, smoking a cigarette. Manny leans a little farther over and sees that there are four more accompanying him: two at the door, and two just before the train tracks.

He touches his temple with the tips of his pointer and middle fingers with his eyes closed.

"*Sleep,*" he whispers.

The five Nerps fall lifelessly to the ground. Two of them snore loudly. Manny lets out a soft giggle as he listens. Again, he touches his temple, closes his eyes, and says, "okay, meet me in *exactly* thirty-minutes, starting now...don't be late..."

He leaps up the steps to his mother's apartment.

As soon as the door opens, strong arms grab him and lift him from the ground.

"Oh my *GOSH*, Manny! I'm *so* glad to see you! I knew that you'd be here soon! I could just *feel* it!"

Rock squeezes him as tightly as he can. Manny can't help laughing.

"Oh, *Manny.* Are you okay? *Where* have you *been* all this time?!" Grea squeals.

His mother approaches and peeks over Grea and Jhenda's heads; they have also rushed to embrace him at the door. She piles in with them as they all hug and make sentimental noises. They back away and spend a few moments looking at Manny. He looks mostly the same, but there's something intangibly different. His energy and presence have completely changed. They can feel that he possesses something silently powerful.

He steps inside and closes the door.

"I'm fine you all, I'm perfectly fine!" he says with a wide grin.

"I just don't know how much more of this disappearing and kidnapping I can take!" Martha says with her hand on her chest, a bit jokingly, but still sincerely.

"I've been in the Outskirts. Studying. Listening. *Preparing...*" Manny says.

"Preparing? Preparing for *what*?" Rock asks with his face twisted.

"It's all around us, can't you see it? And feel it? Aren't things different?" Manny responds.

"Well, yes, things are very different...I honestly didn't think that they could get any worse, but they have," Grea says.

Manny motions for them all to sit down as he does the same. Once seated, he lets out a long, slow sigh.

"So, tell me. Tell me what's been going on since I was taken that day?"

"It's been terrible, Manny, just *terrible...*" Grea blurts out.

"Terrible how?" Manny asks.

"We're followed everywhere. And, they question us...I *hate* it..." Grea says.

"Question you? About what? And who exactly are...*they*?" Manny enquires with his eyebrows lowered.

The group looks sheepishly at one another as Manny waits for a response.

"Grea? Who are *they*?" Manny asks again, impatiently.

"Some guys from the NRP...three in particular..."

Manny's demeanor changes. He's noticeably angry. He thinks back to the Sabbath when Jonah was taken.

"The IE has been closed down until further notice, they say," Martha adds.

"The Awareness Tracts...they...they have you in them now. A picture of you, and they all say, *"wanted for questioning,"* and, *"if you have any information concerning the whereabouts of Emmanuel Kohen, please inform the blah blah blah...*" Jhenda says as she pulls one from her pocket and shows it to him.

He studies it carefully.

"Nerps have been crawling around here for days, watching us," Jhenda continues.

"We know it's because they're looking for you. We haven't told them anything, I mean, about what you can do. Is that why they want you?"

Manny is still studying the tract. He grunts as he slaps it down on the table, leans his head back, and closes his eyes. He leans back forward and rubs his forehead, then gazes at the floor in thought.

"It's not safe for me here anymore. I'm going to have to stay in the Outskirts from now on. That's the safest place for me...off the grid..."

"Manny...no! You can't! It's far too dangerous out there," Martha quickly objects.

"Things are different now. It's more dangerous for me here than it is out there. That's where I've been for the past couple of weeks. I've been fine. I don't want you to worry—I don't want any of you to worry. I know what I have to do."

"No, no, no! Mom is right...it's *way* too dangerous! We're coming with you, Manny," Rock protests.

Manny shakes his head.

"Now wait a minute, I've put you all in enough danger as it is. I can't let..."

"We're *not* taking no for an answer, Emmanuel Kohen..." Grea interrupts, sternly.

He's only heard her speak in this tone a handful of times, and each one of them was equally treacherous.

"We're coming..." Jhenda reaffirms.

He looks into each of their eyes.

Rock first; he sees an unshakable fierceness and determination. Then Grea; he sees her tenacity and willingness to follow him to the ends of the earth. Finally, Jhenda; he sees her courage and bravery—her wisdom and her ability to lead while following.

"*Okay...*" he says with a half grin, knowing that it will be impossible to deter them or convince them otherwise.

Rock pumps his fist. Grea clasps her hands together with a nod. Jhenda simply smiles and leans back into her chair.

"You can come with me. But regardless of what happens, there's *no* turning back after tonight. You all understand this, right?"

They look at each other, then look back at him and nod.

"*No* turning back," Jhenda says.

Manny lets a gust of air exit his mouth and smiles at her.

"*No turning back...*"

51. COMMAND

MARTHA SMILES, OVERJOYED to see them all together again, completely aware that they'll be safer if they stay that way.

Grea happens to glance over at Martha, who's been pretty quiet in the midst of their excitement. Rock and Jhenda notice too. Manny is looking at her while she clasps her hands and grins back at him with her eyes glistening.

"What about you, mom?" Manny says softly.

She leans forward to position herself in her seat better then scoots back again.

"Oh, I can't go to the Outskirts. My health and strength are restored, but I'm still an old lady at heart," she says touching her chest.

"I was afraid you'd say that...but I knew you would..." Manny replies.

"But..." Rock starts to say.

Martha lifts her hand in Rock's direction and shakes her head without looking at him, sensing that he'll object.

"I'll be fine, honestly. I don't think they're as worried about me as they are you all," she says.

Manny looks into her eyes as she curls her lips into another smile.

"I'll be fine," she mouths to him.

He nods in response, trusting her judgment.

Another few moments pass, then Manny looks down at his watch.

"Okay, we have to *go*, seriously. It's almost time..."

"Time for *what*?" Rock asks.

"Just trust me. You'll see."

Manny walks over to the window and gazes down at the train tracks just in front of the building. He sees that the Nerps are still lying on the ground, fast asleep. He walks back to the center of the room.

"Grab whatever things you may need and let's go guys..." Manny urges.

"Hey, some of us are *girls*," Grea says with grin.

Manny smiles back and hunches his shoulders.

"Okay, *you all,* then...better?"

She laughs and pushes his shoulder before jogging down the hallway to grab her belongings.

They scurry like hamsters around the apartment, gathering articles of clothing that have been left there since they first began to frequent Martha's apartment. Shoes, bits of rations, and toiletries are all stuffed into large bags with drawstrings. Manny periodically looks out of the window, at his watch, and then his mother—in that order. Her hands are interlocked and pressed snuggly under her chin. He can see and feel her worry, but remains silent.

It doesn't take the others long to pack their things, mostly due to their excitement. In the back of each of their minds, they are finally about to take a peek into Manny's increasingly mysterious world; maybe they'll even get a glimpse into the supernatural realm.

Three large duffle bags sit in the hallway now.

Manny's friends stand in the living room and gaze at him the way that the Remnant children gaze at the IE as the trains climb Sinai. Manny smiles at Martha. She smiles back, more out of an unspoken obligation than actual happiness. He walks to her, kneels in front of her, and places both of his hands on her shoulders.

"It's going to be okay," he says softly.

Martha stares into Manny's eyes. He looks away, but glances back periodically, trying to not look for too long. He knows that she's going to cry—he can feel it coming like water building up behind a cracked dam. She whimpers, nods, then closes her eyes to slow her tears.

"I always hate to see you go," she says with a broken voice.

He hugs her and pulls her head onto his shoulder.

He stands up, moves back a step, and then takes her right hand with his left, pulling her from her seat until she's standing. He reaches out for Jhenda with his free hand while looking at Grea and Rock, signaling with his head for them to do the same. After they've joined hands, he looks at each of them, slowly transitioning his gaze around the circle, and finally dropping his head into a solemn position.

They each follow suit.

"Creator, we thank you…for who you are, and not just for what you've done. Thank you for keeping us. Thank you, for keeping me. Thank you for…keeping my mother…"

He squeezes her hand tightly as he says the words.

"You've done some amazing things lately. Well, always, but I guess I am just recently realizing it. I thank you for that too. You've shown me your power. In all of these weeks of studying and experiencing you, you've taught me a lot…it's been so wonderful, and I honestly don't feel like I deserve it…"

He pauses and fights back tears himself. The knot in his throat begins to grow, but he continues.

"I know that this is just the beginning of many more things to come. Help me to just trust you. To learn more about you. And most of all, to be used by you. Help me to yield daily, and to surrender daily, so that your plan can be accomplished."

He opens his eyes and looks at his friends before closing them once again.

"Thank you for my friends. We ask for you to watch over us as we take this next portion of the journey together, into the Outskirts. Open their eyes and their minds to the things that you've shown me over the past few weeks. I know that you'll be faithful to do it. Prepare us for all that's ahead, the good and the bad. I'm certain that we'll encounter both, and I'm not afraid anymore. Continue to show us, teach us, and explain to us just how great, powerful, and *REAL* you are..."

Again, his eyes open, but this time he fixes them on his mother.

"As we go down this path, I plead with you to watch carefully over my mother. Comfort her heart and give her a deeper confidence in you. Let her know for sure that she will be taken care of no matter what. She's been faithful to care for me my whole life, so please be faithful and care for her too...besides Jhenda, Rock, and Grea...she's all I have..."

His voice trembles and tears drip down his cheeks. Martha is crying as well, mainly because of the gratefulness in her heart. Hearing her once dismissive and hard-hearted son praying such a bold, sincere, and touching prayer is inexplicably moving. The moment is nearly too much for her; her prayers have been answered.

~ ~ ~

At the same time, the floor beneath them rumbles gently. Rock feels it first, then Grea and Jhenda. All three of them look up and see Manny staring at his mother, then they look to each other. Rock shrugs. Grea and Jhenda interlock their arms as the rumbling increases.

"She's all that I have...and I *need* you...to *keep* her..."

Manny's voice becomes a bit firmer and more intimidating. He doesn't even blink an eye. The floor starts shaking with the magnitude of an earthquake's aftershock. Martha is looking around the room and also at Manny. The windows rattle. Small tables and chairs around the room begin vibrating hard enough to move about the floor. The wind has returned and is blowing through the small apartment; a swift breeze that causes their clothing to flap.

Manny yells over the wind with all of the might that he can muster:

"I COMMAND THAT PROTECTION AND PEACE REST HERE…"

No sooner than the words leave his mouth, a bright light flashes from the ceiling, and there are two loud thuds that sound like small explosions. Manny falls onto the couch, Grea, Rock, and Jhenda onto the ground, and Martha into her son's arms. Something has impacted the living room floor right next to them. The light is too bright for them to see. There is a high-pitched ringing sound suddenly. They all cover their ears and squeeze their eyes shut tightly until it dissipates.

When it does, Jhenda is the first to scream.

Followed by Grea.

Martha yells, then buries her head into Manny's chest.

Manny's eyes and mouth are wide open as he looks at the sight.

The only thing that Rock can manage to say is, *"WH… WHAT?!"*

52. WATCHERS

TWO LARGE BEINGS are kneeling on the floor, both with swords in their hands.

Even in their stooped position, they are over six feet tall. If they were to stand, their heads would easily puncture the ceiling. One is a metallic bronze color; an absolutely beautiful creature. He is a male, with long, woolen, black hair, and a thick beard. The other is made of what looks like crystallized red rubies—a woman. The surface of her skin appears as jagged as a cluster of mountains as viewed from many miles in the air; she looks like she has been chiseled from a large block of precious gemstone.

Their armor and swords couldn't possibly have been forged on earth. They're made of a metal that not only reflects light, but also seems to produce it. The armor and swords create high-pitched tones that modulate like musical notes. Two distinct sounds are being made, and are oscillating in perfect harmony.

The beings lift their heads. Both of their eyes are the clearest white light that any of them have ever witnessed. Both beings gaze at Martha.

"Who...who *are* you?" Martha asks nervously.

The metallic bronze entity speaks:

"I am Peace..."

The crystallized red ruby being follows his lead:

"...I am Protection."

In unison, they say:

"The Witness has summoned us—we are here to obey his command, which has reached the Creator, *Yahweh*."

As they say the name **Yahweh**, they bow their heads in reverence.

"*Watchers...*" Manny says, as the epiphany comes to him.

They both look at him and nod. He nods back at them.

In the very next instant, they both stoop lower to the ground, thrusting their humongous legs deeper into the floor and causing the room to shake again. Then, they leap into the air. In a smooth motion, they sheath their swords and stretch both hands above their heads. The flash of light in the ceiling appears again leaving a large gaping hole that they can all see through; it's more like a supernatural portal of some sort that allows the Watchers to pass through the ceiling without destroying it.

The sky is filled with stars.

The sight is breathtaking.

Protection and *Peace* fly into the air and hover about fifty yards above Martha's building, keeping watch. They soar in a circular motion; angelic guards. The ceiling slowly re-materializes until it looks as though it was never disturbed. The whole room is awestruck. None of them have any words. Each mouth hangs open in silence, except Manny's.

"*Just the beginning,*" he says confidently.

They're speechless still.

"Okay, we've *really* got to go now…"

Rock, Jhenda, and Grea grab their bags as Manny and Martha embrace each other.

"You're protected," he says to her, looking toward the ceiling with a grin.

She just smiles at him, with a few more tears and a tighter hug.

"I love you, mom," Manny says softly.

"I love you more," she gently responds.

As they reach the last step in the stairwell, and as Rock pushes open the door, a train stops right in front of them.

"Come on, *come on*! Get in!" Manny says, looking at the limp bodies of the Nerps as he zips by and climbs up the train's steps.

His three friends follow, rushing onto the train.

Grea glances at the train's conductor as she passes by him; she squints, then stops dead in her tracks.

"*Denzi*? Is that *you*?" Grea says with surprise bursting from her voice.

She hugs him tightly. So does Rock. They take a moment to introduce Jhenda.

"What are *you* doing with this…train?!" Grea continues.

"Connections my friends, *connections*! Keeping rations for the NRP has its benefits!"

"Let me drive!" Rock says with far too much excitement, and seriousness, in his voice.

"Rock, just sit down," Grea says with a shove to his back.

The train pulls away. When it's a few hundred yards past the apartment building and almost at its cruising speed, the Nerps begin to awaken. One of them shakes his head, lifts his face shield, and scratches his eye. The one next to him stretches, yawns, and then catches sight of the train. He taps his comrade on the shoulder and points at it. The other drops his head and shakes it sorrowfully.

"Damien isn't going to like this…"
Another Nerp approaches from the front door of the building.

"He'll have our *heads*…"

53. HOUSE OF YOD

HOURS LATER, THEY arrive just outside of the Outskirts, close to where the train tracks end.

"My friends, be safe. Please be safe," Denzi says to the group as he slows the train to a complete stop.

They hug Denzi again as they each exit the train. Manny stops just outside of the door and turns back.

"Denzi, I can't thank you enough for everything," Manny says sincerely.

"Emmanuel, my friend, *please* let me know if you need anything else. *Anything*. Will you do that?" Denzi says as he taps at his temple with a smile.

"I will Denzi…thank you…and, you be safe too…"

They heart-salute each other. The door closes. The train leaves.

~ ~ ~

The four companions stand at the edge of a large open area, watching the wind carry bits of snow under the moonlight.

"Follow me…this way," Manny mumbles as he starts to walk.

The sound of their bags rubbing against their backs creates a cadence that matches their footsteps. They're silent, with very few comments and noises other than a cough here and there, and a moment when Jhenda pauses to rest and drops her bag. Manny picks it up for her and says, "I've got it."

It's been about an hour since they first started walking. All of them are tired, but no one says anything about it. They hear sporadic howls off in the distance; far enough away for them to not feel immediately threatened, but close enough for them to all wish that they were somewhere inside instead of out amongst the elements.

"There," Manny says.

They each look up. He's pointing at a small structure that's just a few yards in front of them. They stop and drop their bags, panting from both fatigue and relief.

"Now what?" Rock asks.

"Well, we prepare, and we wait for instructions," Manny says.

"Prepare? Prepare how?" Rock continues.

"We study, we research, and we allow the Creator to give us the power we need for whatever may be ahead, because something is *definitely* coming," Manny responds as he slaps Rock's chest with the back of his hand.

Manny lifts a bag and starts to walk toward the small shack.

"Come on, there's lots of stuff in here—lots of information that I'm sure we'll need to know."

"What is this place?" Jhenda asks.

"It's Jonah's. He was living here I think, apparently for a long time; maybe even since Star Fall. He's taken lots of notes, written down dreams, sketches, research, wisdom that he's received directly from the Creator...all types of stuff..."

"Wow, I can only imagine what information is in there. Jonah is one of the smartest and most spiritual people in the world—*has* to be! I can't *WAIT* to pick his brain...well, read his brain..." Grea says, skipping toward the cabin.

Rock and Jhenda grab the other bags as Manny picks up another; Grea forgot about them out of excitement.

They reach the structure and Rock inspects it carefully.

"What's this?" Rock asks, pointing at the symbol on the door.

"It's Hebrew, isn't it?" Jhenda responds.

All of them look at her.

"Well, it is actually…how'd you know?" Manny says with a light chuckle.

"A lot of times we pick up old books when we're collecting. Sometimes I tuck them away when nobody's looking."

"Ah, that's why she's so smart and perceptive. I knew there had to be something. Makes perfect sense now…" Grea says.

"Well, you're right. It's Hebrew. It's a **Yod**—the first letter in the Hebrew name for the Creator…*Yahweh*…"

"Have you named this place yet?" Rock asks.

"Named it? What? Why would I name it?" Manny responds.

"Well, I mean, it *has* to have a name, right?" Rock continues.

"A name? I mean, maybe? I guess I haven't really thought about it…"

Rock picks up a clump of soft ice and crushes it in his hand.

"Well, we have to give it a name…" Rock says as the ice falls back to the ground.

"The House of Yod," Jhenda blurts out.

Again, they all look at her.

They all pause in perfect quiet for a few moments, contemplating.

"I like it," Grea says, breaking the silence.

"See, that wasn't so hard, now was it? *The House of Yod*," Rock says as he pats Manny on the back just before picking up a couple of bags and entering the hut with Jhenda and Grea.

Manny is left standing there alone for a second. He shakes his head and laughs, happy to have the company of his friends again finally.

He looks up at the sky.

He spots a star and grins at it.

He imagines having a personal audience with the Creator for just that sliver of time.

In the next instant, he realizes that he's *always* had a personal audience with him.

"Maybe I *don't* have to do this alone after all…huh?" he says, still looking at the star.

He chuckles again, then follows the others inside.

54. THREE

"IT'S CHANGING AGAIN," Manny says as he looks out of the single window in the very back of the shack.

He presses up against it with the back of his hand and feels the warmth. He watches the sun's light as it radiates and creates a rainbow effect on the windowsill. Jhenda and Grea are both just waking. They yawn, stretch, and then stand. It's still very early.

Books, notebooks, and loose papers are scattered all over the room. Rock is still on the couch with an open book on his chest. His mouth is completely open and he's snoring very loudly. Manny turns and looks at him. Grea and Jhenda notice too. He looks at them and makes a face. They giggle.

Manny floats into the air and hovers just over Rock's body.

"Rise and shine…" Manny says.

Rock grunts and rolls over.

Manny speaks again.

"Hey, *rise and shine*, I said…"

Rock moans and tosses his arm into the air motioning for Manny to leave him alone. Soon after, his snores continue.

Finally, with a burst of wind that lifts the covers off of Rock's body, Manny yells:

"*GET UP!*"

Rock jerks really hard, looks up, and sees Manny hovering about three feet above his face. Manny's body is parallel to his and his arms are folded. Rock is paralyzed as he watches Manny gently suspended in the air like a kite without a string.

"How do you even *do* that?" Rock says, scratching his eye with is pointer finger.

Manny laughs, "by not sleeping all day!"

"I *don't* sleep all day," Rock retorts.

"You sleep all day...*every* day," Jhenda says while Rock rubs his face with both hands, trying to fully wake himself.

"Oh, *quiet*—it's because I'm such a diligent researcher. I *need* my rest!" he responds, holding the book that was on his chest up in the air.

They've been in the Outskirts for a few weeks now, and they've been immersing themselves in all of the information that they can, just like Manny has been. Each of them has a favorite spot. Rock's is the couch, for obvious reasons. Manny likes to sit in the corner of the main room. Jhenda and Grea normally sit together at the table in the corner.

They spend hours reading Manny's golden Grandeurscript, or *the Goldenscript,* as they sometimes call it, along with all of the other notebooks and materials left by Jonah. It's rare that they take breaks. They end up getting so pulled into the information and their resulting discussions that their minds remain engaged for hours at a time.

Today is just like the days before it. They're each in their favorite spots and fervently researching.

"So, let me get this straight," Rock says, "the *Shedim* and the *Watchers* are pretty much the same, but the Shedim are just... fallen Watchers? They're demons?"

"That's right," Jhenda says.

"And they're spiritual creatures, so they have to have a physical body to inhabit so that they can function and do things on earth, right?" Rock continues.

"Right," Manny responds.

"Well, how do they get bodies to use? How do they choose one?"

Manny thinks.

"Well, I think there's more than one way," Grea adds, "the primary way is possession—they have to find a person that's spiritually and mentally weak enough to be overpowered, or, maybe through…"

"*Through conjuring…*" Manny interrupts.

Grea looks over at him just as he looks back at her in self-inflicted astonishment.

"*That's it! That's it!*" Manny exclaims as he jumps up from the corner.

"What's it?" Rock asks, completely lost.

"*Conjuring!* I'm willing to bet that's exactly how the three guys from the NRP were inhabited by such powerful spirits. I know that they are under the influence of Shedim—the darkness is all over them, I could feel it, even back then, before all of this. Conjuring. It was planned. It was calculated. They summoned the Shedim and became hosts, probably through some ancient ritual. That has to be why they're so powerful…"

Manny grabs a notebook from the table.

"Right here! Jonah knew it all along…he wrote this most recently…"

He reads:

"Three of the *fallen* have come to Naza…chosen of the Shedim…of Helel himself…they are extremely powerful and dangerous…one, born of unnatural and unclean means…one willing vessel… and one unwilling, yet selected and forced…these three are the hands of Helel in the earth…"

"Gosh, it's like a riddle," Rock says during a brief pause in Manny's reading.

Manny continues:

> **"Levi, inhabited by *the Slivanathan*. Polus—I sense *the Mulgaroon* within him. Damien is filled with the most sinister Shedim of them all; *the Bel'uvial*…these three have been conjured according to ancient, hidden knowledge…"**

"All of those are demons; they're fallen Shedim. I read about them yesterday. I remember those three names specifically… they're really high-ranking from what I can recall," Grea says.

"Exactly," Manny responds, "those have to be the three spirits that inhabit them."

"I remember seeing them at the IE," Jhenda says, "I could sense the darkness in them too. I could just, *feel* it. I mean, I would always get a sense of people's vibes, you know? My whole life. I didn't know that I was actually sensing the spirit-world…I thought I was just, you know, *different*…"

"You were, Jhenda. We *all* were. We were all chosen before the universe was created. We're spiritual beings first. We didn't just start existing when we were born. We've been preparing for this for all of eternity, and didn't know it…"

Manny closes the book and sits back down in the corner. They all get quiet, thinking about everything that was just said.

"Everything has a spiritual component. We can't forget that," Manny continues, "just like, we always hear, *patience is a virtue*, right? Look in the book about the Watchers; *Virtues* are actually in the hierarchy of the *Messengers and Watchers*. There's an actual spiritual entity tied to Patience. I bet that if we could see emotions, thoughts, and all of these intangible parts of our day-to-day lives in the spiritual realm, we'd see that they all have a physical representation…some tangible property, energy, or a *being* that interacts with us…"

"Well, it makes sense," Jhenda says.

"It does, but it's kind of scary too. Knowing that my words, thoughts, feelings, and *everything*, are so much more than just words, thoughts, and feelings," Rock adds.

Manny nods in agreement.

"Well, I just know that I would LOVE to see the Way and the Cloud. You make them sound so amazing! I hope I get to *spirit-lapse* one day. Do you think I have the *Yahweh Gene* too?" Rock asks.

Grea laughs.

"Rock, if you have the Yahweh Gene, then we *ALL* have it—*trust* me…" she says.

They all burst out laughing, then there's another silent pause.

"Locating Jonah is going to be critical…" Manny says, solemnly.

"Gosh, sounds familiar," Rock says.

"Déjà vu," adds Jhenda.

"I know it, but it's true. He's important to this whole matter. There was more; there were things that I don't think he had a chance to finish telling me…"

"Well, at least we have all of this stuff to research and learn in the meantime," Grea says, looking around the room.

"True, very true…" Manny says.

"So, where do we go from here?" Jhenda asks.

"Honestly, I have no idea," Manny answers.

"Now *that's* reassuring," Rock responds sarcastically.

Manny stands up again and walks to the window. He looks out and sees how far away everything is. They're literally out in the middle of nowhere, in a small abandoned cabin, with nothing except each other.

"I know that the Creator will, I don't know, *guide* us—show us, or tell us what to do, somehow…"

Manny looks at his friends.

"I just…I just *believe* that…"

Another pause.

"Wow," Rock responds.

"Wow what?" Manny says in return.

"I never thought I'd see this day…*ever*…not in a million moons…"

"What are you talking about?" Manny asks.

"The day that you'd start sounding like *her*…" Rock says, pointing at his sister.

Grea simply smiles.

"Me neither," Manny responds with a grin.

Manny and Grea exchange a look of acknowledgement and respect. She wiggles her nose at him to lighten the moment. He chuckles.

"Well, I guess we may as well keep going. Help me dig through this pile. I don't think we've looked at these papers yet," Manny says.

"That sounds good, but…" Rock interrupts.

"Here we go, I can feel it coming," Grea says with a roll of her eyes.

"What, I haven't said anything!"

"You didn't have to…you're rubbing your stomach," says Grea.

Rock looks down at his hand moving in a circular motion over his belly.

"I haven't eaten all day! And that's another thing: what are we going to do for *food* all the way out here? I mean, we're *BURNING* through these rations, and we have *no* idea how long we'll be out here I'm sure, right?"

"I've thought about that. Oh, and correction, *YOU* are burning through the rations," Jhenda responds.

The group laughs.

Jhenda continues, "but don't worry, I know of some places not far from here. There are Waywards who are willing to trade all over the Outskirts—some of them owe me favors, and I know where to get stuff to trade for food, water, medicines...whatever we may need..."

"Problem solved," Manny says.

"Hey, it pays to be a Scavenger," Jhenda responds with a smile.

55. WE MUST

AT THE IE in the darkness of what was once Jonah's office are the three servants of Helel. Levi lights two candles that sit on a shelf against the wall, Polus paces in the center of the room, and Damien sits at the desk with his hands pressed together in front of him.

"Damien...what *issssssss*...our plan?" hisses Polus.

Damien rocks in the chair; it makes a wooden creaking noise as he does. Levi and Polus both look on, waiting patiently for his response.

"We will continue the same efforts as before; we will search every inch of this rotting city hub if we have to. The witness and his companions can't be far away. They're just children! Under normal conditions, we would have tracked them by now, but they have a covering over them—a shield, it seems...*he's* protecting them..."

Damien looks toward the ceiling with a smug face.

"For that reason alone, we won't be able to pinpoint them with telepathy, or dark magic, or a summoning this time...we'll have to find them on foot..."

Damien stands and walks to one of the bookshelves. He leans on it and rubs his head in thought.

"Polus, you cover S&G, Naza, Salem, and Samaria. Levi, you take the Outskirts."

"Why are you having him cover so much ground?" Levi asks.

Polus and Damien smirk at each other.

"He has a...*special skill*...that allows him to do so, quickly and effectively."

Damien picks up one of the candles, walks back to his chair, and takes a seat. He removes it from its holder, tilts it to the side, and allows the black wax to drip onto the table.

"The Outskirts are harsh lands; you are better equipped to navigate the unforgiving terrain, Levi..."

"And when we find them, Damien?" Levi asks.

There's a long pause.

"*Destroy* them," he says as he places the candle back into its holder.

"We must *kill* them at this point...too much is at stake..."

Damien places the tip of his finger into the center of the wax spot left on the table, which has now dried.

"As for me, I will go directly to the key. I know where to find him. He has exactly what we need...he knows the secret..."

Damien's entire hand starts to radiate with a warm, yellow light that pulses in unison with his heartbeat. The dry, cool wax begins to heat up again as Damien touches it. It glows like yellow embers and makes sizzling and popping sounds. Seconds later, it becomes red hot and bursts into a small flame right on the table. Damien lifts his finger. The three men look at the small circle of fire as it continues to increase in intensity. The room glows and their shadows sway on the walls. The burning wax sinks into the table and drips through it onto the floor like golden, fiery drops of water. Once it hits the floor, it creates a small puddle, which cools and returns to its black, waxy form. A sizeable hole remains in the table.

"I'll be back in a few days. Complete your assignments in the meantime," Damien says as he stands, leans onto the table, and peers through the hole.

The men leave the office together.

56. TONIGHT

"So Manny, what do you think may be coming?" Jhenda asks.

Manny looks at her and sees her concern. It's been another long day of studying and researching. Earlier in the day, they all went deep into the Outskirts and bargained with a couple of Waywards for rice, beans, and water; Jhenda was able to find a few cans of gasoline and oil that they were willing to trade for.

"What exactly are we being prepared for?" she continues.

He closes the Goldenscript and turns to her.

"I'm not totally sure, but I know that it's something important. And something *very* dangerous I would imagine…that's what I feel…"

Grea walks up next to them.

"Well, good thing that we have each other. Between us and the Creator, we have some pretty good odds."

~ ~ ~

This is a weekly dialogue amongst the group that takes different forms and uses different words; a question and response of worry, followed by robotic reassurance. It's been two full months, which have felt more like two years, since the small army first moved into the House of Yod, as it's been affectionately named. They saturate themselves in the literature that Jonah has left, but none of them more than Jhenda; not even Manny.

"She's like a machine," Rock comments at one point.

The terms spirit-lapse, the Way, and the Cloud, have become a part of their working vocabularies. The only significant amounts of time that they spend outside of the House of Yod are the periodic journeys into the deeper parts of the Outskirts to trade, as Jhenda guides them. Even though the weather has changed and it's warm again, it's still quite dangerous. Wild animals and the Waywards run the territory.

Waywards are Remnants who do not follow the obligations of the NRP and are cut off from receiving rations. The majority of them reside in the Outskirts, but some are closer to the city hubs. An even smaller percentage of them may be found actually living in some of the city hubs, in abandoned buildings, alleys, or under bridges; however, the NRP tries arduously to regulate these practices.

For the most part, they just try to make the best living that they can through bartering, and occasionally stealing. Some are dangerous, but most are harmless. They can still cause a great deal of unease until it's determined which category they fall into: dangerous or harmless. Those who are dangerous are known to terrorize travelers, are assumed to be cannibals, and are believed to perform ritualistic sacrifices in some cases, but that's largely presumed to be an old wives' tale. The Outskirts have been known to test the might and sanity of even the strongest Remnants, so those wives' tales aren't *too* outlandish.

Manny however has an additional outlet, one that's developed unexpectedly. He finds himself writing now—often. He's taken after Jonah. There's a pile of blank notebooks within the house that the group found not long after they first arrived. Manny puts them to good use. It eases his mind and gives him a chance to vent, without technically venting.

~ ~ ~

"Have you heard anything lately, Manny?" Jhenda asks one evening, after everyone else has fallen asleep.

She sits at the corner table next to the oil lamp, reading through the notebook with the heading that reads, *"History of the NRP."*

Manny is on the floor with his back resting on the wall, writing in one of his notebooks. He looks up at her.

"No, I haven't. Not in a while."

She nods.

"I figured. You would've told us if you had."

He nods too.

"I wonder what you write in those sometimes."

"Oh, do you?"

"Of course. I wouldn't dare try to read it though."

"Why not?"

She looks at a large stack of materials sitting in front of her.

"Well, I think I've got plenty to read for now…"

They laugh.

He stands up and walks over to the table to sit with her. She slides the chair next to her out and smiles as he sits down.

"You know, I always figured that you'd start becoming exactly who you're becoming eventually," Jhenda says.

He scrunches up his face at her.

"What do you mean?"

"I mean, I remember the first day that I met you, which wasn't all that long ago I guess…I could just tell. I could tell that there was something different about you. I could tell that you belonged down on the floor section with everyone else at the IE, and not up in that skybox…"

He looks down with a grin.

"I don't think that I belong down there—even still."

"I do. I'm sure there were people there who were just like you. Not knowing all of the answers, but just having a sense of the truth...the truth that rings inside us all, but that we tend to ignore. Most of us anyway. You're one of the ones who has been brave enough to stop ignoring it."

"Maybe, I suppose," Manny says unsurely.

Jhenda stares down at the table for a second.

"You know, I think that's one of the main things that I enjoyed about the IE. It may even be the only reason that I went at all..."

"What's that?"

"Everyone was different, but they came together, trying to find that truth...which made them all the same I guess...in a way..."

"Yeah, I supposed I liked that too..."

"I mean, people of all backgrounds and understandings, coming to pray and believe in their own way. Jonah was *so* good at facilitating that...and making everyone feel welcome...not judged, or wrong...even me," Jhenda says.

"He definitely was," Manny says, a little sadly.

She looks at Manny and sees his expression change right before her eyes at the mention of Jonah's name. She places her hand on his shoulder.

"He's going to be okay. We'll find him."

He looks at her and offers the best half-smile that he can manage.

"As soon as that Voice of yours starts speaking up that is..."

They both laugh lightheartedly.

"Well, Emmanuel, I'm going to get some shut-eye. We should probably go out and get a few supplies in the morning. What do you think?"

"That sounds good."

He grins at her.

She grins back.

"Night, Manny."

"Night."

She blows out the lamp's flame and crawls into her sleeping bag. Manny sits there in the dark for a few more minutes. Thinking.

After a short while, he feels his way back to his corner and wraps himself in the same thick blankets that were once in his room in his mother's apartment. He's fast asleep nearly as soon as his eyes close.

~ ~ ~

He's aware of himself and his surroundings. He can hear himself breathing. He can feel his heart beating. His eyes pop open and there's nothing but darkness all around him; a terrible, consuming darkness.

A sharp image suddenly appears. He's looking at himself, trapped inside of a large transparent bubble, feeling its walls and yelling, but hearing no sound.

"Am I dreaming?" he thinks to himself.

"I have to be..."

He continues watching. He gets frustrated, wraps his arms around himself, and crouches down inside the bubble. He begins to glow a bright, blue fluorescent color, then he quickly stands and flings his arms open at the same time. A burst of energy and light expands from his body and the bubble bursts.

He sees himself start to walk. The darkness around him turns into the scenery of the Outskirts; he's walking toward the House of Yod. Once he reaches it, he hesitates for a moment and looks from side to side nervously.

"What am I doing?" Manny thinks to himself as he watches the scene play out.

He's still looking at everything happen from a distance.

Finally, Manny watches himself walk inside of the safe-house.

It's bright and sunny outside, but as he closes the door behind him, a large shadow is cast over the entire house. Something flies in circles over the small building and its shadow completely overlaps it. As Manny looks up, he sees a beastly and grotesque creature circling overhead. It is like a dragon, but far more hideous. Immediately, Manny tries to yell to warn himself, but he's still unable to produce any sound. His consciousness is suspended in the air outside of the house, with no ability to do anything except see all that's happening.

The beast breathes a huge blast of fire at the House of Yod and Manny watches himself run out of the door just in time to avoid being consumed by it. He continues to run through the field, and then into the woods.

The dragon gives chase, burning the entire forested area that's full of leafless trees in its pursuit of the Witness.

From the sky above, a single voice cries out as he flees:

"MANNY! YOU MUST GO! TONIGHT!"

Then another:

"EMMANUEL KOHEN! GO NOW!"

Then thousands more join in—the voices of men, women, and children, all mingled together and shouting:

"Manny!"
"Go!"
"Tonight!"
"EMMANUEL!"

"HURRY!"
"NOW!"
"TONIGHT! GO!"
"EMMANUEL KOHEN! NOW!"
"MANNY!"
"TONIGHT!!!"

All of the voices suddenly stop.

Manny looks at the wooded area after it's been set ablaze.

The dragon-like creature circles above it, perhaps ensuring that Manny is dead.

All of the fire begins to recede and collect in the center of the forest.

The flames intensify, then turn bright blue.

When the dragon notices the phenomenon, it flies to the center of the forest also, hovering directly above it to further investigate.

Just then, a huge beam of blue light shoots up from the blue flames and begins to burn the dragon.

It shrieks and makes terrible noises.

Manny's consciousness is now just above the creature.

It looks up into Manny's eyes while it burns and begins to disintegrate.

In its final moments, it now has the collective voices of the thousands which Manny heard just a few moments ago.

It says one final word:

TONIGHT!!!

~ ~ ~

Manny jumps violently, only to open his eyes and see his friends standing above him. He's sweating profusely and breathing as heavy as a man can possibly breathe.

"What happened, Manny? What did you see?" Rock asks.

He wipes his forehead and looks at the moisture in his hand.

"TONIGHT!" he yells.

57. NO MATTER WHAT

MANNY IS FRANTIC. He darts around the room like he's trying to find a time bomb before it explodes. The others watch him nervously, not knowing what to expect. Finally, Grea grabs him by the shoulders.

"*MANNY!* Listen, calm down…breathe…what happened?"

"I saw…*I saw it!* Something…it's coming! *Tonight!*"

"Manny," she says.

His eyes frantically move from one side of the room to the other. His hands are all over the place as he tries to explain.

"It was *here*…it came! It was him! One of them! I'm not sure which…we…we *have* to go…we *have* to get ready…"

"Manny…" Grea says again, even more calmly this time.

She holds his cheeks with both of her hands.

"Breathe…" Grea says.

He stops talking.

"Relax…" she continues.

His posture slumps and his face drips into her hands like soup into a bowl.

"Now, what happened? Think. If the Creator showed it to you, then you already have the answer—*inside.*"

He takes two more deep breaths, closes his eyes tightly, and focuses on remembering the dream.

"It's…it's Levi…the Slivanathan; he's coming here, *tonight*. He's not far away…maybe another hour or so…"

"Okay, okay. What else did you see?"

Though his eyes are still closed, his friends can see them searching around for something behind his eyelids like he's in REM sleep. Suddenly they stop moving and he pops them open. His mouth opens at the same time.

"What...what is it?" Jhenda says.

Manny takes two steps back and starts to look queasy.

"Manny, what? Tell us!" Rock says out of anxiety.

Manny looks at them each uncomfortably.

"We have to—*destroy it*...we have to destroy the Shedim that's in Levi..."

"Wait...*what?* Destroy a *Shedim?* Aren't they eternal beings? How in the world do you destroy demons?" Rock blurts out.

"Manny, okay, wait a minute...we haven't read *ANYTHING* about that, and I've done *LOTS* of reading. Have you seen it anywhere?" Jhenda says.

"No," Manny says dryly.

"So, what do we do, Manny? How do we do it?" Grea asks.

He looks at her, full of worry.

"I don't know..."

Rock flops down onto the couch and covers his head with a pillow.

"Oh, well this is just *PERFECT* then, isn't it?"

He laughs hysterically, overcome with nervousness and fear; it's his only response.

"We have to fight with an ancient demon, which is an *ETERNAL BEING*, mind you...and then *kill* it..." Rock says, then bursts out laughing again.

"Not to mention, Manny is the *only one* with any type of powers, and not even *HE* knows how to destroy it, because, hey... it's one of the first created beings in the universe and has been around for *MILLIONS* of years...and is probably one of the three most powerful ones of its kind...but that's not a big deal at *ALL*, right?! I guess it'll be knocking on the door in about forty-five minutes and saying, *hey guys, ready to fight to the death?* Oh, hey there Slivanathan! Sure, we were expecting you! Hold on just one second, let me grab my notebook full of *GIBBERISH* from fifteen years ago..." Rock says.

His frantic laughter of denial erupts once again.

"Okay, maybe we can..." Jhenda says, attempting to think of a solution, but her sentence ends and drifts off into the abyss; she's just as lost as the others.

"I'm sorry, guys...I don't know what to do..." Manny says as he drops his head and walks to the window.

Grea interjects, "listen, if the Creator showed this to you, and if it's happening tonight, then it means that we're already prepared. That *has* to be the case. If it wasn't, it wouldn't be happening..."

Everyone remains silent, thinking about Grea's words.

"We just have to trust that everything that's happened and that we've learned up to this point has been orchestrated, planned, and is all that we need..."

Grea walks over to Manny and puts her hand on his shoulder.

"Our human knowledge will only take us so far...remember?" she says to him.

"*...acknowledge the Creator, and our path will unfold,*" Manny whispers with his head down and eyes closed.

He breathes out of his nose, looks down at the ground for a second, and then up into Grea's eyes with a nod.

"Okay, great! *Our path will unfold*...that's *awesome!* But what do we do in the meantime?" Rock asks, sarcastically.

Manny scratches at his neck and leans his head to the side, thinking.

"Okay, well, I have to make sure all of you are out of harm's way. He's probably going to come to the House of Yod first, I mean, he'll have to. So, we definitely don't need to be inside when he does..."

"How about we hide where that large ditch is just outside? It's about fifty yards away or so; maybe a little more. That's far enough for us to be safe, but close enough for us to see what's going on," Jhenda follows up.

"Yes, yes! Good thinking Jhenda; that'll be perfect," Manny replies.

"Okay, but what about you Manny?" Grea says.

He thinks again. In a few seconds, he smiles as an idea comes to him.

"I know just the place…"

"Where?" Rock asks.

Manny points to the sky.

"Ah, okay; you're going to do your *superman* thing…" Rock says.

"I sure am…who knows, maybe it'll intimidate him?" Manny responds.

"Worth a shot, I guess," Rock responds.

"Okay, perfect! Well, that settles it…and listen…I need you guys to promise me something…*NO MATTER WHAT*…okay?"

"Promise you what?" Jhenda asks.

"Just promise me…" Manny reiterates.

"Okay, okay, we promise," Grea interrupts.

"Whatever may happen, I don't want you to come out and try to intervene. It may get bad, but I need you all to stay safe."

"But Manny…" Rock interjects.

"No *buts*, Rock. I need you guys to stay safe…"

"Guy and girls, you mean," Grea says, while smiling through her worry.

Manny half-smiles through his own worry in return.

"Guy, and girls…" he says.

He turns and faces Rock who is still on the couch.

"Rock, make sure you take care of them out there, okay?"

Rock nods his head.

"All right, that's our game plan..."

Manny looks at his watch.

"We'd better go ahead and get into position. It won't be much longer..."

They walk out of the door and enter a dimly lit scene, fixated under a canopy of stars that's stretched out above them.

Manny lifts into the air.

His friends walk in the opposite direction and nestle themselves down into the hollowed-out earth, as close to each other as possible.

58. DO YOU SEE THIS?!

IT'S BEEN HOURS. A loud rumbling noise cuts through the silence.

"Eww!" Grea says as she hits Rock on the arm.

"What, I'm hungry!" Rock responds.

"You're *always* hungry! Be quiet!" Grea whispers loudly.

"For what? No one's coming. It's been a *whole* lot longer than an hour by now…"

He rolls over onto his back and looks at the night sky with his hands underneath his head in a relaxed position.

"We might as well go back inside. This is *pointless*…"

"He might be right," Jhenda says.

"Oh gosh, not you *too*," Grea says sympathetically.

"I mean, it's been a while now; *well* over an hour, like Rock said, and we haven't seen the slightest sign of anyone, or anything."

"Finally, someone else with some sense…" Rock says.

"Quiet, Rock. You know, you always think you know *everything*…"

"Me? *Me?!* You've lost your tiny mind—*YOU* are the know it all…"

"No, I don't know it all. No, no, no, I just know more than *YOU*…"

As the two go back and forth, they don't notice the look of surprise and fear that has leaped onto Jhenda's face. She looks off in the distance squinting slightly.

"*Guys…*"

They continue to argue and ignore her.

"*Guys...*"

They still pay her no attention.

"*HEY! Will you two cut it out and look?!*" she whispers forcefully at them, striking both of their arms and pointing toward the house.

A large man, who looks to be the height of the door itself, is walking toward their quaint home. He's wearing a large cloak that's far too heavy for the semi-warm weather and light breeze.

"*Oh goodness, oh goodness...this is it, isn't it...*" Rock says, nervously, still rolling over and adjusting his body.

"Shhhh, be *quiet*," Jhenda says, looking at him intensely.

~ ~ ~

Levi walks along in the darkness and sniffs the air periodically. There's a beaten path that's been traveled repetitively ahead of him; he notices that the ground is more pressed down here than in other places. He follows it. When he lifts his eyes, he sees a run-down shack not far away.

"Hmm, this must be it; I can smell them...they *stink*..." Levy grunts.

He stops about twenty yards away from the door and looks around.

The night is dead silent.

"It's *too* quiet," he says.

"Hmm...I wonder..."

He sniffs the air. Searching. Sensing.

"They have to be close..."

He looks at the doorway of the house and sees that there's some sort of marking on it. He continues walking toward it to get a better look at the emblem through the darkness. He stops again and sniffs the air.

"They're close. They *have* to be…"

He's directly in front of the door. He studies the mark, its curves—its faded blue coloring. He lifts his hand and touches it with his fingertips. A sizzling sound is created and he snatches it away. He looks at his hand.

It's burned.

"*Ahhhh!*" he yells, flapping his hand in the air to cool it.

The more he does, the hotter it feels.

He looks down at his hand again and realizes that its completely on fire. Smoke emits from it uncontrollably as he drops down to his knees.

"*AHHHHHHH!*" he screams even louder.

He digs his hand down into the ground and scoops handfuls of dirt onto it until the fire is put out.

He releases a roar of anger.

Now, a ripping; a tearing.

He grunts and groans.

His already large frame bulges and expands even more. His thick coat tears as two leathery wings rip through it, and a long reptilian tail thrusts itself out of the back of his pants. He stands to his feet, completely transformed into a dragon-like creature, roaring loudly and terrifyingly into the air, and creating a few bursts of flame as he does.

Rage and hatred course through his veins. He's at least twelve feet tall now. His skin looks plated and reinforced like that of a rhinoceros. His legs are as thick as an elephant's. His greenish-gray body casts a long, dark shadow onto the House of Yod, and the smoke from his nostrils rises up like steam from a pot on a stove.

"*OH…MY…FREAKING…GOODNESS…DO YOU SEE THIS?!*" Rock says with his hand over his mouth, trying his best to remain quiet as they look on.

Neither Jhenda nor Grea respond; they're astonished at what they're witnessing.

Levi, now fully converted into his *Slivanathan* form, one of the chief Shedim, is just under a hundred yards away from them. They have seen the pictures for months, studied his traits, read about his history; but to witness this ancient demon in person is something that no amount of studying could have prepared them for. After a few more horrifying roars, the Slivanathan begins to swiftly scan the perimeter, certain that his prey is nearby.

Finally, he looks again at the House of Yod.

He raises his massive paw, with long talons extending from his crooked fingers, and prepares to destroy the building.

59. LIES

A SOUND LIKE that of a low flying airplane can be heard in the air. The Slivanathan pauses from destroying the House of Yod and slowly turns his head.

The sound gets gradually louder.

Seconds later, a blue flash of light appears on the Slivanathan's chest and he stumbles backwards.

A loud thump, and then a painful roar.

Gasping for air, the Slivanathan falls to the ground and rolls twice.

Grea, Rock, and Jhenda are completely confused. They heard the noise and saw the flash of light too, but have no idea what just happened. Their mouths hang open as they continue to watch.

The Slivanathan looks up with a groan, and sees Manny slowly descending from the air above until he's finally hovering just inches above the ground before him.

"*YES!*" Jhenda says accidentally, and then covers her mouth, as Rock and Grea both grab her arms.

"*SORRY!*" she whispers.

~ ~ ~

"Levi, that's *enough!*" Manny yells at the beast as he stands up.

"Ahhh, Emmanuel Kohen—*THE WITNESS*...we finally meet..."

Levi's voice is extremely low, very pronounced, and clearly not of human origin. It's more of a gravelly rumble than an actual voice, but his words are clear and precise. His diction is quite impressive, in fact.

"We've been looking for you, Emmanuel. There is business that we must...shall we say...*tend to*..."

"And what business would that be, Levi?"

"Ahhh, *customary* things, of course...such as you giving us the *secret*..."

"The secret?"

"Yes, Emmanuel! Let's not play games, *boy!*" Levi yells harshly.

The whole time that he's speaking, he's walking closer to Manny, very slowly.

"You have received something from...from *him!*"

Levi points to the sky and looks up with disdain.

"And we require it of you. We need to know what you know. We need to know what he's *shown* you. We need to know the secret of, the *Yahweh Gene*..."

"And why would I leave the presence and protection of angels to commune with demons, Levi?" Manny says, confidently, still hovering, and with his arms crossed.

"Oh...my boy, you know just as well as any of us, that **WE ARE ANGELS TOO!**"

With those words, Levi swipes at Manny's head and stomps at the same time. As he does, the earth shakes violently and causes the ground underneath Manny to rise rapidly, nearly hitting his legs, but Manny drifts aside. Levi just misses striking him in the head. Manny flies out to Levi's side, then blasts him in his rib cage with a ball of blue energy from his hands that makes Levi stagger.

Levi laughs through the pain and places his hand on his side.

"*EMMANUEL!* Don't you see?! He's *USING* you...he's been *USING* us *ALL*...for ages! *ALL OF US!* ALL of his creations. He claims to love us so dearly, yet he gives us rules that we cannot keep! He gives us limitations that we were designed to surpass! And then he teases us with riddles, and swoons us into doing his bidding...it's all a game, boy...don't you see it?!"

"Those are *LIES*, Levi, and you *know* it!"

"*LIES*?! Foolish child! *HE IS THE MASTER OF LIES*! Where do you think they came from?! *WHERE*?! He is the Creator of *ALL THINGS* after all, isn't he?"

Levi chuckles and fixes his face into a sinister grin, realizing that his words are penetrating Manny's heart and mind, at least a bit.

"Don't pretend that you haven't wondered. Don't pretend that you haven't thought of these things, in the recesses of your mind. Your doubts. Your fears. *HIS LIES*!"

Levi blows a burst of flames from his mouth at Manny, which he again somehow manages to evade. Manny clenches his fist tightly and it begins to glow blue. Then, he punches toward Levi's body and the monster hunches over, feeling the effects of the telekinetic blow.

He laughs again, holding his belly and coughing simultaneously; he pauses for a moment to spit out some blood.

"You've felt it, haven't you, Emmanuel? You've felt the questions creep in. Why does he allow such horrible things if he's such a good Creator? Why does he have his creations to perform his will—is he not *CREATOR* enough to perform it himself? He has ALL power...yet he forces you...and all of creation...to be a part of his schemes and plans...and for what?! To what end? What is he *really* trying to accomplish?!"

"Quiet, Levi! You don't know what you're talking about!!!" Manny yells in frustration.

"I don't know what *I'M TALKING ABOUT*?! How dare you! I've been here for MILLENNIUMS! THE NERVE OF YOU... YOU WEAK AND FOOLISH CHILD!!! Why do you think we left in the first place? Why do you think we followed Helel? *HE IS*

A JEALOUS CREATOR! HE ONLY LOVES AND CARES FOR HIMSELF! Not us! Not his children! **NOT YOU!!!**"

Levi violently flaps his wings downward and roars loudly in anger.

"You're a *FOOL* for thinking that he does! He only allows and admires his *own* jealously, but if you were to be jealous as *he* is, and therefore *truly* in his image, *HE WOULD CURSE YOU INTO DAMNATION FOR ALL OF ETERNITY FOR IT! IS THIS THE LOVING AND FORGIVING CREATOR THAT YOU SERVE?!*"

Levi stretches his wings and flies into the air quickly; too quickly for Manny to avoid him this time. He grabs Manny's body and squeezes him, then tosses him to the ground like a rag doll. Manny impacts the dirt with a loud *clunk*. He holds his shoulder in pain as Levi flies just above him.

"Stop being a *pawn* in his *irrational* games, Emmanuel Kohen! They are dangerous games indeed, and they will only get you *HURT!*"

Levi ceases his wings from flapping and drops to the ground. He plants one of his feet into Manny's back with a thud. Manny screams in pain. Multiple ribs and both of Manny's shoulder blades break; Levi can feel the crushing and crunching of Manny's bones under his foot as he rotates it back and forth, grinding him like a bug. There's severe damage to Manny's spinal column as well.

The Slivanathan stretches out his arms and wings, tilts his head up to the sky, and releases a bellowing laugh of triumph.

"I gave you a chance, Emmanuel! I gave you an opportunity to join us, and you *refused! THIS IS YOUR OWN FAULT!*" the Shedim roars.

Levi presses his foot down even harder into Manny's back, crushing him even more.

~ ~ ~

Unable to contain herself any longer, Grea jumps up from her position and runs toward Manny and Levi.

"*Grea, what are you doing?!*" Rock yells.

He gives chase, and so does Jhenda.

Levi hears the disturbance and looks over at them.

"Ahhh! Your little friends have *FINALLY* decided to stop being *COWARDS* and join the celebration!"

"*NOOOO!*" Manny yells with a broken voice as blood spatters from his mouth.

When they are close enough, Levi dips his shoulder low and then whips one of his wings toward the trio. The impact knocks all three of them to the ground. Manny stretches his hand out toward them. He's in so much pain that his arm trembles like a leafless branch in the winter wind. Levi takes in a deep breath and releases a hellacious blast of fire at them. Grea lifts her hands in an attempt to block it, certain that her efforts will not prevent her from being burned alive.

She feels the warmth of the fire.

She sees the bright reds and oranges lunging toward her face; she's closer to the Slivanathan than the others.

And then, everything stops.

Everything.

60. COME ON

GREA'S EYES ARE still closed.

Her hands are still raised.

The extreme warmth is still there.

The illumination created by the fire is still prevalent and intense on her face.

But the flames appear to have stopped in midair.

Not completely, but they move slowly; so slowly that they don't seem to be moving at all.

She opens her eyes. She feels herself pulling away from, herself.

An invisible force removes her consciousness, her soul, from her body, much like oil being separated from water. She looks behind her. Her brother's body is still on the ground, but she sees a version of him made of a translucent blue light standing up and looking at his own hands in shock; it's like his ghost is standing next to his corpse. Jhenda has a version of herself standing next to herself too, looking at Rock with her mouth open. Jhenda's soul stands up. Everything in the universe has slowed down. She sees Levi's blast of fire still blazing toward them at the inverse of lightspeed.

"Have we...have we *died?*" Jhenda asks, with fear and confusion in her voice.

"No, we're not dead," Manny says as he approaches them, "these are our *light-bodies...*"

"What? I thought...I mean, we read it, but...I mean...I thought...I thought only *YOU* could do this, Manny?" Rock says in utter bewilderment.

"I thought so too, but apparently, so can you..."

"What does this mean, Manny?" Grea asks with a trembling voice, much like her brother's.

"It means, that, well...it means that *the Creator* hears, and *he* answers..."

"Why do you say that?" Jhenda asks.

"I asked the Creator, many weeks ago, when we first came here—to give you all whatever it is that he's given me: to give you the *Yahweh Gene*..."

They look at him with surprise.

"I've asked every night since then...and, well, I also asked just now..."

Manny points over at his body.

"Wow...*wow!* This is...this is..." Rock stutters.

"This is pretty *AWESOME!*" Jhenda says excitedly as she hops into the air a few inches, then slowly floats back to the ground.

They chuckle at her.

"Okay, so wait...wait...I've read about this a lot. So, are we about to...*WHERE'S...THE WAY?!*" Rock exclaims.

Manny laughs, lifts his hands, and motions for him to calm down.

"It's somewhere around here, hold on. It will appear soon," he responds.

"I think I see it!" Grea says, pointing behind Manny.

A large black hole is fixated in midair, a few feet away from Manny's body. It looks like a portal into the vastness of the universe, with stars illuminating inside of it; an opening in this dimension that leads to the next, and *all* dimensions.

"Okay, so how do we do it?" Rock asks.

Manny smirks at him.

Without warning, Manny turns, gets a running start, and dives into the opening head first.

The three friends look at each other, speechless.

"You go next," Grea says to Rock.

"Oh, no, no, no... *YOU* go..." he responds to her.

"Stop being such *wusses*," Jhenda says, nudging them both as she hurries past them.

Void of any reservation whatsoever, she takes off running, and dives in. Rock shrugs at Grea, and then jets after her. He swan-dives into the center of the abyss behind Manny and Jhenda.

"Oh, boy... well, great! *Perfect!* This is just *perfect*..." Grea says, throwing her arms into the air, and then letting them drop to her sides.

She walks up to the opening and peeks in. As she does, her brother's hand quickly appears from within the Way, grabs her arm, and snatches her inside as she yelps.

"Come onnnnnn!" Rock says, as they are whisked away together into the veins and bowels of eternity and time.

61. COME QUICKLY

THEY TRAVEL SO fast that none of them can make any sound initially. But once accustomed to their speed, they're able to scream cheers of joy and excitement. They zip past stars that look like streams of tiny decorative lights along the walls of the tunnel.

Then they see it, as they shoot out of the tunnel and into the brightest and bluest sky imaginable.

All four of them slow down to a gentle hover. The sun is blindingly brilliant, but does not hurt their eyes. Thick, fluffy clouds extend as far as their eyes can see, and so do the millions and millions of people standing on them. All races, all ages, together, in harmony. Singing, laughing, talking, and dancing. They look down at the multitude.

Small children wave at them jovially.

Elderly people gaze up in their direction with warm smiles.

Jhenda cries; she's never seen such beauty and accord.

"This is it...*the Cloud*," Grea says in amazement.

"I can't believe it...well, I guess I have to...now that I can see it," Rock responds.

Manny looks at them and grins.

"*There they are! You all, come quickly!*" someone says.

The voice comes from somewhere beneath them.

As the four companions look back and forth attempting to identify it, they see an old man flailing his arms. He's sitting down with his legs crossed. Three younger men who are sitting near him stand, then help him up. The man speaks again once they see him:

"Come! Come, *quickly!*"

Without their control, the four friends are drawn to the four strangers on the cloud, increasingly faster by the second.

"Wait...*wait*..." Jhenda utters fearfully.

At the moment of impact, Manny, Jhenda, Rock, and Grea close their eyes and brace themselves.

Then, a bright flash of light.

62. WRITE!

ROCK OPENS HIS eyes first. He's sitting on a wooden stool with a piece of parchment and crude writing tools in front of him. There are other men around him. Each of them is at a similar, small writing station.

"*How?*" he thinks to himself as he looks at his hands, realizing that they aren't his own.

The old man from the Cloud bursts into the door. He walks by swiftly as Rock follows him with his eyes. As he does, he catches a more in depth look at the men sitting at the other writing stations. They make eye contact with each other. As they do, it's like they can feel one another's presence, even though they are in different bodies; one is clearly Jhenda, and the other, his sister.

The older man sits at a desk toward the front of the room. He looks at each of them. His aura feels every bit like Manny's.

"We must complete these scrolls, quickly! The time is at hand…" the old man says.

His language is foreign, yet they understand every word.

"The Creator has spoken to me, clearly! His words are living within us!"

The man stands and walks around the room, shouting praises and clapping his hands.

"Write these words! Write them and do not miss a *single* one!"

Jhenda looks up at the aged gentleman and can almost see Manny's soft eyes glancing back at her from within him. She can't explain it, but she knows it's him. They exchange a smile, then he points at her parchment. She nods and prepares to transcribe. The man steps to the front of the room and decrees his words with joy and power:

"Those who have passed on are not gone forever! They will live! They *are* alive! Hope is not lost! No! Hope is *never* lost!"

He claps his hands again.

"Awaken! All of you who have transitioned to the higher realms! Let your songs blare in the skies! The earth has received your frail flesh, but your souls are being born again in this beautiful cycle of everlasting life! Your consciousness lives like seeds that have been spread by the winds!"

With their heads down in concentration, they listen to the old man speak. He recites certain words and phrases that are strangely familiar to them; more than likely passages from the Grandeurscript that they've heard at some point but don't know by heart. They write them as quickly and accurately as they can.

The old man walks over to Rock, or rather the soul of Rock in an ancient man's body, and shakes his shoulders. Rock responds with excited laughter. He takes a few more steps and he is back at the front of the room, near the carved out opening in the wall, which is the doorway.

He gazes out of it.
His mood suddenly changes.
No more joy and excitement, but seriousness and a solemn demeanor.
He turns to them, and says his words more slowly and carefully:

"Those of you, full of righteousness...full of love... full of peace and hope...hide yourselves away. The wrath of the Creator is sure to fall upon the wrongdoers of the earth. The entire universe will reveal every evil, every iniquity, every fault... nothing shall be hidden from the *Great Eye*..."

They write with hearts full of anxiety.
The man crouches down low to the ground and rolls over into a seated position; he looks to be in tremendous pain.
Each of the others gets up to try and help him.
He thrusts both of his hands out.
"No! *NO!* Stay where you are! *Write!*" he demands.
They slowly return to their seats and pick up their quill pens.
The man speaks even more slowly than before now:

"When the time has come, the Creator himself will battle with the dark forces that have tortured the world and its inhabitants for millenniums. The pitiless sword of the Great Eye shall destroy the wickedness of the serpent, *Slivanathan*. It will flee but shall not be delivered from the Creator. The dragon of air, land, and water shall be killed, once and for all..."

Another bright flash of light fills their eyes.
Then complete darkness.

63. SWORD

THEY'RE BRIEFLY IN the Way again, moving quickly, but slow enough to be heard when they yell at each other.
"What was that?! A *spirit-lapse?!*" Jhenda says.
"Yes!" Manny yells in response.
"A sword! That's how we kill the Slivanathan Manny! A sword!" Rock screams.
"I believe so! That's what I heard too! Well actually, that's what I said, I guess!" Manny responds.

~ ~ ~

They stop suddenly. They're in a small house, standing outside of a very old wooden door. There are bits of hay on the floor.
"Where is..." Rock says.
"*SHHH!*" Grea says, covering his mouth, "*listen...*" she whispers.
All four of them place their ears to the door.
There's a man inside crying, full of sorrow. Rock peaks through a crack in the door and can see the man on a bed, completely alone.
"*Why!? Why have you forsaken me?!*" the man sobs as he buries his head into the covers on the bed and weeps for a few moments.
They can hear the entire conversation from outside.

"I AM HERE..."

A powerful, non-human voice declares the words.
They back away from the door, terrified.
"It's him," Manny whispers.
The Voice that's become so distinct and unmistakable to Manny is speaking inside the room. The man on the bed falls to the floor and bows his head in reverence.
The Voice continues:

"Look on the Slivanathan, which I created, just as I also created you. He has the strength of thousands of elephants. Look at the power within his core. Listen to the flames rumble within his bowels—fire forms from within him, and he can set all of the forests of the earth ablaze with one breath. His tail is like that of an oak tree; mighty and strong. Sturdy. Unbreakable. A matchless creature, fashioned by my own hands. His skin is impenetrable armor of iron and steel; he is magnificent! He is one of the first of my creations, but his pride and his strength have become too great for even him; let the Creator draw his sword and bring the great *Slivanathan* to his knees!"

A plummeting feeling comes over all of them.
"Whoa...WHOA!" Rock says, as his body feels like it's being sucked down into the floor by an intense gravitational pull.
He reaches for Jhenda's hand.
She takes it.

Again, a flash of bright light, then complete darkness.

~ ~ ~

Inside the Way, they are wafted through eternity once again.

Deep within themselves, they hear the same powerful and commanding voice that they heard outside of the man's door moments ago—the same voice that Manny has grown accustomed to over the past few months:

"My word is alive within you, and sharper than even the slimmest and strongest blades fashioned by the ironworkers of old...slicing through the very spirits and souls of all mankind and creation, and the flesh of every created being that has ever been birthed in the depths of my thoughts..."

They glance at each other.
Then, it speaks again:

"MY WORD...YOUR SWORD...
MY WORD...YOUR SWORD..."

The echo continues until they approach a small speck of light in the midst of the darkness all around them.

The circle grows rapidly as they speed toward it.

Finally, they pierce through it, covering their faces with their arms.

64. DO YOU HAVE IT?

THEY STAND IN the field, staring at each other—and at the Slivanathan.

"His *Word*? Our *Sword*? What does that even mean, Manny?" Grea asks.

"It means...*everything*..." Manny says with a grin as he looks at himself on the ground, and the demonic beast standing atop of him.

"Everything has been preparing us for this! We've been studying and preparing the whole time you all. I kept thinking that we needed something else, something additional...but we don't..."

He pauses and looks back at his friends.

"We already have the Creator...we already have his *word*... we've been using it the whole time..."

"How have we been using it? And how do we use it now?" Jhenda asks.

"We *believe*...and we *speak*..."

"That's it?" Rock butts in.

"That's it," Manny responds, "I think I knew it all along. That's what I've been doing. When I say certain things, and I really believe it deep down inside, it happens *immediately*...it's been happing all along, but I'm just now realizing it..."

Manny looks up into the sky with a huge smile on his face as if he's just won a prize.

"I think I get it...the *Yahweh Gene* makes the supernatural happen immediately...when we can completely believe it without a hint of doubt...that's how *this* is happening right now as a matter of fact!" Grea says excitedly.

"Exactly! This spirit-world...this higher level of vibration and reality has *always* been available to us from the very beginning...we just...*I* just didn't fully believe it. But now it's real to me...it's real to *us*..."

They look at each other again, reassuring one another with their silent nods.

"Okay, so what now?" Rock asks.

"We finish this. That's what," Manny says, looking over at the Slivanathan's atrocious frame again.

They each approach their own body.

Before stepping back inside, Manny looks back at Grea.

"Hey..." he says.

She looks at him.

"It's on you first...*don't* hesitate..." he says.

She nods, but neither of them looks away just yet.

He stares at her intensely and says:

"Do you have it?"

"I've got it," she answers with a grin.

65. COME OUT

THEIR SOULS BEGIN to fuse with their bodies again. Grea's consciousness gradually becomes aware of the intense heat that's close to her face. She can see the brightness of it just beyond her closed eyelids.

Out of pure reflex, her hands straighten with her palms facing toward the fire, just as normal time resumes where it left off before their spirit-lapse.

She feels a coolness come over her—an extreme coolness.

A large blue force field that's ice-cold forms from her palms; a translucent, impenetrable shield.

The fire blasts directly into it but can't pierce it.

It all happens within milliseconds.

"Whoa..." she says, looking at her hands in amazement.

By now, Rock is standing, and so is Jhenda. Rock blasts the Slivanathan with a burst of energy from both of his arms—bright blue energy waves.

Stones and pebbles rise up from the ground, combine with the plasma waves that are emitting from Rocks arms, and collide with the Slivanathan in the very center of his chest.

The Slivanathan stumbles backwards.

While all of this happens, Manny writhes on the ground in pain, now finally free from their enemy's gigantic foot.

Jhenda looks over at Manny and exclaims:

"HEAL!"

When the words leave her mouth, Manny's body snaps into alignment with a series of loud pops and cracks, the blood pouring from his nose and mouth recedes like an ocean at low tide, and he shoots up from the ground like a flower that has just gotten its first taste of sunlight.

Jhenda turns back to the demon and begins moving her hands and arms in a circular, concentric motion that looks like an antique form of Kung Fu. Wind circles her with increasing speed. Then, she thrusts both of her arms toward him and screams forcefully in a form of attack—the wind suddenly rushes away from Jhenda and blasts the Slivanathan like a thousand rockets.

A tornado-like system forms around the beast, encircling him. He cannot escape it. His cries are loud and harsh as the walls of wind keep him confined.

Grea, now standing, thrusts her arms toward him also, channeling even more wind in his direction to keep him restricted.

Rock runs toward him and stops just twenty or so feet away. He raises both of his arms like he's lifting something from his waist. Columns of earth rise at both of the Slivanathan's sides. Rock clenches his fists tightly. The earth wraps itself around the Slivanathan's wrists like stone shackles. His arms are rendered useless. Holes in the ground form beneath the Slivanathan's feet and swallow his legs up to his knees as he drops down into them. The ground becomes solid again, trapping him.

The Slivanathan fights, breathing fire from his mouth and snout in a rage, but to no avail.

He's entombed.

~ ~ ~

Manny watches on, motionless. He can feel heat on his face all of a sudden, which quickly cools again within seconds. This cycle is repetitive. He sees a pulsing blue tint cast onto the ground in front of him and on his clothing. Manny takes another look at his friends and sees a sight that he's not expecting.

Grea's body is a fluorescent blue color and pulsing with energy. The same is true for Rock and Jhenda. Manny catches a glimpse of himself in the face of his watch; his face is the same fluorescent blue—his entire body is in fact. It brightens, then darkens, then brightens again, just like the light he sees emanating from his friends. They look at one another and see the amazing transformation that they've gone through. After a few moments, the intensity of their glowing features dies down and returns to normal.

Manny approaches the others.

They watch the Slivanathan's movements diminish.

"This is crazy! Can you believe it? Did you know?" Rock says, looking at his hands in personal admiration, "it's like, I knew *exactly* what to do! What was that? How was that possible? This is *sooo* crazy!"

Manny touches Rock's arm.

"It's happened! It's finally happened! The *Yahweh Gene*...it's in *you*..." Manny responds as he points at Rock's chest.

"I feel like I can—like I can just *FLY!*" Jhenda exclaims.

"Well, actually, I think we can," Grea says.

Manny nods in agreement with a huge smile.

With one last, forceful attempt to free itself, the Slivanathan jerks its arms and legs. It pulls with all of its might and releases a large burst of flame into the air above its head. The roar is powerful. The stone that entraps it doesn't budge. The shield of wind doesn't break.

He bows his head and breathes heavily, looking at the ground, and then at the group of young super-humans before him.

He lets out all of the air in his lungs.

He slouches into his position, defeated.

The group approaches Levi, who is still permeating with the spirit of the Slivanathan. He looks up at them and snarls as they draw closer.

After they're standing directly in front of him, the whirlwind that's circling around the Slivanathan stops; only the stone shackles remain fixed tightly around his limbs. Manny takes another step forward in front of his friends. He lifts his hand toward the face of the Slivanathan, who towers several feet over him.

Manny takes in a deep breath and releases a bellow into the night sky that shakes the very ground under them:

"SLIVANATHAN, COME OUT OF HIM!"

Levi's body trembles, aggressively. The others back up a few steps. The Slivanathan cries with a loud, terrifying voice and begins convulsing; its back arched awkwardly, its head pointing down at the ground and jerking, and its arms and legs uncomfortably stretching farther and farther toward its back.

Manny lifts his other hand toward Levi and roars again:

"COME...OUT...OF...HIM!"

Levi's head snaps back and points up to the sky. A dark creature flies out of his mouth—a phantom-like winged entity.

It zips into the air above them so quickly that it creates a whistling sound in the wind. Manny quickly reaches out for it as if it's right in front of him, then he clenches his hands and arms closed.

When he does, the spirit becomes trapped in midair, fighting to free itself.

Manny yells with intensity and squeezes with all of his might as he begins to glow fluorescent blue once more. He grits his teeth. He crouches down a bit, forcing all of his energy into his hands and arms.

As he does, just moments later, fire with a bluish tint encircles the demonic power in the air. It makes a noise, a horrendous shriek that none of them have ever heard that's painfully piercing. Rock, Grea, and Jhenda cover their ears with their hands to try and block out the sound.

The creature speaks with a voice that echoes across the open land:

"Wait... *WAIT!* Think of all that we can give you! WE CAN GIVE YOU THE WORLD, EMMANUEL KOHEN!!!"

The Shedim laughs maniacally.

"This whole pitiful *WORLD* can be yours Emmanuel!!! We can all rule it...together! You'll be like us! You'll be like...THE CREATOR!!!"

Manny continues to squeeze his hands and arms together with all of his might.

"I CONDEMN YOUUUU!" Manny yells, trembling as he strains his arms.

Realizing that his efforts are futile, the Slivanathan taunts Manny with the little bit of time and life that it has left:

"DAMIEN IS COMING...
DAMIEN IS COMING!"
"ALL HAIL HELEL!"

It makes the piercing sound again while more of its body catches fire.

The blue flames fully consume the Slivanathan, covering its entire grotesque figure. The heat rages on until he completely turns to ash in midair.

The embers fall down and fizzle out before they reach the ground.

The terrifying screech is now gone.

The desert is quiet.

~ ~ ~

Manny breathes heavily, crouched over, with his hands on his knees and his eyes closed; his friends come to his side.

Levi, now free from the stone restraints and the size of a normal man once more, rests on the ground on all fours.

"Manny, are you okay?" Jhenda asks while touching him on the back.

He nods, still too tired to speak.

His eyes move to Levi.

He looks at him, surrounded by broken stone, his clothes ripped to shreds. His body as frail as a man who hasn't eaten in days—trembling; rubbing his face with one hand and holding himself with the other.

Manny stands up straight and approaches him. The others follow. Once close enough, Manny gently places his hand on Levi's shoulder. Levi jumps at first, startled. Manny touches it again and lightly rubs it to comfort him.

"It's okay now," Manny says to Levi.

The tears come.

Levi's body quivers as his cry pours from him, completely overwhelmed with thankfulness.

"It took *over* me...I couldn't control it! I tried, but I...I just couldn't," Levi responds after his crying has died down and he's able to speak again.

"I know," Manny responds.

"You're free now...you're *free*," Grea says, crying also.

Rock holds his hand out to Levi who looks up, sees it, grabs a hold of it, and allows Rock to pull him up into a standing position. He cradles himself with his arms again, this time with a wide smile and a few tears still streaming down both of his cheeks.

"I don't feel the chains anymore...in here..."

He touches his head.

"Or...in *here*..."

He touches his chest, above his heart.

Jhenda covers her mouth with both hands, consumed by compassion and pity.

Levi stares into Manny's eyes with the deepest gratitude one can imagine.

"*Thank* you," he mutters as he begins to sob again.

Manny cries with him; his chest rising and falling with each burst of emotion.

Multiple feelings rush through him like stray bullets:

Relief.
Humility.
Gratefulness.

Pity.
Joy.

Manny grabs him and hugs him as tightly as he can.

66. TELL ME MORE

INSIDE THE IE, there are various black candles lit inside of Jonah's office again.

"Levi has fallen, I can sense it..."

Damien's voice is filled with vexation as he sits in the large chair behind the desk. In his hand, he's holding a vile containing a sample of blood, obviously one of those collected by the Medics for the NRP. He twirls it around in his hand, looking at it, studying it thoroughly. Polus is standing in the corner next to a man seated in a chair with a large bag over his head and rope tied around his neck, arms, and legs. The man's sniffling and sniveling can be heard from underneath the bag.

"...but *we* have the *key*," Damien continues.

His words are nearly drowned out by the whimpering.

"*QUIET!*" Damien yells has he strikes the desk with his clenched fist.

The man jumps; the yell and bang on the desk startle him.

He fights with himself to remain quiet and calm, with very little success.

"*Take it off of him,*" Damien says, as he motions with his hand for Polus to remove the covering from the man's head.

When it's taken off, the man jumps in his seat once more— his eyes search the room frantically, attempting to orient himself and adjust his eyes to the dim lighting.

"So...*Doctor Ahmad*, tell me more about this...hmm...what is it called again?"

Damien picks up a crumpled piece of paper that's on the desk in front of him.

He studies it.

"...ah, yes...that's it...*THE YAHWEH GENE...*"

As he finishes his sentence, Polus radiates.

A bright yellow energy surrounds him and his body starts to morph.

Polus releases a low hum.

From his stomach area, a foot appears.

An identical version of himself steps out of his original body.

And then another.

And another.

There are eventually five versions of Polus standing in the room, all glowing with the same yellow light. One sits next to Dr. Ahmad. One steps over to the window and looks out. Another leans on Damien's desk and stares at Dr. Ahmad. One stands in the center of the room and rubs his chin. The final one stands by the door and places his hand on the handle.

Damien laughs, extremely pleased by the look on Dr. Ahmad's face.

Dr. Ahmad watches on in terror and becomes hysterical, but too frightened to scream—the lump in his throat makes it impossible for him to produce any sound.

He continues to look on in total shock.

"Yesssssss, Doctor...tell ALL of usssssssssss..."

Each version of Polus says the phrase. Their voices are out of sync slightly, creating a very dark and twisted mood in the room; the atmosphere is unbelievably eerie.

Panic, fear, and shock grip the doctor at the same time, with three separate, but equally frigid hands.

Dr. Ahmad faints and slumps over in his chair as Damien's eyes glow yellow and his demonic laugh continues.

67. THE OTHERS

At the exact same moment, inexplicable things are occurring all over the world.

[NEW TIBET]

A CHILD IS in bed fast asleep.
 He hears noises outside of his bedroom window.
 He wakes up, listens, and becomes afraid.
 He continues to listen as people run past his window.
 He goes to his parent's room and wakes them.
 He warns them that something is happening outside.
 His father gets up first and goes to the boy's room to hear for himself while his mother puts on her robe and shoes. The father comes back and rubs his son's face. He looks at his wife and nods.
 Within minutes they are outside following the crowd. They jog with them for about fifty yards and stop outside of a small hut. There are hundreds of people standing at the doorway and the windows, looking inside at a glowing blue light that's coming from within.
 The small boy leaves his parents and wiggles his way through the crowd. His parents call his name, but he doesn't respond. He's determined to see what's inside. He crawls between and around adult legs until he reaches the doorway.
 Finally, he sees it.

There are older men, who are obviously monks dressed in their traditional garb, arranged around the room. They're all crouching on their knees on the floor, raising and bowing their bodies in harmonization, and clutching Grandeurscripts to their chests.

In the center of the room is a young boy, about his age.

A fluorescent blue light encompasses him as he levitates in the air with his legs crossed and eyes closed.

[NEW EGYPT]

IT'S EVENING. A woman and her daughter are working in the New Egypt Agri-Fields. They collect grains most mornings and store them away—they've done this for years now. They help to supply their entire town with grains and crops for fair bartering rates.

Their system works well, but every so often, men come to town and attempt to take their grains for unfair trading rates—days like today.

"How much do you want for your grains?" the man says with a thick accent as he approaches with his comrades.

"The same price, sir; we will trade for rice...and for water..."

"No, no, no! We cannot do that! You owe us grains from weeks ago!"

The woman is quiet. She looks down and continues harvesting grains, hoping that ignoring them will cause them to walk away.

"Hello! Do you hear me?" he jeers.

His companions laugh.

She continues looking down.

Her daughter is standing closer to the men, looking down and harvesting grains as well. The man makes a few more taunts at the woman. The other men continue to laugh.

The daughter becomes angry, but tries to hide her emotions.

She weeps.

The mother notices.

"Adisa, come here, daughter," the mother says.

The man looks at her. His eyes are beginning to glow with a yellow light.

"Why are her eyes closed? And why is she crying?" he asks the woman.

She ignores him still.

"*Adisa...come to me, daughter...*"

The girl doesn't move. The man touches her shoulder. She jerks away.

"Oh, girl, what's wrong? Do not be afraid. We just want your mother to be fair..."

The other men snicker.

"*You should go,*" the girl says quietly.

The mother drops her basket and approaches her daughter.

"*Adisa, no...*" she whispers.

"What did she say? What did she say to me? Did this child disrespect me?" the man says in an upset tone.

As he does, the yellow light in his eyes becomes increasingly brighter. He lifts his hand to strike the girl, which is now also a glowing fluorescent yellow.

The girl turns to him and lifts both of her hands so quickly that he can't react.

The girl yells:

"*GOOOOOOOOOO!*"

A giant flash of blue light is created from her palms. The light collides with the men and blasts them many feet into the air.

Of the five that were there, three are instantly killed—their bodies burned to lumps of blood, bone, skin, and ash. One of them is so severely burned that he will likely die within the next few minutes. The final man's right arm and leg has suffered third degree burns; he was not in the direct line of impact, but was instead standing off to the side.

He runs with a limp out of the field screaming for his life.

The mother quickly stretches her hand out in his direction, as if catching a small, invisible ball.

When she does, the man stops in his tracks.

She lifts her arm into the air.

The man levitates.

She clenches her fist.

The man catches fire and burns to death in midair while making horrendous noises.

His remains create a black mist of floating embers that remain in the air; a dark creature flies up from the midst of it, and disappears.

Small, black, ghost-like entities rise from the bodies of the three other men as they lie on the ground also, screeching as they do.

The mother walks over to the final man who is not quite deceased yet, stops over his body, and stares at him. The man is bleeding from the mouth and laughing painfully—blood spurts from between his lips as he coughs every few seconds.

His breathing suddenly slows and his eyes widen.

"All hail Helel…" he whispers as the life finally leaves his body.

The mother turns away and hears the sound of a spirit exit him, just as the others.

The mother rushes over to Adisa, kneels, and hugs her tightly.

Adisa is crying profusely.

"I'm sorry...*I'm sorry...*" Adisa says through her tears.
"*It's okay,*" her mother whispers.

[NEW ISRAEL]

TWO TWIN BROTHERS are walking home. It's getting darker by the minute.

"Jude, hurry brother," one says as he speeds up to a jog.

"Why are you in such a hurry, Simeon? We're already late..." the other says as he starts to jog too.

They turn a corner and notice a man looking at them from across the street.

"Do you see him, brother?" Jude asks.

"Yes, I see him..." Simeon replies.

"Do you think?" says Jude.

"Maybe..." Simeon mutters, nearly out of breath.

They keep jogging for another block or so, then reach an alley. Four men quickly run out from it and stop in front of them.

The man that they saw before from across the street has now run up behind them.

"Evening, guys," Jude says with uneasiness in his voice.

"What are *YOU* doing on this side of town, boys?" one of the men says.

"Well, we're going..." Jude begins to say.

"It's none of your business what we're doing!" Simeon says, interrupting his brother's explanation.

"Ah, you're the aggressive one I see...*you* should be more, *careful...*"

As the man says *careful*, his hands begin to glow with a yellow light.

"I knew it..." Jude says.

Simeon uses his arm to push his brother behind him.

"Is that a threat, sir?" Simeon says.

The man doesn't respond. The rest of the men surround Jude and Simeon as all of their hands light up with the yellow, mustard-colored light.

Encircled, the brothers stand with their backs to one another. *"We know who you are!"* the first man says loudly.

"Good...then you also know how this will all end..." Simeon says.

He turns and looks at his brother. Jude rolls his eyes and shakes his head. Simeon hunches his shoulders and tilts his head to the side. Jude responds with a sigh and a nod. The brothers exchange a smile, then turn back to the men.

In the same motion, and at the same time, both of them lift their hands to the sky.

A roaring thunder is created in seconds.

The winds begin to blow boisterously.

The twins snatch down their hands with fierce yells as if pulling down the sky.

At the moment they do, lightning bolts strike all five of the men with a fierceness and quickness that takes each of them by surprise.

The crash of thunder and flash of lighting can probably be heard and seen around the world.

~ ~ ~

All five of the men now lie on the ground, electrocuted, and burned to death.

Small bat-like, ghostly entities fly out of each of their mouths making crying sounds, then disappear into the night sky.

Jude places his hands on his head and paces.

"Calm down," Simeon says.

"I *am* calm," Jude replies, "it's time..." he continues.

Simeon looks into his brother's eyes.

"We must contact the others…" Simeon says as they resume their jog.

68. BLUE ANGELS

"Where will you go?" Grea asks Levi.

"Oh, I don't know. I lived in Samaria many years ago, before—well, before all of *this* happened; I may go back there."

He looks at Manny and grins.

"Thank you, again young man. I wanted to be free, I just couldn't…I just…I…" Levi stammers and looks down at the ground.

"I know," Manny says, "he told me," he finishes, pointing up to the sky.

They embrace once more, then Levi walks away across the desert.

Manny turns to his friends.

Rock places his hand on Manny's shoulder.

Grea and Jhenda hug each other.

A few seconds later, there is a light rumble of thunder and a bright flash of lightning far off in the distance, **to the far east.**

They listen to it and watch the sky briefly, then they look back toward Levi as he continues to walk.

"Is it over?" Jhenda asks.

"I think it's just beginning," Manny responds.

"Come on, let's go…" Manny says as he rises into the air and his body starts to glow bright blue again.

Rock lights up and joins Manny in the air, and so does Grea.

"Neon blue hair, huh? It looks *GREAT* on you! It's so…fitting!" Rock says as he looks at his sister.

Grea squints at him and blows in his direction. A wind forms and joins with her breath, carrying Rock several feet away from his original position.

Manny and Grea both laugh as he strains and struggles to fight through the wind and fly back to where he was.

"*Not* funny," Rock says.

"Where are we going now, Manny?" Jhenda asks, as she glows and rises into the air with them.

He smiles, says nothing, and bursts off into the air at the speed of sound, leaving a streak of blue light behind him.

"This is the wildest thing...*EVER!* He looks like—like a, *blue angel*," Rock says, still watching Manny's flight trajectory.

"And...he's *clearly* not going to slow down for us...we'd better catch up," Grea says.

They look at each other with smiles as wide as their faces, then take off through the air, with joyous shouts as they go.

0-1. MORE TO TELL
─────────────────────────

THE DISTRESSED AND suited man adjusts his tie and shifts his weight on the stool.

"And that's how the story ends, and *begins*...I suppose..."

He coughs a couple of times then scratches his face.

"I'm sure you'd *love* to hear more...and there's so much to tell—so much! *Far* more than I can fit into our time today..."

There's a light tapping, and then a scratching noise on the wall behind him.

"So, little time. How ironic. I've got *all* of eternity. But you don't...not *yet*..."

He turns and looks at the wall, and then turns forward again.

"We'll talk more, I hope...I look forward to it...it's *all* that I have to look forward to from now on..."

The man stands up from his stool, turns to the wall, and walks toward it.

"*Sooo* much to tell—so much to tell!" he says, clapping his hands together and then immediately scratching his head, nervously.

As he approaches the wall, it transforms into a large gaping hole. Cries of terror and agony pour through it, faintly at first, and then increasingly louder. Soon, a stairwell made of burning stone appears. Inside of the hole as far as the eyes can see, there are the tormented souls of those who once walked the earth lining both sides of the stairwell.

There are large, hideous creatures engaging in repulsive sexual acts and torturing the people. Bodies hang from the ceiling and the walls by chains and ropes. There's a lake of lava, swirling, with boats guided by skeleton-like figures. The stench is unbearable: sulfur, smoke, and burning flesh.

Just as he fully enters the cavern, the man looks back.

"So much more to tell…"

The wall suddenly closes up.

The cries, screams, and noises dissipate until there is complete silence.

Silence.

End.

*Thank you, tremendously, for taking
the time to read my first novel.
Now, I undoubtedly need your
help, if at all possible.
Please, share this story with someone.
In fact, with everyone that you can.
Tell them all about this book.
And please, write a review.
I'm proud of you.
I believe in you.*

-NJ Scribe

ACKNOWLEDGEMENTS:

To "the Creator," thank you for expressing a piece of yourself to me, in me, and through me. I'm humbled.

~ ~ ~

To my mom, Queen Angie, thank you for the gift of writing; I'll love you forever.
 To Mammy, Nanny, Lyd, and TJ! We did it! Get ready! I'll love you forever.
 To my dad, Willie Suggs, thanks for offering what you could; I'll love you forever.
 To my Pastor, thank you for accepting me, embracing me, loving me, covering me, encouraging me, teaching me, challenging me, correcting me, and stretching me.
 To King's Chapel, Vine Swamp, St. John's (Dover, NC), G-RDA, The Park (Charlotte, NC), Temple of Refuge (Charlotte, NC), and KCC, thank you for the spiritual foundation and for allowing me to stretch my wings.

~ ~ ~

To Rob Laray and 'Tai Shelby, your contributions have meant the world to me.

To Kate, Alice, and Gina! I couldn't have extracted better editors/proofreaders from the universe! Your insight and guidance were invaluable!

To the team at Damonza.com (*ESPECIALLY* Damon, Chrissy, and Alisha), thank you SO much for the awesome cover and formatting (and PATIENCE); you rock!

You're each just as much a part of this as I am.

~ ~ ~

To KJ, Riss, Reau, Mal, Jenz, Leez, Krys, Bake, Dubb, Fred, Quincy, Hicks, Cope, Flex, Nick, Wooley, Tad P., Mr. J., Tito K., Dino M., G. Herb, T. J. Shelton, Mr. Heath, Chubb M., Jimmy C., Sara H., Lena W., Jon O., Cigi D., "MD" Damoin, "YC" Cherry, J. Beighle, P. Murphy, Kashi W., Brook D., Kera S., Yves C., Kim L., "Perifam", Shondell J., Christy J., Trev E., Mama V. Grice, Neet B., Rev. L. Nixon, Ma Mary, Mama Pat W., Ma Hardy, Ma Bert, Elder and First Lady Ward, the Koonce family (Ann, Bettie, Trish, Bernice, etc.), my family and friends, my social media tribe, creatives, *indigos*, *star-children* worldwide, and MANY others whom I can't possibly compile into a complete list:

THANK YOU!

Thank you for loving me, being patient with me, pouring into me, praying for me, and believing in me, while letting me be... me! You've *ALL* inspired me. You've helped to shape my personality and destiny. Thank you...for *you*.

Thank you to all of my NW Elementary, Bynum Elementary, RMS, Kinston High School, UNC-Charlotte, and ECU teachers/professors/mentors, and so on.

To Charlotte, NC, Greenville, NC, Raleigh, NC, and *ALL* of North Carolina, thank you for being the best locale(s) in the world.

~ ~ ~

To Kinston, NC, thank you for raising me. **Always home.**

~ ~ ~

"Granny," this is for you.
... Rosa Mae "Lossie" Bell Simmons...
I miss you. I love you. Thank you. My beautiful rose.
"He brought you out, all right..."

To my fellow dreamers, writers, authors, artists, entrepreneurs, creatives, etc.,

*I started this book in 2011.
I didn't complete it until 2017.
Never let go of the vision that's
buried inside of you.
It's there for a reason.
Someone needs it.
I'm proud of you.
I believe in you.
Now,* **finish it...**

...we need you.

-NJ Scribe

Oh, I almost forgot.
My question, concerning the truth, which I mentioned in the beginning is...

(next page)

Do you have it?

Book two, coming soon...

:)

2.0

Made in the USA
Columbia, SC
28 November 2017